RENEGADE

RENEGADE

J. H. Sanderson

Paperback ISBN: 978-1-300-69617-9
Hardcover ISBN: 978-1-300-86078-5

To T. Michael Flynn, Burton W. Porter, Gerry Tavares, and David Dwyer, four luminaries in the Golden Age of Lyndon Institute faculty, without whose influence and inspiration this effort would never have been attempted.

Acknowledgements

I would like to take this opportunity to thank all of the people who helped the Roadhouse Sons continue on with their adventures, and who made *Renegade* possible, with a special thanks to the following people:

To Fred Bramante, the godfather of the New England music scene for his help with contacting Jay Jay French to write the music foreword, and to Deborah Osgood for her assistance in facilitating that reconnection.

To Jay Jay French, not only for his wonderful foreword, but also for the fantastic telephone conversations and the opportunity to tell, and retell, my wrestling stories.

To Todd Mattingly, former officer of the Metropolitan Police Department of the District of Columbia. Despite the increased demands of all law enforcement agencies in Washington, D.C., during the presidential inauguration, he still found time to write the law-enforcement forward for this book.

I would like to give a belated thank you to Officer Martin Kolb of the Peterborough, NH, Police Department for his help as a forensic and law enforcement advisor for my previous work, Book One of the Roadhouse Sons series, *Dangerous Gambles.*

Last, but not least, I would like to thank my core team for everything they have done, once again, to make this vision a reality. To my Big Brother, Tony Heyes, for sharing stories and tequila, as well as for making certain that everything was told, and written, correctly. To Dave Costa, Phil Hoefs, and Steve Smith for their music to inspire me when I was staring at blank pages. To Mia Moravis, for her invaluable help in editing, promoting, and encouraging this work, and for helping an idea find the light of day. And finally, to our Phantom Editor, Mr. Objective Man, for his help in making certain that continuity was not lost, and that the weave of this tale did not come unraveled.

Author's Foreword

The world of *Renegade* is darker and far more threatening than the Roadhouse Sons previously encountered in *Dangerous Gambles*. Betrayal, danger, and death, which before had merely been an unfortunate byproduct of their foray into the world of espionage, now confront them as harsh realities.

That's not the only problem they face. They find that the threats from without to the American way of life are echoed by threats from within. Nonconformity is suspect and persecuted; flirtations with fascism fuel an effort to preserve a sense of ersatz security—and liberty. However, I believe that darkness cannot exist without, at least, the knowledge of light. Therefore, whenever the Roadhouse Sons were faced with corrupt officials or individuals seeking, for their own ends, to manipulate venerable institutions, such as the American Legion, our heroes also discovered individuals whose personal integrity would not allow such sinister deeds to succeed.

These champions of the American way of life didn't need to be told what to do. Their innate sense of respect for freedom and liberty were their motivators. I used the American Legion to illustrate this point because it is an organization founded to support not only American veterans, but to encourage American values. Despite controversial incidents in their early years, the Legion has established itself as one of the premier organizations promoting patriotism and American ideals. For me, therefore, it was a logical choice to use that institution to illustrate the need for we Americans to constantly remain on guard in order to preserve our liberties, and to go forth, within the framework of our Constitution, in ensuring that our liberties are not infringed upon.

I also attempted to illustrate an albeit precarious balance of the angst and frustration of youth, as expressed by the nascent Punk Rock movement and its seeming polar opposite, Up With People. Yet, opposites can sometimes be counterparts. Despite the efforts of people to purport the latter as a participant in Moral Rearmament,

Up With People was not, and is not, a religious organization, but rather one that seeks to use music and dance as a means of positive expression, and for its touring youth to contribute to the communities in which they visit and perform. Up With People provides to the world's young people the opportunity to realize their own unique voice, to travel outside their communities and connect with the world. For many "Uppies," their tour is their first opportunity to find that expression, and to do so in an environment in which they realize that there are others like and unlike them. The Punk Rock movement, while certainly coarser and less refined than Up With People, provided many young people with the same opportunity. It was a movement that was so fitting for allowing youth to put their feelings into words, and they were able to connect with others that felt their era's angst in the same way. Just as some cast members of Up With People weren't quite as wholesome as their images suggested, neither were all Punkers as jarring and dissident as stereotyped. After all, no matter what group in which we might find ourselves, we are still—ultimately—individuals.

But, lest the reader worry that *Renegade* is solely an allegorical study and narrative of human nature, I assure you that you'll have fun. I've tried to make this book a bit interactive. In two cases, I've provided plot clues in the form of codes. In one instance, the key to solving the code is quite apparent. In the other, it is far more obscure. For the first, I will say that the clue to the solution, in fact, also provides its own possible red herring. For the second, such a warning isn't necessary; the key to its solution is obscure enough that you'll be on your toes to even notice it.

In either event, enjoy!

Music Foreword by Jay Jay French

In the forty or so years of touring in the rock world (thirty-eight countries to date), the experience of having both worldwide access to power due to some politicians loving my band, and concurrently worldwide scorn by some members of society hellbent on destroying our power to perform in front of millions of people, has always fascinated me.

Finally, Jason Sanderson comes along with a premise that, while it seems farfetched, in reality could be happening right now.

While the series could just as easily have been about an international pro wrestler, Jason instead took it into my world.

A rock band as spies is almost too perfect—total access and no suspicion.

Metal bands can be loved by both the left wing (musicians are the dreaded "artists" born to rebel) and the right (who love the chest-thumping patriotism that many represent). It takes a wrestler (someone who truly understands this unique dichotomy) and a talented writer to take this notion of a band flying under the radar, to pull off this fast-paced, highly entertaining and intriguing novel, a must-read for anyone who loves rock and suspense.

Bravo, Jason. I only hope that you haven't blown the cover off any one that I know...

Jay Jay French
Guitarist
Twisted Sister

Law Enforcement Foreword by Todd Mattingly

As a former member of the Metropolitan Police Department of the District of Columbia, I served thirteen years as a sworn Officer (1996 -2009). During my time, I assisted and responded to many different scenes, from homicides to auto accidents to working in the Command Center during the Chandra Levy investigation to the Metro area Sniper investigation. Being an officer in the District of Columbia allowed me to witness great cases, and to witness many events that most agencies would not experience in terms of crime and events.

Today, I am a civilian. Since 2009, I work as specialist in the Chief's Office for the Capitol Police, a federal agency. I am behind the scenes and now able to read, monitor and witness history in a different realm altogether—the federal agency I work for deals with the lawmakers of the United States, not so much crime on the streets.

Being in law enforcement for almost seventeen years has been the most rewarding life experience ever. It takes special individuals to volunteer to take up the shield and protect citizens, regardless of personal risks. When I made the decision to become a police officer, I knew that I wanted to make a difference. I knew that I wanted to make my mark on life by serving in a capacity that I would be proud of, in a way that I'd feel accomplished so many times and to be greatly rewarded with honors by my superiors. The training that I was afforded was endless, and the training that continues afterwards is training that would save your life, and those of the people you have to protect.

This book is set in the late 1970s. Of course, a lot has changed in the world of police work—specifically, city police work. The technology and forensic science have grown leaps and bounds! And DNA plays a major role in solving crimes these days versus back then. It's important for the reader to know, though, that the forensic science aspects in this book are right on target, for the manners of response and the processing of crimes. That accuracy makes a huge difference to me, and to readers everywhere, especially since TV shows make this work look quick and easy.

This book is enticing and leaves me wanting more. I look forward to reading the whole series. As I read "*Renegade*," I could almost put myself in the scenes. I joined MPDC at a time when the city's crime was out of control, murder rates were extremely high, and the use of force among officers was constantly questioned by the Department of Justice, and by D.C. citizens. The book has a provocative angle of sorts, in that the Roadhouse Sons are stuck in a world where everything is out of control, they never know if a crime's being committed, even against them, and the citizens are just as discontented as they were in real life. "*Renegade*" leaves visuals in my mind, truthful ones that I've lived, and J. H. Sanderson should feel proud of his work.

Todd Mattingly
Specialist, Chief's Office
Capitol Police
Washington, D.C.

Table of Contents

CHAPTER ONE

"Unquiet"

This wasn't what he thought dying would feel like. Instead of lingering in a bed in a sterile hospital, lonely in some nursing home, or even in a comfortable bed surrounded by greedy heirs and fat grandchildren, he felt the wind caress his cheeks as it blew through his hair. He was strangely calm, even oddly reflective. He looked, for the last time, upon the magnificent colors of the sunset as it cast its glow upon the city of Seattle. He was glad that this would be his last vision. The war effort had dimmed the lights of Seattle, giving all who loved the evening skyline a sense of loss, as though grieving a longtime friend. But the setting sun reflected off of the buildings and gave the appearance that the lights were on. He felt the thrill of relief now. He was grateful that his last memory would not be clouded by grief.

He relaxed. All of his earlier tensions ebbed away. The arguments, the fighting and the shouting all seemed like they happened to someone else. The accusations no longer rang in his ears and he no longer vainly uttered his denials. He wiped the corner of his mouth where he felt a trickle of blood, then chuckled as he realized what he was doing. Soon it wouldn't matter anymore.

He thought about what they were doing in his apartment now; going through his things, laying bare the mementos of his life for the world to see. Would they appreciate them as he did? Or consider from whence they came and what recollections would be associated with them? He doubted it. They weren't the sentimental types.

He vaguely remembered an engagement he had the next day. He was supposed to meet Chris for drinks. With regret, he realized that he hadn't informed his friend of the sudden change in plans. But that was all right. Chris would find out soon enough. That probably wouldn't make any difference, either. Not to him at least. Not anymore. That very thought made him smile. Nothing would make any difference to him anymore. He was free at last. Free from the threats hanging over him. Free from the retribution that he feared so much. Free from the rough hands that had grasped at him. He relished that freedom. The

only surprise was the end. The end had come much quicker than he'd thought...
almost as quickly as the pavement that rose up to meet him.

* * * * * * * *

Cameron awoke with a start, drenched in sweat. His breath came in sharp gasps. He realized that he'd kicked away the blankets during the night, but the sheets remained, encasing him in a tight shroud, unable to move. His anxiety grew. Finally disentangling himself, he arose from his bed and walked around the room, the feel of the carpet on his bare feet a reminder that he was, in fact, alive. Cameron leaned against the bureau and took deep breaths, hoping to allay his angst. He trembled, and gripped the top of the bureau to steady himself. Was this a dream? It was easier to believe so.

It was just a fucking dream.

A dream that came more often of late, though with occasional variations, but always essentially the same. The building was on fire and he was trying to get his friends out but, to his horror, he discovered that the door by which they tried to exit kept bringing them back into the burning building. He tried screaming warnings to everyone, but the sound of the fire drowned him out. He tried putting out the fire, but every effort seemed to cause it to flare up more. He noticed a figure standing in the center of the room, and as he attempted rescue, the roof collapsed in a raging inferno. Dust, ash, and smoke filled his nostrils. The heat of the fire caused him to stumble backward. Suddenly the flames blazed all around him. It was at this point when he always awoke, sweating and shaking as he was now.

Cameron breathed deeply, filling his lungs with cool, fresh air.

It feels so good to breathe...

He inhaled again, this time holding in the pure air as though it were anointing him. Cameron exhaled slowly, at last feeling relief. Returning to the bed, he pondered reading a book, but decided against it. For some odd and inexplicable reason, he always felt comfortable in the dark after that dream.

If it's dark, then there isn't any fire...

Childish reasoning, he knew, but reasoning that worked for him and kept sheer panic at bay. Cameron spread out on the bed, his arms and legs draping over the side. In the darkness, he heard Chuck Lamont, the Roadhouse Sons' manager, snoring softly. Snapper, the band's roadie, coughed and rustled about in his sleeping bag, safely tucked in his customary spot under the table. Neither had roused from their sleep, so Cameron knew that he hadn't cried out this time like he'd done so many times before.

That counts for something, I guess.

He lay on the rumpled sheets, feeling the cool air against his skin. He grappled with his psyche, exorcising the dream from his head.

Focus on the good instead…

The bed, for instance. Cameron was so grateful to be sleeping in a bed—not the ground or in the back of a truck—a luxury these days.

Ever since the Soviets had attacked and invaded the United States the summer before, everything careened on a steady downhill slide. Military setbacks were competing with another bane of the morale of the American people—rationing. Rationing was imposed almost immediately. Americans sorely missed easy access to coffee, sugar, meat, and dairy, all of which were, in reality, a very pointed diversion from the real objects of the rationing—gasoline and rubber. The government had adopted, with minor revisions, the rationing system from the Second World War. Included in this enterprise were restraints on nonessential travel, which restricted the Roadhouse Sons' tour stops to within a fifty-mile radius on any given day. However, the government eventually informed the band members that since they were contributing to the morale of the country, their work was considered a boon to the war effort. The restrictions were lifted somewhat, and the band was able to travel farther afield, as long as they did so only on state highways and no more than two hundred miles a day.

Since very few other organizations, including some of the more famous acts, were able to enjoy such freedoms, Cameron suspected that Chuck had used his vast catalog of connections to acquire relaxed treatment for the band. That said, Cameron thought it best not to ask. To do so would bring him face to face, once again, with the reality that had turned his life upside down, a reality with which he had yet to make peace, and which he constantly tried to avoid, but to no avail. With a resolute sigh, Cameron reluctantly admitted to himself that once the thought was reawakened, there was no other way to respond than to reflect upon it.

Was it really only seven months ago that my life effectively came to an end?

Upon quick calculation, Cameron realized that it was. The previous September, Cameron and the other members of the

Roadhouse Sons were recruited by the government—against their will—to penetrate bootlegging operations and illegal drug rings. In the process, they uncovered evidence of possible Soviet penetrations into the very operations they were monitoring. As they gathered information about smugglers, they serendipitously uncovered information about a possible Soviet double agent working beside them, blatantly in their midst. The entire situation erupted into the horrid inferno, constantly replayed each night in Cameron's dreams. Two friends dead, one nearly killed, and someone special—someone who may be gone forever.

And Jack shit in the plus column. I need a smoke…

Cameron fumbled on the nightstand for his cigarettes and matches. Realizing that he had only a few of each, he left them there.

Scratch that idea. It's harder and harder just to have a goddamn cig…

His hand came to rest on the old and battered paperback western, *Sackett*. He found it while packing up Doug's belongings just before the band left Vermont. Cameron had never been much of a western fan, but reading and rereading this dog-eared copy of the Louis L'Amour classic had proved to be a bit of a comfort for him. How many times had he read it already—two, maybe three? He decided to go into the bathroom to read, so as not to wake Chuck and Snapper. As he arose from the bed, he realized that, too, would be impossible.

Fucking blackout.

Following the Soviet declaration of war and the subsequent assaults on the US and Europe, the American government was thrown into turmoil. To their own and everyone else's chagrin, high-ranking government officials realized that they had spent so much time preparing for a nuclear holocaust that they no longer had any idea how to address a conventional war. Thus, civil defense agencies decided to do what generals traditionally had done throughout history: they fought the last war. Dusting off even more World War Two restrictions, the officials mandated blackouts for all coastal lights, street lamps, traffic lights and even motor vehicle headlights. The American people threw themselves into this with gusto, grateful to somehow contribute to the war effort. However, America's citizens endured a subsequent face-slap as the Pentagon announced that, while these actions were patriotic, they were unnecessary since modern fighters and bombers used radar and radio signals to locate targets and weren't dependent upon artificial light, unlike the bombers utilized in World War Two.

Nevertheless, blackouts were still required and not just on the coast, but nationwide. Gradually, Americans began to suspect the true reason for them. The Soviets had invaded Alaska and targeted the community of Barrow, home of the national petroleum reserve. This coincided with two important international incidents: increasing unrest in the Middle East, and Mexico's unwillingness to cooperate with the US in improving our own oil production. Hence, Americans were forced to conserve the domestic oil supply. How better than via mandatory blackouts, which reduced the demand for electricity, allowing it to be used in more essential areas, such as hospitals, military installations, and defense operations.

Cameron closed his eyes and added blackouts to his litany of bitches. He debated throwing on some clothes so he could sit outside in the fresh air, but remembered Chuck's elaborate alarm systems, which was always activated when the band retired for the night. Cameron had no idea how to disconnect the alarm system or, for that matter, how to activate it again, so he abandoned the idea of night breezes. Smiling to himself, he added Chuck's crazy ideas to his litany.

I know, I'll count my bitches instead of sheep.

He proceeded to do so, mentally itemizing each and every gripe and grudge, until he fell into a fitful sleep. As he drifted off, a sound pulled him from his slumber. Cameron lay perfectly still, wide-awake once again.

Cameron discerned Chuck's faint outline in the other bed, and heard Snapper rustle about once more. He was beginning to think he'd imagined the sound.

Great. I am crazy.

Then he heard it again, a faint scratching coming from the door. He slowly glided off the bed and grabbed one of his boots. With cat-like tread, he walked on the balls of his feet toward the door.

The Roadhouse Sons were occupying the second floor of an old motel. The front wall in each room was comprised of the typical cheap veneer-and-plywood door and a large faux picture window— the kind that, ordinarily, allows in ample light from the parking lot, had the patriotic owner not honored the blackout law. The drawn curtains only served to heighten the effect of the ebon gloom.

Cameron carefully avoided positioning himself in line with the door, instead squeezed himself into the section of wall between the door jamb and window molding. He heard the noise again, even clearer. He wondered if he should wake Chuck.

It was a scuffling sound, followed by, perhaps, a mutter. Cameron was tempted to look through the door's peephole, but resisted.

It's so friggin' dark! And they could shoot me.

Whoever was outside likely had a gun, and there was Cameron, positioned directly in the line of fire. The door would be scant protection against anything but the smallest-caliber weapon. Realizing that he could probably get a better view through the window, Cameron moved quickly to the far wall.

Slowly and painstakingly, he pulled back the curtain. Since the room was at the end of the balcony, there was nothing to the left of the window, so he could see the walkway outside the door. The light from the motel's neon sign cast a vague illumination upon the walkway.

Blackout laws don't apply to this guy's sign, I guess...

Cameron couldn't discern much more than the balcony railing and the shapes of several cars parked below. The stars were partially obstructed by surrounding buildings and, despite the cloudless sky, there was no moonlight either, leaving the balcony bathed in a darkness that could send any skeptic's imagination reeling.

Cameron was tense, remaining perfectly still. He breathed through his nose to avoid panting, but each breath was deafening to his own ears, and he was certain that his exhalations would give him away. His eyes adjusted to the meager light. He could sense some regular shapes of the outside—trees, buildings, cars. He couldn't really see anything.

He heard the sound again, this time followed by a clatter. There was no movement, or so he thought. Suddenly, he noticed something clamber along the railing and disappear. Cameron heaved a sigh of relief.

Probably a damn cat!

He scolded himself and returned to his bed, dropping onto the mattress with a weak groan.

"I bet it was a raccoon." Chuck's voice came out of the darkness so suddenly that Cameron jumped, stifling a startled cry.

"Fuckin' ay!" hissed Cameron. "You scared the shit out of me!"

"Cats don't make any noise." Chuck yawned, ignoring Cameron's agitation. "Dogs make all kinds of noise, though. Raccoons make that chattering sound. I bet he found some food or something someone left around. Good thinking with the boot and where you stood, by the way."

Cameron said nothing, but just sat there, wishing he could be swallowed up by the darkness. Chuck was awake all along.

"You had that dream again," came Chuck's disembodied voice, issuing a statement instead of asking a question.

"Yeah," confirmed Cameron. "How did you know?"

"Easy to recognize," said Chuck.

Cameron began to answer, but Chuck cut him off.

"Not now," he said, a note of finality in his voice. "Don't wake up Snapper. We'll talk in the morning."

Cameron persisted, only to have Chuck scold him more vehemently.

"In the morning!" he reiterated. Cameron knew not to push the issue. Once Chuck made a decision, there was no room for debate. Cameron reclined on his bed, too tired and agitated to argue.

Chuck yawned. Cameron heard him roll over and, within minutes, Chuck's gentle snore resumed. Cameron was trembling, partly from his waning adrenaline rush and partly from sheer anger. Chuck had been awake and left Cameron alone to face potential danger. Cameron realized his anger, unabated, was not really aimed at Chuck; this anger was far too vast to fire upon just one object. This anger spewed forth from Cameron's viscera—for what had happened to his life; for the lack of control he had over it, no matter how hard he tried. The extent of his anger was tempered only by his acknowledgement of its futility. Cameron reminded himself once again that he had, seven months ago, made a choice that was absolute and irreversible. He felt his anger give way to fatigue so strong that he lapsed into a heap, as though embalmed by that fitful sleep once more.

CHAPTER TWO

"Hag-ridden"

One of the earliest effects of the war was the closing of interstate highways to all civilian and nonessential personnel. This mandate fulfilled President Dwight D. "Ike" Eisenhower's vision of better enabling the quick transport of military supplies, as well as allowing highway straightaways for use as potential airstrips and emergency evacuation routes. While this new regulation was a major inconvenience for the average individual, many supposed it would be an economic godsend for the small communities and businesses that were bypassed for years by Ike's aptly monikered National System of Interstate and Defense Highways. Many of these hamlets, however, had been simply struggling to survive *before* Ike's mandate. Once cross-country traffic was shunted to the highway system, businesses in those towns located tantalizingly close to the interstates were unable to capitalize upon its virtues, without the means to expand and improve over the years. The irony, therefore, was that now, with this sudden and new commerce opportunity presenting itself in the form of increased local traffic, these businesses weren't adequately equipped to take advantage of it. Additionally, the limitations imposed by the war on both money and building materials rendered the opportunity doubtful of ever being realized. Forced like all civilians to travel the smaller state highways, the Roadhouse Sons now found themselves in such an ill-fated establishment, the Gaston Diner, in a small Missouri town off of US Route 40, within sight of I-70.

The band members were seated at adjoining booths eating breakfast. The Roadhouse Sons consisted of guitarist and front man Cameron Walsh, and his pack of merry men. Rich Webster slapped the bass guitar while Clyde Poulin, guitarist and occasional keyboard player, set the ladies drooling with his onstage high jinks. The boyishly sweet, but married, Evan Dixon played drums and held down the rhythm along with Rich. Chuck Lamont fulfilled the duties of band manager and occasional guitarist whenever he could muster the time, and Phillip S. Napier, known to the band as "Snapper," was their new roadie.

"You look like shit," said Rich, still looking down at his plate. He pushed the powdered eggs around on his plate and reached for the salt. Cameron looked Rich in the eye, but didn't answer. He just sat there and looked down, staring now into his cup of instant coffee. He reached for the Cremora, but changed his mind. It wouldn't make the pale brown liquid taste any better, nor would it cool the abysmal beverage.

At least it's really hot…

He'd told the waitress that he didn't want sugar, so none was provided. These days, no dining establishments would waste their rations, sugar or otherwise, by placing them on the table if no one wanted to use them. Avoiding the hassle of requesting one measly packet of sugar, Cameron heaved a weary sigh and blew on his coffee. He considered responding to his band mate's remark, but decided against that, too. Rich didn't notice; he sliced off a bit of the mystery meat on his plate and held it up, staring at it before venturing it toward his mouth, all the while shifting uncomfortably in his chair.

I'll bet he drew the short straw!

In an effort to conserve money, the Roadhouse Sons didn't have the luxury of individual rooms on this trip. All six of the boys had to cram themselves into two rooms. On several previous occasions, though, they were forced to share only one room, or divide themselves up between one room and the van. Comparatively speaking, two rooms for the six of them was a luxury.

The boys didn't mind staying three to a room, as long as the rooms had queen-sized beds. One could sleep on top of the covers in a sleeping bag in the middle, while the others slept on either side under the covers. However, more often than not, the rooms had twin beds, which meant that at least one person had to sleep on the floor. For this, they drew straws. Judging from Rich's inability to sit still, Cameron guessed that he was the lucky one this time.

"Floor duty?" Cameron asked, yawning. To his surprise, Rich shook his head.

"No," he grumbled. "That fucking mattress was like sleeping on a sack of old army helmets. German helmets. The pointy kind."

"Pickelhaubes, or should I say, pickel*hauben*!" said Snapper, smiling and gulping his Tang.

"What?" asked Rich, stretching his arms over his head.

"The pointy helmets," Snapper explained, wiping his mouth. "That's what they're called."

Rich shrugged in response. "This doesn't taste like Spam," he grumbled again. He cut another piece of meat with his fork. "I'd almost say this was the real thing."

Chuck, who'd remained silent until hearing this, finally spoke.

"Probably canned ham," he said, shoveling scrambled eggs into his mouth.

"I thought that's what Spam is," Rich replied. Chuck shook his head.

"No. That's made with other stuff."

They all stared at him. Rich, fork poised halfway to his open mouth, looked horrified. Chuck rolled his eyes.

"I mean like pork shoulder, ham hocks, corn starch, water, and salt, for crying out loud! I wasn't talking about the disgusting parts of the pig."

The boys muttered their relief and voraciously resumed their meals.

Chuck smiled mischievously. "They save those for hot dogs!"

Rich looked up, mouth agape, and dropped his fork. He grabbed his glass of Tang and guzzled it down. He'd had two hot dogs the night before.

From the next booth, Clyde and Evan burst into laughter. Chuck laughed silently, shoulders heaving. Cameron blew on his coffee again.

"Pitiful!" he muttered, teasing Rich. Cameron turned his attention to Chuck. He noticed some time ago that whenever Chuck was in a good mood, he ate with great enthusiasm and held his fork the way a child would, by clenching the handle in his fist. Today was the first day in a long while that Cameron saw Chuck do this, and so enthusiastically that his food wasn't reaching his mouth.

I wonder what's up with him?

"What's the matter with you?" asked Snapper, lighting a cigarette. Cameron ignored him and continued sipping of his coffee.

"He's hagridden," said Chuck, mopping his plate with his toast.

"What's that?" Snapper asked.

Chuck downed the last of his coffee and threw his napkin on his plate.

"Back in the old days, that's what farmers used to call horses and animals that were out of sorts," he explained. "They used to think that witches came by in the middle of the night and rode the animals all night long, leaving them worn out and exhausted the next morning. They explained knots in horses tails and manes as put there by the witches to hang on as they rode."

"And that's what you think is wrong with him?" Snapper smiled.

"Yup," said Chuck, retrieving a toothpick from his shirt pocket "He's got all the signs. He's lethargic, cranky, with hollow eyes, matted hair, he's off his feed, and he smells like a barn."

"Neigh!" Cameron whinnied, grimacing.

"The prosecution rests," said Chuck.

"Of course, I could just be getting a crappy night's sleep," murmured Cameron, resting his chin in hand. "That and I'm going out of my mind with this creeping cross country. For Christ's sake, if we're going to be stuck in these little towns, can't you at least get us booked in some clubs or something?"

Chuck cleared his throat and returned his toothpick to his pocket. He put both hands palms down on the table and looked Cameron in the eye. "We've been—"

"And as far as me smelling like a barn," Cameron interrupted, clearly perturbed, "when was the last time anyone said you smelled fresh as a daisy? Would it kill you to get us a place that has hot water? I haven't been able to take a hot shower in almost a week!"

"The water situation is out of my control." Chuck was sullen. "When they shut off the power—"

"Out of your control!" snapped Cameron. "What the hell is the point of having a manager if you aren't going to get this shit straightened out? You're supposed to be taking care of us and managing our careers, not coming up with excuses!"

Cameron glared at Chuck. Chuck maintained his composure, his body language and expression relaxed. Only the slow drumming of his fingers on the table betraying any sign of annoyance.

"Is that all?" asked Chuck quietly, his voice calm. Cameron sipped his coffee. He knew that he was out of line. The band's manager was the picture of tranquility, but one never wanted to be the subject of Chuck's focus if he became vexed. Like the others, Cameron had learned to recognize the early warning signs of Chuck's irritation. First, he would lean back, draping his left arm over whatever support was behind him. His right hand was always flat on the table in front of him or on his lap. Next came the drumming of his fingers, then the lowering of his head. The boys knew to run for the hills if Chuck's movement surpassed that. Cameron was fully aware that he'd pushed Chuck to stage two already. It was time to back off.

"Good," said Chuck calmly, but with nary a trace of a smile. "I know it's frustrating but, trust me, we're working on it. McIntyre is up in Columbia right now trying to get us booked someplace." Chuck's assistant, Barbara McIntyre, usually traveled ahead to upcoming concert venues to handle the advance work. Lately though, she was sidetracked with necessary administrative work relating to the band's other, more clandestine, activities.

"I know you need to rehearse," continued Chuck. "I know you're going stir crazy. I wasn't looking forward to a cross-country road trip, either. I did that with my family when I was eight and still can't figure out why I didn't kill them all in their sleep. The only benefit this trip has over that is that you boys don't kick the back of the seat and make my mother scream profanities."

Don't pacify us. We're not ten years old.

"As for the water thing," Chuck sighed. "Man, just suck it up and live with it. If you have to take a cold shower, take a cold shower. A lot of people are doing a lot worse. All I can say is sometimes life sucks and that's all there is to it. When life kicks you in the gut, try and catch your breath as quick as possible and move on."

Cameron nodded, sighing and resolute.

"Yeah. You're right…"

They sat in awkward silence. The remaining band members suffered the same frustrations as Cameron. While they fully understood Chuck's explanation and sentiments—they'd all arrived at the same conclusions on their own—they had no idea of how to heed Chuck's dismal advice.

The band was suddenly aware of how conspicuous their silence, as well as their mere presence, rendered them. Several diner patrons repeatedly glanced in their direction. It wasn't the Roadhouse Sons' appearance that made them noteworthy; they dressed in the usual fashion of young men without office jobs, and none of them were fans of outlandish getups or loudly colored outfits. The reason they were so noticeable rested on one simple fact—their lack of familiarity with the area and their resulting and collective fish-out-of-water demeanor.

If any one of them would draw attention as a stranger in town, though, it was Rich. He was the exotic one. His dark complexion and dark hair, combined with his Fu Manchu mustache, suggested some Oriental or Native American heritage, and his closed nature only added to the air of mystery about him. Cameron, dressed in a tee shirts and jeans, was of average height with wavy, dark, shoulder-length hair and a full mustache. Indeed, he wasn't rough on the eyes, but there was nothing about him that would be worthy of inordinate attention. That luxury belonged to Clyde, the gorgeous golden boy of the band. Other than a scar he incurred during a mission and which he occasionally kept covered, he dressed similarly to Cameron, though much more suggestively. His long, wavy, sandy-brown hair, piercing eyes, fabulous physique, and just-fell-out-of-bed lustiness made women of all ages swoon. The cherub-faced, curly-haired adorable Evan and shaggy-haired, wiry Snapper didn't evoke terror or suspicion in anyone, either. Regardless, they still garnered stares.

Cameron took a final sip of coffee and lowered his cup, inadvertently and loudly banging it to the table. He glanced around sheepishly. No one said anything, nor did anyone seem to notice. Chuck dabbed at his plate with his fingers, corralling toast crumbs hither and yon on his plate. This was a habit that Cameron found particularly annoying, but one that Chuck acquired during his time in the army; there was no way that anyone was going to break him of it. The awkward silence continued until it was mercifully broken by the timely arrival of their waitress.

"Can I get you boys anything else?" she asked with a fond smile.

You're why we eat here, even though there's no bar!

The waitress was a kind, decent woman, and took it upon herself to make up for the low-quality food by taking a genuine interest in her customers. She alone was the entire dining room staff. Along with the cook and one busboy, she was in perpetual motion when the place was busy.

"I think we're all set." Chuck smiled back at her and thanked her, as did each member of the band. With a wink and another smile, she presented the bill with a flourish and hurried back to the counter, where an elderly couple waited to pay for their food. Chuck grabbed the bill and studied it closely, shaking his head disapprovingly.

"Are they trying to rip us off?" Snapper whispered, leaning in to take a look.

"No," muttered Chuck. "But I think they're ripping themselves off. No one is taking into account the higher cost of food due to rationing. This whole thing didn't come to six bucks. Those are prewar prices, for crying out loud. OK, boys. Pony up!"

The band pooled together their money and gave it to Chuck.

"You guys take off, if you want." Chuck slid out of the booth. "I need to talk to Cam for a minute."

Cameron groaned inwardly, anticipating a tedious reproof about his bad attitude.

It won't be the first one.

He was relieved when Clyde and Snapper remained while the rest of the band left the diner and returned to the hotel. He, Chuck, and the boys went to the counter and paid the bill.

"Oh, and this is for you," Chuck said with a smile, handing the waitress another dollar. "I don't like leaving tips on the table. Too much of a temptation for someone to grab it. Especially nowadays."

"Why thank you, young man!" she said, beaming. She dropped the dollar bill into a large jar next to the register. "That was very generous!"

Cameron noticed the jar for the first time. It was a large jar, the type usually filled with pickles or mayonnaise. This one was cleaned and one-third full of loose change and some dollar bills. It was also adorned with red and blue stars, and decorated with a hand-written label.

"Alaskan Refugee Fund." Cameron's voice was barely audible, but very little ever escaped the waitress.

"My brother and his wife used to live in Barrow," she explained, her light and cheery tone now quiet and distant. "He worked as an engineer with the oil company. She was a schoolteacher. She quit teaching when they had their daughter. They named her Millie."

The waitress spoke in short, crisp sentences, her voice constricting as she struggled to maintain composure. Cameron could tell it was a losing battle.

"Millie would have been two on Valentine's Day," the woman said, before her speech was choked with an anguished cry. Chuck reached out and gently touched her arm, knowing that there was nothing one could say at such a time. Providing comfort and solace would alleviate her distress, and remind her that her grief was understood, even if it was too heavy laden for words.

Barrow was the first spot on American soil occupied by the Soviets. No one had been able to escape. From there, the invasion unfolded with blitzkrieg-like speed, swift and total. However, the

Soviets, having rapidly expended their element of surprise, underestimated their foes. The Alaskans were able to mount resistance and evacuation strategies. Their progress, though, was soon disrupted. Missiles launched from submarines in the Bering Sea and Bristol Bay struck Anchorage as well as Fairbanks, attacking both cities and the US Air Force base.

American citizens fleeing the combat areas made their way to Juneau as best they could. In the confusion, there had been efforts to get the women and children relocated to camps in the Pacific Northwest. Refugee centers were almost entirely devoid of men, except for those who were elderly, infirm, or otherwise unable to participate actively. It was not unusual, therefore, for women to deliver to the refugee stations their children—tagged with the names and addresses of relatives in the continental US—only to disappear back into the wilderness to fight. However, the governor of Alaska, as well as the leader of the Alaskan Red Cross, toiled with great difficulty to discourage this phenomenon. The dilemma escalated in the ensuing months as US and Soviet forces fought for each and every one of the Aleutian Islands, with official rights of possession shifting almost daily.

An attack on the city of Yakutat destroyed the small airport there, as well as wreaking havoc on the roads connecting Juneau to the rest of the state. This forced refugees to attempt evacuation by sea, which in turn forced the United States to supply the resistance via ship and other military seacraft. Soviet submarines severely harassed the unarmed fishing and relief vessels operating in the Gulf of Alaska. This led many, in and out of Alaska, to attempt drastic evasive action by moving over land or via air, either of which often resulted in death by exposure or crashes. These events exacerbated the burgeoning frustrations of Americans and Canadians. Cameron winced as the related news stories flashed through his mind.

A cold shower isn't that much of an inconvenience. I feel like such a shit.

With Herculean effort, the waitress regained her composure and forced a smile. Cameron reached into his pocket and withdrew the paltry sum of change. He dropped it into the jar, grimacing at the pathetic *clink* of the nickels and pennies as they landed on their brethren coins.

Literally, the proverbial drop in the bucket...

The waitress smiled and nodded an adieu. They left the diner. Clyde and Snapper, quite sullen, decided to return to the hotel.

Cameron sighed and lit a cigarette. He awaited Chuck's imminent lecture. Not that he minded, really; he enjoyed a grand rapport with Chuck. It was seldom that the two would ever truly butt heads, but he knew that Chuck wanted to talk privately and there was no putting it off. He was right.

"First off, let me say that I am going as stir crazy as you." Chuck led the way down the sidewalk in the opposite direction of the hotel. "I'm not pissed at you, or even irritated with you for grousing and grumbling about the current situation. To be brutally honest, I figured you'd have gone off the deep end long before this—"

"Man, I just want to *do* something!" Cameron insisted.

"I already told you! We're trying to get some bookings elsewhere," Chuck assured him. It was well known to the band that Chuck hated interruptions, but this time, he didn't reprimand Cameron for his. The lack of admonishment suggested to Cameron that Chuck was up to something.

"Well, that's good, I suppose," muttered Cameron, grinding out his cigarette.

"I thought that would make you happy!" exclaimed Chuck. Cameron shrugged.

"That isn't all I've been thinking about," Cameron explained. Chuck walked in silence. Eventually, they arrived at a small park. Cameron remained standing, despite his manager's gesture toward the benches.

Chuck sat, making sure that he maintained a clear view of the entire park, and anyone who arrived or departed. At the moment, there was no one within their immediate proximity. On the other side of the park were people playing Frisbee and riding bikes. Chuck gestured again for Cameron to sit next to him.

"Well, fuck it!" snapped Cameron. "Back in Vermont, we went through months of your stupid-ass spy boot camp, and more months of training and briefings, and all that hassle and pain, only to be left out in the cold with nothing? Why, man?"

"You boys are sources," Chuck explained, his voice still hushed. "Sometimes you're not called on to do anything for a while. Sometimes, sources are used just once and that's it. Sometimes, they're called upon all the time."

"So where the hell do we fit in?" demanded Cameron. "Are we just one-hit wonders, or what?"

Chuck folded his arms across his chest. He gazed across the park. A young mother with her baby in a pram crossed along the far end of the lawn, stopping to allow bicyclers to pass in front of her. Cameron shifted impatiently, but Chuck didn't notice. A car passed by. Chuck eyed the vehicle. Cameron couldn't discern why, and his annoyance with Chuck's silent treatment grew. He was about to speak, but Chuck beat him to it.

"Do you think that I would still be here, if that was the case?" Chuck asked, his gaze now back on the bicyclists.

"Well, I sometimes wonder if you're working with us to make up for all the shit that went down before."

"Oh, right!" laughed Chuck. "The government doesn't honor its Indian treaties, we've still got POWs missing in Vietnam, there are refugees stranded in the Alaskan Front, but they're going to lose sleep over a cover band from Vermont. You figured it out! I'm busted!"

"Do you have to say it like that?" Cameron muttered, lowering himself to the bench. It was a rhetorical question. Chuck patted him on the back.

"Don't worry, Cam, old man," Chuck said, cheerfully. "The fact is, we realize everything you guys went through, and not just those of us who trained you, either. We also realize that you didn't know the full extent of the danger you'd be facing. When you did realize it, you didn't try to back out, even though it cost you dearly. That takes balls, man. I, for one, don't regard that commitment lightly. It speaks volumes that certain other people don't, either."

"Then what the fuck are you going to do with us?" demanded Cameron.

"Believe it or not, we've got a chance to appear in a USO tour. I'm hoping to hear word on that soon from McIntyre."

"A USO tour? Playing for the troops?"

"Yeah," said Chuck. "But it hasn't been easy to arrange."

"Why not?" asked Cameron. Chuck grinned and shook his head.

"You have to be invited *and* have a clean record to get into a USO tour," Chuck explained. "And let's just say you guys aren't exactly choirboys."

"True, but we aren't that bad, are we?" asked Cameron. Chuck nodded with a laugh.

"As far as that batch of brass is concerned? Yes, you are, or were, to be specific. They don't want *anything* on your record, especially in the last ten years. But we've been working hard to get things cleaned up for you, and we're pretty sure that we've got it all taken care of. If we're lucky, we should be hearing from the powers that be pretty soon. Like I said, your presence has to be requested, and since you guys aren't as well known as the bigger acts, it's doubtful that anyone outside of the Northeast would request you. So, we've had to be a little creative with that, too. But if it all works out, you'll have plenty of work. McIntyre's been working really hard on it because we think you'll do some serious good there."

"How, exactly?"

"From a practical standpoint, a cover band will help the USO quite a bit. The famous acts that Roadhouse Sons cover are too expensive for the USO to contract and transport for visits to all of the camps and bases, but you guys aren't. With your band, they get hit songs of *several* of the famous acts, all in one show. That's a virtual happy pill, good adrenaline for the troops." Chuck hesitated, then cleared his throat for emphasis. "Your other talents can be used there, as well."

"How?"

"If you're on a morale tour, for instance, you'll have ample opportunity to talk to some of the soldiers and hospital personnel, right?"

"That's right, I guess. Yeah."

"You'd also hear a lot of what they had to say."

"I'm with you."

"That could include information about black propaganda pushers…"

Cameron furrowed his brow, evaluating Chuck's statement. "Really?"

"You remember black propaganda?"

Cameron's memory rewound to the weeks of briefings and meetings during Clyde's recuperation from the previous year's explosion. The rest of the band worked with a variety of experts who trained them to recognize overt and covert forms of propaganda designed to inspire or demoralize targeted groups. The band surprised their superiors by responding to these concepts quicker than most neophytes. Subsequently, the boys were asked to formulate and stage a presentation regarding how they utilized music to influence audiences during their shows. One evening's presentation also featured a performance demonstration. The band was amused at the mass of slack jaws in the audience, especially when Clyde was given free reign. Cameron smiled fondly at the memory.

Consider yourself influenced.

"Black propaganda occurs when the enemy attempts to or succeeds in passing false information from false sources, via messages, commentary, or ideologies, for the purpose of embarrassing or defaming the opposing enemy, and undermining morale among soldiers and civilians."

"Good boy!" Chuck's smile beamed.

"And, the black propagandist has to presume willingness of the recipient to believe the information and that its source was credible."

Chuck's smile was now a beacon. "You sold me! If we can sell it to the others, we'll be golden."

"Your bosses?"

Chuck's smile waned. He was suddenly pensive.

"Not quite. Even though it's actually not one, the USO functions like any other government agency. They're partnered with the DOD and, theoretically, we all work for the same side, but nobody plays in their house without them maintaining control. That's understandable. Fortunately, though, we've got people on the inside who have a lot of influence. If they say it's a go, then it's a go. But if they say there's no way in hell, then the whole idea is off."

Cameron said nothing. He gazed at the scene before him. A small park in the middle of a small town. A civil war monument stood in front of him, and the American flag unfurled in the breeze. Children rode by on their bicycles. People wandered up and down the sidewalks, stopping to chat or window-shop. If Cameron didn't know better, he could have sworn it was any other day in any other town in America. He could even pretend that the red, white, and blue bunting decorating the town's buildings were hung for a holiday or special event, not the outpouring of patriotism in response to their country under attack.

But the war burst into his thoughts and he couldn't help but think about the related inconveniences—the shortages, the rationing, and his myriad complaints about these egregious impositions. But then he recalled the waitress at the diner. He thought of the people forced from their homes, of the families perpetually terrified and worried and the emotional duress endured when no word on their relatives and friends ever arrived.

Cameron's petty complaints faded, but his resentment grew for the mere fact that they were forced to attempt normal lives during the reality of war and the unspoken, but omnipresent, threat of a nuclear attack. He loathed that the children he saw playing in the park had to grow up with this. He bristled just thinking about a woman who had to collect money for refugees in the hopes that she was somehow doing something for her family. He resented that American men and women who had done nothing to provoke an enemy attack were forced to flee their homes, become guerillas and form a Resistance—and do so on American soil. Most of all, Cameron resented the fact that he was sitting on a park bench, feeling the breeze and the warmth of the sun. He felt like he was making no difference.

"I said we'd talk about it this morning," Chuck said, interrupting Cameron's thoughts.

"Talk about what?" Cameron asked.

"That dream you've been having," Chuck said. He looked away from Cameron and glanced down the street. "Tell me about it."

Cameron hesitated, fumbling for the right words. Even though the images in the dream were as clear and lucid in his waking state as they were in his sleep, he still found them incredibly difficult to describe. Slowly and with great caution, Cameron revealed to his manager the nightmare that haunted him. As he was about to describe the dream's horrific finale, Chuck interrupted him.

"And every time you think you're about to die, you wake up, right?"

"Yes. How did you know?"

"I've had the same kind of dreams," he explained, still looking down the street. There was an odd tone to Chuck's voice, almost as if he was talking to himself and unaware of Cameron's very presence. "I've had friends that had the same kind of dreams. Especially after going through shit like we went through."

"You mean, like in the army?" Cameron asked warily. Chuck rarely, if ever, spoke of his service to his country, and inquiries about it were often met with either terse responses or firm orders to ignore the subject altogether. There was no such response this time. In fact, Chuck's shoulders sagged noticeably, and his face wearied before Cameron's eyes.

"Yes. And other times."

"Like when?"

Chuck looked at Cameron.

He looks so sad...

"Let's get something straight once and for all. My story isn't for me to tell or for you to hear. I give you the benefit of my experience, not the *Sturm und Drang* of my testimony. Do I make myself clear?"

Cameron said nothing. He just nodded, having learned from his own experience that Chuck didn't favor verbal interaction when he was in such a state.

"I told you then, and I'll tell you now. You did the best you could. You did better than I've seen others do, and *you* didn't have a fucking clue what you were doing. You pulled everyone out of that mess that wanted to get out of it. The ones that didn't make it out with us ended up that way as a result of their own actions. You can't do anything about that. No one can. Let it go."

"How? How do I do that?" Cameron leapt from the bench, clearly agitated. Chuck glared at him.

"Shh! *Sit down!*" Chuck hissed.

Cameron remained standing, stouthearted and stalwart. Chuck jabbed at the bench with his index finger. Cameron sat, if for no other reason than to prevent Chuck from breaking his digits. Chuck held Cameron's gaze for what seemed to Cameron like an eternity. At last, the elder spoke.

"You constantly remind yourself of this conversation, that's how. You remind yourself when you go to sleep. You remind yourself when you wake up, from that dream or otherwise. And you remind yourself every time you eat, drink, piss, and shit. Just like the rest of us."

Cameron leaned forward, studying Chuck closely. Cameron wanted to push further. He could knew by the set of Chuck's jaw that doing so would be a mistake. Cameron's inner compulsion won the battle against his will. The question would not go unanswered.

"Why don't you ever talk about what you did?"

"Because I don't think about it," Chuck replied without hesitation.

"Ever?"

"Ever."

"Why?" Cameron asked, his voice a whisper. "I could use some advice on this."

Chuck stared straight ahead.

He's clenching his teeth...

"You're right," Chuck said. "You could. You got a lot of training before, but it was all theory. You need some practical work now, some hands on training."

"Like what, exactly?"

Chuck didn't answer for several minutes. Once again, he behaved as though Cameron wasn't present. Chuck's gaze wandered about the park and the surrounding streets. He smiled at the antics of the children on their bicycles, and watched the swallows swoop and dodge the ground and each other. Cameron fought the urge to reiterate his question.

"You guys did good work in Vermont." Chuck spoke so suddenly that Cameron was startled. "You were recruited to collect information on a drug ring and you did it. You helped shut the ring down, and you uncovered the source location of the merchandise. But let's face it. Your success was due almost entirely to pure chance and shit luck. Any arguments?"

Cameron hesitated, then shook his head.

"You lost only one member of your team, and only one other member of your team was seriously wounded. That's very good, but also largely luck. A logical, trained agent would not have attempted such cowboy antics, thusly endangering themselves and others. Are there any arguments with that?"

Again, Cameron shook his head.

"You need to be trained in hand-to-hand combat," Chuck continued. "And in proper procedure and protocols. I need to give you the complete training we Feds receive, but I'm working under very severe handicaps that make all that difficult to accomplish."

"Like what?"

"Number one. Clearly we are not at our training facility," Chuck replied. "We are here in Missouri. We are a rock band. We are on a road trip to only God himself knows where. Number two. In our midst is one Philip S. Napier, whom we affectionately refer to as Snapper, and who has not experienced even one iota of what the Roadhouse Sons have been through. He cannot fathom the full extent of what we're involved in. If we suddenly plunge him into our real world, it may very well shock his sensitive system and result in trauma, hysteria, and possible bed-wetting, the last of which I do not want on my conscience."

Snapper was an old pal of the band's, brought on board following the death of their treasured friend and roadie, Doug Courtland. Snapper was one person whom Cameron and the boys knew at length, and trusted implicitly. They worked vehemently to convince Chuck and McIntyre that Snapper was someone worthy of invitation into their fold. After initial resistance, and following a thorough background investigation, Chuck and McIntyre finally agreed to hire Snapper.

"So, what do we do?" Cameron asked. Times like these frustrated him the most. He knew that something needed to be done and he possessed the eagerness to do it. The frustration of waiting for the opportunity for action to arise exhausted him. Cameron wanted to plow ahead, but realized that his potential maneuvers were the cowboy antics to which Chuck referred.

"By the way, this is part of your lesson," Chuck smiled.

"What is?"

"Waiting," Chuck replied. "Agents on TV and in the movies get into exciting, nail-biting situations at the drop of a hat, but the fact is that you wait, and you wait, and you wait, and then you finally get the chance to hurry up and wait some more. You wait for all the leads you've been following to guide you to another clue. You wait for people you are following to make a mistake that lets you snag them. You wait for the fates to smile on you so you don't go completely stir-crazy waiting for all of your waiting to pay off. If another assignment is waiting for *you*, you complete all of the briefings, training, and preparations for it. And if, after all that waiting, the gods end up really pissed off at you, you're stuck behind a desk doing administrative shit and waiting for paperwork."

"Sounds like a blast," muttered Cameron. Chuck whistled and shook his head.

"Granted, we've got our assignment. They haven't been too pushy about things. They want us to do a reconnaissance tour for right now, partly so Macintyre and I can schedule and execute more of your training." Cameron's eyebrows rose to his hairline. "And, for example," Chuck grinned, "you have to learn how to make a drop, how to locate a drop site, things like that."

Having never actually done so, Cameron briefly described the instruction that Chuck's predecessor, Dwyer, had provided during the band's initial recruitment in Vermont. He also took the opportunity to inform Chuck just how much their new and brief history had impacted his life. Cameron reiterated how the Roadhouse Sons had been arrested in Vermont on a series of phony charges made by a disgruntled club owner, who the band had discovered was cheating them. While the boys were detained, they were approached by a group of individuals who offered them the opportunity to get all the charges dropped, but on the condition—that they cooperate in full with the federal government. Reluctantly, they agreed and were sequestered for several months and taught various rudimentary espionage skills. The band successfully uncovered a smuggling ring, but at the expense of two lives. Gordon Dwyer, their original manager, had been killed, as had their roadie, Doug Courtland. One of their recruiters, D'Lorenzo, had been recalled to face misconduct charges. Clyde had been seriously wounded and bore a scar to prove it. In addition, they had uncovered evidence of a possible double agent who had betrayed the United States and compromised national security, thereby enabling the Soviets to attack the United States and at the same time had recruited another double agent—for whom Cameron had developed romantic feelings— and assigned her to Europe.

"You should write a screenplay," Chuck said glibly. The tables were turned with the look Cameron gave Chuck.

"Oh, don't be upset with me. All that was fine, for what it was worth."

For what it was worth!

"Obviously, you have to know a lot more than that. You'll be in worse situations, believe me. None of us can afford to rely on luck to save your bacon ever again. Do you understand what I'm saying?"

Cameron nodded. A knot was growing in the pit of his stomach.

Oh, no…

"We'll schedule more training, Cam my man."

"When do we start?" Cameron's throat was so dry that his question croaked forth from his throat.

"When I give it the green light," Chuck smiled. "Now, in the meantime, head back to the hotel. I've got to be alone."

With that, Chuck rose and made his way across the park. For several moments, Cameron just sat there, watching Chuck walk away. Finally, he stood and stretched, basking in the warmth of the spring sun and relishing the cool breeze blowing on his face.

As he started to walk toward the hotel, he felt the undeniable sensation that he was being watched. Cameron paused at a crosswalk. As he looked down the street in both directions, he noticed from the corner of his eye that someone was watching him. He didn't give it much thought since he was a stranger in this town and was, therefore, bound to attract attention from the locals. Still, there was no need to take chances. Once across the street, he paused to look in one of the store windows, and then pretended to pick something up off the ground. As he stood up, Cameron saw that the person had also crossed the street.

Cameron moseyed down the sidewalk, stopping to read the various posters for local events. Potluck dinners to raise money for the war effort, war Bond drives, blood drives, a wrestling show, and a notice for a missing orange-and-white cat named Morris were among the placards posted in the windows. Cameron kept walking at a leisurely pace.

Several few blocks down was a display of plastic Memorial Day bouquets and wreaths in the window of a hardware store. Cameron paused to examine the faux flowers, and glanced back up the street from whence he'd come. His pursuer had paused three doors away, and was bending down to tie his shoelace, thus preventing Cameron from seeing his face. With the man momentarily distracted, Cameron seized the opportunity to evade him and ducked inside a convenience store. He walked to the far end of the establishment, and from there he had a perfect view of the sidewalk in front of the store. Also to his benefit was the sun's position. Cameron knew that the brightness of the outdoors rendered it almost impossible to see inside the store. That, coupled with the customers milling about inside, made it easy for Cameron to avoid casual detection.

Cameron's pursuer passed the store window without pausing. Cameron caught a fleeting glimpse of the person. It was a male, approximately Cameron's size, clean-shaven, with short hair, sunglasses, a blue baseball cap, and a light blue windbreaker. The man made no effort to come into the store. Cameron felt foolish. He decided to look around the store a bit before heading out. He glanced at the magazines near the counter. Looking up, he noticed that the shopkeeper was giving him a dirty look. Cameron decided to make a quick purchase.

Pulling out his ration book, he realized that he had two extras for tobacco products.

I'll just buy a pack of cigarettes.

"Are these yours?" the shopkeeper asked, studying the ration coupons and eyeing Cameron suspiciously. Cameron was about to retort when he realized that he would only be asking for trouble.

"Yes, sir. They are," he said. Cameron conjured a sincere effort to be polite and to hide his anger. "Would you like to see my license?"

CHAPTER THREE

"Living in a New World"

"They bombed Pearl Harbor!" Clyde was stricken, yet fascinated. He stood in the doorway of Cameron's room, bracing each arm against the doorframe, his breathing labored as though he'd just run a marathon. His face was drawn and pale. Snapper could see that Clyde was shaken to the core.

"They did that years ago, man!" Snapper said with a slight chuckle. "You're watching too many reruns of *Get Christy Love*."

Clyde rushed over to the television and turned it on. The snowy black and white reception showed the *ABC News* logo. Frank Reynolds's voice repeated earlier reports of a Soviet attack on Pearl Harbor.

"Initial reports indicate that the missiles were fired from a Soviet Yankee-class submarine," came the authoritative, yet calmly assuring baritone. Clyde listened to the hypnotic voice report of yet another attack on American soil. Despite his panic at the thought of a pending nuclear assault, Clyde couldn't help but feel his terror allayed at the sound of that voice emanating from the television set.

Reynolds turned slightly to retrieve new reports handed to him by off-camera staff. "We've received confirmation that no, I repeat, *no* nuclear warheads were launched."

Snapper muttered something to himself. Clyde ignored him. The reception on the television was fading and the screen began to roll. Snapper leaned over to adjust the set, causing the reception to briefly fade to a snowy static, so he adjusted the rabbit ear antennae.

Frank Reynolds was back. "Initial reports say that the targets all appear to be military in nature, with no civilian casualties reported." At that moment Howard K. Smith's clear, sharp voice broke in. Clyde wondered if the networks paired these two news anchors on purpose; one offered calm assurance, the other offered reserve from false security and complacency. As though reading Clyde's mind, Smith began to ask Reynolds the questions that Clyde himself was pondering.

"Frank, no doubt you and our listeners have drawn the same parallels to the Japanese attack in World War Two," Smith said, looking at the camera despite the man seated next to him. "In that event, the Japanese severely damaged the Pacific fleet. Can you give us any word on whether or not that is the case in *this* attack?"

Reynolds paused for a moment and looked down as if to gather his thoughts before answering his partner. Clyde surmised, though, by the way Reynolds eyes darted off-camera, that news staff were relaying information verbally, rather than from the Teletype.

"No, Howard. We don't have any confirmation of damages at this time," Reynolds replied. "But our sources do tell us this. It appears that the majority of the fleet had already been deployed to search for any Soviet naval presence, as well as to accompany the convoys en route to the islands."

After Alaska, Hawaii had been the next area most affected by the war. The majority of Hawaii's food and materials were shipped in from the mainland either by air or by sea. Soviet aircraft and the Soviet Navy had severely disrupted these routes. American bases in the Far East, such as Guam, Iwo Jima, and the Philippines, had been able to turn to Southeast Asia and Australia for supplies, as those routes weren't affected as severely. However, with the Soviets learning early on how to disrupt the American ability to effectively track their submarines, the Battle of the Pacific was proving to be a cat-and-mouse game between the two navies, with neither effectively gaining the advantage.

Snapper watched Clyde's shoulders sag. The reporters continued talking, keeping Americans informed of nothing as they awaited more information. Clyde thrust his face in his hands and began to tremble.

"Man, are you OK?" Snapper asked. He was aware that the news was serious; America was at war, after all. Regardless, Clyde's reaction nonplussed him. Clyde didn't respond, but rubbed his face, as if to rub away the outside world, abruptly stood up, and walked out. Snapper hesitated for a moment, then ran after him, squinting through the sudden emergence into sunlight. Clyde was already halfway toward the stairs to the parking lot. Snapper ran to keep up. Clyde did not want company. The very manner in which he walked made that clear to Snapper, but the roadie realized that Clyde shouldn't be left alone. Snapper hung back, Clyde still in his sight.

Clyde reached the parking lot and pushed past an elderly couple who grimaced at him disapprovingly. Snapper, following stealthily, nodded and smiled embarrassingly at the old folks, hurrying on to remain on Clyde's trail. Clyde reached the sidewalk and headed north. It was just past high noon and quite warm. Clyde's rapid stride created a sweat for Snapper; it was a chore just keeping up with him. Never once did the guitar player look back.

They continued along the sidewalk until it ended. Clyde kept walking, right onto the shoulder of the road. Snapper followed as they passed various businesses, shops, sheds, and parking lots. Eventually, they reached a vacant lot and what appeared to be an abandoned garage. As if on a mission, Clyde crossed the lot and walked to the back of the building. Snapper made his way carefully to the corner of the building and peeked around, pulling back as a rock struck the wall next to him, spraying tiny bits of cinderblock and stones. Figuring Clyde had finally spotted him and was warning him away, Snapper pressed himself against the side of the building and remained there, wondering if the guitar player was going to look for him. When Clyde didn't show himself or call out, or use any other means to acknowledge Snapper's presence, he wondered if Clyde realized he was even there.

Snapper carefully peered around the corner once more. Clyde was picking up small rocks and throwing them against the back of the building. There were no windows or doors, or anything that could incur damage. Clyde hurled a rock as hard as he could. After it rattled against the building, he bent down and picked up another. He aimed at nothing in particular, but simply continued throwing stones against the back of the building. Taking a chance, Snapper stepped out a bit farther and watched Clyde. The guitar player didn't acknowledge him. Snapper moved cautiously toward Clyde.

Clyde threw rocks, one after another, in rapid motion. Snapper saw that Clyde was breathing heavily, perspiration soaking his shirt. He muttered, throwing stone after stone, diving down to gather and fling new ones at rat-a-tat speed. It reminded Snapper of the arduous toe-touch coordination training in gym class at school. Snapper sidled up to Clyde and picked up his own stone.

"Mind if I join you?" Snapper asked, cautiously. Clyde said nothing. Snapper threw his stone and watched it bounce off the wall, leaving a small white mark at the impact site. Nonchalantly, he examined the wall. A host of small white marks were spattered all over it. Snapper realized that this wasn't the first time that Clyde had performed this ritual. He was about to speak when Clyde beat him to it.

"She'd have been four on Valentine's Day," he spat, hurling the stone with all of his might. It struck the wall with a loud crack, creating a small cloud of dust then ricocheting off to the right.

"I thought the lady said she would have been two," Snapper said. Clyde didn't seem to hear.

"Fucking war!" Clyde hissed, increasing his firing speed. Snapper watched, fearful that Clyde would make himself dizzy and fall over.

"Man, you're going to hurt your arm!" he said, trying to get Clyde's attention. It was no use. Clyde continued to bend and stand and throw with all of his might. Snapper watched him stumble; Clyde was indeed making himself dizzy. The guitar player's breathing became labored, a dark stain of sweat now on his back.

"Fucking Commies!" Clyde snarled, his teeth clenched tight. "Fucking bastards, fucking bombs, fucking wars. Fuck, fuck, fuck!"

With each expletive, Clyde's movements became faster, and with the final one, the result that Snapper feared finally happened. Clyde lost his balance and fell forward, face-first into the gravel. Snapper hurried over to help him up, but Clyde had already rolled over onto his back, his arm across his eyes.

"Get the hell away from me, man!" Clyde warned. "I want to be left alone."

"I was just trying to see if you're all right!" Snapper protested.

"I'm fine!" Clyde reproached sarcastically. "I'm friggin' fine. I'm lying here on the ground, just fine and dandy. I had a place to sleep. I had a good meal and I'm lying here with the warm sun shining down on me without a care in the whole wide world! My life couldn't be better if Farah Fawcett was in my lap right now. I'm fine, fine, fine, fine, FINE! I'm so damned fine I could shit a pink Twinkie. Can't you tell? Isn't it obvious how perfectly fine everything is? Am I in a refugee camp? Am I being shot at? Are they dropping bombs on my ass? No, no, and NO! So, therefore, everything is just plain old gloriously fucking *fine!*"

Seeing Clyde's actions reminded Snapper of times when his own uncle would take a large block of wood and spend literally hours pounding nails into it, covering every square inch. When the nails were flush, Snapper's uncle continued to pound away until he could swing his arm no more. "Survivor's guilt," Snapper had once heard someone call it. Snapper's uncle had been the sole survivor of an attack on his unit during the Korean War. The uncle was sent home with a Purple Heart and an artificial leg, along with a depression that would sink him into long periods of seemingly unreasonable and abstruse melancholy.

What Snapper couldn't understand was why Clyde felt this way. He had known Clyde for a while—even though they weren't close friends—and he knew that Clyde had never fought in war. None of them had been called up in the draft in Vietnam; thankfully, they'd all just barely missed it when it expired in 1973.

Clyde pushed himself up, releasing a long and weary sigh. He rose first to his knees, then fully upright. Snapper eyed him solicitously. Clyde swayed slightly, but quickly regained his balance, then bent over, head toward the ground.

"Are you all right, man?" Snapper asked, running up to him.

Clyde finally acknowledged the roadie's presence.

"I'm OK," he replied, nodding his head. "Just thought I was going to be sick for a minute, that's all." Clyde picked up a handful of rocks and, once again, commenced to throwing them against the building, with even more force this time.

Snapper stood watching him for a while, listening to the clack of each stone rebound off the cinderblock. Finally, predominantly out of boredom—and fellowship—Snapper picked up some stones and began pitching them. Just as he finished his first throw, a black-and-white police car came around the corner. Snapper's gut wrenched.

"Shit," he muttered, stones falling from his hand. A short bulldog of an officer, dour in visage and demeanor, emerged from the driver's side of the vehicle and sidled toward them.

"What are you fellows doing?" the officer spat. Clyde made no effort to acknowledge the officer, instead, continuing to throw his arsenal of stones. Snapper fought his own annoyance at the officer's questioning of the obvious, and muttered a response.

"Nothing," he grumbled, immediately realizing the inadequacy of his reply.

"Sure looks like something to me," the officer replied, irritatingly officious. He turned his attention to Clyde. "Son, why don't you put those rocks down and step over here a minute?"

Clyde threw a stone and was about to throw a second when he suddenly looked at the officer, as though noticing him for the first time. He turned back to the wall and paused for a moment, as though to finish his second throw. Snapper felt nauseous, convinced that Clyde would challenge the officer's authority. To his great relief, though, the guitarist dropped the stones, wiped his hands on his jeans, and walked right up to the policeman. The officer, squint-eyed and stolid, paused before speaking, to see if Clyde was defiant or compliant. He realized that the young man wouldn't cause any trouble, and asked his question once more.

"I'll ask you again, young man. What are you doing?"

Clyde shrugged.

"I'm just throwing rocks at an old building," he explained. "What's the big deal? I'm not hurting anybody. I'm not doing anything wrong."

The officer shook his head, casually resting his hands on his hips.

"Well you see, son, that building you're talking about isn't abandoned. It's owned by a Mr. Bob Larabee, and he reported it being shot up out back. We just got a call that someone was out here doing it again. Did you see anyone else out here?"

"No," Clyde admitted, his breathing becoming rapid. "Since I've been here, it's just been me and Snapper. But I wasn't shooting anything. I was just throwing rocks. You can see where I threw them. I thought it was abandoned, I swear. I didn't break any windows or anything. I didn't think I was doing any harm!"

"He's telling the truth," offered Snapper in agreement. "I was there with him today. We were only throwing rocks."

"And why were you boys throwing rocks, might I inquire?" pontificated the lawman.

Clyde defended his actions, imparting to the policeman his sentiments about the news of the bombing of Pearl Harbor, and of his growing frustrations over the current state of affairs.

"I thought that was kind of a constructive way of getting it out, instead of doing something stupid like going on a bender," Clyde explained. "Like I said, I didn't think I was hurting anyone."

"There are other ways of dealing with frustration," the policeman said. "Enlisting, for one!"

Clyde sighed and shook his head, tapping his chest.

"Classified 4-F," he replied, sadly. "Heart murmur. I tried that back when this shit started. Thought Cameron was going to have a fit."

"Who's Cameron?" the officer asked, squint-eyed once again. "I thought you called him Snapper?"

"Cameron is the front man of my band," Clyde explained, kicking his toe into the gravel. "Snapper here works for us. He loads the truck and sets up our equipment and stuff."

The policeman nodded.

"So you're a musician," he asked. "What kind of music do you play?"

"Rock and roll," Clyde stated proudly, making the sign of the horns with his left hand. "I'm with the Roadhouse Sons." Snapper noticed the policeman's upper lip curl, almost imperceptibly, but the grimace ceased as quickly as it appeared. Snapper recognized the prejudice, though, and his dislike of the officer was complete.

"Would you fellows mind putting your hands against the car, please?" the officer asked, mildly. Clyde and Snapper realized that this was a command, not a request.

"Am I in any trouble?" Clyde asked, his face ashen. He didn't move.

"I received reports of someone firing shots against this building and want to make certain you boys aren't carrying firearms. Now, put your hands on the car and spread your legs," the officer said firmly.

Snapper glanced at Clyde and nodded, both deciding to comply. The officer told Snapper to stand against the front of the patrol car, while Clyde was told to place his hands on the trunk. The guitarist was patted down first. Clyde tried to steady his breathing while the officer placed his hands against Clyde's chest. The policeman didn't spend much time on Clyde's upper body, possibly due to the fact that he was wearing his signature tight tee shirt, which left nothing to the officer's imagination. The officer then tapped the toe of his shoe against Clyde's ankle. Clyde spread his legs.

"Don't you need, like, probable cause or some something to do this?" demanded Snapper.

"We received a report of someone shooting at this building. The description of the person matches your buddy here," the officer replied patiently. "To me, that adds up to probable cause." He resumed his search of Clyde.

"How'd you get that scar on your arm?" the policeman asked. Snapper saw Clyde's face flush at the mention of his gunshot wound. He steeled himself, anticipating Clyde's response.

"I got hurt at work," Clyde muttered.

"You told me you were in a band."

"Sometimes we play in some rough places," Clyde explained.

"Do you have anything in your pockets that I should know about?" the officer asked. Clyde shook his head.

"Excuse me," the officer asked. "I didn't hear that."

"No," Clyde grumbled, spreading his legs further.

"Would you empty your pockets, then?" the policeman said to both of them.

Clyde and Snapper complied with the lawman's order. Suddenly, they heard a voice calling out.

"HEY! What's going on?"

Snapper looked up. There was Chuck, striding across the street with great determination, his expression a mixture of annoyance and concern. Snapper couldn't decide if he should be relieved or even more distressed about his manager's arrival. Just then, the officer grabbed Snapper's arm. Snapper decided he was relieved. The policeman halted his search of Snapper's belongings and marched up to Chuck.

"I'm Officer Beecham," the lawman stated pompously. "Who might you be?"

"My name's Chuck Lamont. I'm their manager. What's going on here?"

"I'm investigating reports of vandalism, and arrived to find these two throwing rocks at this building."

Chuck tossed a furtive glance at Clyde and Snapper. They looked at the ground, clearly having noted the expression of exasperation on Chuck's face.

"Do you guys have an explanation for this?" Chuck demanded. Even the police officer flinched at the sound of Chuck's voice.

Snapper remained silent. Clyde repeated to Chuck the very explanation he'd provided to Officer Beecham. Chuck just stood there, hands on his hips and legs apart. Snapper wondered why this stance was so popular on this day.

"Well, don't let me interrupt, Officer. Do your duty."

The officer turned back to his business at hand and continued to pat down Clyde down. He found the card that confirmed Clyde's 4-F classification. He turned his attention to Snapper, and finished examining the contents of the roadie's pockets. Snapper carried some loose change, cigarettes, a pack of matches, and the band's ration books. The officer flipped through the books, as though searching for contraband hidden in the pages.

"Would you like to see my identification?" Chuck asked, still maintaining his stance. Officer Beecham nodded. Chuck tossed him his billfold. The officer opened it, immediately noticing Lamont's firearm permit.

"You have a gun?" the policeman asked. Chuck nodded and described his firearm. The officer scrutinized Chuck's permit.

"Do you want me to bring it into the station for you to see?" Chuck asked, exasperated again. The officer shrugged.

"You don't have to. Of course, it would be nice if you did. I just don't see why a rock band should have to carry a firearm."

"We've been in some places where it might've come in handy," Chuck said with a smile. "You know how some clubs can be. However, I only use it then. I don't carry it everyday."

Officer Beecham nodded. He returned the billfold to Chuck without looking at him.

"You folks obviously aren't from around here," the policeman said to Chuck. "So where, exactly, are you staying?"

Chuck named the hotel and told Officer Beecham how long the band intended to stay in town.

"Do you want to take them in?" Chuck asked.

"No," Officer Beecham said. "The fellow that owned this building was just afraid that someone was trying to send him a warning, if you know what I mean. This is a whole new world now and not everyone in it's nice. To be honest, with the tighter security, now I've got a lot more serious things to deal with than some rock throwing. No serious damage has been done, no windows broken or anything, so I'll tell him it was just someone horsing around and that *you* won't do it anymore." Officer Beecham pointedly gazed at Clyde. The guitarist nodded his head in agreement.

"Like I said earlier, there are other ways of dealing with your frustration," the officer continued. "I might have a few suggestions, if you're serious."

"Like what?" Clyde asked. He gathered up his personal effects and filled his pockets.

"There's going to be a meeting tomorrow night at the American Legion," Officer Beecham said. "We're trying to get some community projects going to help with the war effort. If you're serious about wanting to help, I'll release you into your boss's custody and he can bring you. Are you willing to do that?"

Clyde knew that this was more than a casual invitation; it was more of an informal condition of probation. Refusing wouldn't fly. He nodded in assent, albeit reluctantly. Chuck nodded, as well. The officer smiled, as though he himself had just saved the world.

"All right then," Officer Beecham said. "Looks like this whole thing was a little misunderstanding and we've got it all sorted out. You fellows have a nice day."

The policeman turned and walked away. Snapper could swear that Officer Beecham practically skipped. The policeman crawled into his cruiser. As he was about to close the door, he paused, looking at Clyde.

"I'll see you tomorrow night," he said. The note of warning in his voice was palpable. Snapper was nonplussed by this man's ability to be simultaneously reasonable and dogmatic. It was, in a subtle way, a frightening combination.

Clyde watched the cruiser pull away. Chuck came to his side.

"I don't want to hear a word," Chuck said, through clenched teeth. "We're going back to the hotel, *now.*"

The manager turned and stormed across the lot, back in the direction from whence he'd come. Clyde and Snapper followed suit.

"Thanks for following me, man," the guitarist said in a low voice. "Sorry I wasn't better company, but I just had a lot of stuff running through my head. I needed to work it out."

"Do you come here a lot?" Snapper asked. He knew that the myriad pockmarks on the cinderblock wall were Clyde's work.

"Yeah," Clyde admitted. "I went over there when I had a ton of crap pressing on me. I just throw rocks until I'm too tired to think, then I come home."

"You thinking about the bombing?" As soon as the words had escaped his mouth, Snapper realized that this was a stupid question.

"Yeah," admitted Clyde again. "The bombing, the war, the whole FUBAR of it all, and the fact that I'm here listening to the damned TV advertising Post Honeycomb cereal like nothing's wrong in the whole friggin' world. Just like it did a year ago."

"Is that what's bothering you? That we're trying to still be normal?"

"Yeah, that's what's bothering me!" hissed Clyde. "The fact that we're trying to be normal, and I don't know if we're ever going to be normal again. Every time I think about how it was last year, I'm afraid it won't be that way next year. Hell, I'm afraid there won't *be* a next year, sometimes!"

"Me, too, if it makes you feel any better. I think we all do."

Clyde shook his head.

"There's got to be some way," he muttered, shaking his head.

"Some way to what?"

"Some way to shit peach ice cream!" snapped Clyde. "I don't know! Some way to make it all stop. To make the fear stop, to make the guilt stop, to make the bombs stop! To make it all go *away*, so I can spend my Saturday afternoon's watching Dick Clark babysit a bunch of kids who think they can dance, without wondering if I'm going to be vaporized by some fucking nuke!"

Clyde stopped and rubbed his face.

"That's all I want, man," he said. "I want the shit to stop."

"You, me, and everyone else," sighed Snapper. He privately mused over Clyde's expressions of defecating desserts amidst the guitarist's plea for peace.

They caught up with Chuck and all three made their way back to the hotel. Just as they arrived, a patrol car pulled out of the parking lot.

"What was he doing here?" Snapper wondered. It was the dutiful Officer Beecham.

"He's checking to make sure I told him the truth," Chuck retorted, heading for the stairs. The guitarist and roadie sheepishly followed, saying nothing.

"Where are the others?" Chuck asked them. He opened the door to his room.

"The last time I saw Cameron he was with you," Clyde said.

"I think that the others took the van to get some air in the tires and get some oil," Snapper offered. Chuck, pensive, rubbed his chin.

"All right," he said at last. "When you see them, tell them to stay here. You guys stick around, too—" Just then he was interrupted by the ringing of his telephone. Hurrying inside, Chuck answered it. He left the door ajar, allowing the boys to hear his side of the conversation.

"Hey! Where are you?" he asked, pausing for the response at the other end. "Right. I know where that is. OK, stay there. I'm on my way."

The boys watched from the doorway as Chuck quickly changed his shirt and grabbed a well-worn "boony" flopped-brim soldier's hat from his duffel bag. Tucking his shirt in his jeans, he grabbed a pair of sunglasses and hurried out. They followed him with their gaze, hovering near the doorway. Almost to the stairs, Chuck turned around and came back to them.

"Snapper! You got a cigarette on you?" Chuck asked.

"Yeah," said Snapper, shaking one from his pack. "But I thought you didn't smoke?"

"I do today," Chuck smiled, tucking it behind his left ear. He turned and hurried down the colonnade.

"Where are you going?" called Snapper.

Chuck turned full circle with a smile on his face.

"Out!"

CHAPTER FOUR

"High Anxiety"

Cameron sat on the bridge, sipping his Coke. He watched the cars and pedestrians pass by. The wide rail that separated the street from the walkway made a nice perch to watch anyone approaching him from either side. He took only small sips to make his Coke last, not because he'd just used up the last of his sugar rations, which he had, but because he needed to appear to be simply relaxing. Cameron's eyes followed a pickup cross the bridge and continue north along the street. As he did so, Cameron saw that his shadow was still perched on the park bench, perusing a newspaper. Cameron snickered.

You must have that fucking thing memorized.

He wished that he had a newspaper, as well. This casual observation was the most tedious thing he'd ever experienced. He tried to ignore how bored he was. He felt the warmth of the sun on his back and watched the water as it flowed under the bridge. The sensations produced a hypnotic affect, and Cameron knew that he shouldn't become too relaxed. To do so would possibly allow his "friend" to slip away unobserved. Cameron looked away from the water, turning his head in the directions of the various sounds of people approaching. With his peripheral vision, Cameron saw the other fellow doing the same thing. Something about the other man's actions led Cameron to believe that this person was not a leisurely bench patron. The man glanced about too furtively and purposefully. This didn't make Cameron feel any better.

For a moment, Cameron debated whether to get up and walk around again, but thought better of it. He'd told Chuck where he was and had been told to stay there. So he did just that.

But damn, my ass is falling asleep!

Rocking back and forth slightly, he tried to maneuver himself into a comfortable position, but try as he may, the bridge rail was still not going to conform itself to Cameron's posterior. Espying the man on the bench, Cameron resented him even more. Realizing that his "shadow" was not any more comfortable than he, Cameron smiled just a little.

Suddenly, a police car veered around the corner and slowed down as it approached Cameron. Two officers in the front seat pointed at him and began to roll down their window. Then the officers noticed the fellow on the park bench. The man looked toward them and dropped his paper. The stranger didn't wave or acknowledge them in any way, but once the officers noticed him, they said nary a word to Cameron and drove away.

Weird.

Cameron casually turned his attention back to the river. His "friend" resumed reading his newspaper.

Cameron tensed. This waiting was driving him crazy. He knew that he needed to do something, but he wasn't entirely certain what that should be. In an effort to control his frustration, he began swinging his legs a little faster, but realized that he projected frustration and impatience, so he stopped. He didn't have a watch, so he had no idea just how long he'd been waiting for Chuck.

After the next gig, I'm getting a Timex. Takes a licking and keeps on ticking.

He again fought the urge to swing his feet. He looked up and saw someone walking toward him. Cameron tried to remain calm, but this new stranger, like the one on the park bench, was wearing sunglasses and a hat. This gave Cameron cause for concern. He casually sipped his soda, as much to quench his thirst as to have something handy in case he needed a weapon. The stranger rubbed his nose as he approached and fiddled with his sunglasses. Cameron relaxed. It was Chuck.

Chuck paused in front of him.

"Hey buddy, you got a light?" he asked, taking the cigarette from behind his ear. Cameron hesitated a moment before answering. Chuck pulled down his sunglasses. Cameron could see his eyes and knew that Chuck was serious.

"Yeah, sure," Cameron replied, fumbling in his pocket for matches. Leaning forward to help shield the flame from the wind, Cameron whispered to Chuck.

"What the hell are you doing?"

"I'm just asking for a light, man, that's all," replied Chuck, taking a deep drag and then trying to stifle a cough.

"You look like your face is on fire," muttered Cameron. Chuck furrowed his brow and looked at the sky.

"Needed an excuse to stop for a casual chat," Chuck replied with a cough.

"I can never figure out how you guys do this," Chuck whispered, taking a much smaller puff. Cameron rolled his eyes, and before he could answer, Chuck continued.

"That fellow over there's the one you were talking about, right? Just nod if I'm correct."

Cameron nodded, taking a sip from his soda.

"We're talking low enough so he can't hear us unless he has a really good listening device, which I doubt he does. Have you seen any cars following you guys?"

"Nah," said Cameron shaking his head, then spitting over the handrail of the bridge.

"That habit is as nasty as this one," grumbled Chuck, eyeing his cigarette and taking another puff. "Has he made any contact with anyone else that you've seen?"

"Nope," smiled Cameron, watching Chuck flick his tongue to get rid of the taste of tobacco. Cameron told Chuck about the police car. Chuck leaned on the rail, considering this new information.

"So, we know he is at least known to the local constabulary if he isn't working with them," he said, pensively. "But you haven't seen anyone else? Any cars passing by repeatedly?"

"No."

"Then he's probably working alone, since there doesn't seem to be any surveillance car traveling around with him. When did you notice him?"

"Right after you left the park," Cameron said, lighting his own cigarette. "Followed me down the street and made me suspicious, so I ducked quick into a shop to see if he'd keep on going. He only went as far as a few shops and waited for me to come out."

Chuck pursed his lips, weighing the information.

"Well, he didn't follow me, so that would suggest that he isn't an agent, or at least isn't one that's very well versed in his subject," mused Chuck.

"What makes you say that?"

"If he were an enemy agent, he would have followed me," coughed Chuck. "Which raises the question of why follow you?"

"I don't have any fucking idea," muttered Cameron, slowly swinging his legs once again. "Not a single clue."

Chuck turned to toss his cigarette into the river and glanced at the man on the bench. The man raised his newspaper up higher as Chuck looked in his direction.

"We also know that he is an amateur at this as well," Chuck said, hopping up next to Cameron.

"How can you tell that?"

"You never do anything to draw attention to yourself. You always keep your movements natural."

"Like taking up smoking?" giggled Cameron.

"Kiss my ass," grumbled Chuck. "Tell me what you did to try and shake him."

Cameron casually told Chuck of how he'd wandered about town, into and out of shops, and down various streets with the other fellow never out of sight.

"Why didn't you try getting back to the room?"

"If he was trying to find out where we were staying, he wasn't going to learn it from me," explained Cameron.

"Smart. Why did you call?"

"I thought you should know about it and I needed help to get rid of him. So, what do we do now?"

Chuck thought for a minute. He stretched.

"We split up and head out," he explained. "I'm going to head through the park and up that street on the other side. You wait about three minutes and then head up this one. Go two blocks and then cut down the first alley or street that you come to. I'll be waiting at the other end."

"I don't have a watch," Cameron pointed out.

"Ask Santa for one this year," Chuck replied. "In the meantime, count to one hundred and eighty."

With that, he patted Cameron on the back and hopped down, pausing to take a quick sip of Cameron's soda.

"I backwashed in that," snapped Cameron.

"So did I," smiled Chuck as he handed the bottle to Cameron. Chuck headed across the bridge. Cameron watched as Chuck continued through the small park and passed the man on the bench. The man pulled the paper back a little to watch Chuck pass, but neither man acknowledged the other.

Cameron looked skyward and began counting. At least this was giving him something to do. He counted on, absentmindedly bringing the soda bottle to his lips, but catching himself just in time.

He could never be sure if Chuck was kidding or not. When his count approached one hundred sixty, he too hopped down from the railing and stretched his legs. Counting to one hundred and seventy, he noticed the man shift his newspaper. Stretching once more as he counted to one hundred and eighty, Cameron started across the bridge. He whistled as he walked, but realized that this behavior was just too obvious. He knew from watching movies, as well as trying to avoid detection by jealous boyfriends, that a studied nonchalance was never effective, so he simply continued walking. Approaching the corner of the nearest building, he glanced back and saw the man fold his newspaper and rise from the bench.

For a moment, Cameron considered stopping right there at the corner and seeing what the man would do, but thought better of it. Chuck had given him specific orders and this was no time for improvisation. He continued walking at an even pace, pausing once in a while to look at the window displays. He reached the first corner and stopped to let traffic pass. Looking both ways, he noticed that his shadow was still behind him.

Cameron crossed the street. A thought struck him like a lightening bolt. What if something had happened to Chuck? What if this guy was working with others and they'd grabbed Chuck? What would he do then? Cameron imagined scenarios, discounting each one as soon as they formed. His anxiety escalated and his breathing accelerated.

Slow down. You're going to make yourself sick.

Cameron maintained his pace as he moved along the sidewalk. Finally, he reached the second block and was about to continue to the next corner when he noticed an alley between two buildings. Remembering Chuck's instructions, Cameron ducked down the alley and ran. He contemplated tossing the soda bottle, but remembered that it was a viable weapon. Halfway down the alley, Cameron came to another, wider alley. This was obviously a cross way for delivery access to the stores. He paused briefly to look both ways, and saw, with great relief, that Chuck, hat and sunglasses now removed, was leaning against a building to Cameron's left. Chuck beckoned Cameron and motioned for him to be silent. Behind them was a small door. Chuck's foot kept the door ajar. He pushed Cameron inside.

Before Cameron could ask what they were doing, Chuck closed the door noiselessly and held his finger to his lips. Cameron studied the surroundings. The room itself was dark, but light appeared through an open door on the far wall. Cameron could see they were in some sort of storeroom, but he couldn't discern its purpose. Rows of shelves, many of which were empty undoubtedly due to the war, lined the walls, with other shelf units scattered throughout. Muted voices came through the open doorway, but no one entered the room. Chuck pressed Cameron against the wall. He gripped the doorknob with both hands, putting one foot against the doorjamb as leverage to keep the door from being pulled open. Cameron saw the knob turn, but Chuck gripped it even tighter. Cameron put his Coke bottle on the floor and was about to grab hold of the doorknob as well, but Chuck shook his head. Whoever was on the other side of the door shook the doorknob and then stopped. Chuck didn't release his grip or remove his foot.

Several minutes passed. Chuck pressed his ear against the door, then motioned for Cameron to follow him. Chuck carefully opened the door enough to look out. When the coast was clear, he stepped out, pausing briefly behind the door to check the other end of the alley. He motioned to Cameron, who followed him out. Chuck quietly closed the door behind them.

The stranger was now almost at the end of the alley, but was moving quickly toward them. Chuck pointed in the opposite direction from whence they'd originally come, and pushed Cameron. The two men hurried back to the smaller alley, then hurried down to the opposite street, keeping the buildings between them and the stranger. They paused at that corner, and as they did so, saw the other man emerge on the opposite side of the street. The stranger quickly crossed, but completely ignored them.

Cameron was about to say something when Chuck interrupted him.

"Come on, let's go," he said, then dashed between two parked cars and crossed the street. Cameron waited for a pickup truck to pass, then followed his manager. They hurried to the end of the block, careful not to run, then rounded the corner. The stranger was continuing along the sidewalk, looking from side to side and occasionally pausing, but never once looking over his shoulder. Cameron noticed the man's shoulders sag and his pace slow.

Don't expect sympathy from me.

To Cameron's surprise, Chuck never slowed down or made any attempt to hide from view in case the stranger noticed them. They continued this way for several blocks until the stranger turned right.

Chuck turned down a smaller side street that ran parallel to the stranger's route. Cameron examined the buildings for possible escape routes. There was a fence blocking his view. Cameron anxiously picked up his pace. Chuck didn't hurry, but didn't instruct Cameron to slow down.

Reaching the last building, they peeked around the corner and saw the man heading diagonally across the street to a one-story white clapboard-and-brick building, which he entered via a side door. Cameron was able to get a good look at the building.

In the front was a small yard, divided by a cement walkway. On one patch of ground was a young tree. On the other was a white flag pole, displaying the American flag. Also in front was a large sign identifying the building as an American Legion Post. Cameron was about to ask Chuck what they should do next, but Chuck shook his head.

"Let's get back," Chuck said. "There's nothing to see here."

Cameron wasn't so willing to dismiss the man that had spent so much time following him. He cast one last look at the building, wondering why any of its inhabitants should be taking such an interest in him.

"My throat's dry," said Chuck. "Give me the last of that coke."

"I haven't got it," said Cameron. Chuck stopped and faced him, looking concerned.

"What did you do with it?" Chuck demanded. Cameron shrugged.

"I must have left if somewhere."

"Where did you leave it?" Chuck demanded. "Think carefully."

Cameron mentally retraced his steps. When did he last have the soda?

"I think I left it in that storeroom," he said, finally. "Yeah, I set it down when I thought you would need help with the door. Why?"

"Because when you use someplace as a hideout, you never leave any trace behind," Chuck said, sternly. "You never leave anything out of place and never give anyone a reason to think something is out of place, or that someone had been there."

"Should I go back and get it?" asked Cameron. He hoped he didn't seem facetious. He genuinely regretted having made such an abysmally stupid mistake. Fortunately, Chuck shook his head.

"No, I doubt there's any need for that," he said. "Something like that could easily be put down to one of the guys that works there. But make damn sure you never, *ever* do that again. You might not be so lucky next time."

CHAPTER FIVE

"Gloom, Despair, and Agony on Me"

Chris Simms was a timid little man and the last person one would expect to be the road manager of a rock band, especially of an emergent punk rock band. He had no idea why he was selected for this job, but knew that it was in no one's best interest—especially his—to complain about it. His superior, Jack Stanley, the actual agent and manager of the band, dubiously entitled Boney Jack, was not at all a tolerant individual. The best way to avoid him, Simms had discovered, was to relentlessly pursue whatever assignments Stanley gave him, even ones as mind-numbingly tedious as this one. Slowly, Simms went through the stack of mail once more, setting the pile he'd just examined off to the side to avoid including it again in this inane search. He knew it had to be here. It was supposed to have been sent already. He would be expected to produce it very soon. The thought of not being able to deliver did not appeal to him.

When he was satisfied that he'd turned over every correspondence stone, he carefully pulled another stack of mail toward him and scrutinized each letter, envelope and post card. Simms had already searched through them all at least three times, each time without success yet; still, he kept going back, convinced that there was something he'd overlooked. Yes, it was possible that the item that he so tediously and meticulously sought had been lost in the mail, or hadn't been sent yet— if at all—but it was no use employing such excuses as a defense. Responsibility for any failure was his alone to bear, and that realization made him even more anxious. Simms reasoned to himself that the large amount of Boney Jack fan mail made it impossible to notice everything at once. It *was* here. He would relax, listen to *real* music—as opposed to what those punkers played—and begin searching again.

Thus, with trembling hands, Simms poured himself a glass of wine, one of the few benefits of this job. He inhaled the rich aroma of the robust Chianti and felt, more than smelled, the essence of its pungent bouquet. He held the glass up to the light and smiled as the liquid illuminated into a deep, ruby red. He hesitated before sipping it, enjoying the anticipation more than the action. When at last he put glass to lips, the warm liquid virtually kissed him, as appreciative of him as he was of it. His timidity ebbed, his anxiety now dissipated, as the warmth of the wine spread throughout his body. Simms set his glass down, walked over to the turntable, and placed the record of his favorite tenor on the stereo, the volume of which was set at slightly less than one-quarter of the dial. The band hated his music almost as much as he hated theirs; the lower Simms kept the volume, the less violated his sensitivities remained, having fended off the inevitable boisterous complaints.

After a deliberately indulgent moment, Simms drew a deep breath and returned to the task at hand. He sat at the table and proceeded to examine each piece of mail once more. His confidence now increased, he calmly and carefully read and reread the addresses and return addresses on each envelope. He slowly opened the envelope and reviewed the letters and pictures therein. He even inverted and shook each envelope, just to be sure he'd revealed all of its contents. He found himself humming along with the stereo, the ardent voice echoing and complimenting the warmth of the wine. He became lost in the music and permitted himself just one moment to relax.

Christopher Simms mused over why he'd garnered this position. He was a man of culture and sophistication. As road manager, he had the ability—and responsibility—to provide a buffer between his clients and an innocent and unsuspecting world. This was no easy task. Boney Jack, both the band and the eponymous lead singer, were intent upon devoting themselves to living the stereotypical lifestyles of rock stars. Their reading material consisted primarily of lurid, pornographic magazines and tabloid coverage of other bands. It was these articles that they pursued with great relish, absorbing with fascination each account as a personal challenge to surpass the excesses about which they read. Simms was surprised to discover that they insisted upon having copies of whatever daily local papers were available. He soon realized, though, that they were not interested in current events; it was the latest curfew schedules, and which Seattle clubs were permitted to be open on what days, that captured the band's attention.

Simms seethed with resentment at the very thought of the band going to clubs. As road manager, he was required to accompany them, and it was usually on these outings that his humiliation became nearly intolerable. The band's erratic and destructive behavior kept Simms constantly engaged with club owners, waitstaff, and managers, keeping the peace and avoiding unnecessary attention by both press and police. Initially, Simms believed that the band was not responsible for their actions, being under the influence of alcohol and whatever other narcotics they'd ingested. Over time, however, he realized that their behavior was far more calculated than he'd initially thought, and he discovered that they *wanted* to see how far they could push people before someone snapped.

As Simms sipped his wine, he indulged in the one fantasy that kept him going—that one day *he* would wake up and be told that at least one or more of the band members had not. Their constant and ever-increasing drug consumption assured him that this was a distinct possibility and, he admitted to himself with a sly smile, it was the reason he had long ago ceased the hopeless task of trying to discourage their sybaritic behavior.

The sudden pounding on the door caused Simms to start, and he spilled his wine. As the angry voices emanated over the music, he shuddered as he saw how closely the dripping wine and the resulting puddle on the floor resembled fresh blood. The pounding grew louder and Simms hurried to the door, leaving the mess behind. As he approached, the pounding became louder still and he knew that it had to be a member of the band. He also knew that they wouldn't hesitate to break the door down. Fumbling with the lock, he pulled open the door and narrowly missed being struck by a fist that, seconds before, had been pounding to get his attention. Instinctively, he raised his arm to deflect the blow and shut his eyes as he anticipated contact. His blood went cold as he heard the familiar cruel laughter of his main tormentor.

Simms cautiously opened his eyes and instantly wished he hadn't. Jack Preston, known as Boney Jack to his adoring fans, stood in the doorway, his right fist poised in the air. Boney Jack was as skeletal as his moniker indicated. Slightly over six feet six inches tall—in interviews he always insisted: "Six, six, and one sixth, baby! I'm the living Mark of the Beast!"—Boney Jack towered over most of his associates, which meant that he would have to tip his head to speak to them, causing his wavy, raven hair to fall forward, giving the effect of a hooded cowl. The thick, dark brows and dark circles under his eyes, the result of too little sleep and too many drugs, highlighted his hazel irises. The skin on his face was sallow and drawn tight against his high cheekbones, with his dark clothes only adding to the macabre effect. Whenever Simms looked at him, he was reminded of a ghoul.

"What's the matter, Chrissy?" Jack laughed, coldly. "You know I'd never hit you! At least not when you're looking."

Boney Jack pushed his way into the room, knocking Simms into the wall. Two more members of the band, lead guitarist Jack Quinn and bass player Jack Ralston, followed their lead vocalist over the threshold. The press had dubbed them "Three of a Kind," but the truth was that they couldn't have been more different. Boney Jack Preston was the sworn enemy of anything conventional and accepted. Jack Quinn was almost devoid of personality, habitually acceding to dominance and to anything suggested to him or demanded of him. Jack Ralston was as narcissistic as Preston was anarchistic, carefully using all of the connections made by the band to ensure a future for himself once the eventual—and some would say, increasingly inevitable—breakup of the band occurred. Simms had long ago learned of Ralston's "casual" inquiries with record companies and producers and other musicians with whom they'd worked. Logic would dictate that Simms carefully monitor Ralston's actions to guarantee that no jeopardy would befall his and the band's livelihood, but Simms knew that the band's disintegration would likely be his only salvation, so he did nothing to prevent that course.

"Reading your fan mail, Chrissy, or more likely ours?" Jack asked striding over to the table. With a grand swipe of his arm, he sent the stacks of letters to the floor, and some into the puddle of wine. Horrified, Simms ran to the table to try and retrieve the letters. As he dropped down to his knees, Preston gave Simms a shove in his backside with the toe of his boot, sending the road manager face-first onto the floor.

"Yes, I'm reading your fan mail!" Simms cried in exasperation. "Making sure that all of the requests for pictures get answered and all of the lovelorn young ladies get your heartfelt and well-worded responses."

"Fuck that," Jack said, taking another swipe at the pile. "Who needs that shit?"

"You do, for one," snapped Simms. "That is, if you want to keep selling records and tickets and living the lifestyle to which you've become accustomed."

"Crass materialism, that's all it is," yawned Ralston, grabbing the bottle of Chianti and guzzling it. Simms felt tears burn his eyes. That wine was nearly eight years old and he'd acquired it very recently, at great expense and with great difficulty, despite his connections. It was one of the few means of escape available to him, and watching it rush down the gullet of the bass player nearly caused Simms to shriek. The only reason he didn't give in to that impulse was because he knew this was what they wanted. By denying them that satisfaction, he would deny them their prize and therefore, ultimately, win this battle of the wills.

"Corporate sellout," Ralston continued, a trickle of wine dribbling from the corner of his mouth. "Sacrificing our artistic integrity for the sake of sponsorships and filthy lucre. I hate them and their money!"

"Is that why you spend it so fast then?" snapped Simms. "Are you trying to shove it away from you as quickly as you can?"

Ralston's face twisted in rage as he approached the kneeling man. This Jack was almost as tall as Preston, but his features were fairer and his build stockier, almost Nordic. A clean-shaven face and long, sandy-blonde braided hair coupled with a pair of bright green eyes could not have rendered Ralston more different in appearance to Preston, but like his fellow musician, Ralston was just as devoid of compassion. Simms steeled himself for the blow he knew was coming, until Boney Jack interceded.

"Don't touch him," laughed the singer. "We've got other shit to do right now."

"What do you want in here, anyway?" demanded a relieved Simms, gathering up the scattered envelopes. He looked up as Jack walked past him, expecting another swipe at the table or at him.

"How many times have we fucking told you about playing this music so loud?" Preston shouted, stopping in front of the record player. Simms attempted to struggle to his feet, only to have Ralston push him back down. Simms watched as Jack dragged and screeched the needle across his treasured album. Simms knew that they were expecting him to react to the ruination of his prized record, but he knew what was coming and the scratch wouldn't make any difference. As expected, Boney Jack removed the record from the stereo and examined it carefully, then turned it over to examine the other side. Simms waited, refusing to give him the satisfaction of a response. Annoyed, Jack glared at him and snapped the record in two. Throwing the shards in Simms's face, Preston stormed out of the room, with the other two dutifully in tow.

Simms stayed on the floor until he heard the door close. He rose to his feet. His record was shattered and Ralston had the Chianti. Simms didn't feel the despair that they'd no doubt hoped to cause him. He'd been through far too much in his life to allow these petty thugs to, despite their constant effort, reduce him to what the more professional sorts had been unable to accomplish. Instead, Simms felt frustrated and annoyed that he was constantly subjected to this type of behavior. He knew, though, that he wouldn't be forced to endure this forever. If he could only find what he was looking for—find *it*—he would be free even sooner. Retrieving a cassette recorder from the drawer of his desk, he inserted the earpiece into his left ear and pressed the play button. He smiled as, once more, the soothing sounds of Mario Lanza calmed his soul.

CHAPTER SIX

"Hopeful, with a Chance of Danger"

Cameron and Chuck followed the sidewalk's path. No one spoke. Cameron rued his mistake even more.

I left that friggin' bottle behind...

Chuck suddenly broke his silence. Cameron was long since used to and no longer caught off guard by Chuck's sudden bursts of speech, and equally as sudden periods of silence.

"Have you been keeping an eye on Clyde?" Chuck asked. "I mean, have you noticed him acting strangely?"

"You mean stranger than usual?" Cameron chuckled.

"I'm serious, man," Chuck responded, his voice stern. "This isn't any time for humor."

Cameron was taken aback. He searched his memory for any odd behavior on Clyde's part.

"Well, he's been different since getting shot," Cameron admitted. "He's been more withdrawn and touchy, but I just put that down to nerves. I mean, let's face it, man, he got shot and there was the explosion, and they never found Doug after that, and then he had surgery and all. *You* might be used to that shit, but the rest of us are pretty new to it."

Chuck nodded, but said nothing. They walked several more blocks in silence.

"I noticed the same things," Chuck admitted. "I chalked it up to nerves, too. But I'm talking about lately. Have you noticed anything more pronounced? Is he inordinately dejected and high-strung?"

"No," said Cameron. "But I do notice when he hears anything about the war, he gets really moody. He didn't used to. Well, I mean, at least not that much."

Chuck nodded and, per usual, said nothing. Cameron didn't press him about the line of questioning.

"We have to keep an eye on him," Chuck said. He related the encounter they'd had with Officer Beecham over Clyde's rock throwing, and the officer's subsequent edict that Clyde contribute more appropriately to the greater good.

"They didn't arrest him?" Cameron asked. Chuck shook his head.

"No. The officer just gave him a warning not to do it again and strongly suggested community service."

"Wow! You guys must have a lot of pull to get him off like that." Cameron whistled. Chuck shook his head again.

"Didn't have a thing to do with it," he said. "I think Beecham believed that Clyde was just agitated about the war, and frustrated about not being able to do more. He wasn't deliberately trying to cause trouble. With all of the heightened security these days, the cops probably don't want to be bothered with petty stuff like that. Beecham seemed genuinely exhausted and only too happy to leave, once he saw what was really going on."

"Did he give Clyde any guff about not enlisting?" asked Cameron, seething at the memory of his earlier encounter with the storekeeper. Chuck shrugged.

"He did. Clyde explained he was disqualified because of a heart murmur." Cameron stopped dead in his tracks.

"Clyde's got heart problems?" he said. "He never told me that!"

"I don't think it was something he wanted to talk about," Chuck replied, still walking ahead.

"Jesus! Do I need to worry about him dropping dead on stage some night?"

"I'm not a doctor." Chuck stood still and abruptly turned to face Cameron. "But I *do* know that, sometimes, heart murmurs are simply an extra noise, like an additional heartbeat, and no big deal. He probably got a good lecture about it when he had his arm stitched up. That might be contributing to his whole funk, too. Heart murmurs can run the gamut from serious anomalies requiring constant monitoring to the description I just told you, so if he hasn't keeled over on you yet, I doubt that he will."

Cameron, stupefied, stood there for several moments. At last, he resumed walking. By the time he and Chuck reached the hotel, it was afternoon and much warmer outside. They headed toward their rooms. Once again, Cameron regretted leaving the soda bottle in that storeroom, but for a less remorseful reason. He was dying of thirst, and doubted the band had any beer in the room. For a moment, he contemplated drinking water straight from the faucet, but decided against it.

I've never acquired a taste for the cheap stuff.

Chuck and Cameron were about to enter their respective rooms when they heard voices emanating from one of the others. Evan and Rich must have returned, though Cameron hadn't seen the van in the hotel parking lot. A woman's voice suggested that McIntyre might also be in there. He chuckled to himself.

Not necessarily McIntyre.

Chuck decided to check in with the band. His seemingly random knock on the door was recognized by the room's occupants as the given signal from a member of their team. Nevertheless, Rich barely opened the door and peeked out.

"What's the password?" he whispered, with mock seriousness, and then collapsed into a fit of laughter.

"Ballbuster," said Chuck. This only served to make Rich laugh harder, so much so that he had to lean against the doorjamb to prevent falling over.

"Let me in," Chuck said. "We've got work to do."

Stepping inside, Cameron and Chuck found the Roadhouse Sons gathered around the television set, watching the colorful antics of the Roadrunner and Wile E. Coyote. Cameron took notice of McIntyre. She was clearly not as relaxed as the others, a fact that rendered him instantly on guard.

"Have a nice walk?" McIntyre asked Chuck, who shrugged.

"I had an interesting one, if that's what you mean," he replied. He told McIntyre about Cameron's inadvertent adventure and how they'd followed their shadow back to the American Legion Post. McIntyre registered no reaction whatsoever. Her face was a complete blank. This disarmed Cameron even more.

"Then our information was right," she said at last. "Henry Clay's had his eye on some persons of interest. He thinks there's a rogue American Liberty League forming here. If he's right, this could be the beginning of a slacker raid."

"I wouldn't doubt it," said Chuck, sitting on the bed. "It would fit. A rural area, Middle America, very patriotic. The American Legion building seemed to be in good shape, so you can see that it's an active post, no doubt with active auxiliaries, as well. And we have learned from the local constabulary that they are promoting a lot of community service."

"Who's Henry Clay?" Cameron asked. "Is that a code name? I thought he was dead?"

"What's a Liberty League?" asked Snapper. "For that matter, what's a slacker raid?"

"Liberty Leagues are groups of people that have been forming around the country in response to the war effort," Chuck explained. "Encouraged by the American Legion, Liberty Leagues provide a much-needed, and resultantly highly productive outlet for the average American's patriotic zeal. The leagues encourage the growing of gardens reminiscent of the victory gardens of the First and Second World War, and they help organize drives for scrap metal and other items for the war effort. They also work with the Red Cross for blood drives, and offer assistance for the Alaskan refugees. With the growing need for funding, the leagues are also helping to organize war bond drives."

"However," interjected McIntyre, "nationally, there have been reported cases of leagues developing into vigilante committees to monitor suspected subversion. They've caused enough trouble that the National Commander of the American Legion brought it to the government's attention, and the Legion has been working closely with us to monitor all such unsanctioned activity."

"So, what about that other stuff?" Cameron asked again.

Chuck explained further. "Henry Clay, in addition to being the name of a famous statesman, was also the name of the regional director for the USO, as well as a regional director for the American Legion, and a liaison with our agency."

"Slacker was the term they used for people that didn't enlist during World War One and Two. Slacker gangs are groups that conduct slacker raids, and round up people they think should enlist," McIntyre said. "As a rule, these raids only detain people until they either check their status with the Selective Service, or make certain they register. Unfortunately, on a few occasions, these raids were violent and we have reports on some that have actually turned into lynching."

"Lynching?" cried Rich. "Who the hell are they lynching?"

"In most cases, people suspected of supporting the Soviets," Chuck said. "But in a few cases, people that had been conscientious objectors."

The band sat in stunned silence. Chuck and McIntyre continued to brief them. No one interrupted or asked any more questions.

"Do we have anyone working for us that's infiltrated yet?" Chuck asked. McIntyre shook her head. She handed to Chuck the notes she'd been reading.

"Could this guy have been a potential contact?" asked Evan. "It seems like he was trying to monitor something, at least. Or maybe trying to get your attention."

"Not a chance," said Chuck. "It was way too amateurish. He didn't try to avoid drawing attention to himself, and he didn't try to make any direct contact. He didn't even watch to see if he was being followed. For heaven's sake, Cameron even caught on to him."

"Oh, *I* even caught onto him?" Cameron sneered. Chuck's face reddened with embarrassment, a sight the Roadhouse Sons had never beheld. Cameron actually relished it.

"I'm sorry, man!" Chuck back-pedaled. "I didn't mean… Look. You know you boys aren't seasoned veterans, so if *you* were able to see that the guy was up to something, then that confirms to all of us that we know he's not one of our agents, or managed by us."

"You think they're Russian?" asked Rich, rising from his chair to stretch.

"No. Doubtful for the same reasons," McIntyre said. "From the sound of it, we have a home-grown network functioning here. The primary trouble we're confronting is that there are no clear suspects behind any of this. Henry's office received reports from what he calls reliable sources, but he's had little success in acquiring the information they need to launch an investigation."

McIntyre turned to Chuck, then eyed the band members, one by one.

"Have there been reports of any suspicious activities in the area?" Chuck and the band shook their respective heads.

"I've been reading the local papers almost every day," Evan replied. "The police logs haven't reported any serious crimes, just a lot of traffic violations, bootlegging, drunk and disorderly, that sort of thing. There were some house fires, but they weren't deemed suspicious, and they didn't amount to a lot of damage."

"Anything that struck you as unusual in any of the articles?" McIntyre asked. "Anything that you wouldn't expect to find in a small town newspaper?"

Evan thought for a minute, then shook his head again.

"No, not really," he replied. "Mostly wire service stories about the war, articles about local boys in the service, public service announcements and public interest articles. So normal it was almost boring."

"In the file, you'll see that Henry noted similar activity to what Evan's just reported," McIntyre explained. "Henry's sources are highly credible, but there's no mention of anything at all unusual in any area police reports. In fact, investigations underway are usually dropped after a short time, due to lack of evidence, or citizens choosing not to press charges."

"Police intimidation, you think?" Chuck said. McIntyre shrugged.

"Hard to tell," she said. "But I doubt it."

"Why not?" Cameron asked.

"We've questioned a few of the sheriffs and police chiefs in this part of the state. They're frustrated by this, too. Since many of their officers are enlisted, the remaining personnel aren't adequate to cover their jurisdictions. Responding to the slacker raid investigations sap their resources, especially when the victims change their story, or drop all charges as soon as the investigation starts."

Chuck closed the folder and handed it to Cameron, who perused it pointedly and quickly, and passed it on to Evan. Evan studied the file and passed it to Rich, who in turn passed the file to a reluctant Clyde. Once each member of the Roadhouse Sons took a turn studying its contents, the file was passed to Snapper. McIntyre, who'd been silent during all of this, finally spoke.

"Were there any articles on local businessmen, or area businesses and groups?" she asked, looking directly at Evan. Evan nodded.

"Yeah. Nearly every day, they pointed out a couple of people from around here."

"What did they mention in particular?" she pressed, leaning toward him. Despite the fact that Evan was a happily married man who desperately missed his wife and child, there was no denying that McIntyre, by her body language alone, could elicit a physical response from him. It was not a sexual response, by any means. It was a sensual response. McIntyre was the type of woman who caused one's senses to flare. She was a catalyst of sorts, and conveyed a certain electricity. It had little to do with the fact that she certainly wasn't rough on the eyes. It was her economy of purpose. She could very easily be someone who was "too much," yet she gave away so very little. It was that quality alone that always kept the boys on their toes.

Evan cleared his throat and recounted the articles for the matter at hand.

"Well, they talked about how long each one had been in the area, how long they had been in business, and how involved they were with the community. That sort of thing."

"Did they mention anything else about them?" McIntyre asked. "Was anyone cast in an unfavorable light? Any hints of previous scandal?"

"The papers didn't really convey anything like that," Evan continued. "Sometimes they'd mention if someone had a son in the military, or how active they'd been in some of the drives the county held, but nothing personal about any of them."

"We might want to take a look at some of those articles together," Chuck said to Evan. "You might be surprised."

"What do you mean?" asked Snapper. "Secret codes or something?"

"You could say that," Chuck smiled. "Though, it would be more like subliminal advertising, I'd expect. I bet they say nice things about people that are loyal Americans and not so nice things about those they think aren't actively supporting the war effort."

"You mean like slander? But I didn't read any indication of that kind of stuff. I do read the papers carefully like you told me to." Evan, his brow furrowed, was trying not to sound defensive, or be offended. Chuck shook his head.

"No, nothing that obvious, Evan," Chuck explained. "It's more a case of what they don't say, as opposed to what they do say. Articles about people or groups ill favored by the press can be less detailed and shorter, maybe have less photos. Little things like that help shape opinions, causing people to regard one person or business more than another."

"Is that what you guys were referring to when you told us about black propaganda?" asked Rich. "Because it sure sounds like it."

"Yes, it is." McIntyre continued, "Advertisements, interviews, and reports all have the purpose, not just the effect, of swaying public opinion."

"Is that why you guys are always reminding us to stick to 'Just the facts, ma'am' when we're writing our reports?" asked Clyde, showing off his best Jack Webb impersonation.

"Yes." McIntyre smiled wryly at Clyde, who blushed—a reaction he rarely, if ever, elicited around women. She turned to

Chuck, then gestured to Cameron with a nod of her head. "Speaking of which, Chuck, don't forget to have this little escapade formally documented."

"You're reading my mind, beautiful," Chuck said with a smile all his own, and a pointed look at Cameron. "I was just about to say the same thing." He turned his attention to Clyde.

"And I want a full report of *your* adventure today, too," he said, smacking the guitarist on the bottom of his sneaker. Clyde, lollygagging on the bed, responded with a heavy sigh and a roll of the eyes.

"What happened with him?" asked McIntyre, surprised and concerned. Chuck, eyebrows raised, glanced at Clyde, who knew he had to take the cue. He sheepishly related his events of the day, replete with the arrival of the punctilious but equitable Officer Beecham.

"That's why I'm making sure he only watches cartoons from now on," chimed Snapper, with more than a dollop of self-importance. "News about the war gets Clyde upset."

"It doesn't matter if I can see it on TV or not!" snapped Clyde. "I can still think about it, can't I? You can't monitor my mind, you know! I still hear about it everyday!"

"I'm just trying to help," replied Snapper, now on the defensive. "You don't need to keep trying to find out more stuff and agonize over it! You're right, we see and hear enough of it everyday. You don't have to go looking for it."

"I don't need a babysitter!" Clyde snapped. "For crying out loud, you'd think I was in danger of doing something stupid from the way you all act!"

"All right, guys, calm down," interrupted Chuck. His voice was calm, but firm. "Snapper, I want a report from your perspective, too."

"Me?" cried the roadie. "What for? Why can't you go with his?"

"Both of you, and I, will have to submit reports. It's protocol, especially because local law enforcement personnel were involved," Chuck insisted. "This little episode is bound to show up on someone's radar eventually, and when it does, it'll be a good thing to have a nice, neat little paper trail explaining what led up to it and how we dealt with it."

"Is that really necessary?" asked Cameron. He lit a cigarette and grabbed the ashtray off the table. Both Chuck and McIntyre nodded.

"Absolutely. We file reports for everything. This shouldn't be lost on you," Chuck averred. "Not much different from the army in that regard, and that's beneficial. It helps to cover your butt in many situations, and goes a long way in preventing any potential problems down the line. You know all this. You know you do."

Cameron knew that Chuck was right; he didn't like it, but he knew it.

Benedict Arnold in front of everybody?

McIntyre knew what made Cameron tick. The boys had a rough day already. Chuck wasn't jumping in to settle things down, so she elaborated.

"If your actions are challenged, or if there's a question involving adherence to protocol, your reports stand as facts of the related events. That's why we're such sticklers for these things, especially if we're operating covertly. Also, since we, in this situation, brushed with other law enforcement agencies we have to file a report. If we don't file a report and they do, their report stands as fact of the situation, and our memories, if we're called to testify, stand as conjecture. Memories fade over time, a lot quicker than pen on paper. Our reports eliminate conjecture and confusion. In this particular case, Cameron, we don't know who your shadow was. With a total lack of information thereof, we have to operate in a fashion as detailed as possible, so if we hand this investigation off to another team, we don't give them a scanty file like this one. So, welcome back to school, fellows. You still get to do reports. This isn't new news. You all know that."

"Can I have my mom write me a note?" moaned Clyde, pulling a pillow over his face.

"I'm trying to sympathize," said McIntyre, with only half-hearted sincerity. "But, no. Stop acting like you're in third grade. You have to suffer on your own."

"Oh," laughed Chuck. "I like that part."

"Are you...? Man!" Rich, who'd been gnawing on a guitar pick, dashed it to the floor, nose upturned. Chuck nodded enthusiastically, and burst forth an outright guffaw.

"I envision it frustrating the shit out of some little uptight, ass-clenched bureaucrat's desire to nitpick us for not submitting the proper paperwork. I often think that half the reason they have us do all that administrative work is to see what doesn't come in. By making sure everything's submitted in proper order, I have denied them...the pleasure...of trying to make my life miserable!"

"How do you people have time to fight the Russians?" muttered Snapper.

This caused Chuck to laugh even harder. "We people? You're one of *us* now, son!"

McIntyre rolled her eyes heavenward. She cleared her throat once, then again.

"*So*! How do we handle Cameron's shadow?"

"The gods have smiled great opportunity upon us. I'm going to take advantage of Clyde's condition of release." Chuck smiled knowingly. "I'm going to see what there is to discover when we go to that meeting tomorrow night. I am very confident that it will be something fruitful for us all."

"Chuck, I don't endorse that idea," McIntyre said, emphatically. "I know that it was a condition of Clyde's release, but it could only make things worse for him. If he's so wrought with frustration that he's vandalizing buildings, then putting him in a situation where he'll be further confronted is just asking for trouble."

"For the record, I did not vandalize anyone's building," insisted Clyde, without removing the pillow from his face. "Well, not intentionally, anyway."

"That's not the point," McIntyre insisted, her professional mien in full force. "I don't believe that complying with this particular condition will do you any good, Clyde. With all due respect, it certainly won't help our mission any if we have to spend our already limited resources monitoring you to prevent you from going off the deep end."

"Do you have any other suggestions?" Chuck asked, nonchalantly.

McIntyre now leaned toward Chuck. He, though, was long since immune to her impact.

"When you take in your firearm, like Beecham told you to do, take your credentials with you," McIntyre explained. "Let them know that your dog's bigger than their dog."

"I really don't want to tip our hand just yet," Chuck replied. "If there's a rogue group maneuvering, they're at least working with the full knowledge, if not cooperation, of local law enforcement, as evidenced by their deference to Cameron's buddy."

"I still think it will be a big mistake if you and Clyde go to that meeting," McIntyre insisted. She nodded toward Clyde. "If he's not thinking straight, then he's likely to compromise the situation. He's too close to it, not to mention a potential loose cannon."

"But I don't think it'll be like that at all," Chuck assured her. "He'll be with me."

McIntyre averred her position with a crisp retort. "You're taking an inordinate risk. I can see putting him where they can see he's trying to be a good boy, but relying on him to remain calm in a potentially volatile situation is tempting the fates."

"I'll be there, too!" cried Snapper. "I mean, I know that I haven't done anything serious with you guys yet, but I think I can help here. Especially if Chuck's there, too."

McIntyre wasn't mollified by any means, but Chuck continued to insist, in his provocative and effusive manner, on his course of action. Ultimately, she had no choice but to concede, with no further objection and albeit reluctantly.

"Well, I'll at least let our superiors know about this," she stated. Chuck nodded his head.

"I was about to suggest that," Chuck conceded. "Now...I'm hoping you have some news for us?"

"Good news and bad news." McIntyre sighed. "Which do you want first?"

"I could use some cheering up," Chuck replied, sardonically.

"The good news is this. All systems are go for us to put the Roadhouse Sons into the USO program."

"That *is* good news!" said Cameron, bolting upright from his chair.

"What's the bad news?" asked Rich cautiously.

"The bad news is this. There isn't another tour starting up any time soon."

The Roadhouse Sons, much to McIntyre's chagrin and Chuck's amusement, moaned and uttered expletives, while Clyde pulled his ever-present pillow tighter over his face. Even Chuck smacked his palms against his thighs in abject annoyance.

"Do you have any idea when they'll be starting another one?" Chuck howled. McIntyre shook her head.

"The USO tour musicians, other personnel, and gear are subject to the same travel restrictions as those of regular citizens. That makes it difficult to plan logistically and transport everyone, even those folks headed for the army bases. There are two tours in this district right now that are about to leave, but they don't have any openings. There are tours elsewhere, but there's no way for us to get the band there in time for their departure."

Clyde, despondent about even more bad news, disgustedly rose from his seat, pillow still in hand, and changed the channel on the television set. He plopped back down on the bed. Before either Chuck or McIntyre could respond, a special report was broadcast.

CBS News correspondent, Robert Pierpoint, announced corrections to earlier reports, confirming that there were, in fact, civilian casualties in the Soviet attack on Pearl Harbor. Horrifying images flashed upon the screen. Ambulances and rescue workers were driving through crowded streets, dodging fire and human beings, while more of humanity, in various stages of shock, wandered about aimlessly. Theses images, and more of burning vehicles and shattered buildings singed into the psyches of the Roadhouse Sons, as scenes they'd associated only with war movies played out before them. An American paradise was now in ruin. As Pierpoint continued describing the indescribable, Clyde rose from the bed and ran to the bathroom, slamming the door behind him.

Before anyone could react, they all heard something never heard before.

Clyde was sobbing.

CHAPTER SEVEN

"No Excuses"

"You're not making excuses!" Jack Stanley exclaimed, with a hint of amazement. Christopher Simms glanced up from the ever-present stack of mail he was forced to examine ad infinitum, and gave Stanley a quizzical look.

"I've never known that to be particularly effective," Simms answered, resuming his arduous task. Jack Stanley admired that attitude. He was not innately patient, and it was a trait that he was forced to develop when he decided to enter the music business, and especially when he decided to manage a band himself. It helped that he was able to surround himself with competent associates to handle the issues that seemed tailor-made to aggravate him.

Jack Stanley was a man whose life and circumstances had hardened both his will and his resolve. This enabled him to deal with the petulant demands of his clients. Reporters, hoteliers, and studio chiefs referred to him as "the man who held the leash of Boney Jack," though, in actuality, he only held the purse strings. To the band, though, such tethers were one and the same. On the rare occasion that a band member bristled with demands for autonomy, Jack Stanley would contentedly allow them their folly of responsibility for their own affairs, including bar tabs, limousine rentals, damages to hotel rooms, etc., the situation of which always quickly resulted in the band member's return to the status quo.

Stanley wasn't unrealistic, however. He knew that, for all of their nonchalance about finances, the band demanded certainty that they were not being cheated. He obligingly, therefore, accounted for every dime by keeping detailed records of all their royalties, transactions, and expenses. Content that they would be able to live in the style to which they'd become accustomed, the band allowed Stanley to handle everything else. In order to do so, he demanded from his associates the same attention to detail that he demanded from himself. Hence, in this instant, he was brought to the chair opposite Simms.

"You're absolutely right, it isn't," said Stanley. "That is why I'm happy you're not pursuing that road." The statement fell flat, revealing neither pleasure nor displeasure. Simms shook his head and looked up from the pile of letters yet again. Stanley looked about Simms' office and espied clear evidence that his associate wasn't merely trying to elicit the illusion that he'd been working. Everything was organized according to a system. All postcards were in one pile, with letters and envelopes in separate piles. A white linen tablecloth was spread out on Simms's work surface.

Simms ignored the statement, and instead began scrutinizing another stack of mail. Stanley studied his associate carefully. There was no outward signs of panic, but Simms seemed a bit unsettled. His movements were purposeful, studied, and formal. Stanley was quite pleased with this example of efficiency, though he made no effort to show it.

"However, I must admit I do have a concern that is bothering me," Simms replied, still working.

"What would that be?" Stanley said, sitting down, legs crossed.

"What if there's been a mistake?" Simms said, looking up. "What if they got it wrong? Suppose we're wasting time looking here when we should be looking elsewhere?"

Stanley didn't answer at first. He regarded Simms in silence, watching the other man grow increasingly uncomfortable. Stanley bounced his foot in the air. Finally, he spoke.

"I have considered that same possibility," he said. "However, all of my sources say that it was mailed from Anchorage shortly before the last assault. It should be here. Anyhow, I've had no contact with them since the assault and have every reason to believe they never made it out. Checking with them is therefore out of the question."

"Well, at least Anchorage certainly helps to narrow my search," Simms smiled. "War zones do not require postage or provide postmarks. The war zone markers were the first place I searched. Unless, of course, they mailed it to someone else first?"

Simms sounded foolish even to himself; he'd examined everything at least three times, and knew that he'd narrowed nothing.

"Are you being facetious?" Stanley asked quietly. Simms shook his head.

"No, I'm being practical," he explained. "I can't help but think that something has gone wrong somewhere, and I feel we should be retracing our steps."

"There is no indication that it was lost in Anchorage. It was supposed to have been mailed out before the assault. Can you give me any reason to believe that it was lost here?"

Simms hesitated before answering. Stanley noticed Simms tremble.

"Well, yes, frankly."

"And what is that?"

Simms considered his answer for a moment. Finally, he related to Stanley the incident involving the band spilling his wine and destroying his record.

"What on earth does that have to do with anything?" demanded Stanley. Simms held up a stained letter and some envelopes, the ink on them a blur.

"Is it possible that the information we're looking for could have been washed away?"

Now it was Stanley's turn to be silent and uncomfortable as he examined the damaged correspondence.

"We had both better hope not," Stanley said at last. "You're certain you've gone through everything?"

Simms looked up, deadpan, and gestured toward the myriad cartons stacked against the far wall.

"Each piece. Three times."

Stanley turned his attention back to the wine-stained postcard, and held it up to the light.

"Which one did it, by the way?"

"It is always instigated by the singer," Simms explained. "He is also usually in the company of the other two Jacks. Once he commences, the others join in. And the bass player walked out with the bottle of Chianti."

As Stanley eyed the postcard, visions of kicking someone began dancing across his mind's eye. He wasn't entirely certain whom he was kicking. Not that it mattered to him, anyway. Simms paused and spoke again, albeit a bit haltingly.

"Are you…are you certain that…that they are really worth the aggravation of putting up with them?"

"For the time being," Stanley said curtly. He often had to defend his decision to be associated with the band, and was frankly growing tired of it. From his peers, it was frustrating. From his subordinate, it was intolerable. Simms didn't respond, and Stanley wondered if his associate caught the exasperated note in his voice.

"They are one of the most successful and popular bands in the Northwest," Stanley replied automatically. "Their popularity, and their revenue, makes them a tremendous asset to me. Enough of an asset to outweigh their liabilities."

Simms looked up and gave a nod of acceptance to that explanation, then continued laboriously with the task at hand.

"If you're so convinced it's not here, then why do you continue looking?" Stanley mused.

"Because I think that every possibility should be examined," Simms replied cautiously. "As much as I think it might not be here, I can't be entirely certain that it isn't."

"That position is to be commended," Stanley stated imperiously. Simms braved a smile at this encouragement, until Stanley continued. "That is, if indecision is to be considered a virtue."

Simms face paled. He quickly resumed his task as Stanley continued.

"As I said, other things sent from the same period, and place, have arrived. Everything indicates that *it* would as well. I have no reason to think otherwise."

"But Alaska is in turmoil," Simms pleaded. "The resistance, the assaults, the counter-offensives, all of that adds up to chaos! Just because some things weren't affected doesn't mean that everything was unaffected. Accidents happen. Are you absolutely certain that they didn't make it out of Anchorage?" Simms pressed.

"Yes," replied Stanley, flatly, his visage a cold mask.

An awkward and palpable silence overtook the room. Stanley cleared his throat.

"Speaking of the band, they're due for their publicity appearance this afternoon," Stanley explained with an evil smile. "You must corral them to their photo shoot and interview. Needless to say, make certain they're at least coherent when in front of the cameras. We don't want any repeat of their Seattle debut."

Simms's memory flashed to Boney Jack's first television interview following their arrival in Seattle. The lead singer was his usual surly, truculent self and refused to respond to any of the interviewer's questions. The other band members were too starstruck with the heightened media attention to be able to utter more than a few syllables, except for the bass player. Still intoxicated from the night before, Jack

Ralston commandeered the reporter's microphone and proceeded to embark on drunken philosophizing that even embarrassed the rest of the band. While not directly involved with that debacle, Simms was well aware of the resulting fallout bestowed upon his superior, and he had no wish to see it repeated. Before he could say anything, the phone rang. Stanley motioned for Simms to answer it.

"Hello, yes," Simms said, his tone serious, his features blank. Soon, however, things began to change. His eyes became wide and his jaw dropped.

"Yes, yes of course," he stammered. "I understand, absolutely. I'll try and put you through to him right now."

Placing the caller on hold, Simms turned to Stanley.

"You better take this," Simms explained. "This is damage control beyond what I can do. It's the police and they are demanding, by name, to speak with you."

Stanley dropped the postcard and motioned for the receiver.

"Hello, yes. Yes this is he," Stanley spoke in his practiced, detached manner. "What seems to be the problem, officer?"

Simms watched Stanley's initial reaction match his own, but Stanley's face then flushed crimson.

"He did *what*? Yes, yes, I understand. I'll be right there!"

With that, Stanley slammed down the receiver and stood up.

"What happened?" Simms asked, cautiously. "They didn't give me any details, just insisted on speaking with you personally."

"What happened? Those idiots decided to visit a local elementary school, unannounced, and interrupted a student assembly!" Stanley raged as he stormed to the door. "I'm going down to the police station. Call the attorney and have him meet me there. Their assets might outweigh their liabilities, however, the scales are beginning to tip!"

Simms allowed himself to smile only after he heard the door slam. Then he dialed the number he'd put to memory and explained the situation to the band's legal counsel.

"No, I'm afraid they neglected to tell me which station," Simms replied, his smile growing wider. "I hope that won't delay them being released."

CHAPTER EIGHT

"My Country; Right or Wrong, My Country"

Clyde felt the intent stares of strangers on his back. For the first time in his life, he feigned insouciance.

Chuck had instructed Clyde to make a point of immediately locating and greeting Officer Beecham. To do so would clearly indicate to the officer that they'd complied with the unofficial terms of Clyde's release.

Clyde spotted Beecham, who was deep in conversation with another attendee. He took a deep breath, mustered his confidence, and strode across the room toward the officer, hand extended. Beecham acknowledged Clyde with a nod in lieu of a handshake, thanked him for coming, and returned to the conversation with the other person. Thrown off guard by Beecham's casual demeanor, Clyde turned to leave. Just then, the officer spoke.

"Where's your other friend?" Beecham said, his low and casual tone nothing short of augural.

"He was still getting ready when we left." Clyde pressed his hand against his leg to keep his own tone steady. He knew that dealing with law enforcement was nothing like dealing with women, but he decided to impart the same charm.

"He said he'd be right along." Clyde mustered his widest grin.

"I certainly hope so," Beecham said, gazing at Clyde quizzically, as though parsley was stuck in the musician's teeth. Once again, the officer turned away abruptly and resumed his conversation. Clyde, dumbfounded, stood there for a moment, then sped away, looking for Chuck.

Spotting the manager on the far side of the room, Clyde made his way toward Chuck. The room was incredibly crowded, and he made sure that he politely interacted with anyone he had to pass. Never in his entire life had he been forced to exert so many niceties; the Red Sea always parted in his presence. Not so was the case here. Several people gave him dirty and derisive looks. To them all, though, Clyde offered a sheepish smile, but inwardly bristled at the manner in which he was being treated. He was, after all, there on forced march, and accommodating these people by trying to blend in, as well as enduring their rejection of his efforts.

"Lose the macramé belt," Chuck had advised him before they left the hotel. "Get a belt from one of the other guys, if you really need one, which I doubt. I swear, you paint those things on."

Clyde protested vehemently, albeit in vain, that he shouldn't be forced to change who or what he was. Chuck was unmoved by the guitarist's banal philosophical bromides.

"You have to be accepted by them. You have to blend in," Chuck explained. "You can't do that by sticking out like a sore thumb. While you're at it, try and find a pair of jeans that doesn't have those tears in the thighs."

At that suggestion, Clyde was even more determined.

"This is who I am, man! I found myself and this is who I am!" he cried. "If they can't accept that, the hell with them! Give me one good reason why I should change."

"Because they have to think that you're sympathetic to their cause and compatible with their views. There's no way that you can accomplish either one if they think you're going to try and seduce their daughters, or for that matter, their wives!"

"I don't see you making any big changes," Clyde pouted.

Chuck ran his fingers through his thick ebon locks. "Long, curly hair, past my shoulders, remember?" Chuck smiled and held up a clump off hair, showing off his new look. "Do you think I just got sick of putting it in a ponytail? That reminds me, be sure to brush your hair, too."

"You sound like my mom," Clyde snapped. "Do you want to check and make sure I washed behind my ears?"

"I have perfect faith that you washed behind your ears." Chuck raised an eyebrow. "Didn't you?"

After several more attempts at arguing his case, Clyde realized the futility of his objections and allowed Chuck to properly outfit him for the meeting. A pair of newer jeans replaced his favorite ones. A belt was abandoned entirely, and his skintight tee shirt was replaced by a less formfitting baseball jersey borrowed from Cameron.

"It used to be Doug's," Cameron explained. "They didn't have any place to send his effects."

Clyde held the shirt reverently, conjuring a mental picture of the dead roadie, then slipped it on over his head. It was indeed a bit large, much to Chuck's relief, and it definitely ensured that the young man would be less conspicuous. Clyde, though, was visibly uncomfortable.

"What's the matter, now?" Chuck demanded.

"Feels so loose," Clyde mumbled, shifting inside it.

"Your skin is tight enough." Chuck sighed. This was almost as bad as outfitting a girl. Clyde's pouting lips protruded further. "Look at it this way," Chuck said. "For once, you're leaving something to the imagination." Clyde was not pacified in the least, and Chuck had reached the end of his rope. "Besides, if you keep wearing your skintight clothes and we decide to put a wire on you, it will stick out worse than your nipples, and suddenly showing up later in something like this will attract even more attention. If you start off wearing loose clothing, they won't think anything of it. Now shut up and stop pulling at that jersey."

Chuck had them arrive early. He wanted to reconnoiter the surroundings. They agreed to split up, but maintain visual contact with one another at all times. Clyde did as he was told, and found himself bored out of his mind so early on that he looked for Chuck, merely to have someone with whom he could strike up a conversation.

Once he'd managed to cross the room, Clyde saw Chuck talking with another fellow who was standing with his back against the wall. Clyde reluctantly veered in another direction. Prior to their arrival, Clyde was informed at his briefing that Chuck would scout on his own, and that he was not to be interrupted from conversations unless there was clear and present danger.

"But what am I supposed to do?" Clyde had asked.

"Wander around, look like you're trying to meet people, read some pamphlets. Find out about the volunteer projects Beecham mentioned. You're supposed to be looking for opportunities to serve your country. We can be pretty certain that the police have mentioned you, especially if they invited you to this thing. You'll have a better chance of getting noticed if I'm not holding your hand." Clyde, now duly instructed, examined with ersatz zeal the framed pictures on the walls. Also as instructed, he remained in Chuck's general vicinity. Clyde checked the wall clock. Snapper was instructed to arrive thirty-five minutes later, to keep Beecham and associates on their toes.

Chuck was confident that upon their very arrival he and Clyde would attract attention. He was right. Almost immediately after they stepped across the threshold, Chuck knew he was being watched. He headed toward the wall placards honoring the long lists of Legion past officers and post members who had died in service to their country. In doing so, he struck up casual conversations with several people. Chuck then made his way to the opposite wall. There hung memorial photographs of Legion members bedecked in uniform, some in dress and some in field. He lingered over these. He didn't want to merely give the impression of genuine interest; he was, indeed, engaged in his desire to know more about these local heroes.

Chuck hailed from a legacy military family of many generations, documented as far back as the Civil War. He joined the army as soon as he graduated from high school in 1964. Just as Chuck had surmised, President Johnson announced an increase in troop strength in Vietnam the very next year. Chuck had a hunch that it would be just a matter of time before he was called up and deployed to the Far East, and he was right. He found himself there before the year was out.

Chuck rarely spoke about his experiences in Vietnam. He would neither confirm nor deny if he was involved with any campaigns, offensive or otherwise. He bristled that the national zeitgeist was assenting to a negative stereotype of the Nam vet. He loathed the very idea of talking about that time in his life, plain and simple. He did, however, welcome the resulting solace in the memories summoned by looking at the Legion photos of soldiers standing by their combat jeeps, proud with commitment to their companies, and visibly stouthearted in their loyalty to their country. Examining each face, Chuck wondered if he'd ever seen any of these men in person. If so, at this point, there was no way to be certain, so he didn't dwell on it. Just then, his peripheral vision caught a male figure approaching.

"Traveling down memory lane?" the man asked. Chuck turned from the wall to the man. He immediately realized that the person standing before him was Cameron's infamous shadow. He was wearing different clothes, but there was no mistaking that face.

"Yeah," Chuck said with a smile. "I was there in '68."

"Tet?" the other fellow asked, his voice dropping to a conspiratorial tone. Chuck nodded.

"Kien Giang." Chuck's tone was equally as hushed.

"Mekong Delta, wasn't it?" the man asked. Chuck nodded. The other man squinted. Chuck surmised that the man was trying to trip him up, but then realized that he was simply struggling with his memory.

"That was…I Corps, right?" he said, finally. Chuck smiled.

"Close," he replied. "MR-4. I take it you were there, too?" The other man nodded.

"Yes," he said. "We got caught in that, as well. Not far from you, in fact, in Tam Ky. We were ready, though. We got hit on the second day, so we'd heard about the rest of you getting nailed."

Chuck eyed him suspiciously.

"Then you and I must have been in two different wars," he said. "Tam Ky is nowhere near where I was. It's on the coast seventy kilometers south of Da Nang. Not only that, you guys got hit before we did."

Cameron's shadow smiled.

"Just making sure you weren't blowing smoke up my ass," the man replied, extending his hand. "The name's Brody Aldrich."

"Lamont," Chuck replied, taking Brody's hand. "Chuck Lamont."

The two exchanged lighthearted war stories. Brody pointed to several photographs, citing former members of his unit.

"Most of them are gone," he said. His solemnity resounded in Chuck; it was a sensation he'd fought ad infinitum, and sometimes, to little avail. "Some of them are back here, though," Brody continued. "They've settled down with families, not like what the news reports would have you believe. None of them have gone crazy yet."

"Wait 'til their kids are teenagers," Chuck muttered, his hand cupped to his mouth. Brody laughed jovially.

Chuck turned away from the photographs just in time to catch sight of Snapper framed in the doorway, accosted by two older men. Per his instructions, Snapper hadn't altered his appearance in any manner. His hair was still slightly disheveled, and he hadn't shaved or changed his clothes from the previous day. He was the antithesis of the two clean-shaven men in uniform who greeted him.

"Excuse me," Chuck said. "I see one of my friends just arrived. I better get over there."

Brody pondered the commotion at the door.

"Is he a friend of yours?"

"Yeah," Chuck replied. "He works for me, and so does that fellow over there."

Chuck pointed at Clyde, who was still consulting the lists of Legion members and former officers. He, too, noticed Snapper's arrival, and cast a furtive glance at Chuck.

"What are they doing here?" Brody inquired.

"Well, they're not eligible for military service, so they're looking for a way to do something helpful. Officer Beecham recommended that they come here and see what opportunities were available. I'd better get over there and vouch for my friend."

"I'll come with you," Brody offered.

Chuck and Brody strode toward the entrance. After assuring the Legion members that Snapper wasn't there to cause trouble, they brought him inside. Chuck introduced Snapper to everyone met thus far, and Brody managed to engage them all in small talk to get acquainted. Chuck monitored the boys' interaction, occasionally finishing one or the other's sentences to avoid the inadvertent disclosure of covert information. For all the time he spent with the band, Chuck still remained vigilant about them keeping their cover. Most inquiries were, thankfully, innocuous enough to allow the boys to provide the majority of the answers.

Chuck wondered when all the hobnobbing would stop and the official business at hand would start. At last, a man appeared at the podium and called the meeting to order. At that, Brody took his leave.

As they sat down, Chuck observed the people sitting behind the podium. Uniforms indicated which men were members of the post. Officer Beecham and three other men in regular dress were seated with the officially clad men. Chuck wondered if they represented community leadership of sorts; the other men on stage seemed to defer to them, despite their own uniforms.

The man at the podium cleared his throat and tapped the microphone. He proceeded to speak in an inordinately loud manner.

"He wouldn't have to do that if he put his mouth against the mic," Clyde muttered. Chuck shot him an admonishing glance. As the man welcomed the attendees, the PA system emitted a piercingly loud hum and crackle, which intermittently interrupted the speaker.

"Sounds like a short in it to me," Snapper whispered to Chuck. He didn't answer Snapper. Instead, he kept his eye on the stage and on the men fumbling about in a cabinet nearby in a feeble attempt to adjust the PA system. Several minutes passed. Finally, one of the men shrugged and turned to the speaker, shaking his head. Clearly annoyed, the speaker waved a dismissive hand at them and they pulled the plug on the microphone.

"I apologize for that, ladies and gentlemen," the man resumed. "Let us now say the Pledge of Allegiance and the Lord's Prayer."

Clyde was disappointed when the meeting consisted of updates on blood drives, bond drives, and the requisite spaghetti supper. He'd hoped that the Liberty Leagues and slacker raids mentioned by Chuck and McIntyre would be the primary subject matter. One of the men seated near Officer Beecham was an extension service staff member from the state college, and provided how-to tips on victory gardens. Another was from the Red Cross and thanked the Legion members for their efforts in organizing the blood drives and fundraisers for the Alaskan Refugees. The third gentleman never approached the podium. As the speakers fielded questions and announcements from the audience, Snapper stifled the urge to yawn. Clyde inwardly screamed from boredom.

At long last, Beecham rose and walked to the podium. Clyde and Snapper noticed a subtle shift in Chuck's position. They took that as a pointed cue to pay attention.

"Ladies and gentlemen," Beecham began, his voice firm and his demeanor proof that he was well accustomed to public speaking. "I do not need to remind you of the dangers and threats facing our country. The war we feared is now upon us, and our very life as a nation is threatened. We in the contiguous United States could suffer what is happening in Alaska, where the Communists are herding American citizens into concentration camps, as did Hitler and his Nazi regime."

Clyde's mind flooded with horrific images described to him by his father who, with his own military unit, had liberated one such camp. Clyde was instantly terrified by these memories and, despite wanting to signal to Chuck that he somehow needed relief, he remained still. He knew it was ludicrous to seek reassurance that these atrocities were a lie. Now completely agitated, sweat trickled down his back as Beecham blathered on at the podium.

"We must remain on guard against all possible threats. We in law enforcement cannot be everywhere at all times. We need you, our citizens, to be our eyes and ears. Report *all* suspicious activity to us immediately. Keep your eyes and ears open and remain alert. Do not decide the importance of anything you report. *We* will ascertain the facts and a subsequent course of action." Officer Beecham provided examples of suspicious activity, such as curfew violations, and unknown or unrecognized persons lurking in unlighted areas. He finished with an ominous flourish. "Leave no stone of suspicion unturned."

Beecham opened the floor to questions. Several attendees raised their hands and called out, asking if situations they'd experienced were indeed a cause of concern. Officer Beecham calmly and patiently addressed each person's inquiry. He showed no irritation toward anything asked of him. Clyde wondered if, prior to becoming a police officer, Beecham was an entertainer or politician.

"What about the slackers?" a male voice called out from the back of the room. Clyde noticed that Officer Beecham stiffened ever so slightly, and was puzzled by it; the question seemed perfectly reasonable. Beecham, though, recovered quickly and responded.

"In this community, we have had, and continue to have, a strong show of support by our young men, who have registered with the Selective Service. They've given us no cause for concern. The question of slackers is a good one, but for another reason."

The officer had Clyde's undivided attention. Beecham had spoken about the need to be on guard against Communist sympathizers, and Clyde was certain that this was the moment in which Beecham would announce a slacker raid.

"We've got enough on our plates monitoring the bad guys," Officer Beecham concluded. "There is no need to worry about our good guys. We've all heard rumors and reports about vigilantism. I urge you not to participate. Remember, if you witness suspicious behavior, tell us. Do not enforce the law yourself. You will cause more harm than good."

Another male in the back of the room demanded to know why. Clyde turned around, but couldn't identify the speaker.

"You cannot take the law into your own hands," the policeman insisted. "We are a society based on laws, and freedom, and justice! A principle of justice is innocence until proof of guilt. If we violate that principle, then we are doing the Communists' work for them. Let them do it in Moscow. I don't want to see it in Missouri."

Beecham's speech incited heated discussions. Some were in favor of his instructions and sentiments, while others vehemently opposed them, the latter of whom claimed that his ideas simply gave the enemy ample room in which to operate. Clyde attempted committing to memory who took what side in the argument, but it was impossible, as people talked over and tried to outshout one another.

The moderator returned to the podium. Clyde was grateful for the short circuit in the mic wires; the snapping and crackling helped to squelch the arguments. Beecham, the frustration on his face so clearly evident, resumed his seat. Clyde was a bit nonplussed; Beecham couldn't have possibly thought that the subject matter wouldn't at all excite his audience. At last, the moderator delivered some semblance of order to the proceedings and introduced the third speaker.

"Ladies and gentlemen, I would like to introduce Robert Pecham, who would like to say a few words."

A flaccid round of applause was issued as the man rose from his chair and stepped up to the podium. He appeared to be in his early forties. His short, dark, slicked-back hair betrayed just a hint of grey at the temples, making his already brilliant blue eyes seem even more stellar. He was bedecked in a dark grey suit with a freshly starched white shirt, and wore a red tie adorned with regimental stripes. The dimple on his chin matched his dimpled smile, which displayed his perfectly straight, white teeth. He stood at the podium like a Hollywood idol, beaming his smile around the room, gracing in turn each section of seating, drinking in the weak applause and intoxicating himself with even the scantest hint of adulation. When the last of the egregiously awkward clapping ceased, Pecham spoke in an ingratiatingly unctuous, warm tone, imparted for the effect of instilling confidence and comfort. Unfortunately, the actual result fully exposed the fact that Pecham didn't possess one ounce of interest in anything about any of the attendees. Clyde hated him instantly.

"Thank you, ladies and gentlemen, for having me here tonight." Pecham's voice was as thick and as oozing as treacle. He paused momentarily to clear his throat, then gripped the edges of the podium and took a deep breath. He looked out over the room, his face no longer displaying appreciation for the imagined adulation.

"Here comes the fire and brimstone," Clyde whispered to Chuck. Chuck fought a reactionary smirk, and kicked Clyde's foot to quiet him.

"None of us need be reminded that we are enduring difficult times," Pecham began, his voice soft and firm. "Indeed, these very speakers that have addressed all of you this evening are eloquent reminders of that troubling fact. Most of us here remember the first time we grew victory gardens, or engaged in scrap metal drives, and tried to raise money to buy creature comforts for soldiers fighting on the front or for refugees driven from their homes by the winds of war."

Pecham, arms elevated in heavenly gesture, paused to allow the images of which he spoke to clash into the minds of his fellow Legion members. Even Clyde traveled memory lane back to the times when his parents and grandparents told their tales of the Second World War. Lost in reverie, he involuntarily jumped in his seat when Pecham spoke again.

"Yes, ladies and gentlemen," Pecham pontificated. "We did our utmost to contribute to the efforts of our country when we were called upon to fight the evils of the Axis as they threatened our very way of life. We did so willingly, and responded generously with both men and materials. We fought in Europe and in the Pacific so that we would not have to fight on Main Street."

Much to Clyde's annoyance, Pecham indulged in another dramatically pregnant pause.

"But now we are faced, once again, with the need to supply creature comforts to soldiers and refugees. We are once again faced with innocent people being driven from their homes and suffering hardships and depravations that you and I, secure here in our homes and communities, can only imagine."

Pecham's voice trailed to a soft whisper, then rose to sudden force.

"Now, *we* are faced with this peril in our *own* country, on our *own* doorstep. It is our *own* people who are driven asunder by the enemy, imperiled in their homes, and violated into enduring unimaginable conditions! We can no longer convince ourselves that we are safe behind the two oceans, and thus removed from the threats of the outside world. That illusion has been ripped from us! And we will never, *ever* again be able to delude ourselves with a false sense of security."

With each syllable of emphasis, Pecham chopped the air with his hand, holding it still as each beat completed. Clyde mused to himself that Pecham's hand—indeed, his whole arm—had transformed itself into a giant accusatory finger pointing right at the heart of the audience. Snapper shifted in his seat. The hall was completely silent. Clyde reminisced again, this time revisiting his high school days. He recalled with amusement the headmaster who at an assembly reprimanded the entire student body for the actions of a misguided few. That was the very first time that Clyde understood the meaning of collective guilt. He wondered how many here in the Legion hall were experiencing that same feeling. Here they were, no doubt about to hurry back to their living rooms to watch television, or enjoy a cold beer and grumble about the rationing and restrictions. Images of American men and women—not to mention children—fighting for their lives or suffering untold deprivations made the discomforts and complaints at the meeting seem petty in comparison.

"Extreme situations demand extreme actions," Pecham told the audience, his visage gloomy as his voice grew increasingly morose. "The government is waging a war for which we were woefully unprepared. Can you imagine the tremendous effort required to bring this nation to the state of necessary preparedness in order to prevent the Soviets from gaining further inroads? Can you? Not to mention the sheer fortitude needed by *us* to drive the Communists from our shores! Ensuring the future requires the full commitment of every true and loyal American in order to survive, let alone *win*."

"Again with the chopping hand," Clyde mumbled. This time, Chuck glared at him.

The audience murmured agreements, heads nodding emphatically. One man cried, "Here, here!" Invigorated by this positive response, Pecham continued.

"One would think that, when called to patriotic duty, any red-blooded American enjoying the liberty and protection of the United States of America would respond to that call without *hesitation!*"

The sudden clamorous affirmations that erupted from the crowd startled Clyde to the point of agitation. Even men on the stage applauded. Pecham affected a dignified pose, once again gripping the sides of the podium and looking out over the crowd, this time feigning not to notice their adulation. He stood there, his head atilt, as though hearing esoteric messages from a voice inaudible to everyone else.

"Yes, you would!" Pecham whispered, his voice sotto voce with a maudlin hint of sorrow. "Yet there are, even in these times, men and women who are not willing to shoulder their share of the burden. They hear the call. They receive the requests. They tell themselves they'll do it next time. But when will next time come? Now, I do not mean to cast aspersions on the fine people of this community. I know of your past, of your tremendous sacrifices. I do not mean to impugn your patriotism, for in the past, when called upon, you have always responded with alacrity. Our inability to meet the goals of our latest war bond drive in no way indicates a dampening of your fervor. I understand the burdens you face. After all, haven't I helped many of you with your businesses or your homes, even so far as to acquire favorable rates on your loans?"

Snapper and Clyde shared knowing glances. Snapper, cupping his hand to his mouth, whispered, "That's a veiled threat looming, if I ever heard one!"

Pecham paused, eyeing the crowd intently. With no warning, his beaming gaze returned.

"Frank!" Pecham smiled broadly, pointing to a man in the crowd. "I know you couldn't have purchased your usual amount of war bonds, due to that new house of yours; significantly more expensive than you thought, yes? A sizeable dwelling of approximately twenty-eight hundred square feet, yes? Twenty-nine? Did you opt to install the pool, or decide to postpone that? I don't remember what you decided."

Clyde heard the man, Frank, mutter a response. Snapper nudged Clyde and whispered, "This guy's a real pri—" Clyde snapped his forefinger to his lips and shushed Snapper just in time. Pecham continued to smile as though he were personally responsible for all toothpaste advertisements. He looked down at the bewildered and betrayed Frank and winked. He then chuckled, as though scripting his own private joke.

"Isn't it amazing how we can still go on with our lives, even in wartime?" Pecham asked rhetorically. He continued, all the while beaming his smile at the crowd. "I know we're going to do everything in our power with this latest war bond drive to make certain that we'll always be able to do just that. Now remember, you don't have to wait until the bond drive commences. You just stop in and see me the next time you're at the bank. You know I'm always there, always ready to talk with you. And now it's time to bid you adieu. This meeting is running long and I don't want to be responsible for any violations of curfew. Lord knows we don't want to make unnecessary trouble for Officer Beecham, now do we?"

Pecham concluded his remarks with several niceties directed at various audience members, and by evoking random chuckles from others. He left the podium and made his way through the crowd, pausing to shake hands and speak as necessary. He didn't seem to notice Clyde, Chuck, and Snapper at all, and exited the premises through the main door. The crowd continued to mill about, and some left, while others headed to the rear table for coffee and doughnuts. Clyde and Snapper, with only a look, sought Chuck's guidance for what to do next.

"Wait here. Stay inside and stay close," Chuck whispered. "I'm going to talk to Beecham for a minute." With that, he approached the stage and attracted the officer's attention. Beecham leaned toward Chuck, clearly irritated, but remained attentive to whatever was being said to him. From where they stood, Clyde and Snapper were unable to discern Beecham's verbal reply, but there was no mistaking the shaking of his head. The officer turned and stormed off in the opposite direction.

"Let's go," Chuck said as he returned.

"What did he say?" asked Clyde. He and Snapper fell in step. Chuck shrugged.

"Nothing much," he replied. "We can talk about it on the way home."

Clyde read the warning in Chuck's response. This was nothing to discuss in a crowd of people. Once outside, Chuck headed in the opposite direction from whence they arrived. They crossed several streets and no one spoke until they were several blocks away.

"That was pretty weird," Snapper muttered. "Why did we even bother going over there? People just ignored us, except for the old farts that gave me a hard time."

"We were supposed to get an idea of who might be behind some of the suspicious activity going on around here," explained Chuck. "I think we did our job."

"What the hell are you talking about?" demanded Snapper. "We didn't talk to anyone at all, except for the conversations you had."

"Keep your voice down," Chuck warned. "As a matter of fact, I've got three people that bear further examination."

"No doubt one of them is that Pecham guy," sneered Clyde. "I had him pegged for a used car salesman, but I suppose being a loan officer at the bank is probably the same."

"He isn't a loan officer," clarified Chuck. "He's the president of the Cole County Farmer's Bank, according to Officer Beecham."

"Well, then, that explains how he knew about that guy's house," grumbled Clyde. "And speaking of Beecham, what is he anyway? Is he like the sheriff or the police chief or what?"

"He was the lieutenant in the police department here in Gaston," Chuck explained. "But he's the acting sheriff now. The sheriff was called up when they mobilized the national guard."

"So he's just holding the job 'til the other guy comes back?" Snapper asked. Chuck shook his head.

"No. Until they get around to holding the election," Chuck explained. "Some of the folks were talking about how frustrating it is to have to wait for the election next November."

"Why are they waiting until then?" Politics were lost on Snapper.

"They don't want to go through the expense and hassle of holding a special election just for this, so they're going to wait until the general election next year, maybe."

"Maybe?" asked Clyde. "I thought next year was an election year." Chuck slowly shook his head.

"Listen to the news, and not just about the war, man," he sighed. "Haven't you heard they're thinking of suspending the elections because of the war?"

"What the fuck?" whistled Clyde. "No! I hadn't heard anything like that. I just sort of figured it was always done and that was it. Why are they thinking of stopping it?"

"It's not definite. It's still being discussed," explained Chuck. "But a lot of people are concerned with how we can have an election at all when one of our states is occupied by enemy forces. They think that it would be bad for the war effort. It might give the Soviets a chance to try something else."

"But, wouldn't that be illegal?" asked Snapper. "I mean, Carter would have to declare martial law or something for that to happen, wouldn't he?"

"I'm not a constitutional lawyer," Chuck replied.

The three men walked on in silence, Chuck directing and redirecting Clyde and Snapper through myriad streets and alleys. It was Clyde that broke the silence.

"Carter wouldn't do anything like that, anyhow," he grumbled. "He—"

"Listen to me and listen good," Chuck interrupted. He stopped dead in his tracks, whirled around, and faced them. "I don't care what your political opinions are, or whether you two even have any. *Keep them to yourselves.* Do you understand me?"

"Hey, man! I'm not allowed to have an opinion?" Clyde demanded. "I thought this was still a free country."

"It is," Chuck replied. "But we don't ever—and I mean *ever*—express our political opinions publicly, *especially* now."

"Why not?" Clyde insisted, furious at this seemingly arbitrary suppression of his conscience. "Is that like a violation of policy or something?"

"Not policy," Chuck explained, trying to be patient. "Common sense. People are on their last raw nerves. Anything could set someone off. We're supposed to conduct surveillance. Nothing else. Understand?"

Retorts and arguments raced through Clyde's mind as he fought the instinct to aver his position. He realized, though, that Chuck was right, and simply nodded in agreement. Chuck nodded in response, paused with furrowed brow, and then spoke.

"Have you guys noticed anyone following us?" he asked in a low voice. Snapper and Clyde shook their heads.

"No, man. I haven't," said Snapper. "Why? Have you?" Chuck shook his head.

"No. I haven't either," he drawled, still pondering. "I can't help but think that they made note of our departure. I was sure they'd have us tailed."

"Well, maybe it's just your imagination," said Clyde.

"No. You told me once that Dwyer talked about game rules, right?"

Clyde nodded. "Yeah. What about 'em?"

"What Dwyer called game rules are really something else," Chuck said. He huddled closer to them. Snapper and Clyde followed suit. "We call them Moscow Rules."

"What the hell are those?" Snapper whispered. "I thought we were fighting the Russians."

"They're rules for working in the same arenas as the Soviets. Everyone in this field, including spies heading to Moscow, learn them," Chuck continued. "It's too much to explain right now. I will tell you that one of the rules is to always trust your gut. Right now, my gut is telling me something is very, very wrong. Let's get back to the motel." Clyde and Snapper stood there, dumbfounded at Chuck's sudden divulgence. "*Now!*" Chuck hissed.

The three of them hurried along the darkened streets. Chuck's maneuverings and navigation had taken them roughly parallel to the route they needed; they quickly reached the motel. The band truck and the van were still parked in their usual spots. McIntyre's car was gone. Chuck quickened his pace, running up the stairs, the other two in close tow. They entered their hallway and examined the floor at the bottom of each door to their rooms. The lights in each room were off. Chuck unlocked the door to his room and turned on the light. The room was in shambles.

Chairs were knocked over and the mattress on one of the beds was askew. The closet doors were opened, and coats and shirts yanked out and strewn about. A large stain had seeped into the carpet. Quickly, Chuck knelt down to touch it. The substance was clear. Chuck smelled his fingers. It wasn't beer.

"It's not blood. Probably water," he muttered. He stood up and walked toward the bathroom, pausing only at his duffel bag to remove his gun from its shoulder holster.

"Check your room!" he commanded. Clyde hurriedly produced his key and unlocked his door. His room was in the same condition.

"Hey!" Clyde whispered, sotto voce.

Chuck entered, carefully examining the room. He found no evidence indicating why the rooms had been ransacked. He turned to Clyde and Snapper, both still standing in the doorway.

"There's another one of the Moscow Rules you need to remember," Chuck said.

"What's that?" Clyde asked.

"Murphy is *always* right."

CHAPTER NINE

"The Gathering Storm"

He sat alone in his office and poured himself a drink, one for which he felt he'd earned every drop. After leaving orders with both Simms and the front desk that he was not to be disturbed under *any* circumstances, he'd drawn the shades and sat in silence in a rapidly darkening room.

Jack Stanley's day had been a nightmare, beginning with the phone call from the irate police sergeant. The hysterical teachers that were at the station when he arrived, soon joined by even more irate and hysterical parents, did nothing to make the situation better, especially when some of the parents tried to accost him. Even the intervention of the police didn't make him feel any more secure. However, any relief he felt when the squad room was finally cleared of the screaming—and potentially violent—crowd, soon turned to despair when he realized they had left to speak to the press, who had gathered outside the station. Eventually, the Boney Jack band's lawyer arrived, and attempts were made to get the band released into Stanley's custody. After much argument, they were detained until a judge could post bail. Pleas and insistence by both lawyer and manager fell on deaf ears.

"Public urination, public drunkenness, indecent exposure, disorderly conduct and sedition," recited the desk sergeant, reading the police report. "Your clients aren't going anywhere anytime soon, I'm afraid."

"Sedition!" cried Stanley. "What are you talking about? They interrupted a school assembly, for God's sake! How can that be considered seditious?"

"It was not just a school assembly. It was a school election," the sergeant replied. "It was an exercise by a public school system to demonstrate the democratic process and allow the students to vote on a resolution supporting the armed forces and decide how to use the money they'd raised in a fundraiser for the war effort."

"I understand that things are at a great patriotic fervor right now, but interrupting a school election can hardly be considered seditious," insisted Stanley. "Not even Joe McCarthy would be able to make that argument!"

"The one who calls himself Boney Jack openly declared: "Fuck the vote!" to the entire student body, and advised them that voting was simply the government's way of fooling them into complacency." Stanley felt his chest tighten. "He then accused them of funding the murder of women and children by sending their funds to the troops." Stanley went numb as he heard the sergeant read the report.

"The subject was then joined by his companions in smashing the ballot boxes, declaring that once the war was over, we wouldn't be wasting our time this way anyhow because we would all be cogs in the Soviet machine."

Stanley put his head in his hands, wishing that he were any place else but there. He sat in silence and could only hope to formulate a defense. Stanley, with a surreal, detached feeling, heard the sergeant continue with the police report.

"The subject then urinated on the ballot boxes and the ballots, as well as on the American flag while shouting 'Long live anarchy!' and 'Down with the government.' That is quite an argument for sedition, I would say."

Stanley's stomach churned with anger and frustration as he realized the implications of his clients' actions. This incident wouldn't be sloughed off as a publicity prank. This time, Stanley was afraid that Boney Jack Preston had really gone too far. Images of the intricate consequences made him physically ill.

"The government has not passed any sedition laws or even suspended habeas corpus," the lawyer declared angrily, though weakly. "Attorney General Bell isn't even considering asking for it! The most you can hold them on is disturbing the peace."

"That is something you will have to argue before a judge," the sergeant snapped. "Those are the charges we're holding them on until a judge says otherwise! If you want to earn your retainer, mister, then you come back tomorrow when they get arraigned." Stanley halfheartedly mustered a protest, but didn't wait to hear what the sergeant had to say. If the man was worth anything other than negotiating settlements out of court, he would realize that arguing the case in front of a police officer instead of a judge was pointless. The realization that incompetents surrounded him caused Stanley to seethe even more. He would have to achieve a final resolution to this situation alone. Without excusing himself, Stanley simply stormed out.

Stanley spent the ride home trying to fashion damage control. The negative publicity would turn a lot of people against the band, but at the same time possibly help cement their credibility as an antisocial group tapping into the frustrations of youth scared by the prospect of being drafted, and terrified of the thought of a sudden nuclear attack. These same youth were angry at a world they felt they had no control over. That was a demographic that Boney Jack had been aiming for, but their commercial success and notoriety, ironically, compromised their credibility. Once this episode made the news, Stanley realized, everything could change. If he was smart and remained calm, it could be changed for the better. Memories of the objections that religious leaders and parent groups made about Elvis Presley when he first gained national fame raced through Stanley's mind, heartening him.

For all of its unpleasantness, this situation had the potential to be a marketing gold mine. With careful manipulation of the media, he could downplay the anti-American perceptions enough for the band to still play in public, and still attract the emergent punk crowd. Stanley would have to consider his steps carefully and remain exceedingly circumspect. However, at present, he had far more serious problems to deal with than potential record sales.

Boney Jack, man and band, never seemed to consider the collateral damage that their actions brought. In the past, such situations were dealt with by agreeing to pay for settlements or deductibles, or even with a quiet payoff to a manager or other victim. This time, however, he knew it was impossible for the solution to be that simple.

The band had enjoyed a growing popularity with some members of the armed forces, and there was indication that the Alaskan resistance was broadcasting recordings of their single, "Dead Reds," to harass the enemy in occupied territory. Stanley had been working very hard on channeling that popularity into a new publicity opportunity for the band, only to realize that opportunities were, in all probability, vanishing in front of his eyes; the problem at the school cost them armed forces support.

If Stanley thought his day couldn't possibly get any worse, he was sadly mistaken. Upon his return to the hotel, Simms, with a worried look and a phone message, was waiting for him in the office suite. Stanley quickly briefed Simms on the situation with Boney Jack and made it clear he was not in the mood for questions. Knowing his associate's dislike of their client, Stanley was somewhat pacified, noting that, for once, Simms was not visibly gloating over their predicament. Taking the phone message and storming to his own suite, Stanley felt his blood run cold when he saw the number he'd been instructed to call. As he dialed the number, he told himself that he was just imagining things, projecting his emotions onto a situation that didn't merit it. He was wrong.

"I assume you haven't received the present we mailed you," said the voice on the other end of the line. There had been no exchange of pleasantries, or introductions.

"No we haven't," said Stanley nonchalantly. "But you know how mail is these days. Things are always getting delayed. It hasn't arrived yet, but I'm sure it will very soon."

"No it won't," they said flatly. Stanley felt his heart sink. "Your friend decided it was too valuable to mail, so they thought it would be best to bring it to you in person."

With that, Stanley dared to hope that it was still on its way and that everything would work out.

"They must be coming by bus, then," he said, trying to conceal his eagerness. "If they had been coming by boat, they'd be here by now. The last ship bringing refugees from Alaska arrived a few days ago. If they left Anchorage before the assault, they would have probably been aboard."

"They didn't get out of Anchorage before the assault," the caller stated tersely. Once again, Stanley felt the ground cave beneath him. "It appears that they were caught in the bombing and evacuated during the recovery efforts. We have just learned that they were severely injured. Their injuries were too severe for the hospitals there to address. They were held in Juneau until their conditions stabilized, then were sent to Seattle for further treatment."

"Do you know which hospital?" Stanley asked.

"The army medical center," the caller replied, making no effort to conceal any irritation. "You know perfectly well that all evacuees are quarantined until they have a thorough check performed on them. The process is designed to frustrate espionage efforts and the smuggling of stolen property out of the war zone."

Stanley trembled as the caller spoke, grateful that he couldn't be seen.

"I see," Stanley whispered, after a brief pause. "It will be difficult to get into the medical center, you understand. Special passes are required, and one's only able to visit relatives. Even the Red Cross has a hard time getting in. It will be a challenge, but I think I might be able to work out something."

Stanley held his breath, praying that the caller wouldn't suggest a publicity visit to the hospital, thereby forcing him to recount the day's incident. He knew it would be impossible to keep it from them, but wanted to be able to provide a clear plan for addressing it before being confronted about it.

"But, you forget, they *are* your family," the caller reminded him. Stanley could almost see the cold sneer accompanying the words. "We will provide to you the information you need to request the necessary permits. Wait for our instructions." The click and buzz on the other end of the line seemed more ominous than usual. Stanley's hand trembled as he returned the receiver to its cradle.

Refilling his glass, he searched his mind desperately for silver linings in the storm clouds gathering over his head, however thin those linings might be. First, he knew that the press would be extensively covering this egregious situation with the band, and no doubt, negatively.

"This is going to be a PR apocalypse," he mumbled to himself. But the situation could still be played to his advantage. He laughed sardonically as he realized he wouldn't have to spend a dime on publicity, for a little while at least.

"I don't give a damn what you say about them," Stanley said to the empty room. "Just make damn sure you spell their names right."

He also realized that he could throw Simms to those lions, and maintain the image of a disappointed daddy to the press. The image of Simms trying to defend the band while they simultaneously turned on him went a long way toward cheering Stanley up. However, it was short-lived. This was of no consequence right now, as the other, more pressing matters, such as the situation surrounding the package, loomed over his head like the sword of Damocles.

The caller said that the messenger was bringing the package himself, but did not tell Stanley where it could be retrieved. Stanley cursed them for taking such a risk. It was almost inevitable that once they were put into a hospital or mobile medical unit, their belongings would be collected. That would, for all intents and purposes, guarantee that the package had been taken. Or had it? The caller hadn't indicated if anything had happened to the package. Could this mean that, despite this unforeseen circumstance, everything was still going as they'd planned? A chill ran down Stanley's spine. Not necessarily so. He was not merely expected to retrieve the package any longer. He now had to find out if it was ever there in the first place. His higher-ups were onto the situation.

The image of storm clouds grew darker and heavier as Stanley contemplated the potential tempest about to break around him. In other circumstances, he would have scheduled the band in a publicity tour to gain access to the hospital, as he'd done so often in the past with other situations. The faces of the angry people in the police station, and the angry mob that had formed outside in the parking lot when he left, morphed themselves into visages of angry American soldiers, and pushed through all of his other thoughts.

Indeed, Boney Jack's antics this time might have permanently jeopardized their usefulness—an outcome far more serious than a drop in record sales.

Stanley drained his drink. The warmth of the bourbon didn't offer him the comfort he was hoping for.

Perhaps things were not really as bad as they seemed, he tried telling himself. He decided to keep repeating that until he believed it. He refilled his glass and sighed heavily. This was going to take a while.

CHAPTER TEN

"Déjà vu"

This was all too familiar to Cameron—being loaded into the back of a car and brought in for questioning by men in suits who refused to explain why they were detaining him. The only response to his demand for an explanation was the appearance of a snub-nosed revolver. Cameron knew, before even entering the building, that the Roadhouse Sons would be taken to a room, sat at a table, and left alone. However, there were differences this time that caused him concern.

The first was the way their captors had arrived. There was a knock at the door followed by a pronouncement that whoever was there was from hotel maintenance. When Cameron opened the door, he questioned these strangers about their none-too-regular maintenance uniforms.

"We're with the FBI," one of them declared. When Cameron asked them to provide their credentials as proof, the door was kicked in and a fight ensued, with two of them stuffing Cameron's face into the floor while a third pointed a gun at Evan's forehead. Once Cameron was handcuffed, the men searched the room. Cameron heard similar sounds from the other room, suggesting that Rich was going through the same ordeal.

The second oddity that Cameron noticed was the intruders' lack of concern for how they transported the boys. The three band members were ordered into the back of a car—unattended. Once on the road, the boys were also permitted to speak however they pleased. The two men in front—one with the gun pointed at them—conversed freely with one another and even asked questions of Cameron, Evan, and Rich. Cameron was even free to look out the rear windscreen. It was this, more than anything else, that convinced Cameron these men were not at all who they said they were. His hunch was confirmed when, as their car pulled out of the parking lot,

McIntyre was driving in. Cameron, in an effort to get her attention, waved frantically as the two cars passed one another. Looking out the rear now, he was relieved to realize that he'd been successful. McIntyre was now a few cars behind, following them. The men in the front seat had simply surmised that Cameron was flirting with a pretty woman, and they didn't notice that same pretty woman was following them.

They drove the car in a direct route into the parking area of a building unfamiliar to the boys. The men in this car, as well as four men in the other car, failed to notice McIntyre trailing them the entire way. Finally, Cameron, Rich, and Evan were brought inside and left in the same room together.

No way are you guys feds.

Rather than feel comforted, Cameron was now even more wary. The sheer amateurism of their acts suggested that these men might be part of the vigilante gangs that the boys had been apprised of. Regardless of the men's affiliation, there was no denying the fact that they were careless, which guaranteed mistakes, and ones with serious consequences.

After sitting Cameron, Rich, and Evan at the table, the two interrogators left the room. The boys waited a few moments after the door closed to see if the men would return. When no one did, Rich was the first to speak.

"Who the hell are they?" he demanded in a harsh whisper. Evan and Cameron looked at each other.

"Did they identify themselves to you?" Cameron asked. Rich shook his head.

"How'd they get into your room then?" asked Evan. "You didn't let them in, did you?" Again, Rich shook his head.

"Hell, no!" Rich snorted. "I was lying on my bed and heard all the commotion in your room and got up to see what was going on. I opened the door and four guys rushed in and started kicking the crap out of me. How'd they get into your room?"

"They knocked and said they were from maintenance," Cameron explained. "I opened the door a crack to see what they wanted and they asked me to open up. I told them I thought they were dressed pretty fancy for janitors and they said they were bureau boys. I thought it was a joke and asked to see their credentials and that's when they kicked in the door and you heard the commotion. Then we ended up here."

"You guys think they're really feds?" asked Rich. It was the others' turn to shake their heads.

"Not a chance in hell," insisted Evan. "Just look at how they've done things so far. Feds would never have made that many mistakes."

"Yeah, I thought it was pretty bush league, too," agreed Rich. "Besides, didn't Chuck tell us—" He was interrupted by a loud cough from Cameron, signaling they shouldn't say too much.

"We don't know exactly who we're dealing with and how amateur they are," Cameron whispered. "Let's not give anything away on our end." The other two nodded in agreement. Just then, their interrogators returned.

There were three men. Two of them were middle-aged and slightly heavyset. Each had short hair, though one sported a military buzz cut. All were dressed in dark suits with white shirts. In addition, Buzz Cut wore a tie and carried a notepad. Two of the men sat opposite the boys. The third just stood there, momentarily confused, before heading out of the room and returning with another folding chair.

Yep. Professionals all the way.

"Okay," said Buzz Cut with a cough. "We want to ask you some questions about what you're doing here."

"You broke into our rooms and dragged us here," snarled Rich.

The man ignored him.

"Specifically, we want to know why you have been staying here for as long as you have without applying for any job, or displaying any visible means of support."

"We've got a job," Cameron said. "We're musicians. We've got a band called Roadhouse Sons and we've been playing gigs from the Northeast to here."

"Then what are you doing in Gaston, Missouri?" Buzz Cut leaned forward.

"We're waiting for clearance from the USO to go on a war bond tour for the troops." It was Evan who spoke this time, calmly and evenly.

"Why are you waiting for clearance?" Buzz Cut asked. Cameron noticed that the man was not taking any notes, despite the holding a notepad.

"Gas and stuff is rationed," Evan pressed on. "Even the USO only puts together tours when they have the rations to send the performers out."

"So, you're just hanging around here doing nothing while you're waiting," asked one of the longer-haired men. He was about Cameron's age, but a bit out of shape, and wore a suit with the top button of his shirt unfastened and his tie loose about the collar. The man had a toothpick in his mouth; he kept chewing it and moving it around with his tongue. Cameron wanted to gag.

You I'll call Toothpick.

"I guess," Cameron replied. He knew these men were trying to bait him. He was not going to play along. McIntyre had followed them and he was confident that she would know how to get them out of this.

"Why are you here and not in Columbia?" asked Buzz Cut.

"When we arrived in Missouri, this was the farthest we were able to travel on our permits," Evan stated. "We're only allowed to travel about a hundred miles a day, or less. When we reached our daily limit, we were here in Gaston."

"That was weeks ago," the third man snapped, lunging forward. "What are you still doing here then?"

"Roy, why don't you be quiet and let me handle this?" Buzz Cut said, visibly irritated. Roy leaned back in his chair and proceeded to sulk. Rich eyed Evan. Evan nodded imperceptibly. These men were amateurs.

"Again, why are you still here?" Buzz Cut asked.

"We don't want to waste our rations," Cameron explained. "It takes gas and tires to drive up to Columbia, and we don't know for sure what we're supposed to do. So we wait here till they call us. What's the problem with that?"

"Don't get flip with us, son," snapped Toothpick. "We're the ones that ask the questions around here!"

Where in the hell is McIntyre?

"So, exactly what are you doing with yourselves while you are waiting for this call to come in?" Buzz Cut asked finally.

"Just waiting," Evan said with a shrug. "We stay in our hotel rooms and stay out of trouble. That's it."

"You stay in your hotel rooms and stay out of trouble," Buzz Cut repeated. Cameron seethed at this amateur's pomposity and annoying technique, then seethed even more when he realized how effective it was.

"Or you just stay out of sight," sneered Toothpick. Cameron pictured himself shoving that toothpick down the man's throat.

Calm down. He's not worth the effort.

To their credit, none of the band members made a reply. The other men shifted disconcertedly in their seats. Cameron realized that by staying silent, the boys had frustrated a plan. For the first time since the onset of this intrusion, Cameron felt confident. The band obviously knew what they were doing. These guys didn't. As quickly as Cameron's confidence arose, however, it left. If their interrogators were rattled that easily, the situation could become dangerous.

Buzz Cut left the room, followed by the others. The three band members whispered to one another, but stopped when the door opened. Toothpick returned and sat down opposite them. He crossed his arms, staring silently at Cameron. It was everything Cameron could muster not to laugh aloud at this sophomoric attempt at intimidation,

Why not have some fun with it?

Stretching out his legs, Cameron then crossed them in a grand gesture, and leaned back in his chair, arms folded behind his head. Looking at Toothpick, he smiled.

I'm not falling for your bullshit, little boy.

As expected, Toothpick's face became darker and he took a deep breath. His eyes narrowed to slits. Cameron's smile grew slightly wider.

I will play you like a Strat and let you know it.

Cameron's smile grew a little wider. This caused Toothpick's eyes to widen, and he shifted uncomfortably in his chair. Cameron saw his adversary jut out his chin and stare back, menacingly. Cameron sighed languorously, but betrayed no other reaction. Toothpick was not so composed.

Toothpick rose from his chair and kicked it away. He leaned all the way over the table and slammed his hand down hard. He was about to say something to Cameron when the door flew open.

"What the hell's going on in here?" Buzz Cut poked his head in the door. Over his shoulder, Cameron could see some other men trying to look into the room.

"This guy's giving me an attitude," insisted Toothpick. "Look at him!"

Buzz Cut looked at Cameron, who shrugged his shoulders, a confused look on his face.

"Get out here, now!" demanded Buzz Cut.

Cameron pointed at himself, a surprised look on his face.

"Me?" Cameron asked, innocently. Buzz Cut, clearly annoyed, shook his head.

"No! *Him!*" he replied disgustedly, pointing at Toothpick. Toothpick sulkily complied, giving Cameron a warning glare as he left the room. After the door shut, Evan spoke.

"That probably wasn't a smart move," he whispered.

Cameron shrugged again.

"Who cares?" he replied. "I'm done playing their games. I've been through this enough times for real. These yahoos aren't going to rattle me."

Before Evan could reply, Buzz Cut returned, slapping his pad of paper and pen down on the table.

"I want you fellows to write down your names and dates of birth," he instructed.

"What the hell for?" demanded Cameron.

"Just do as I ask," said Buzz Cut. Cameron noticed he betrayed no emotion, neither annoyance nor impatience.

"What for?" repeated Cameron once again.

"We're going to check with the draft board to make sure you boys are registered with them, that's all."

"I'm not giving you anything," Cameron snarled, crossing his arms.

"And just why not?" asked Buzz Cut. "What have you got to hide?"

"Nothing," insisted Cameron. "It's just none of your business if I'm registered or not."

"Then if you've got nothing to hide, you shouldn't be afraid to give me your information."

"I'm not afraid of anything. I'm just not going to let myself be bullshitted into surrendering my personal information."

"If I'm requesting information in an official capacity, then you are obliged to provide to me said information."

"What official capacity?" Cameron snorted. "You clowns haven't shown us one piece of identification telling us who you are. You want something, then you give something. Show your credentials. Just who are you, anyway?"

"I don't have to answer to you," Buzz Cut said. "I'm duly authorized to collect information on suspected persons in this county, and I am duly exercising my duties as directed in my orders."

"What orders?" Evan insisted. "Authorized by whom? You want information, you better be providing some!"

"You fellows are not in any position to dictate terms to me, or anyone else," Buzz Cut replied, calmly folding his hands. "I don't think you fellows appreciate how much trouble you're in. Your actions have been very suspicious, and you have been heard uttering un-American and disloyal phrases."

"What un-American phrases?" Cameron demanded. "You've never heard us say any such things!"

"We've got witnesses that are willing to testify that they've heard you fellows utter a Russian toast at a local bar, followed by the words 'in case we lose.' That is detrimental to the morale of the people, and undermines the war effort."

"No one ever heard us say any such things, because we never have," Cameron retorted. He did, though, recall an instance when the Roadhouse Sons said that exact phrase. However, it was not in a public setting.

"But we have witnesses who are willing to say that you did," Buzz Cut stood up, smiling curtly.

"Then your witnesses are as full of shit as you are," Cameron said.

"The burden of proof will rest with you." Buzz Cut's voice took on the unctuous quality of a used car salesman.

Despite his best efforts to the contrary, Cameron felt himself bristle.

"Innocent until proven guilty," he replied, menacingly.

"If you say so," Buzz Cut said, sitting down.

"That's the basis of American justice," snapped Cameron, slamming his hand down on the table. He felt the sting of the contact, but registered no reaction to the pain. He realized that he had already given his interrogator enough of an opening to use against him; he wasn't going to hand over any more.

"If you say so," Buzz Cut repeated, a content smile on his face.

So, you think you're so smart because I betrayed a weakness. Well guess what, sonny boy? So did you.

"I say so," Cameron averred, his voice quiet. Even to himself, he sounded impotent and defeated.

"I suppose you'd also expect a trial by a jury of your peers, wouldn't you?" Buzz Cut laughed. "Well, that might be hard, finding twelve draft-dodging subversives. You might have to settle for twelve honest and upright citizens from Kennesaw County, all of whom have relatives off fighting for their country, so you boys can sit here and enjoy yourselves."

"That isn't how it is and you know it," snapped Evan, with Rich echoing his sentiment.

Buzz Cut was unperturbed. Folding his arms behind his head, he leaned back in his chair.

"Maybe I do; maybe I don't," he smiled. "If you boys want to play rough, then you will have to carry the burden of proof."

"The burden of proof rests with the prosecution," grumbled Cameron. Buzz Cut laughed.

"You've got all the little old answers, don't you, son? Well, you're just like any other Saturday-night lawyer. You know just enough to think you can stay out of trouble, and just little enough that you don't know how much trouble you're in."

"I haven't gotten myself into jack shit," said Cameron. "I repeat. The burden of proof will rest with you."

"It's not going to rest with me," Buzz Cut assured him. "I pass this off and never have to worry about it again. That's how it goes. It rests with—"

"Says who?" Cameron demanded.

"Says the honorable Clifford Allen Lewis, prosecuting attorney for Kennesaw County, and one of the directors of the bureau." Buzz Cut delivered this information in a schoolyard singsong style of voice. This made Cameron shudder. He made a mental note of the prosecuting attorney's name.

"Now," Buzz Cut said, sitting up in his chair. "Why don't we stop wasting time and just give me the information that I want. Okay, son?"

Cameron stared at him for a moment. Once again, Cameron was being buffaloed into an untenable situation. He absolutely refused to cooperate. Holding his breath, he made a difficult decision.

"I'm not saying another thing without a lawyer present," he spat.

"Then you are officially invoking your Fifth Amendment rights," smiled Buzz Cut. For a moment, Cameron wondered if he hadn't hoped Buzz Cut would say just that.

"I'm invoking whatever rights protect me from being interrogated by some fat, fascist fuck like you," Cameron replied. Buzz Cut continued to smile.

"Now, if you were innocent and didn't object to me verifying your draft registration, you wouldn't need a lawyer, now would you?" Cameron made no reply. Buzz Cut was unfazed.

"We could go to all the trouble of trying to find you a lawyer at this time of night. No telling how long that could take. He would simply tell you to cooperate with us and make life easier, just like they've done with everyone else. Or, if you want to just avoid all that hassle, you can tell us what we want to know and you'll be free to go." Cameron said nothing. Buzz Cut turned to Evan and Rich. He asked the same question of them. When they, too, refused to cooperate, Buzz Cut's smile faded. He quickly gathered up his pen and unused note pad.

"Have it your way," he muttered as he got up to leave the room.

Just then, the door flew open and one very angry policeman entered.

CHAPTER ELEVEN

"Assume Nothing"

Chuck hastily strode across the motel parking lot to the registration office, with Clyde and Snapper in tow. Suddenly, a car approached, horn blaring, and screeched to a halt immediately behind him. Startled, Chuck spun around. His adrenaline at high threshold and hurling expletives, he pounded on the hood of the vehicle.

"Hey!" cried a female voice. It was McIntyre behind the wheel. Her expression was frantic. Without waiting for further explanation, he jumped onto the car and slid into the passenger's seat.

"You guys stay here!" he ordered Clyde and Snapper. "Go to my room and lock the door. Don't open it for *anyone* 'til I get back!" Without waiting for a response, Chuck slamming the car door as McIntyre sped away.

Clyde and Snapper, utterly perplexed, did as they were told and without hesitation. They ran back across the parking lot and locked themselves in Chuck's room.

"What the hell is going on?" Chuck demanded.

"The guys have been picked up," McIntyre replied, checking the rearview mirror. Instinctively, Chuck did the same.

"Picked up? By the police?"

"I very much doubt it," McIntyre replied.

She described the events that unfolded earlier that evening. Upon returning from Columbia, she noticed two vehicles leaving the motel parking lot. In the first car, two men sat in the front seat, one of them turned around, as though talking to someone in the back seat. As she passed the car, she saw Cameron seated in the back. Two males were seated in the back with him. When Cameron saw McIntyre, he waved and gestured, pointing with his thumb erect. She realized that he was alerting her of the presence of a gun.

"I thought you and the others were in the second car," she explained. "But when I passed them, I could only see two males in the front seat."

"What did you do?"

"I followed them!"

"Do you think it was local law enforcement?"

"Not once did they bother to look in the rearview to see if they were being followed!" McIntyre shook her head in disgust.

"Then it wasn't the cops," Chuck grumbled. "It wasn't the feds, either, obviously."

"Any guesses?" asked McIntyre.

"Not yet. Anything else?"

"Both cars headed downtown and parked in front of a building in the government complex by the courthouse. The police station is right there, but they didn't go inside."

"*All* the government offices are there," pondered Chuck. "Do you think this is official?"

"Wouldn't someone have notified us?" McIntyre asked incredulously. "They wouldn't just spring that on us. That would be crazy!"

"One would hope. Did you actually see anyone with a gun?"

"Yes. The man in the passenger side of the first car exited the vehicle. He had a gun. He instructed Cameron and the guys to exit the car on the same side."

"What about the men in the other car? Did they have any weapons?"

"If they did, there was no indication of it."

"Did they take Cameron and company into the police station?"

"No. All of them walked across the parking lot and entered another sort of mod building with a glass door inset in the middle of a concrete wall."

"They parked in front of the police station, but didn't go in," Chuck repeated. McIntyre nodded. "Intimidation factor?" she asked.

"You bet. Parking in the government complex in front of law enforcement headquarters makes people nice and nervous. They lead them elsewhere to confuse them and mess with their minds."

"It's very likely not official," said McIntyre. "That means we can't employ official measures to find out what's going on. Any ideas?"

Chuck was sullen. They drove on in silence. McIntyre had learned a long time ago that Chuck wasn't ignoring her; when he was mute, he simply had nothing to say. So she said nothing, leaving him to his thoughts.

At last, McIntyre reached the government complex and pulled into the parking lot.

"Both vehicles are still here," she said, pointing toward the cars.

Chuck sat bolt upright. "Which building did they enter?" he demanded.

"That one," she said, gesturing toward a small, three-story building on the north end of the parking lot. She parked a short distance from the building.

"Wait for me here!" Chuck jumped out and hurried into the police station. McIntyre backed into a nearby parking space and positioned the car in a manner that allowed her to monitor the entrance to the police station and the building into which the Roadhouse Sons were led. The car keys remained in the ignition and she checked her holster with a pat to her side. She was ready for a rapid escape, if necessary. She scanned the parking lot as she waited.

The complex was quiet, as was the street. Curfew was moments away, and only official vehicles were on the roads. The parking lot itself was well lit; other buildings housed several county offices, as well as multiple federal offices. Security in this enclave was paramount.

McIntyre scanned the area vigilantly as she waited, glancing frequently at the dashboard clock. She drew no attention to herself, behaving nonchalantly. Ten minutes had passed since Chuck left.

Just as she was becoming nervous, Chuck emerged from the police station, followed by a uniformed officer. Chuck motioned for her to follow them as he and the officer hurried across the parking lot, the officer quickly outpacing him. Putting the vehicle in gear, McIntyre inched along, following them.

The police officer reached the glass door of the smaller building before Chuck did, and practically yanked the door off of its hinges as he opened it. He barged inside without waiting for Chuck to catch up to him and the door closed just as Chuck reached it. The door's self-locking mechanism prohibited Chuck's entry into the building, despite his struggle to open it. McIntyre parked the car and jumped out. By the time she ran the length of the short walkway, Chuck was pounding on the glass so vehemently that McIntyre feared he might break it.

"Hey!" Chuck yelled, his face against the window. "Hey! Let me in! I'm with him!"

"What the hell is going on?" McIntyre shouted.

"I'm not sure!" he shouted back, still pounding on the window. "That was Officer Beecham, the one I told you about, remember? He's the one that questioned Clyde and Snapper. I told him what happened and I thought he was going to explode."

"Why?"

"He turned red and stormed out!" Chuck hollered.

"Did he say anything?"

Chuck pounded on the glass for emphasis. "Not a damned thing!" With a final pound on the window, Chuck threw his hands up, exasperated. "Where the *fuck* is he?"

McIntyre cupped her hands on the glass and peered into the building. She saw lights on near the door and others set intermittently along a narrow corridor. She could discern that people inside were moving around. No one seemed to realize that she and Chuck were outside trying to get in; if anyone did notice, they certainly didn't acknowledge it. McIntyre was about to start shouting, when one of the men in the corridor happened to look in her direction. She flashed her brightest smile and waved, beckoning the man to the door.

"Someone's coming," she said, taking her position next to Chuck.

A man opened the door.

"I'm sorry," he said. "It's after hours. We're closed." He was about to slam the door when Chuck grabbed the handle.

"We're with Officer Beecham."

McIntyre eyed the other man. Though Chuck had directed no real threat at him, the sharpness and tone of Chuck's voice advised against denying them entrance. The man, unused to being challenged, looked at Chuck, befuddled. Chuck said nothing, his gaze at the other man direct and unyielding.

McIntyre counted in her head, *Five, four, three, two, one…*

The man waved them inside. With no further regard for the man, Chuck stepped inside. McIntyre followed, flashing one last smile. The man closed the door behind them, sputtering officiously.

They stood in what appeared to be a reception area. McIntyre realized that the corridor she'd seen from the window was not the only one; it ran from the door to the rear of the building. Another ran perpendicular to the first. Chuck and McIntyre saw no one else in the immediate vicinity, nor was there anyone in either corridor. They could, however, hear voices.

"Do you know which way he went?" Chuck asked the man.

"Where who went?" the man asked as he drew closed the window blinds on the glass door. McIntyre couldn't discern if the man was sarcastic or stupid. Neither could Chuck, who calmly repeated the question.

"Where Officer Beecham went." Chuck glanced down the corridors. Nothing raised his suspicion.

"He went that way," the man said, pointing down the hallway McIntyre had first seen from the outside. "But I wouldn't go down there, if I were you."

"Why not?" Chuck was nearing the end of his patience.

With Chuck concentrating on the other man, McIntyre concentrated on their surroundings. With the blinds drawn, she could no longer see outside. Inside, any doors that were closed when they arrived remained so. Still, she knew that anyone could be on the other side of any closed door—and with a gun pointed at them. For mere reassurance, McIntyre hugged her arm to her side. Her gun was at the ready.

"He was looking for Mr. Lewis, and Mr. Lewis doesn't like to be interrupted when we're conducting an interrogation," the man continued.

"Interrogation?" Chuck snapped, stuffing his face against the man's astonished mug. "Exactly who the hell do you think you are? You're not associated with the police. What is your authority? The feds?"

The man stammered his answer.

"The-the county prosecutor's off-office. We keep an eye on un-American activities. Just like the House Un-American Activities Committee."

"That was abolished by the House of Representatives four years ago!" McIntyre said calmly. Chuck burst into laughter and pointed at the flummoxed man, who blushed at his own ignorance.

Before the man could retort, a door in the first corridor opened. An older, heavyset male entered the hallway. Clearly affronted, he shot a disapproving grimace in their direction.

"What is the meaning of this ruckus?" the older man bellowed, sneering down his prominent, aquiline nose. McIntyre inspected him from afar. He was a short, heavy-set man, approximately five feet six inches tall. His white hair was laced with traces of gray, and he was clean-shaven. He stood with his stomach pushed forward, as though deliberately drawing attention to his paunch. He waddled down the corridor toward them. As he approached, McIntyre noticed that he was replacing the cap on a small white bottle.

"Three of my employees were abducted this evening. An eyewitness stated that they were forcibly escorted into this building," Chuck said firmly. "I just spoke with the police, who stated that my employees were not detained in any official capacity. I want to know where they are!"

"I'll thank you not to raise your voice at me," the older fellow said, sniffing disdainfully. "I'll have you know that I'm Clifford Allen Lewis, the prosecuting attorney for Kennesaw County, and I have full jurisdiction in this matter."

"Jurisdiction over what?" demanded Chuck. "Are my employees to be charged with an offense? If so, why weren't they detained by the police, legally and within their rights?"

Lewis blinked rapidly, as if such a form of communication was the epitome of defiance of one's inferiors.

Chuck closed his eyes, his patience waning. "Where are my men?"

Lewis sniffed.

"I don't see why I need to answer that question." As though for emphasis, Lewis unscrewed the cap from the white bottle, inserted the bottle tip into his nostril, and squeezed.

McIntyre stifled the urge to laugh.

"You don't need to answer, Lewis!" came Officer Beecham's voice from the doorway of another room. "Your friends are right here, Chuck. They're free to go."

Beecham stepped into the hallway, and with a ceremonious sweep of his arm, presented Evan, Rich, and Cameron. Cameron and Rich passed him cautiously. Evan, however, behaved in a completely uncharacteristic fashion. For just a moment, he stood face to face with Beecham, then glared at him and walked away. McIntyre was agog; she'd never seen Evan challenge another human being.

"There. See?" sniffed Lewis at Chuck, beaming with grand satisfaction. "There was no need for your outrageous behavior. I inform you heretofore that this incident is not to be forgotten anytime soon. You may very well regret this impertinence."

"I think this has gone far enough, Clifford," said Beecham. His voice was menacing. "I'll vouch for him, and these men, too. You don't need to worry about it."

"I'll be the one to decide that—"

"Leave it alone!" the officer warned as he led the Roadhouse Sons past the older man.

"What?" the elder man asked. Chuck and McIntyre glanced at each other, brows furrowed. Lewis's expression and demeanor had changed suddenly to one of innocent misunderstanding.

"Weird," McIntyre mouthed to Chuck. He nodded, their exchange unnoticed by the rest.

"I said let it go," Beecham repeated, his voice booming. He turned to Chuck and the band.

"Do you all need a ride?"

"We don't need a ride," Chuck muttered, hiding his disgust. "We have our own car. Are we going to get in any trouble for being out after curfew?"

"No," Beecham assured them. "I can give you an escort back, if you'd like." "You don't need to go to the troub—"

"The affrontery! I endured outrageous accusations about unjust detention, and here you are, flagrantly disobeying curfew!" scoffed Lewis with another derisive sniff. "You have strange double standards, if you ask me."

"Who asked you?" snapped Chuck. "Do you have cots here for us to sleep on? No? Then we don't have much choice about being out after curfew, do we?"

Lewis, visibly shocked, feigned backward, as though he'd just endured a blow to the face. As he stumbled, he blustered and flailed fantastically.

"Why are you so upset? I make no accusations! This is inappropriate behavior! And from someone claiming to be unjustly detained!"

"Now is not the time, Clifford!" Beecham roared.

McIntyre and Chuck eyed each other in disbelief. The band members looked on as though they were witnessing a circus sideshow. Cameron began humming "Entrance of the Gladiators." Evan and Rich turned red suppressing their laughter.

"Time to go. We'll be just fine," McIntyre said, opening her arms and corralling the boys toward the door. "Thank you for everything. C'mon fellas. We don't want to be out any later than we have to."

McIntyre hustled Cameron, Rich, and Evan to the entrance and jostled them through the door. Chuck seethed at Lewis, turned on his heels, and stomped out the door. He looked at McIntyre, who nodded toward the boys. Chuck took the cue and marched them toward the car. McIntyre closed the door, making sure that she heard the lock mechanism click. If the door opened behind her, she wanted to know it.

She lagged behind, hoping to overhear anything Beecham and Lewis might say as they left the building. She dropped a quarter from her trench coat pocket, and bent down to retrieve it, checking over her shoulder to see if anyone else had left the building. No one had. She could barely discern the silhouettes of Beecham, Lewis, and several others moving about in the first corridor, but no one headed toward the door. She hurried down the walkway and jogged casually to the car, where she found Chuck questioning the boys.

"I'm telling you, man! That's what they said!" Cameron was insisting. Evan and Rich nodded enthusiastically.

"I'm telling you, it's not possible!" McIntyre heard Chuck say. "I'm not discussing it outside here. Get in the car."

"But, man, you've got to listen to us!" Cameron was holding fast.

"Not here!" Chuck hissed. Cameron hesitated, debating whether to press the issue. To McIntyre's relief, he chose not to and climbed into the back seat of her car. The others followed suit. Chuck climbed into the front passenger's side, shaking his head all the while.

McIntyre slid into the driver's seat and started the ignition. She turned on the radio, the setting of which played not music, but static, which enabled them to talk in the car, undetected by audio surveillance devices.

"All righty," sighed Chuck. "Tell McIntyre what you told me."

McIntyre looked in the rearview mirror. The expression on Cameron's face was nothing short of sheer frustration coupled with exhaustion. She anticipated his usual defensive demeanor, which often resulted in a battery of additional confrontations. Hoping for Cameron's cooperation was naïve at best, but McIntyre waited optimistically. Thankfully, after a deep breath, Cameron began his narrative and explained how he, Evan, and Rich were assaulted at the motel, and dragged, for no apparent reason, into purported custody. He then described how they were questioned, leaving no detail to McIntyre's imagination. When they deemed it necessary, Evan and Rich would elaborate or clarify. She was impressed with their collective recall abilities while subject to duress. Chuck's expression revealed the same, and McIntyre was relieved. She knew that Chuck was finally able to relax a bit. When at last Cameron completed his report, Chuck questioned the boys once more.

"So, they literally said they were with the Federal Bureau of Investigation?"

All three of the musicians shook their heads.

Cameron spoke first. "No! They just said they were with the *Bureau* of Investigation," he insisted.

"No *Federal*," Rich chimed in.

Evan spoke next. "He said their agency gave them the authority to question us and take us in if we resisted."

"How did you resist?" McIntyre queried.

"That's just it!" Cameron exclaimed. "We didn't. At first, they said they were with maintenance, and when I opened the door all the way, they said they were with the Bureau. When I asked for their creds, they kicked the door in and tore the place up. Then they dragged us downstairs."

"I didn't even get a chance to say *anything!*" shouted Rich. "I heard the shit going down in his room, and they jumped me when I came out my door."

McIntyre drove the car through the darkened streets. They sat in silence, waiting for Chuck to speak. He said nothing.

Eventually, and much to the boys' relief, McIntyre broke the silence.

"Well, there's no denying it. It's total bullshit!"

"That, my dear, is an understatement." Chuck had weighed in at last. "But who is this Mr. Clifford Allen Lewis, and why is he covering up bullshit?"

"From the way everything was going down, I felt sure it was one of the vigilante groups you've talked about," said Cameron. Evan and Rich agreed.

"First, it was obvious that they were only using intimidation and didn't have any legitimate authority," Evan said.

"And judging from Beecham's reaction, the police have no idea what Lewis is doing," added Rich.

Cameron weighed in. "It seems to me that they're running their own show!"

Chuck turned so abruptly to look at them that the musicians sat aback.

"Very good," he murmured esoterically. "That's exactly what we're thinking, too."

Cameron's gut wrenched. The unctuous tone and timbre of Chuck's voice set him on guard.

"So what do we do now?" he ventured.

Chuck rubbed his eyes, weariness wafting over him.

"I'm not sure. Clyde and Snapper aren't briefed on this yet."

"Yeah. They need to know what happened," McIntyre said through a yawn. Despite their collective and evident fatigue, Cameron knew that the Roadhouse Sons were not about to call it quits.

As they pulled into the parking lot of the motel, the light was on in Chuck's room. The band's room was still dark.

Chuck was pleased. "They stayed put!" He turned to the Cameron, Evan, and Rich. "Do any of you have keys to the truck?" They shook their heads.

"The keys are in the room," said Cameron. "I don't carry them around since I sold the Mustang."

Cameron attempted to hide his resentment. During the band's previous assignment in Vermont, he'd grown attached to the yellow Mustang Grande. It was issued to him when he and the band were recruited to work with McIntyre and Dwyer, and he had many a pleasant memory of it. When the Roadhouse Sons left Vermont to tour, there was no way that they would be able to secure adequate rations for an extra vehicle. Such an extravagance would draw undue attention to a struggling cover band. At first, Cameron resisted the order to sell the Mustang, but he soon realized that he was fighting a losing battle. Although the title and registration were in his name, he understood completely that this was ultimately a case of "the Lord giveth and the Lord hath taken away." And so he sold it. Evan and Rich sold their cars, as well.

In the vehicles' place was a converted van, roomy enough to store luggage and equipment. On more than one occasion, it was utilized as a camper. Funds remaining after the purchase of the van were originally intended for the purchase of a more reliable truck. Everyone decided, though, that it would instead be less costly to make repairs on the existing truck.

"I think we should move the van and the truck closer to our rooms," said Chuck. "I want to keep an eye on everything until we get out of this town."

"Do you think they're going to try anything again?" asked Evan.

"They just got challenged in their own den," Chuck observed. "If they're trying to throw their weight around, they're not going to let it go without retaliation. If word got out that they didn't respond, they'd lose their intimidation factor. We'd be stupid not to be on our guard." McIntyre parked the car, and the boys moved their respective vehicles, as instructed. Chuck motioned for them to be silent, and instructed them to follow him and McIntyre to the room.

Chuck knocked on the door in signal fashion. Cameron saw the slightest of motion at the curtain, but saw no shadows. The door opened, revealing Snapper silhouetted in the portal. He held the door open just enough for everyone to squeeze inside, then quickly closed it. The room was neat as a pin. Cameron soon discovered the reason for the lack of shadows in the windows. Both the table lamp and the standing lamp were set almost flush against the window, providing illumination to the room itself, but no backlight in the room to reveal the movements of any occupants.

Clever. I'd never have thought of that.

After their latest ordeal, Cameron was relieved to know that his fellow musicians were adapting to their new and sudden vocation. They were employing learned tactics, and following their intuition. That was a very good sign, indeed.

Chuck cleared his throat. "All right, gang. Listen up!"

He and McIntyre briefed the boys, recapping the day's incidents and the subsequent conversation in the car. Snapper and Clyde were clearly relieved to have the band in one place again. Chuck revealed no relief; he pressed the boys with more questions.

"You said they claimed to have heard you all say a Russian toast?" he asked. "Where would they have heard that? Did you say it out loud in a bar or something?"

"No fucking way!" declared Cameron. "We're not that ballsy."

"Are you sure about that?" Chuck settled on the edge of the bed.

"I'm positive," Cameron insisted. "We might make jokes privately, but we'd never say anything like that in public."

"Are you sure you didn't say it sometime when you were drinking? You know, say it and not remember it?"

"Man, we don't spend enough money to get a buzz, never mind get drunk," explained Rich. "Besides, we know things have changed now that we work for you. We don't even get hammered like we used to. Hell, we can't afford to do that shit anymore."

Evan asked, complete with groan, "Could the room be bugged? That would be Vermont all over again! I don't think anyone's checked since we got here."

Chuck arose from his perch. He motioned for everyone to continue talking, then beckoned McIntyre. The two of them searched the room, concentrating on the peripheries of doorjambs, and on wallpaper, carpet and paneling seams. Clyde and Snapper offered commentary on the meeting they'd attended, and the others did the same. Occasionally, McIntyre or Chuck threw in a question. They proceeded to the bathroom, then checked all of the obvious places, including the backside of pictures and mirrors. They carefully unscrewed the mouthpiece of the telephone receiver, and quietly opened the drawers of the nightstand and other furniture. McIntyre examined the curtain rods while Chuck ran his hands along the tops of the window frames. Cameron watched their every move, memorizing the ritual. Finally, Chuck and McIntyre sat down.

"If this room is wired, it's a damn good job," Chuck said.

"Should we check the other room?" asked Cameron. Chuck nodded and instructed Cameron and Rich to follow him. Clyde, Evan and McIntyre waited as the others performed the ritual surveillance sweep of the other room. At last, the three stood in the doorway. From the looks on their faces, it was clear that their sweep had the same results.

"Nothing," grumbled Cameron.

"They're either really good, or you guys just don't remember what you said in public." Chuck's demeanor was admonishing, his tone judgmental.

"We didn't forget anything," insisted Cameron, bristling at Chuck's insinuation. "I told you we'd never say anything like that in public."

"Why would you say it at all?" snapped Chuck, making no effort to hide his vexation.

Cameron roiled, but checked his temper.

"Maybe you're used to this." He was surprised at his own level of calm. "You've been in a war before. You know what it's like to have a threat hanging over your head, and you've lost friends. We haven't. This is all new to us and it's pretty damned scary, if you want to know the truth. Yeah, we said the Russian toast. It was a *joke*. It's our way of whistling past a very big, dark, scary fucking graveyard at night. I'm sorry if someone overheard it and it caused a problem. We thought we were safe in our own rooms! Guess again!"

To everyone's surprise, Chuck nodded. Cameron had expected their manager to verbally tear him to pieces with the same accusations he'd heard from Buzz Cut.

"I was seventeen during the Cuban Missile Crisis," Chuck said. "I lost about five pounds after that because I was too nervous to eat, and couldn't sleep anywhere except in my basement for almost a week afterward. Yeah, I know what you mean. For what it's worth, I would have figured you'd have been safe here, too."

"So, why aren't we?" demanded Rich.

"I wish I knew, man. I really do."

"Do you think another guest could have overheard them?" asked McIntyre. "These walls aren't that thick and these guys get a little loud when they've had a few drinks."

"It's a possibility," Chuck agreed. He turned to the boys. "Do you lads remember the last time you might have said it?"

"No, man!" Rich replied. "Sometimes we say it; sometimes we don't. It depends on our moods, I guess."

Chuck rubbed his eyes. "That doesn't narrow it down any. There've been some guests in and out of here recently, but they were traveling through, so they couldn't have been the witnesses Lewis referred to."

"If he even has witnesses," snorted Cameron.

"I take it you don't believe he does?" Chuck studied Cameron carefully.

"I don't believe it for one friggin' minute," the musician replied.

"Why not? You're not denying that you said it. Someone reported it, so there has to be someone somewhere that could be a witness."

"It just seems like it's all a bunch of bullshit intimidation," Cameron insisted. "Lots of threats and innuendos, but nothing with teeth in it!"

"Not yet, anyway, but you're right. There's a whole lot of implication goin' on, and much of it could be smoke and mirrors."

As Chuck spoke, the lights flickered, indicating that motel management was shutting off power for the lights, as they did each evening.

"Barbara, do you have any objections to staying here tonight?" Chuck smiled innocently. McIntyre rolled her eyes.

"Ugh! As if I have any choice!"

"You take the room with Clyde, Rich, and Evan," Chuck sighed. "You've got a gun and so do I. If anyone tries anything, we'll have adequate means of defense."

As they left for their room, Chuck told Snapper to move the band truck again, even closer to their side of the hotel.

"This time, back it in toward your door. There's no way they'd be able to open the hood on that thing without making a racket and alerting us, but with the back toward the open lot, they could easily cut the lock and slide the door up quietly without our noticing."

As the others readied for bed, Chuck positioned himself at the railing while Snapper moved the truck. The motel's street sign was still lit, and the outside lights were on, as well. Chuck had ample light and opportunity to monitor the parking lot and the surrounding entrances. There was nothing to see—no strangers, no unfamiliar vehicles. As soon as the truck was positioned, Chuck returned to his room and called the band members together. He wanted them to survey the premises, and he designated shifts.

"You really think they'll try something?" whispered Cameron.

Chuck laughed. "They've already tried something by nabbing you guys. That didn't work out. As I told you ten times before, they'll be back. I'm dividing your watch into three-hour shifts. McIntyre needs to be fresh for the drive back to Columbia tomorrow, so we guys are going to do the watch tonight. I'll take the first one here. Who wants the second?"

Cameron volunteered and headed for bed to grab as much sleep as possible. He was just snuggling in when the lights went out. Cameron tensed. As his eyes adjusted to the darkness, he wondered if the sudden outage was part of a retaliation plot by Buzz Cut and company. Hearing nothing out of the ordinary, Cameron realized that the lights went off per the usual nightly black out, and nothing menacing or sinister lurked.

Cameron settled back into his bed, with the fear that he'd toss and turn and remain awake the entire time that he awaited his turn at watch or, even worse, that he'd dream again about the fire, of being surrounded in flames.

CHAPTER TWELVE

"Opportunity"

Jack Stanley was in no mood for his clients' perpetually surly attitudes. Having already spent the morning in the unenviable position of experiencing the outrage and contempt of innumerable public servants—from law enforcement to school district representatives to lawyers, lots of lawyers—he'd simply had enough. The lawyers, in particular, set Stanley agog. At first, he was amazed at the sheer quantity of lawyers, all of whom arrived at the hearing to represent the parents of the children in attendance at the assembly. Ultimately, though, Stanley realized that there were plenty of suits to file, and sharks willing to file them. The story had received incredible media coverage and was the talk of Seattle. Any lawyers worth their real or imaginary salt were jumping at a chance to be involved in the brouhaha. From the most respectable firms to the seediest ambulance chasers, all of the legal eagles present were eyeing Stanley with utter disdain. He realized that the situation was going to be a long, drawn out, pricey ordeal before all was said and done.

If the bail hearing was any indication of what was to come, then the experience was slated to be pure torture. Several parents brought children, the youngest ones, who had witnessed the incident. Noting the age of the children represented, Stanley was disgusted by the manipulative maneuverings of these parents. Many children burst into tears when the Boney Jack band members were escorted into the hearing. Stanley had no choice but to remain stoically seated behind his clients as they were formally charged then asked how they would plead. The responses were entirely typical.

Caesare, the band's percussionist, was the first to speak. In a voice so inaudible that he was asked by the judge to repeat his answer, Caesare stated, "Not guilty." Stanley loathingly eyed the spineless drummer. "Probably peed himself when his name was called," Stanley muttered under his breath. Perhaps if Caesare had been allowed to plead last, he could have taken his cue from the others and possibly displayed a modicum of courage. "No," Stanley whispered to himself. The gravity of the situation would hit Caesare like a brick; he'd behave even more pathetically. Resultantly, any display of defiance by the others would seem farcical, at best.

The next to speak was Black Jack Quinn. Stanley almost admired him. Indeed Quinn was defiant, but his defiance was born of conviction, not of affectation, as was usually so evident in the others. Quinn followed his not guilty plea with an uncharacteristic passionate, bitter diatribe on the charges brought against him. Only after the judge threatened to charge him with contempt of court was the lawyer able to calm and quiet Quinn, who returned to his usual flaccid demeanor.

Russ, who refused to state his surname, simply responded with a surly "Not guilty!" and sat down, crossing his arms and attempting his best look of scorn. Stanley thought Russ resembled nothing more than a pouting child, and noticed with amused contempt that the guitar player's herpes sore was flaring up on his lip again.

When Jack Ralston stood to cite his plea, Stanley wanted to escape the room. As expected, Ralston was able to take a simple not guilty plea and transform it into a self-serving soapbox. Stanley watched in horror; he loathed Ralston. The judge advised Ralston to save his defense for his trial, and ordered him to sit down. Ralston abided, and quickly. He shared no glances with his band mates as he did so. Stanley shook his head.

The last to stand and plead was Boney Jack himself. Stanley held his breath, knowing this would be sheer spectacle and pure showboating designed to outshine the others. He was right. Boney Jack stood, the mere act of rising exhibiting his usual graceful, slinking and slithering manner. He reminded Stanley of a lugubriously uncoiling serpent. Initially, Boney Jack refused to plea. Instead, and as Stanley expected, Boney Jack pontificated his vitriol in a tirade decrying the penalty he was forced to endure for exercising his first amendment rights, and he accused the court and legal system of fascist hypocrisy.

When Boney Jack spoke, his voice was just as reptilian as his physical comportment. He hissed in simultaneously silky and harsh intonations. Following his outburst, he proceeded to deliver a torturous soliloquy on the state of American society. The press zealously recorded, in print and photograph, the entire spectacle, and, for a fleeting moment, Stanley wondered whether any amount of the resulting free publicity was worth the cost to his sensibilities. However, there was absolutely nothing that could be done at that time. Repeated warnings from the bench did not quiet Boney Jack's vehement monologue, nor abate it. Finally, upon the judge's orders, Boney Jack was removed from the courtroom and a plea was made on his behalf.

The fact that bail was argued upon endlessly was clearly a harbinger of what would become of the looming trial. With the band's tawdry actions still fresh in townsfolk's collective mind, the prosecutor argued that they should be remanded back into custody and remain in the county jail pending trial, a suggestion that brought cheers from many of the spectators.

The judge restored order in the court and requested testimony of the defense. Stanley was pleasantly surprised at the prowess of the band's counsel, who began his argument by stating that a travesty of justice would occur if the court based its decision solely upon the emotional responses of the populace. He eloquently presented an image of the band members, who were guilty of nothing more than reacting to the intense emotions affecting everyone else in the country, especially those living in such close proximity to the war zone and to military bases. He explained that such proximity included the only Trident submarine base servicing the Pacific, a target unlikely to be ignored by the Soviets. Therefore, he exclaimed, the entire situation was inherently hazardous, and evocative of extreme duress.

"Oh, that's a good one!" Stanley whispered to himself. The courtroom was still. The band's lawyer, gesturing emphatically with great sweeps of his arms pronounced, in a grand finale, that remanding the band to custody would prevent them from fulfilling contractual performance obligations, resulting in the loss of multiple jobs and an adverse effect on the local economy.

At long last, a sum was set and the band members were released into Stanley's custody. Bail was a bittersweet victory for the band. Indeed, they were free to go, but at a high price. Bail itself was set at twenty thousand *each*, and the band *and* management company were required to surrender to the court all of their respective gas and travel rations. Adding insult to injury, all of them were forbidden to travel outside of Seattle's city limits.

Stanley and the band were ushered from the courthouse and escorted by private security hired by Stanley for that very purpose. Security's job was twofold. Crowds and press were prevented access to the band members, and vice versa. That would ensure that the band couldn't make statements that would complicate their defense. Despite the ordeal in the courtroom, Stanley was determined to draw hearty benefit from the incident, and he didn't want anything to impede his plan. The band members were collectively their own worst enemy. Hence, they were the ones to be guarded most. At the first available opportunity, Stanley was planning to launch a carefully crafted publicity campaign. The logistics of the launch were too delicate to be rendered subject to the band's collective caprice. Just as Stanley had anticipated, Boney Jack and his compadres indeed attempted to continue their manifesto as security struggled and stuffed the band members into their limousine. Stanley ordered the driver to take the band straight back to the hotel.

The security detail followed closely. Stanley desperately needed time away from the band and directed the driver to take him to Bellevue, but then remembered that he was now restricted by court order to remain within city limits.

"Never mind. Drive down by the waterfront," Stanley said, his agitation unconcealed. As the car turned around and traveled down the opposite side of the street, Stanley sat back and closed his eyes in an attempt to catch up on sleep. He'd been denied the luxury of slumber during the previous evening, the majority of which was spent placing calls to the band's law firm and fielding phone calls from select media sources. Simms had entered Stanley's office, a look of deep concern on his face. Stanley knew instantly what Simms was about to say.

"There's a call for you, sir," Simms uttered. "Line two."

"Can you take a message?" Stanley snapped, gulping another shot of bourbon. He hoped that the irritation in his voice concealed his fear. Simms shook his head, grimly.

"No, I'm afraid not," he said. "They insist on talking to you now, sir."

Stanley tersely nodded his head toward the door. Simms took the cue and left the room. Stanley inhaled deeply, as though the very air provided the fortitude he needed to endure the call. He raised the receiver to his ear and punched the lighted button on the phone. There was no need for salutations, nor was there an opportunity for them. The caller wasted no time expressing rage about what had transpired, and about the negative attention and publicity drawn to Boney Jack. Serious concern was raised about complications presented by the whole situation, and how future activities could be impeded.

"You realize that those punks have a police record now," the caller said. Stanley ignored the pun and, making one of his own, assured the caller that he was well aware of the band's new record.

"You also recall that they were scheduled to take part in the upcoming USO tour?"

Stanley stated that he was well aware of the tour, and politely reminded the caller of his efforts to secure the band's spot.

"Then you don't need to be reminded that now, with this fiasco in our midst, there is no way they are eligible to take part in it?"

"I assure you, this is only a temporary setback." Stanley was attempting to sound calm and respectful, but keeping his composure required gargantuan effort. "I've been working on a very carefully crafted publicity campaign, one which I'm certain will minimize any negative publicity by turning it to our advantage. We'll be able to schedule a separate simultaneous tour and work as many of the same locations as we can."

"That may be fine for record sales and concert tickets," the caller warned. "Have you forgotten that if they are ineligible to participate with the USO, they are ineligible to enter army bases? That includes army hospitals, not to mention refugee camps. Has your carefully crafted publicity campaign taken this into consideration?" Stanley said nothing. How could he admit that he hadn't even had time to consider a change of clothes, let alone actually implement damage control and set tour dates? His situation would be infinitely worse if he dared to infer any faltering circumspection on his part.

"The time has come to reconsider their viability," the caller continued. "Perhaps they've outlasted their usefulness, reached their point of obsolescence."

"Do you want me to release them from their contracts?" Stanley queried, his tongue practically stuck to the roof of his arid mouth. There was a long pause. At the point when the silence was almost unendurable, the caller finally spoke.

"No. At least not at the moment. We'll advise you of any further course of action. In the meantime, you have much more to rectify than these disrupted appearances. It is imperative that you do so. And immediately." The sound of the caller's last words virtually hung in midair, ominous and taunting.

"I understand," Stanley said, projecting faux confidence. "I will start right away—" The sudden buzz ravaging his eardrums indicated that the call was terminated.

That conversation had disrupted Stanley's sleep the night before. All night he had sat awake, considering option after option, and myriad contingency plans. All to no avail.

Now, he found himself at the Seattle waterfront, his mind as clouded as the sky, his spirits as damp and dreary as the city's famous rain and fog. He glanced out the window, scowling at the passersby—at humanity, really. He had fought innate misanthropy for his entire life, and felt his line of work was perfect for him. But the few people with whom he was forced to intimately interact made him nauseated, and anyone else within reach, especially the media, were just annoying gnats, disposable vermin.

The car passed the Edgewater Inn. He remembered the scandal forever immortalized in Frank Zappa's song, "*The Mud Shark*," of Led Zeppelin and other bands staying there and purportedly forcing a groupie to have sex with parts of a dead fish. Stanley's resentment against all musicians seethed anew. He thought about his own charges. With increasing irritation, he realized that by not returning to the hotel with the band, he'd left them in the custody of Simms. Even in the best of times, his subordinate was unable to exercise much, if any, control over the band. Further adding to Stanley's problems was the realization that with his travel rations turned over to the court, he was wasting precious gas rations on this pointless trip. He had to return to the hotel, whether he liked it or not. There was no other choice available to him. Stanley abruptly ordered the driver to return to the hotel. He exhaled and took stock of his situation.

He was only forty-five minutes from the refugee hospital at Fort Lewis, but was presently unable to venture within its proximity. He managed a highly successful and sought-after band that, at present, wasn't welcome anywhere. In short, he was managing the most lucrative liabilities ever.

Stanley's jaw ached. He was clenching his teeth, too angry to stop. All of his careful planning, the hours and hours of work, the meticulous and artful crafting and machinations were now disrupted, and at the worst possible time. No. He was too close to success to allow things to go to hell in a hand basket now.

Failure would come over his dead body.

"Or someone else's," he muttered.

CHAPTER THIRTEEN

"The Best Laid Schemes o' Mice and Men"

Chuck lay on the bed, his eyes closed. Cameron knew that Chuck wasn't asleep. The occasional sigh and rhythmic shaking of his foot revealed to Cameron that his manager was mulling something over, possibly honing in on a course of action. Cameron continued to read the newspaper, and repositioned himself in his chair so that he couldn't see the toe of his manager's bouncing boot. His attempt to digest information in the article was difficult enough without the additional distraction of flying footwear.

The headline blazed. *TRANSIENTS BROUGHT IN FOR QUESTIONING.* No names were mentioned—not of the band members, or of the detaining organization's personnel—leaving a great deal to implication, interpretation, and one's imagination. The article cited no specific allegations, nor were there any physical descriptions or photographs of the detainees. However, there was no doubt left in the reader's mind that a group of young men staying at a local establishment were questioned by authorities in order to determine their status and intentions. Cameron was willing to bet that there were few people in Gaston to whom that description applied.

He glanced up from his paper. The expression on Chuck's face was absolutely serene, and incited in Cameron the desire to throw something, something made of glass, something that would land with a loud crash. He opted, instead, to vocalize his supreme irritation.

"'They were released, pending further investigation,'" he snarled. "What bullshit!"

"What's incorrect?" Chuck asked, his eyes still closed, arms folded behind and cradling his head.

Cameron hurled the newspaper. The paper fell to the floor, its pages splayed about. "All of it!" the singer cracked. "They didn't mention who detained us or how, or the fact that that they weren't authorized to do it! They made us sound like criminals, for God's sake!"

"I'm sorry," said Chuck, with Zen-like detachment. "Where were any of you mentioned in that article?"

Struggling to control his agitation, Cameron snatched the paper from the floor, rifled through it, and upon locating the article, read it aloud.

"Several young transients at a local establishment—"

"Could mean anyone," Chuck interrupted.

"We both know damned well it means us!"

Chuck shrugged, still prone on the bed with his eyes closed. "You know it. I know it. The guys know it, and I'm willing to bet the writer of the article knows it. However, no one specific was mentioned, so you really can't complain without drawing attention to yourself. The reporter's argument could be that since *you* weren't mentioned, no one else knows it either."

Cameron's angst was not mollified. "I'm going to call that paper and straighten this out right now!" He opened the nightstand drawer and held up the telephone directory, shaking it toward Chuck.

"Hell, I might even write a letter to the editor!" Cameron sputtered as he flipped through the directory. "But I doubt that it would get printed."

"Do we have a guilty conscience?" asked Chuck, smiling slightly. His eyes were still closed and, despite Cameron's palpable irritation, Chuck's body remained completely relaxed.

"Hell no I don't, and you know it!" Cameron shouted.

Chuck's smile broadened into a wicked grin. "Then why are you getting upset about an article that doesn't even mention you?"

Cameron stared at Chuck in disbelief. "You realize that this article is telling everyone that we're somehow suspect and need to be monitored! There's no telling how people will react to it, or what the consequences for the Roadhouse Sons'll be if we stay in this fucking town!"

Chuck said nothing but lay placid, the maddeningly serene expression on his face. Several eternal seconds passed. Chuck finally spoke, almost in a whisper.

"By provoking you to respond out of irritation, they convince people that you respond out of guilt. Would you like to know the best way to totally negate their efforts?"

"Hell yes I would!" Cameron declared, thumping his fist to his chest. The very idea of striking back thrilled him. "What the fuck do I do?"

Chuck employed another dramatic, pregnant pause.

"Nothing. Do...nothing."

"What?" Cameron gasped.

"Do nothing," Chuck repeated. His smile resembled that of the Cheshire Cat. "They haven't actually accused you of anything. The papers plant the seeds of innuendo in readers' minds and provoke responses from their subjects, forcing them to behave according to the accusations, and thusly gaining credibility in the public eye. If you do or say nothing, the papers appear foolish and inconsequential."

"Are you serious?"

"I'm very serious. This is the most basic form of psychological manipulation. High school girls use it on each other all the time."

"So, I'm just supposed to let it go and do nothing?"

"By doing nothing, you aren't doing nothing," Chuck assured him.

"Then what *am* I doing, exactly?"

"Being a grownup," Chuck smiled. "Well...more or less!"

Chuck's glib response only served to irritate Cameron further, even more so as he admitted to himself that Chuck was right. Realizing that he'd allowed himself to be enticed into the exact desired response made him feel naïve and foolish. He sighed in resignation.

"You're probably right. I'll just ignore the whole thing."

Chuck sat bolt upright.

"No!" he warned. "Bad idea! You *never* ignore a provocation from an adversary."

"But you just told me to!"

"I said don't *respond* to it. I never said ignore it."

Chuck smiled and, swinging his feet off the bed, looked Cameron in the eye. He paused before speaking, all the while holding Cameron's gaze.

"By not responding, you steal from them the satisfaction of their anticipated outcome. They can't capitalize on no response from you."

"How is that different from ignoring them?"

"If you ignore them, you negate their existence, which means you're not remaining aware of them, of how they escalate their efforts, or what defines their Achilles' heel."

"Oh. I see!"

"The best course of action is, therefore, not to respond. They can't know it's getting to you. Don't talk about it. If someone asks, don't admit anything, not even that you saw the article. Lull them into complacency. Remember that Moscow Rule."

Cameron arose from his chair and stretched. As he happened to move toward the door, he saw at its bottom a shadow dart past. He ran to the door, silently opened it, and peeked out.

The cleaning lady.

The woman dashed behind her cart and fled into the adjoining vacant room. Cameron nonchalantly stepped toward the railing and basked in the fresh air.

The cleaning lady emerged from the doorway. She was a short, plump woman with long black hair drawn into a tight chignon. She constantly chewed and jiggled her jaw in a manner suggesting the presence of poor-fitting dentures. Her leathery skin, combined with the silver streaks in her hair, gave the appearance of a woman in her sixties. Cameron recognized the signs of "road years" on the woman and figured that, in all actuality, she was likely to be only in her mid- to late forties. The black concert tee shirt with its faded *AC/DC* emblem confirmed his assessment. The woman continually searched for something in the various compartments of her housekeeping cart. She finally returned to the room. After only a few seconds, she exited the room again. She did not acknowledge Cameron at all. Her gaze was directed right before her, never deviating elsewhere.

As a musician, Cameron encountered such behavior all the time, and for a moment, he felt relief. This was familiar territory. He mused over how many times groupies and less-tawdry women used this faux inconspicuous technique in hopes of attracting his attention.

All the time!

Cameron chided himself for his vanity. Suddenly, he recalled situations less manageable, less savory. How many times were other women jealous of the girls to whom he had paid attention and retaliated by informing boyfriends or husbands of potential infidelities? Those vulture types hovered about, comporting the same inattentive, indifferent gaze, but were always alert, soaking in every detail and chomping at the bit to report it all later.

The current situation with the cleaning lady was a bit clearer. Cameron moved with purpose, swaying with the breeze. From his peripheral vision, he saw that the woman was watching him, though pretending not to. She didn't behave as though she were surprised by his presence, nor did she act as though she recognized him. She didn't acknowledge him in any way, shape, or form. When Cameron deliberately smiled at her, she responded with the classic deer-in-the-headlights gape.

Cameron went back into the room and closed the door. Turning on the television, he motioned for Chuck to come to the far side of the room.

"I think I know how they've been able to listen to us," he said, his voice barely audible over the television. "That cleaning lady has been listening at keyholes, I'll bet." Cameron described in detail her skittish behavior and his brief, wordless exchange with the woman.

Chuck nodded. "That's a possibility, but it sounds a little far-fetched to me."

"Consider this," pressed Cameron. "She's cleaning the room next door. She already cleaned it yesterday."

"So? The rooms are cleaned on a daily basis. What's so remarkable about that?"

"The room next door is vacant!"

Chuck's eyes widened and he smiled his wicked grin. "Ahhh. Good, good!"

He mouthed the words, "Is she in there now?"

Cameron nodded. Chuck walked to the television and lowered the volume. He placed his ear against the wall and listened. After a few moments, he turned to Cameron and mouthed "Nothing," then sat down in his chair. He beckoned Cameron to him and whispered in his ear.

"I'll bet she was just doing the same thing I was. Can't hear a sound of anything being moved, so she isn't dusting, walking, or vacuuming in there."

"What do we do?"

"From now on, we never talk without the television on. Turn on the radio, too, for good measure, but don't do that too often."

"Why not?"

"You know this from your days in Vermont. Moscow Rule. You don't want to vary your routine too much. It tips them off that you're onto them. You have to stay within your cover."

Chuck tapped Cameron's knee and motioned for him to follow. Leaving the television on, Chuck stepped outside. Cameron followed and closed the door. The two men walked past the adjacent room. The cleaning lady was still working in the room, and the door was wide open. Chuck and Cameron didn't greet her as they passed. At the bottom of the stairs, Chuck motioned to Cameron to light a cigarette. Cameron furrowed his brow. Chuck motioned again. Cameron attempted to light his cigarette, but the direction of the breeze changed and he had to turn around. In doing so, he was able to casually monitor whether the cleaning lady was watching them. She was. With his cigarette fully lit, Cameron turned around and nodded.

"Thought so," Chuck said. "We'll go for a little stroll and come back. I guarantee she'll have entered our room."

"But we've got the do not disturb sign out!" No sooner had the words escaped his lips did Cameron instantly feel unsophisticated.

Chuck lowered his head and fluttered his eyelashes at Cameron, unsuccessfully suppressing a smile.

Cameron grinned. "I know. That was dumb! But how will we know if she went into our room?"

"The television will be off."

"Really?"

"Housekeeping habit."

Chuck and Cameron continued walking, eventually meandering past their favorite diner, where they encountered Rich and Snapper, both of whom were sourpussed and sullen.

"What's the matter with you two?" Cameron asked.

Neither Snapper nor Rich uttered a word.

"Come on," pressed Chuck. "Why the long faces?"

Rich and Snapper ruefully described the mixed reception they'd experienced upon their arrival at the diner. Both were at a loss as to why their waitress and two of her peers treated them with abrupt and inordinate hostility. Until that time, all of the diner personnel were friendly toward the boys.

Cameron briefed them on the situation with the recent newspaper article. Neither were satisfied.

"If it didn't say our names, then how come people think it's us?" asked Snapper.

"They didn't have to mention specifics," explained Chuck. "There are only about thirty-three hundred or so people in Gaston. Strangers stick out like a sore thumb in a small community like this. For all intents and purposes, you boys are still strangers here."

"It sucks," grumbled Rich.

Snapper didn't hesitate to chime in. "And Chuck, you had us go to that stupid meeting the other night, just so people wouldn't think this way about us!"

"That's the way it goes sometimes." Chuck smiled, his expression wily and sly as a fox. "You can't always predict exactly how people will respond. But you've just given me an idea."

Chuck reminded Snapper of how the hosts at the meeting encountered such difficulty using the microphone. Snapper described the circumstances to Rich and Cameron.

"There was obviously a short somewhere in the mic unit. If I had time, I could've fixed it."

"You're reading my mind," Chuck grinned. "We're going over there and you're going to graciously volunteer your time to do just that."

Snapper grimaced. He was confounded. "You're shitting me, right? They practically spit on me here at breakfast, like I'm a draft dodger or a friggin' commie. They're really gonna love me over there!"

"Maybe. Maybe not." Chuck wrapped his arm around Snapper's shoulder. "You won't be alone."

"I won't?"

"We'll all be there."

"All of us?" cried Cameron. "Have you lost your mind? What could all of us possibly have to do over there? They don't even know the rest of us."

"That's right. They don't know you all. They've got ideas about you planted in their heads by other people. That is fortuitous. Very, very fortuitous."

Rich was livid. "You have lost your fuckin' mind!"

"Not at all." Chuck remained calm. He knew that he had to reassure them. They were all angry and shooting from the hip. "Let's get out of here."

Chuck led the boys out of the diner and down the street.

"Calm down, boys, and be quiet. Pay close attention."

Cameron, Rich, and Snapper exchanged furtive glances, but obeyed.

"When McIntyre checks in with Columbia, she'll likely report that we'll remain here to conduct additional surveillance. The newspaper article works in our favor. The locals' bad attitudes toward you give us a prime opportunity to monitor them. They're suspicious of your every move and it gives us easy reciprocity to eyeball them. We'd be stupid not to take advantage of that."

The boys engaged in a heated debate, bantering about the possible pros and cons of Chuck's idea. Everyone finally admitted that it was the best plan. It had to be; it was the only plan.

"What next?" Cameron asked.

"We head back to the motel." Chuck said. "I'll call McIntyre right away. Then I'll call the Legion, talk to Brody Aldrich, and get us all set up."

"Who's he?" asked Rich.

"He's the fellow who was shadowing Cameron, the one I finally talked to at the meeting. He's involved with the Legion. That I know for a fact. It's pretty obvious that he's involved with the Liberty League. I'm not sure if he's involved with this newspaper stunt, but I intend to find out."

"Why bother if you're not sure?" Snapper was not happy about the plan; he felt like a decoy, like pure, unadulterated bait.

"You don't turn down an opportunity to learn firsthand about your enemy."

"That's dangerous." Cameron stared at Chuck.

"You want safety, wear condoms," Chuck winked. Cameron was not amused. They walked to the motel via an alternate route. Snapper questioned the new route, and Chuck explained that he didn't want to alert the cleaning lady of their return. Cameron's shared his theory about the woman's monitoring activities. Rich agreed instantly.

"Now that you mention it, she does work odd shifts. Sometimes I see her coming out of the rooms at night, sometimes in the morning."

"Have any of you guys noticed anything missing?" Chuck asked. Rich's revelation concerned him. "Anything at all? Think carefully."

The band members confirmed that none of their belongings were missing, nor was there any indication that their possessions were searched. Nothing had ever been out of place. Chuck advised them to set booby traps that would pass unnoticed to the untrained eye. Rich asked Chuck to cite an example.

"You all have long hair. After you know that she's already cleaned your room, put your duffel or guitar case on the table, then lay one or two strands of hair across the clasp or buckle mechanism. You know the drill! Do it in a way that's obvious only to you. If she moves anything, you'll know. The hair will be gone."

Finally, they reached the motel parking lot and continued to their respective rooms. The cleaning lady was nowhere to be found. Chuck and Cameron entered their room. From the doorway, Chuck briefly scanned the area, then elbowed Cameron and pointed to the television. It was turned off.

"I knew it," Chuck whispered.

Chuck turned on the television and then summoned Cameron and the two of them fully examined the room and the bathroom. Nothing was out of place and everything appeared to be intact.

Chuck left the room and went with Clyde and Evan to their room.

"You two check your room right now," Chuck said.

Chuck went back to his and Cameron's room. Cameron anxiously awaited him. They sat in silence for a few minutes before Chuck motioned to him.

"Go round up the guys and tell them to come here."

"All of us?" asked Cameron.

"Yes. Act casual and tell them to bring their guitars and sticks. I just told them all to search their rooms. I acted as though I was just saying hello. Whoever's watching us knows that I'm your manager. It's not unusual for you guys to hang out in my room. For everyone to be in their own rooms this early looks suspicious. Personally, I feel that the good people of Gaston have too much on their minds, so I don't want to encumber them with our goings-on anymore than we have to."

Chuck winked at Cameron again, and with the television still on, he dialed his contact in Columbia. Cameron gathered the boys and they all came to the room and waited, watching Bob Barker flirt with contestants on *The Price Is Right*. Cameron was amazed that the producers of the show were still able to secure good prizes during wartime. He noticed, however, that the show no longer featured cars and vacation trips. The current prizes were necessities and basic pleasures, such as food, appliances, and tickets for inexpensive entertainment, all prizes that focused on simple pleasures to ease the strain of life during wartime.

Good for national morale, I suppose.

Cameron started to doze off. He heard Rich and Snapper step outside for a cigarette. As he felt himself drift further toward slumber, he could discern vague portions of Chuck's side of the telephone conversation. Chuck's head nodded in unseen agreement with whomever he was speaking. Cameron's eyelids were as heavy as lead. He allowed them to close. He had just nodded off completely when Chuck slammed the telephone receiver into its cradle.

"I should bet on my own intuitions. I'd be filthy rich," he said.

"Rosebud in the fifth," mumbled Cameron. Chuck shook Cameron's bed.

"Sleeping Beauty, wake up! I was right! They want us to stay a while and find out all we can."

"Then what?" Cameron yawned.

"Then they've got someone else to take over," Chuck said. "McIntyre says they might have another assignment for us soon."

Cameron was fully awake. He stood up, as though at full military attention.

"Well? Spill!"

"You might have a performing gig."

"Did you say a gig?"

Chuck ignored him and dialed the number for his next call. "Gotta call the Legion. You know. Our plan."

Cameron could not have cared less about any of the current mess.

Upon hearing the word "gig," Snapper and Rich came back into the room.

"We have a gig!" Clyde made no effort to hide the excitement in his voice. Chuck glared at them and mouthed "Shhh!" with his forefinger to his lips as he spoke into the receiver.

"I'm looking for Brody Aldrich. I was wondering if I might be able to leave a message for him. What? He's there? Great! Could I speak to him, please?"

The boys ignored Chuck and huddled among themselves, whispering new plans and discussing possible set lists.

After a brief pause, Chuck spoke again, first offering an introduction, then adding bromides and small talk. He finally cited the purpose of his call, addressing the subject of the faulty PA system, and mentioning that some of his associates were in the music business and could repair the mic units. Chuck smiled broadly. At this point, the Roadhouse Sons' reverie had quelled and they looked at Chuck with mock anticipation. Chuck finalized the arrangement.

"Yes! We can be there this afternoon," he said. "Around three? See you then."

Chuck terminated the call and told Clyde to close the door.

"All righty. Here's the crux of my calls. The first went just as I expected. We're staying here for now. McIntyre's and my reports were delivered this morning, and they'd just finished her debriefing when I called. Obviously, their concern is escalated and we're to collect as much information as we can, including names of persons of interest. Then, our superiors will initiate a full investigation."

"I've got a few names for them." Cameron's sentiment weren't solely his own.

"Really?" asked Chuck. "Who's on your list? Let's hear it."

"One Mr. Clifford Allen Lewis Esquire, for sure," Cameron laughed derisively, snorting for emphasis.

"Yeah, Chuck, and add that guy that was speaking at the meeting," offered Snapper.

"Which one?"

"Oh, what was his name?" Snapper strained to recall the man's name, then clapped his hands and pointed at Chuck. "Pecham! That's it! That Pecham guy who was the main speaker. I'd put him on the list. Right near the top."

"Why?"

"'Cause of the way he used guilt to make people support what he had to say, *and* the way he put people on the spot. It seemed like he was using blackmail to get them to buy more war bonds."

"Blackmail!" Chuck mocked aghast. "That's a mighty strong word!"

"Well, maybe not blackmail. But you have to admit it was pretty shitty the way he would tell people they needed to buy more bonds, and then criticize them for how they were spending their own money! On top of that, he kept reminding them of how he'd helped them all out at some point, letting the whole world know who was beholden to him. That's pretty friggin' slimy, if you ask me."

"It was pretty disgusting to see," said Clyde, shaking his long locks in disdain.

Chuck laughed. "It was grotesque!"

Rich was riled up and ready for the rumble.

"I think we should take a look at the guy who followed Cameron, too. He's doing his own surveillance, and you even said the police knew about it. He's obviously involved in some way."

"Anyone else?" Chuck queried. He looked directly at Cameron.

"The reporter that wrote that fucking article," Cameron snarled.

Chuck grinned. Then he broke into laughter. "Just because you didn't like what they wrote?"

"Hell no!" Cameron insisted. "Because that article wasn't part of the police log. Whoever wrote it had inside information, probably from Lewis. Hell, they could have been there and we didn't even know it!"

"Or they got a statement from someone who *was* there."

"Then they probably have more information. This shit's been going on since the war started, I'll bet." Cameron was livid.

"If they refuse to cooperate with an investigation, they could cite protection of a source. But you're right, Cam. It is worth considering. At the very least, we should check out all of their articles and see if this is their usual subject matter. Anyone else we should add to our list?"

Cameron furrowed his brow. "Though, remember Evan said they usually reported nothing really serious. But still…no stone unturned. Who else then?"

"Officer Beecham," Snapper said with great resolve.

"You mean the officer that questioned you and Clyde?" Chuck asked.

Snapper nodded vehemently. "The one that *harassed* us, you mean? Yeah, that's the one!"

"Is that it?" Chuck pointed to the television. "Turn it up a little bit."

Clyde adjusted the volume knob.

"Well," Chuck continued. "I must say you guys are getting good. Those were reasonable observations, and they mirror the recommendations that McIntyre and I wrote in our reports."

"You were suspicious of Officer Beecham," said Cameron. "I wondered if you were working with him on arranging an investigation."

"That was a possibility at first, but only just," Chuck concurred.

"Why?" asked Evan. "I thought that you're supposed to work *with* the local law enforcement. That was my impression."

"Only if called in on a case, such as a threat to national security. But truth be told, we're called in for homicides most of the time." Chuck raised his eyebrows, a conspiratorial smile curling his mouth. "Mostly, we work independently, shall we say."

Rich battled confusion. "Wait. A minute ago you said working with Beecham was just a possibility. At *first*. Do you trust anyone?"

"Another one of the Moscow Rules. Everyone, and I do mean everyone, is potentially under opposition control. We had no idea what to expect here. Since there are no official documents corroborating any of the reports we've received, from Henry Clay or otherwise, we can only surmise that someone in a position of authority is involved in shady activities with the opposition. When Beecham appeared last night, my suspicions about him increased tenfold."

"A police officer as a potential adversary…" Cameron mused. "It's a bit spectacular, but nothing shocks me anymore."

Chuck took a deep breath, and exhaled slowly.

"Last night, when I went to the police station, I played dumb about your immediate whereabouts and about knowing that you were detained. Beecham was on the phone when I got there. I know he could hear me, but he waited for me to finish talking with the dispatcher before coming out to see me. When I told him what happened, he bolted through the door and ran ahead of me into the other building. Before I could catch up to him, he opened the door and rushed in, but McIntyre and I were stuck outside for several minutes."

Clyde smiled knowingly. "I bet McIntyre was able to get someone's attention."

"She's quite capable of getting attention. But with those guys, I think it was more than a pretty turn of the ankle that brought them to the door. I think Beecham went in first to make sure we wouldn't find anything, and to get you guys out of there."

"Why would he want to get us out of there if they're trying to investigate our supposedly suspicious behavior?" asked Cameron.

"Remember. We're still strangers. Their whole operation could be jeopardized if people who they deem to be the wrong people get wind of their activities. Up until now, they've worked on their own community, people who'll keep their mouths shut out of fear. Now, though, they just blew everything wide open. They did it all by themselves."

Chuck leaned forward and lowered his voice.

"We have to maintain our element of surprise," he said. "They have no idea who we are, or that we're monitoring them."

"Well, what if they catch on and figure out who we are? Any help for us is sitting in Columbia," Cameron said. "Fat fucking lot of good that does us here."

"No!" Chuck was adamant. "We're getting some backup. The superiors know the potential for this situation to escalate. They're not going to risk this operation. McIntyre couldn't give me specifics, obviously, but she did say that she had some information for me that I'll have to keep close. As far as we're concerned, we're on our own until we hand this off."

The fact that danger was imminent hit the Roadhouse Sons like a ton of bricks. They'd barely recovered from the incidents in Vermont.

Not again…

The constant reference to Moscow Rules and talk, talk, talk aggravated Cameron to no end. He needed action. He needed to feel like he was doing something. Inaction stifled him, and the ad nauseum cloak-and-dagger chatter was driving him insane. He fought the urge to leave; he knew that if he walked out, the others would realize just how frustrated he was. He spoke directly to Chuck, his demeanor grave and steadfast, and his tone unavoidably sardonic.

"Let me guess. We wait and we watch. We stay on guard, and stay together as much as possible. Move in pairs at all times."

"What's your beef?" Chuck was dead serious. He held Cameron's gaze. "There's no telling what lengths they'll go…"

"We've been on the road for months since we left Burlington, still playing spy, waiting and waiting, and now we're back in a position of danger?"

A pall of silence fell upon the room as the Roadhouse Sons weighed the magnitude of their circumstances. Cameron's mind reeled. Memories and images of Burlington, Vermont, clashed through his head. Burning buildings, explosions, bodies on gurneys.

Please don't let it come to that.

"I have other news," Chuck said cheerfully.

Cameron was always unnerved and almost frightened by Chuck's ability to shift the gears of his emotions so quickly.

That man's not right.

"I can hardly wait to hear this," said Rich. "What next? Parachute into Anchorage?"

"I hate heights." Chuck smiled; it was that sly, wicked grin again. The boys stared at him, stupefied.

"You guys have a gig coming up!"

The boys looked at Chuck, then at each other. One by one, they assimilated the new information, and the atmosphere in the room lightened, though Cameron could feel that this purported surprise hadn't drastically changed their moods. Chuck proceeded to elaborate on the details presented by McIntyre, but still no real excitement blossomed. There were lighthearted remarks, but no one asked any questions. Chuck, as always, was the only one who flipped the impetuous switch of sudden happiness and basked in the light. Cameron just stood there. He felt like he was in a vacuum, rising, enclosed in a bubble, one that encased him so tightly, he wouldn't bother to escape. The boys certainly weren't distracted from the real meat of the matter—their ominous briefing just moments ago.

That's good. They won't ignore red flags, I hope…

CHAPTER FOURTEEN

"Shadows"

When Jack Stanley was informed that a police detective had arrived to see him, his initial assumption was that the visit regarded the charges against the band. He welcomed the lawman into his office and offered him a chair opposite his own at the desk.

Stanley eyed the chap. The detective was approximately Stanley's age, perhaps slightly older. He sported in his hair a rather obvious permanent wave, and he had a walrus-style mustache. He was dressed smartly in a checked jacket and maroon slacks. Never having been able to accept the casual attitudes that many had adopted as their mode of dress, Stanley was pleased to note that the man's polyester shirt was buttoned all the way to the top, and that he sported a tie. The two bantered introductions and the detective presented his credentials, after which they settled into their seats and addressed the business at hand.

"We have some more questions regarding the death of John Collier," the lawman said. "We're hoping you can answer them for us."

As the actual purpose of the policeman's visit was revealed, Stanley was caught entirely off guard, but years of conditioning had taught him to conceal any rue or surprise. Throughout his career, he'd imparted the self-control of a poker player; to expose one's emotions could have severe consequences. The policeman hadn't altered his own expression at all, so Stanley was confident that he'd betrayed no emotion.

"I'll certainly do what I can, Detective," Stanley assured him. "But I'm afraid I've already told you people everything I know. There's nothing more that could be of any use to you."

The detective disregarded Stanley and withdrew a notebook from his breast pocket.

"I'm sure you're aware of the circumstances surrounding his death, correct?"

Stanley nodded. "Yes, he's the young man that leapt from his hotel room. Tragic, really."

"Why do you say that?" the lawman asked, seemingly confused by Stanley's response. Stanley knew that the detective's inquiry was simply an interrogation tactic, and was unshaken by it.

"He was a young man in apparently good health, with his whole life ahead of him, not to mention such plans for his career. I can't imagine anything so serious that he would have to take his own life to escape it. To simply throw everything away like that can be described in no other way than tragic. Wouldn't you agree?"

Stanley's inquiry garnered no response.

"Speaking of his plans, you had some business involvement with him, didn't you?"

Stanley was prepared for such questioning. He expected it. "Yes. That's correct."

"What was the nature of that business, exactly?"

"It was very informal," Stanley explained. "You see, like I, he was involved in the entertainment industry as an agent, albeit not as well known or as successful as I am, and he was hoping to establish a connection with my agency for some projects in development. We didn't have contact with each other outside of business."

"What was the nature of these projects?"

Stanley thought for a moment, shifting his gaze as he considered his response.

"He said that he had some potential clients who were ready to embark upon a more national level of exposure, and would need some representation. He was hoping that I would sign them."

The detective's head was down. He referred to his notes, pondering the information Stanley had just provided.

"If he was already representing them, why would he need you?"

Stanley smiled. "I can tell you exactly why. He knew that on his own he wouldn't be able to book his artists into any major venue, or secure them a record contract, thus he needed to find someone who could."

"Why do you say he couldn't have done that?"

"The music business is not simply a business," Stanley explained. "It is almost a secret society. You don't simply walk into Capitol Records and become a sensation. It takes work, hard work, and more than that. It takes connections."

"Connections to what?"

"Connections to the record companies, the press, the radio stations, to all of the people and entities needed to take mediocre talent and turn them into superstars. Most specifically, connections to the who's who that can get you noticed and signed, not designated to the circular file." Stanley pointed to his waste bin for emphasis. "Our Mr. Collier knew that he didn't have enough of those connections, and sought an association with someone who did."

"And that someone was you?"

Stanley coyly nodded his head in faux modesty. The lawman gave no indication that he noticed the other's arrogance.

"We know that he lived in Los Angeles," the lawman continued. "With all of the music studios and record labels down there, why would he come up here to Seattle? It couldn't possibly have been just to see you."

Stanley smiled wryly at the detective's blatant insult. This man was out of his league, Stanley surmised, relaxing into his chair.

"The talent he represented do not blend well with the established taste of the Los Angeles music scene," Stanley snorted, and stared at the detective as though the man was an apostate. "They are part of the more recently burgeoning punk culture, a music genre receiving welcome reception here in Seattle more than anywhere else."

"And your managing of successful punk bands attracted his interests?"

Stanley sat back in his chair and raised his eyebrows. "Of course. I am an established member of the entertainment industry and have amassed countless connections in my career, connections that I do not divulge or even share very easily, I might add."

"Why?"

"Divulging one's hard-earned connections virtually gives them away for nothing," Stanley pontificated. "That information has a price. To simply surrender it to someone at no charge is bad business. Even offering a recommendation or a reference to unknown talent needlessly places my own reputation on the line."

"Then his meetings with you were unsuccessful?"

Stanley shook his head. "On the contrary. We spoke several times to discuss his ideas. We agreed to set up an audition for his talent so that I could make a final decision about representation. He had provided me with demo tapes, of course, but I wanted to see them perform live. You can edit and master out rough spots on tape, you understand, but it is much more difficult to hide flaws when performing live. I needed to know firsthand, and prior to agreeing, the difficulties, if any, inherent in refining and representing this man's act."

The detective jotted voraciously in his notepad as Stanley talked. He then opened a manila folder and retrieved what appeared to be notes he'd written prior to his arrival. The investigator reviewed the notes for a moment, then turned his attention to Stanley.

"Did Collier give you any indication that he was troubled? Did you have any suspicions about his state of mind as a result of any or all of your meetings?"

Stanley shook his head. "None whatsoever," he declared, his demeanor grave. "Our meetings were conducted via telephone. Naturally, he seemed nervous, you understand. He'd never before involved himself with business dealings at the national level. He was quite anxious to make a success of his efforts. But he gave me no indications that he was about to take his own life, I assure you."

The detective pondered his notepad once more, then suddenly looked up at the ceiling, as though beckoned by a voice that Stanley couldn't hear.

"According to his appointment book, on the day he died, he had scheduled a meeting with you," the detective said. "Was that to be a telephone conversation, as well?"

"No. That appointment would have been our first meeting vis-a-vis. Inspector, I don't know if you are familiar with me, or with my line of work," Stanley said, his smile condescending, as he managed his irritation. "I manage a great many talents and have offices on both coasts, and in Europe. I can't possibly enumerate the representation requests I receive on a daily basis. I speak of acts who feel that they're ready to grace the stage of Carnegie Hall simply because they correctly identify the E string on a guitar, or gather more than five audience members at a Howard Johnson's lounge. One develops strategies to protect one's self against these assaults on one's sense and sensibilities. My initial strategy is to screen such talent via telephone interviews and subsequent requests. If they're able to meet my professional criteria, I'll consider further investing my personal attentions."

"And things had reached that point with Collier?" the inspector asked. "Since they had asked you to arrange a live audition?"

"Yes. They had."

"You didn't keep the appointment. Why?"

Stanley leaned back in his chair before replying.

"Problems with one of my British clients demanded my personal attention and involved a series of telephone calls to London. My assistant, therefore, called Mr. Collier to reschedule our appointment for the following day."

"His appointment book indicated a meeting the next day with one Christopher Simms. *He's* your assistant?"

Stanley nodded. "Yes, he is. As I explained, circumstances in London meant that I was unsure if I'd be able to attend the appointment. Mr. Simms would attend in my stead, if necessary."

"Would they have met over drinks?" Stanley was visibly confused.

"I suppose that's possible. A three-martini lunch, I suppose. Why do you ask?" This time, the detective responded to the reverse inquiry.

"Collier's appointment book indicated that he was to meet Simms for drinks, and your assistant's telephone number was jotted in. Is that your assistant's usual approach, Mr. Stanley?"

Stanley considered the question carefully before responding.

"Absolutely," he replied. "My own approach is formal and managerial. Mr. Simms's style is casual, and thus, more engaging. He's much better suited than I to a lack of formality. He's less intimidating than I, ergo the talent easily negotiates with him."

The detective wrote in his notepad, with seemingly a bit more gusto. Stanley wondered if his statement was somehow esoterically revelatory.

"I'm surprised you wouldn't have made a point to meet him yourself."

Stanley looked the lawman in the eye. "As I've already explained, I attempted to, but the scheduling went awry. Also, Collier was nervous, inordinately nervous. He was calling me all hours of the day and night. I don't deal well with such manic personalities. I find them exhausting and, much of the time, a *waste* of my time. Such unpleasant tasks are usually delegated to Mr. Simms, and when I couldn't meet with Collier, I was relieved to send Mr. Simms."

The inspector wrote in his notepad. The constant jotting of notes vexed Stanley. He hoped that he wasn't misquoted.

"Is there any indication that Mr. Collier was experiencing financial troubles?"

"I knew from our telephone conversations that he was personally responsible for his band's expenses. But he didn't divulge to me details of his dealings." Stanley chuckled. "Like so many others of his unsuccessful and inexperienced ilk, he thought that all of the publicity photos, event posters, and merchandise would be contributed gratis and with no obligation to the band because, of course, they would become famous someday and generously repay the gifts. Hah! Unless there is some type of sponsorship or investment to defray promotional costs, managers pay for these things out of their own pockets with the hopes of recompense from royalties. If the act is successful, these expenses are recouped with no long-term detriment to the investor. However, in the case of Mr. Collier, the talent's lack of bookings strained him financially, of which he didn't hesitate to inform me."

"Is this why he leapt from his hotel window?"

"I can't say if that's why, or not," Stanley averred. "I said that his expenses exceeded his return on investment. I have no idea if that was motivation enough for suicide. Ascertaining that conclusion, my good fellow, is your job, not mine."

The inspector glared at Stanley.

"Mr. Stanley, was Collier negotiating with any other talent agencies?"

Stanley was losing his patience, but regarded the detective with caution.

"None that I know of, though I never asked."

"Why not?"

"One thing you should know about our profession, Detective, is that nobody keeps a secret. If another agency was considering Collier's clients, I would know about it. No one was."

"If one was, though, would that have been a deal breaker for you?"

"Not in the least," Stanley huffed. "Competition is a part of the music world, a mere fact of life. I would've expected Collier to pursue multiple options for himself and his clients. If he didn't, I'd have no respect for him, nor any faith in his talent."

"Is there anyone who can corroborate your telephone calls to London?" Stanley smiled contemptuously. He wanted this visit terminated, and hastily.

"That may be difficult. The crisis with which I dealt was partly related to the bombings of the day before. Most of my London staff and some of my clients were among the victims of the attack. I was working with the London authorities, providing staff and client rosters, along with possible contact information for families, insurance companies, and so on. I'm sure you're able to contact the War Office in London. They may provide with the name of someone with whom I spoke. For most of the day and part of the evening, I was on the telephone with the War Office as well as the London police and spoke to many people. I'm certain someone must remember talking to me."

The detective said nothing. Stanley wondered why the detective didn't mention checking telephone records, but suspected that the very idea of contacting London authorities set the lawman's stomach churning. In the best of times, interjurisdictional cooperation was difficult and time consuming. To deal with a foreign agency located in a city reliving the Blitz was a prospect only the most naïve would entertain. To expect cooperation on a case involving a suicide in Seattle, Washington, USA was naïve, at best. Stanley could practically read the investigator's mind as the latter reached the same conclusion. However, the detective was not one to reveal his frustrations.

The interview continued for seven excruciating minutes. To Stanley, the visit felt like an eternity, as the detective confirmed and clarified Stanley's previous statements to the police. Stanley showed no concern during the recapitulation, and when the detective was ready to leave, Stanley escorted him from his office and right into the hallway. After bidding a proper adieu, Stanley went back to his desk.

Why were the police interrogating him? Despite the detective's claim, this visit couldn't be attributed to mere clarification of Stanley's previous testimony. There was nothing in Stanley's dealings with Collier that should suggest anything other than a professional relationship. What could prompt law enforcement to surmise that Stanley possessed any other insights into Collier's personal life?

Did Collier leave behind evidence suggesting more than a professional involvement between them?

Stanley poured some bourbon into a glass. He spoke aloud.

"I intend to find out."

CHAPTER FIFTEEN

"Round Two"

The old man ambled across the room toward Chuck, Cameron, and the boys. The man so resembled Archie Bunker that Cameron's heart sank.

Oh, great! This is going to be a hassle. I just know it.

Complete with dark pants, white shirt, and cynical blue eyes, the only difference between this man and the television character was the bald spot atop his head.

He even walks like him.

The man continued toward Cameron, his gait causing him to turn slightly to the side. He stooped as though gravity itself battled the man's forward motion.

To Cameron's surprise, as the man drew closer, he smiled. When at last he reached Cameron and the others, he extended a meaty hand, giving them each a hale and hearty greeting.

"How's it going?" The man spoke with a booming, cheerful voice. "My name's Bob Larabee. I'm the commander of this post. You must be the fellows that Brody told me about. He had to step out, but I'll be happy to help you young fellows."

Chuck indulged Larabee with formal introductions. Larabee looked Rich, Snapper, Clyde, and Evan in the eye and, shaking their hands again, took the time to engage in a brief, personal exchange with each. By the time Larabee returned his attention to Cameron and Chuck, Cameron had a glimmer of hope that being forced to volunteer wouldn't be the ordeal he feared. As though reading his mind, Larabee shook Cameron's hand for the second time, too.

"Thanks a lot for your offer. That system's been giving us a hard time and we just don't have the extra money to get a new one. If you could fix it, that would be a tremendous help."

"Happy to pitch in, Bob," Chuck said with a smile. "We said we wanted to help out around here. That seems like a good place to start."

The Roadhouse Sons glanced at each other, their apprehension waning.

Bob Larabee led them to the stage and showed them the location of the PA equipment.

"It's wired so that it comes through the drop ceiling to the speakers."

Snapper questioned Bob, and upon hearing the old man's responses, the boys chimed in with their diagnoses and solutions.

Bob was impressed. "You all sound like doctors! So what's the prognosis?" He laughed at his own joke. Rich rolled his eyes, and it was Snapper who shot the bass player an admonishing glare.

The boys discussed the situation further, then turned to Bob.

"Do you have any ladders?" Evan asked. "We'll check the wires in the ceiling, while Snapper looks at the console."

Snapper concurred. "I might have to take it apart to examine the connections. Each one might have to be cleaned. I'll do that first."

"We have everything you need," Bob said cheerfully.

The boys proceeded with their plan and worked on the PA system. They tested various elements, and Cameron volunteered to clean up for each of them. As he dusted the console, he looked up and saw Chuck and Bob in a far-off corner of the hall. They were too far away for Cameron to discern what they were saying, and their physical stances prevented Cameron from reading their lips. Judging from Bob's perpetually nay-shaking head and sagged shoulders, the conversation was not a pleasant one.

"Hey!" Cameron looked up. Rich was on top of the ladder. "Hand me some tools. I need a screwdriver. A flathead'll do."

Cameron had turned away from Chuck and Bob for only a moment. He looked back. Both men were gone. Cameron immediately felt a twinge of panic. Calming himself, he assessed the situation. He'd heard no sounds of a struggle, nor had he heard anyone else enter the hall. It was unlikely, therefore, that Chuck had been forced out of the premises against his will. Cameron relaxed, but suddenly remembered the fate that had befallen Chuck's predecessor, Dwyer.

Dwyer was, along with McIntyre, the original recruitment team for the band's counterintelligence network. Dwyer was a protégé of Chuck's, and a veteran agent with many years' experience under his belt. During the band's first assignment, though, Dwyer suffered a fatal mistake. He let his guard down. McIntyre and Cameron discovered Dwyer shot to death in a warehouse. That was Cameron's first—and horrifyingly so—experience discovering a dead body. As far as Cameron knew, Dwyer's case remained unsolved. To make matters worse, neither McIntyre nor Chuck would discuss it with him.

I'll be damned if I'm going through that again.

Cameron yelled aloud to no one in particular.

"I'm going to go look for a broom to start cleaning up this crap!"

The boys happily grunted their various acknowledgements, but were invigorated by their task. They were able to easily and rapidly locate and repair the PA problem, and had enough extra time to improve the PA's setup and perform the required enhancements. They were almost ready to leave, having executed the tasks promised.

Cameron made his way downstairs. As McIntyre had coached him early on, after rounding the corner at each landing, he stood with his back against the opposite wall before descending further. By doing so, he'd minimize the threat of anyone unknown to him who might be lurking below.

Cameron reached the bottom of the stairs and found himself in the Legion's bar. Other than several women cooking in the kitchen, no one else was present. None of the women seemed surprised or startled when Cameron asked them for a broom. They knew why he was there and thanked him for repairing the PA system. They told him the location of the custodian's closet, smiled, and sent him on his way.

The closet was located adjacent to another room, the door of which was unmarked. From behind that door, Cameron heard Chuck's voice. He hesitated, then decided to knock on the door. He barely waited for Bob's booming "Come in!" before opening the door.

"Sorry to interrupt," he said, poking his head in. "Just wanted to let you know we're almost through upstairs."

Cameron's eyes darted about the room. He detected no cause for concern. Chuck was seated and fully relaxed, his arms folded on his chest and his legs extended and crossed upon another chair. Bob sat at his desk, leaning back in his chair. Both were smiling and had been laughing about something. Neither were irritated by Cameron's interruption.

"Is it working now?" Chuck asked.

Cameron nodded. "It was just a loose wire," he explained. "We got that fixed, no problem, and rewired the speakers for you, too."

"How does she work?" Bob asked, clearly pleased.

"Good as new," Cameron smiled. "All I need is a broom to clean up."

Bob beamed. "Well, I certainly appreciate all you boys have done,"

Cameron wondered if Bob realized that it was Clyde who'd thrown rocks at his garage. If he actually knew, Cameron doubted that Bob would be so pleased with the boys.

Better not to mention it.

Cameron turned to leave.

"I think I got us another booking," Chuck said. Cameron stopped dead in his tracks and turned back toward the men.

"These good folks are putting on a fundraiser for another bond drive, but ran into a little bit of a problem. Seems they were going to have a wrestling show, but the promoter doesn't have sufficient rations and isn't able to get a ring down here. So, I offered us up to fill in."

"I haven't wrestled since my freshman year of high school," Cameron deadpanned. "But I think I can take you."

Bob burst into laughter. Chuck arose from his chair.

"That's not what I'm talking about, and *no you couldn't*. I suggested we do our show instead. Bob here thinks it's a good idea."

"Yes, I do!" Bob assured Cameron. "One of the reasons that we considered wrestling was to attract a new crowd. Our members have contributed every idea they can muster, but we can't let the well run dry. We're always looking for new ways to raise money. And to attract more members."

"What do you think?" asked Chuck.

Cameron grinned. "Yeah! That sounds great, but how soon is the gig?"

Bob consulted his wall calendar.

"We've planned the fundraiser for next Saturday. How does that sound to you?"

"It gives us time to rehearse. We can set up right here ahead of time, rehearse, and be ready to go."

"Oh, it won't be here," said Bob. "We were going to have it at the Cattleman's Club just north of town. It used to be a big dance hall and holds a lot more people. It's better access from the roadway, what with the rations and all, and that's easier for out-of-towners."

"Do you think they'll let us set up to rehearse there?" asked Chuck. He, like Cameron, had assumed that the venue was the Legion hall.

"No. They've got other things going on next week," the old man explained. "Mostly auctions and such. There's no way you could play in there while that's going on."

"Could we rehearse here?" Cameron asked. "We won't be that loud and we wouldn't be in your way."

"No. We've got meetings scheduled for nearly every day, and the ladies have a rummage sale."

Always "No," this guy...

"I'd hate like hell to go into a show cold," Cameron insisted. "I know the guys will feel the same way."

"I've got a garage on the other side of town," Bob said. "Its just sitting empty right now. It's a little dirty, but you're welcome to use it if you want."

"That's a good plan," Chuck sighed, relieved.

"Good! I'll go grab that broom and tell the guys. They'll be thrilled."

"Wait for me." Chuck remained long enough for the old man to search his key ring for the garage key.

"I can't seem to find that key, darn it. You all go ahead and I'll bring it to you. See you soon." Bob waved them on, and Chuck and Cameron ascended the stairs.

Upon entering the hall, the sight before them caused Cameron's gut to wrench. Chuck tensed. If he was on guard, Cameron knew the situation did not bode well. Four strange men surrounded the Roadhouse Sons. As Chuck and Cameron drew closer, Snapper's insistent tone dominated the room.

"No! Really, man, it's OK!" the roadie declared emphatically.

"It isn't, son," the man replied. "I overreacted and feel mighty bad about it."

"What's going on?" Chuck shouldered himself between Snapper and the stranger. Cameron stood directly opposite Chuck, hoping that they wouldn't have to break up an altercation.

The stranger, apparently sincere, turned to Chuck. "I was just telling your friend here that I'm sorry about the way I treated him at the meeting the other night. Sometimes, young folks come in here with accusations and try to fight and cause trouble. I wasn't sure if he was one of them or not. I just came down pretty hard on him, warning him to be on his best behavior."

Snapper spoke, this time less adamantly. "From the sound of it, you have good reasons to be suspicious. No offense taken. Really."

"What kind of accusations?" Chuck probed.

"Oh, God. A lot of things," the stranger sighed. "They accuse us of forcing people to enlist, and arresting them if they don't. They say we're monkeying with the war bonds, and not accurate with the money we take in."

Until that point, the other three strangers remained quiet and observant. Finally, one of them spoke.

"That's right. They argue that we don't report everything we get. That's a damned lie! We don't have anything to do with issuing war bonds. That's done through the bank."

Chuck's slight shift in position was a telltale sign to Cameron, who was familiar with his manager's idiosyncrasies. Chuck had just made a mental note.

The third man muttered, "Yes. We just hold the fundraisers for the bond drives. The bank sends people to take pledges and collect the money, then the bonds are issued. We never even touch 'em."

"I thought you get the bonds right when you buy them," Clyde asked, visibly confused.

"Well, you're supposed to," the third man conceded. "The trouble is, we have so many rallies and fundraisers that the bank can't keep up! So, the bank collects the money and issues the bonds when they come in."

"So, why the accusations?" Chuck asked.

"Sometimes people think they've paid more than they actually have. They think the bank hasn't issued the right amount of bonds."

"You guys don't keep record of who pays what?" asked Evan.

The whole scenario sounded odd. Something was remiss.

"I just said we don't have anything to do with it! The Liberty League just hosts the event. We're not in charge of it. But because we do the hosting, people think we've got our hands in the pot, and if there's any discrepancy in how the bonds are issued, they think we've pocketed the extra money!"

Curiouser and curiouser, said Alice…

Sensing Cameron's doubt, the third man continued. "Just look around! Does it look like we've been pocketing any extra?" he snorted.

"Doesn't the bank have records of what they collect here?" Evan pressed.

"I suppose they do. I've never seen them, and I haven't asked to, but they must—"

Bob Larabee's resonant voice interrupted the impassioned discussion.

"I found it!" he shouted, triumph etched all over his face. "Took me a while, but I got it!" Bob laughed and sauntered toward Chuck, handing him the key with a flourish and a bow of his head.

"Found what?" Rich asked, eyeing the key in Chuck's hand. Chuck told the boys about the gig and Bob's offer to use his garage for rehearsal. The band was more than happy to hear the news; at last, they'd be able to perform again.

Bob gave Clyde an amiable pat on the back.

"I think you can show them where the garage is!"

Clyde's blush was so pronounced that Bob guffawed, turning so red in the face himself that the boys wondered if he was about to faint.

"Now don't you worry, young fellow," said the old man, practically weeping. "If I had a penny for every kid I've met in mischief, I'd be richer than Croesus!"

Clyde smiled sheepishly and endured the verbal sparring and jabs of his band mates, all of whom were merciless upon realizing that Bob was the man whose property Clyde had vandalized.

"Now that you fellows are all done up here, go downstairs and get something to eat," Bob offered. "We prepare dinner once a week for veterans and families of servicemen having a hard time making do their rations. We've got plenty of food, so go help yourselves!"

"I'll finish the sweeping and be down in a minute," Cameron said.

The others followed Bob downstairs. Cameron's stomach growled, but he wanted to finish the job. He swept the area where the band had been working and noticed that the stage could use tidying. As he worked, he heard someone approach him from behind. Thinking that one of his band mates was in the hall, he yelled over his shoulder that he was almost ready to eat. The voice that greeted him was not a friendly one. Cameron turned around and found himself face to face with Buzz Cut, Toothpick, and two other men whom he'd never seen.

"Well, look what we have here," Buzz Cut said with a menacing sneer. "Sweeping and housecleaning. Now isn't that nice?"

"With that long hair, I'll bet he'll make someone a nice wife someday," Toothpick laughed. The two strangers laughed, as well.

"He's halfway there, I'll bet." Buzz Cut wasn't going to let up. Cameron was sure of it. "Just give him an apron and some pearls, and we've got June Cleaver right here in Gaston!"

The others laughed even louder. Cameron was livid. Baiting him into a confrontation was bad enough. Two sniveling toadies scoring points with their boss at Cameron's expense was intolerable. Cameron gripped the broom handle tightly, calculating just how close he'd have to be to execute a perfect swing at Buzz Cut's head.

Take out the leader and the rest will run.

Before Cameron reacted, Chuck and Bob appeared in the doorway.

"Can I help you fellows?" Cameron was shocked at the timbre of Bob's voice; it held none of the jovial, cheerful tone as it had before. Buzz Cut's lackeys were alarmed by Bob and Chuck's presence. Buzz Cut and Toothpick weren't concerned in the least.

"We just stopped in to see how things are going," Buzz Cut said, the intonation of his voice suave and smug with sycophancy.

Cameron's ire wasn't quelled.

I could crack his skull...

For no apparent reason, Chuck glared at Cameron.

Seems like he can read my mind!

"Nothing here is any of your concern!" Bob said, shoving his face into Buzz Cut's. "This is a members only club, and none of you are members."

"Neither are they!" Buzz Cut, unmoved by the challenge of authority, pointed to the band members.

"I owe you no explanations," Bob warned. "Your father might own half this town, but he doesn't own this half! Now, I've told you before and I'll say it again. Get the hell out!"

"OK, Bob. Just calm down. Don't get your blood pressure up. We'll leave. Anyhow, we don't want to interrupt your houseboy here."

As they turned to leave, Toothpick spat the wooden sliver in his mouth at Cameron. They strolled past Chuck and Bob, flashing testy grins. When they'd vacated the premises, Cameron continued sweeping in silence. He picked up the debris and dumped it into the wastebasket. He was seething.

"Who were those guys?" Chuck asked Bob. The old man shook his head in disgust.

"That was Chad and Joe Pecham," the old man grumbled. "Bob Pecham is their father."

"The banker?"

"One and the same. The one with the short hair is Joe. That's Pecham's oldest boy. The other boy is Chad. Chad won't dare fart if his brother doesn't tell him to."

"We met last night," Cameron muttered. Bob was confused. Chuck briefly reiterated the events of the previous night. Cameron could see that Bob wasn't pleased, or at all surprised to hear Chuck's account. The older man clucked his tongue in disgust.

"That was their uncle. Clifford is their mother's brother. He pulls that malarkey all the time. That's why he was never appointed as a judge. In Missouri, it's possible to hold a seat on the bench to fill a vacancy until the next election. One of the judges died in a car accident, and Clifford used his influence to make the governor name him for the vacancy. However, he made a total ass of himself on the bench, and his party and several other judges pressured him not to run in the election. Someone else was elected instead."

"What did he do that was so notorious?" Cameron disliked Clifford Allen Lewis to no end; anything derogatory about him was perfect fodder.

"He cast unjustified rulings and sentences that had no basis in the law. Damn near every one of them were overturned on appeal. He proclaimed in public that since he was an acting judge, he was like the captain of a ship and could do whatever he damned well pleased! He didn't take kindly to being forced off the bench, or off the ballot, for that matter. He tried undertaking a write-in campaign, but other than his immediate family, no one in the county voted for him."

"I bet that went over big," chuckled Cameron.

"Oh, God almighty! That was another scene," Bob moaned. "Lewis claimed voter fraud and demanded a recount. He was in the papers for weeks and threatened to take it to court. It held up swearing in any of the winners and was just a huge, embarrassing mess. The Missouri secretary of state stepped in and said that there was no justification to demand a recount because he only got ten votes, compared to the hundreds that the others got, and if he did want to have a recount, he'd have to pay for it himself. Well, that put an end to that, let me tell you! We all figured that he was too cheap to pay for a recount, let alone one where he'd find out he probably didn't really get ten votes!" The old man laughed bitterly. The boys knew that no love was lost between Bob and Lewis.

"So, now what is he doing?" asked Rich.

"He's back in his role of county prosecutor," Bob sighed. "And he's even more of a pain in the ass than he was before. And I don't care who knows I said it, either!"

Chuck patted Bob on the back. "I take it there's been conflict due to adverse opinions about Mr. Lewis." Chuck looked at Cameron and raised an eyebrow.

He's onto something.

"He and his brother-in-law are a little thin-skinned," Bob snorted with indignation. "Adverse opinions make them a little vengeful. More than a few people who questioned his actions had loan applications rejected, or new fees hit their accounts."

"Has he bullied you?" Snapper asked.

Bob laughed. "Not because he hasn't tried, young fellow. I never liked that cuss. When he was elected onto the board of the bank, I moved all my business elsewhere. He's tried luring me in by offering lines of credit and so on, but none of it's worked. I've been around longer than him, or his brother-in-law. I know how they work. They make you a deal, one that ends up with you indebted to them in more ways than one. The hell with that! I drive the extra distance and do my banking in Columbia."

"Do they retaliate against their critics?" Chuck queried.

"Hell, yes!" the old man grinned. "Permits had ways of suddenly being revoked or delayed. Their nephew used to pull people over for mild traffic offenses and issue outrageous fines."

"Who's their nephew?" Cameron was confident that he already knew the answer.

"Beecham. His mother is Pecham's other sister."

"You say he used to pull people over," Chuck pressed. "I take it that he doesn't anymore."

"No, he does not," the old man smiled. "He got a little too ambitious for his own good!"

"What happened?" Like Cameron, Snapper was enjoying this, too.

"He pulled over the wrong car. Thought it was mine and found out it wasn't!"

"Whose was it?" Cameron was about to pop with curiosity.

This is getting better and better!

"A justice of the Missouri State Supreme Court!" Bob burst into loud, gravelly laughter. "To make matters worse, he approached the car, shouting and swearing, and didn't have any explanation for why he was so mad, or why he pulled the justice over in the first place!"

"Is that why he hasn't been named sheriff, just acting sheriff?" Chuck asked. Bob smiled mischievously.

"I won't say yes or no, but I think it's a hell of a coincidence. You guys don't want to hear all our dirty laundry. Come on downstairs and let me get you something to eat." With that, he headed toward the stairs, the band close in tow.

The dining room was no longer vacant. Most of the tables were full, not with the usual bar patrons, but with young women, small children, and senior citizens. They were eating soup and small plates of salad, and each were given one roll. The boys remained by the stairs as Bob entered the kitchen.

"Guys, I can't do this," said Cameron, looking around the room.

"Me neither," muttered Rich. Evan, Clyde, and Snapper agreed.

"You can't turn it down," Chuck whispered. "You'd appear rude!"

"No, we won't," Cameron said. He walked past Chuck to the kitchen door, and motioned for Bob.

"Bob, thanks a lot for the offer, but we're all right."

Bob's smile faded, and his expression turned dour.

"You boys don't have to do that. We've got enough to share."

"Bob, you've got one pot of soup and one big metal mixing bowl of salad, and a lot of people need food more than we do," Cameron replied, just as serious. "We can share our rations. We don't want to take anything from people who really need help. Thanks for the offer, though."

The old man shook his head and sniffed. For a moment, Cameron wondered if Bob was going to weep.

"That's awfully nice of you fellows."

One of the ladies helping in the kitchen overheard Cameron and Bob's conversation. She had a most taciturn expression and Cameron was nonplussed as to what could be vexing her. Nonetheless, he smiled and waved to the women in the kitchen. He shook Bob's hand and hurriedly joined the others to leave. He was stopped short by a woman's voice.

"You wait right there!" It was the woman from the kitchen. She hobbled toward them, holding a tray with cake, all cut and set on napkins.

"I heard what you said, and that was an awful nice thing you did, but we want you to have this."

Cameron was about to protest, but he could tell that the woman would not take no for an answer. Gingerly, the Roadhouse Sons and their management each selected a piece of cake.

"I'm sorry it wasn't more." The woman smiled and hobbled back to the kitchen. Cameron felt a nudge on his arm.

Clyde stood before him with a handful of one-dollar bills. "We're giving this to them so they can buy more food," he whispered. "You got anything to contribute?" Cameron reached for his wallet and pulled out several one-dollar bills and handed them to Clyde, who hurried to the kitchen and handed the money to one of the ladies. The boys watched from afar as Clyde spoke to the woman, who smiled and kissed him on the cheek. He hurried to his fellow musicians and they left the Legion hall.

Once outside, Chuck asked, "Any conclusions?"

No one spoke, but the tension had left each of them. Everyone but Cameron.

"I think this investigation is going to be very interesting. Damn, but I love fresh applesauce cake!" Chuck mused.

Something's up.

CHAPTER SIXTEEN

"Suspicion"

Stanley was not satisfied with his subordinate's answer. It was too clear cut, too dry, and left no room for any other consideration or conclusion. Simms was hiding something.

"Why would Collier have written that he was meeting you for drinks?" Stanley demanded again.

Simms was indignant. "I've already told you! Why must you ask me again?" he snapped. "I have no idea why! I had no plans to meet with him then, or at any other time!"

"You're lying!" Stanley insisted. "Why else would your name be in his appointment book?"

"Do you honestly think I want to jeopardize anything that we're doing here?" Simms hissed. "For God's sake, with this punk band of yours peeing in our pool at every opportunity, the stress is bad enough without adding some unknown variable!"

"Well said," Stanley smiled. "Very well said. Very good. And very rehearsed."

"I've rehearsed nothing!" Simms barked. "I'm telling you the truth! Do you honestly think that for one minute I've forgotten that if anything sinks this boat of ours, I'll drown, too? I don't even have the benefit of any life preserver, as you might have!"

"Neither did Collier," Stanley said with a cruel smile. Simms flinched. What Simms averred was indeed undeniable. If anything went awry, Stanley was, at the very least, valuable. Simms, on the other hand, was entirely expendable.

"And look where it got him," Simms replied, returning Stanley's mocking grin. "I have greater aspirations than ending up a grease stain on Seattle's sidewalks."

"The best laid schemes o' mice an' men…" said Stanley, his voice cold. Simms said nothing. He knew that Stanley would no longer tolerate any defiance; he would construe it as pure, unadulterated insubordination.

"Someone has obviously decided to go off on their own." Stanley spoke with sinister calm. His tone caused Simms to shudder. "Established systems are suddenly derailed…not in just one instance, but several. And key instances, I might add. There is no way that I can consider such events mere coincidence."

Simms remained silent.

"Nor can anyone else," Stanley added. The two men stared at each other. Stanley ended the impasse when he impatiently arose and poured himself another drink. He held the decanter for a moment, examining it. He placed it on the sideboard and walked back to his desk, deliberately pausing after each footfall.

"We have to retrace Collier's steps, beginning with his arrival" Stanley said, matter-of-factly. "Do we have any idea with whom he was in contact?" Simms dared do nothing but shake his head.

"You had me inquire at the hotel already," Simms replied, maintaining his composure. "He had only checked in the day after he called you from Tacoma."

At that, Stanley whirled about, his face riddled with bewilderment.

"Tacoma? I never spoke to him while he was in Tacoma. My only contact with him was when he arrived here in Seattle."

Simms was utterly perplexed. "That's impossible," he said, rummaging through his message booklet. "Here's the carbon from the first telephone message. The prefix belonged to a Tacoma number, not a Seattle one."

Stanley snatched the message booklet from his assistant's hand. He examined the pages closely, comparing the dates and times of Collier's communications.

Collier was indeed in Tacoma three days before he arrived in Seattle. Why had he told Stanley that he'd come straight to Seattle from Los Angeles? Admonishing himself, Stanley wondered how he could have been so sloppy as not to have noticed the differences in the telephone number prefixes. Then he realized why. He never dialed numbers directly; Simms always handled that for him, alerting Stanley when the calls were connected. Stanley sighed with relief, as he realized he never had cause to see the message booklet.

Looking up from the booklet, Stanley glowered at Simms and slammed the booklet on the desk. "Why didn't you tell me about

Tacoma before now? What if the police had asked me about this? What answer could I have given?"

Simms flinched at Stanley's outburst, but quickly recovered.

"I didn't know that it was a cause for alarm," Simms insisted. "I had no idea he wasn't supposed to have been there!"

Stanley ignored Simms and continued to scour the remaining message carbons.

Simms cleared his throat. "Collier had probably reached his travel limit for that day. Travel is often restricted down there, due to the military bases."

Stanley snickered.

"Don't feed me that dribble. If that was the case, how do you explain this message?" He pointed at the booklet and shoved it at Simms, who read the message aloud.

"Have arrived at the airport, will call later from the hotel."

"Is that your handwriting?" Stanley urged.

Simms shook his head. "You know I would always cite which airport and which hotel. That's the part-time help's writing. That day, the band had a photo shoot for the new album cover and I was with them, so she worked."

"Are you certain?" Stanley demanded. Simms nodded.

"I never forget those occasions. They are indelibly imprinted in my psyche—"

"I'm not interested in your editorials," Stanley shouted. Rising to his feet, he grabbed his empty glass and stormed over to the sideboard. As Stanley lifted the decanter yet again, Simms watched with concern.

"You should be careful," Simms offered, cautiously. "You've been doing that a lot lately."

"I have very good reasons for doing this," Stanley said. "I might not have the chance again."

The profundity of the statement hit Simms like a boulder. Stanley was afraid.

"Do you think—"

"I don't have time for idle speculations," Stanley snarled. "We have to find out what Collier was doing in Tacoma. We have to find out before the police do. Do we have anyone available, someone thorough?"

Simms was about to answer, but Stanley left no time for a response.

"Someone...circumspect?"

"More or less," Simms replied.

"Who?"

"Quinn," Simms answered. "He and Ralston were always trying to talk to Collier alone. We know Ralston. He's an opportunist and doesn't care how he goes about it. Quinn, however, is different."

"What about Quinn?"

"Quinn's an odd milquetoast duck but he isn't careless, especially if he's on his own," Simms explained. "By himself, he looks before he leaps. He took the time to evaluate Collier without the rest of them telling him what to think; I'm sure of it. There's a good chance that Quinn's heard something, something useful to us. He likely wouldn't recognize it as such, but we might."

"You're probably right," Stanley said, rapidly draining his glass. He poured one more shot of liquor and drank that just as quickly. "I didn't know they'd been spending time with Collier." He eyed Simms.

"Do you want me to talk to Quinn?" Simms asked meekly.

Suddenly, Stanley seized his suit jacket and stormed from the room, yelling over his shoulder.

"No! *I'll* do it!"

CHAPTER SEVENTEEN

"Eruption"

"That's an order, damn it!" shouted Chuck. His face was crimson.

Cameron stood his ground, his stance that of a ram, head down and ready to butt heads with any lesser opponent.

"I'm not some kid you can ground for three weeks! If I want to go someplace, I'm fuckin' going! You got that?"

Chuck shoved his face into Cameron's, his voice almost inaudible.

"I will not repeat myself."

Chuck's breath was hot against Cameron's face. His eyes were dark, the irises as black as the pupils. Cameron knew that Chuck was angry to the core.

"You are on assignment, a highly dangerous mission. You will do exactly as you are instructed. Nothing else."

"Or else what?" Cameron remained calm, despite his own incredible ire, and maintained a steady gaze nonetheless. He was not backing down.

Chuck stood eerily still; he didn't even blink. "Are you challenging me?"

Cameron couldn't recall ever hearing such menace in Chuck's tone. He remembered the band's original recruitment when Doug was still alive. His roadie—his *late* roadie—challenged their first supervisor repeatedly. The confrontation between the two ended with a loaded revolver pointed at the roadie's chest.

Chuck's hands were in plain sight and empty, but he'd served in special forces during Vietnam and there was no telling what he'd learned. Despite Cameron's adamancy, he knew that Chuck held the advantage. Surprisingly, and to his own amazement, he did not yield. He wasn't sure why a simple disagreement had so quickly escalated to near altercation, but as a matter of principle, and for his own honor and sanity, he had to maintain his position.

I am not going to submit to you, or anyone! Not now, not ever.

Cameron allowed his fury to wane. Inhaling deeply, he stated his desires once again.

"I just want to get out of here and go for a beer. That's all! I just need to get out and relax."

"You'll stay put, like I told you to," Chuck replied, his own ire fading, despite his biting tone.

Are you trembling?

The two stood facing each other. Despite their increasing calm, they remained unyielding in their bearing.

"You're the superman, not me," Cameron said, bitterly. There were times when he admired and trusted Chuck, but in times when Cameron could tell that only the mission held Chuck's concern, he literally hated his superior.

"What the hell do you mean by that?" Chuck's steadfast gaze turned to a formidable glare.

Cameron didn't want to exacerbate the situation further, but he had to make his point.

"Nothing bothers you," he said, accusingly. "We feel pressure, like we'll snap. You sit back and smile. You don't feel anything. You think we're the same way. We're not. We're human!"

"I won't even dignify that with a response."

"I didn't think so. You don't give a shit about me, or any of us."

"You really believe that?"

"You're so full of contempt 'cause I said it out loud. Guilty conscience?" Cameron couldn't stop himself. He plunged into the emotional abyss. "If I got shot right now, you'd probably step over my body without another thought. You wouldn't even bother to kick me off to the side!"

"You can't talk to me that way—" Chuck was furious.

"I can and I did and I will!"

"Don't push your luck—"

"That's what you did to Doug! You even told us to forget about him! *Forget about him!* You didn't even let us go to his fucking funeral!"

Chuck's mouth was agape. Cameron's ferocity was astounding. He'd never imagined that Cameron was capable of such rage.

"Is that what's bothering you all this time?" Chuck was stunned. Utter disbelief shrouded him.

"You treat us like meat. You move us around like pawns on a chessboard! We can't speak up. We can't complain. We're meat!"

Chuck smirked. "Ah, the irony. You don't seem to mind that treatment when it involves groupies."

"You...mother...fucker! You friggin' lunatic..." Cameron, suddenly and eerily calm, went straight for Chuck's jugular. "Is that why you got thrown out of the army—"

In one swift motion, Chuck grabbed Cameron by the jaw, crashing him into the wall.

"You will never *ever* mention my military service again!"

Chuck hissed at Cameron, spittle flying from his mouth. His grip on Cameron's jaw tightened. Cameron heard his mandible click and felt its tendons strain. Pain ripped through to the area below his ears. He panicked.

He's gonna break my jaw!

Chuck was nose to nose with Cameron, eyes ablaze.

"I was getting my ass shot at while you were safe at home jacking off over *Playboy.* You think I'd just step over your body? Like I had to step over the bodies of my buddies? When I was trying to shoot the sons o' bitches that shot *them*? That mission? The one I served in and you didn't? I'm a bastard because I'm not sobbing over some asshole who tried to play hero? That doesn't make me a bastard. That makes me an agent!"

Frantic pounding on the door yanked Chuck from his diatribe. They heard Rich's anxious voice.

"Hey! Open up! What the hell's going on in there? Let me in!"

Chuck and Cameron were frozen in time. At first, neither of them acknowledged the interruption, or the resulting abrupt trek back into reality. After several seconds, Chuck released his grip on Cameron's jaw and strode to the door. He opened it, barely ajar, and before him stood the puzzled, disheveled bass player.

"Cameron and I were having a discussion."

Rich squinted his eyes and attempted to peer into the room.

"What about?" he commanded.

Cameron viewed his superior from behind. He could tell that Chuck's muscles were still taut as wire; he was practically quivering with tension. Cameron worried that Chuck would attack Rich, and attempted to plot how he'd keep the two men apart. Thankfully, the strategy was unnecessary. Chuck opened the door all the way and allowed Rich entry to the room.

Rich cautiously stepped forward. "What about?" he repeated.

"About something I have to tell all of you." Every syllable cracked like a whip. "Go get the others in here."

Rich said nothing. He nodded and, walking backward, retraced his steps out of the room. Cameron could only assume that Rich was doing as he was told because he was fraught with worry; he wasn't the type to skulk away on demand.

Chuck stood in place. He didn't close the door but gripped it so tightly that his knuckles were white. Cameron massaged his jaw. The ghost of Chuck's grip remained. The lower portion of Cameron's face was hot, and his jaw still sore to the touch. As he headed to the bathroom for a cold washcloth, Chuck spun around, teeth clenched and his eyes on fire.

"Don't you fucking move."

Cameron stopped dead in his tracks.

He's an animal!

The Roadhouse Sons appeared in the doorway. Cameron looked at Snapper imploringly.

"Get in here and sit down!" Chuck yelled. His eyes never left Cameron's.

Silently, Clyde, Evan, Rich, and Snapper filed in, one by one, and seated themselves. Chuck slammed the door and locked it. He turned on the television and sat on the edge of the bed. Tension permeated the room. The boys were gravely concerned.

"I want to get something straight right now." Chuck spoke concisely and with even tone.

It's like nothing ever happened!

"I give orders, not suggestions. I don't explain my decisions and there's no reason to. I, and I alone, am responsible for the success or failure of this assignment, and I'm responsible for each of you. If I say no, it's no. If I say yes, it's yes. You all chose to remain in this organization. I repeat, you *chose* to remain. Therefore, you are to behave in a manner befitting protocol. That includes avoiding, either by accident or design, any form of insubordination. Do I make myself clear?"

No one spoke. The boys were numb and confused. Chuck's denunciation was illogical and uncharacteristic, at best. Their angst was increased, due to the previous audible evidence of a heated confrontation between Cameron and Chuck.

"Is that clear?" Chuck bellowed. Evan jumped he was so startled. They all mumbled their assent. All but Cameron.

"I told you not to push your luck," Chuck hissed.

Cameron swallowed hard. He did not speak. Chuck rose to his feet. Cameron held his breath. He felt his panic return, but he remained seated. His only protest was his silence. He was not willing to surrender.

Chuck stood in front of Cameron, lording over him. Cameron's stomach churned, but he said nothing.

"Come on, man!" Rich urged. "Say something!" The others added nervous exhortations. Cameron could not find his voice.

"Yes, Cameron. Say something." Chuck's comportment was as cold as ice.

Cameron stood. "No! It's not clear." His mouth was arid.

Chuck squinted. "What isn't clear?" Chuck hands were clenched, tight as vices.

"Why you don't keep your promises!"

"You're speaking in tongues." Chuck was nonplussed.

"The other day you promised us practical training, including protocol. Why haven't we started?"

"Under no circumstances am I required to explain any of my decisions to any of you."

"Not your decisions," Cameron insisted. "The reasons behind them! You dictate our actions, but you never tell us why your decisions stand. For God's sake, tell us why something is smart or not, so we can figure shit out for ourselves. Of course I'm pissed off! I don't have any idea what to do unless you tell me, or why it's important to do it, because that part you won't tell! When we said we'd stay in for the fight, we were under the impression that we'd always be informed. No such friggin' luck! We're in the midst of even more local woodchuck law enforcement cloak-and-dagger crap for no apparent reason, and with no end in sight. No wonder it's come to blows!"

Chuck weighed Cameron's proclamation. At last, Cameron had said what all the guys were thinking.

Chuck stood eye to eye with Cameron. After several moments, he plopped into a chair, put his elbows on his knees, and put his face in his hands. His very essence wreaked of the fatigue of futility.

This guy's a train wreck.

"If I had any answers, don't you think I would have told you?"

"That's not what I meant," Cameron insisted. "You said I couldn't go out tonight, right?"

Chuck grunted his affirmation.

"You didn't tell me why."

"I don't have to, you fucking bastard!" Chuck's cool was blown. Cameron expecting another brawl at any moment, and the boys braced themselves for the worst. Thankfully, Chuck stayed in his chair, stewing; he didn't make a move.

"Not the decisions. The conclusions!"

Chuck trembled with anger.

"What *led* you to that conclusion?" Cameron spoke quickly. "Why was tonight different from last night? What should we know? We have to be able to draw the same conclusions ourselves? What if you're not there? That's what I want to hear."

Chuck took a deep breath, held it, then slowly exhaled.

"You're right," he whispered. "You're absolutely right." He was silent for so long after his admission that the boys were addled by the quiet. Chuck stared at the floor. When he finally spoke, his customary self-control was restored.

"In our midst there are several persons of interest who are attempting to provoke us into some type of dispute," Chuck began. "By confronting three of us, they seriously miscalculated the results of their actions and exposed their entire operation. They will not risk us revealing that exposure. Conceivably, therefore, they could make an attempt on one, or all, of our lives."

Chuck eyed Cameron directly.

"Despite opinions to the contrary, I *am* concerned about the safety and welfare of our unit. Support is en route, but the longer we wait for the opposition to make a move, the greater chance that such action will be unilaterally against our favor. Going out to a bar to let off steam places us in a position of vulnerability. The obvious combination of alcohol, testosterone, occupational duress, and your inexperience in any kind of combat, factors into my decision to forbid your patronage of such places. Allowing you to go *at this time* presents an unnecessary risk, not only of your safety, but of the success of this assignment."

Cameron's face flushed. He'd reacted foolishly, with no self-control, and with no regard for his superiors. Chuck's struggle to control his temper revealed to Cameron the dire toll his behavior had thrust upon his mentor, his manager, and his friend.

"Look man, I'm sorry about what I—"

"Shut the fuck up! There's no apology and handshake cure! You wanted explanations; I delivered them. I will not permit any of you to place yourselves in needless danger. The job is tough enough."

Chuck forced eye contact with Evan, Rich, Clyde, and Snapper. He didn't look at Cameron a second time.

"I'll spell it out for you. We've got an opportunity to collect information on a serious extortion racket. That includes gathering information involving the theft of government bonds. This information will be used to conduct a full-scale investigation into actions that could do more to undermine the war effort than a Soviet attack on Washington! Attacks by foreign countries unite Americans. Elected officials ripping us off discourages Americans. If anything happens to jeopardize this investigation, we lose the opportunity to stop the extortion racket, once and for all. I won't risk that, or any of you, *if* at all preventable. If that's not safe or comforting enough for you, tough shit!"

Chuck was exhausted. He rubbed his face and slumped over, his muscles flaccid. He was the picture of a man who'd just experienced life's greatest defeat. The boys stared uncomfortably at one another, attempting to divine their collective thoughts.

"If you'd just told me that, we wouldn't have had a fight," Cameron said quietly.

"Do any of you have money for beer?" Chuck asked. Snapper and Evan nodded.

"Go get some. And take them with you. Stay together, go only to the corner store and come right back. No stopping elsewhere for anything. Cameron and I still have some business to take care of."

Evan said, "But don't you—"

Chuck stabbed a finger directly toward Evan.

"That's an order and not one I need to explain to you! Get out, get the beer, and get back. Don't waste time, or piss me off any more!"

"I was only going to ask if you wanted a Pepsi instead," Evan murmured.

"No! If I have to deal with this shit, I want a beer, too. Now get your asses in gear and move!"

The boys left. Cameron was more than apprehensive. He rubbed his jaw.

I don't want to be left alone with him.

"Sit down," Chuck sneered through clenched teeth. "You're not the only one feeling the pressure."

Cameron began to speak, but with his fist in the air, Chuck silenced the singer's commentary.

"There's no room for mistakes. The last thing I need right now is to act as your schoolmarm!"

"I was just trying to—"

"Shut it!" Chuck warned. "Your insisting on explanations was just some sorry excuse you pulled out of your ass at the last minute. You and I both know it."

Cameron sat, shamefaced; Chuck's insights were spot-on. He wasn't easing up. Cameron knew that he deserved the impending onslaught.

"I cited the reason that I forbid you to leave. The least you could have done was cite the actual reason for why you're so damned pissed off and out of sorts. If you pulled something so blatantly stupid and false with me, how would you handle yourself with that gang? You suck at poker face. Your number would've been up, and you'd be susceptible as hell. You and all the boys. Those sloppy racketeers are watching our every move. It would be their dream come true to have you boys separated from the group and vulnerable."

"You're probably right," Cameron said quietly.

Chuck wasn't mollified; he was offended. "What 'probably'? And don't kiss my ass."

"I'm not," Cameron replied, sullen. "I've been thinking about risky situations, too, and that's exactly one that I thought of—"

Chuck snorted in disdain.

"Did I blow things that bad? So much that you won't listen to anything I say anymore?" Cameron demanded.

Chuck, as though swatting at a gnat, dismissed Cameron with a disgusted flick of his wrist.

"I will not repeat this. I don't care if you loathe me. I don't care if you trust me. I don't give one sweet fuck if you're afraid of me. You obey me! No second-guessing me! No thinking it through on your own. You have no idea what you're doing. You proved that tonight, not only with your request to leave, but with your inability to convincingly discuss it."

Chuck's every word was a stinging indictment of Cameron's attitude and behavior. Cameron felt nauseous. He started to speak, but thought better of it. Chuck was right. This was nothing that a simple apology could repair. Cameron, still seated, stared at Chuck, who rested his head in his hands, and sat staring at the floor. The static from the television filled no void left by Chuck's silence. Deciding to risk one more of Chuck's angry outbursts, Cameron spoke.

"I do trust you."

Chuck raised his head. He looked right through Cameron. The effect was daunting, chilling.

"You said you didn't care if I trusted you or not," Cameron continued. He cringed at how insipid his own words sounded. "I said I do trust you. I was frustrated. You didn't seem to trust me."

Chuck rose from his seat and began pacing.

"Man, I'm sorry! What else can I say?" Cameron was almost pleading.

"Nothing! It's disgusting to watch you try. I've got enough shit on my mind right now without you turning into the head sissy for the wah-wah brigade."

"I fucked up! I'm *sorry*! But it wasn't because I don't want to do this. I want to do it better, be the one that you and McIntyre don't have to worry about."

Chuck continued pacing. He ignored Cameron, and Cameron struggled harder to explain himself.

"You've never, ever felt frustrated doing something? Especially something completely different from your entire life? You never flexed your muscles, trying to make it all feel right?"

Chuck rolled his eyes. "Listen, you pantywaist! I wouldn't be here right now if I'd, at any point in my career, army or otherwise, ever pulled your touchy-feely crap. Get out of my sight."

"Then I guess I was wrong!" Cameron laughed. "You're not Superman. You're Jesus Christ! Never did anything wrong. Always knew what to do. Too perfect to be among us mere mortals."

Chuck's jaw clenched. As the color drained from Chuck's face, Cameron gagged. He thought he was going to vomit. For a millisecond, he felt doom. He closed his eyes and braced for the blow, then forced himself to look Chuck straight in the eye. To his surprise, Chuck stopped pacing and turned to him.

"You're right. I did stupid shit and said stupid shit, more often than I'd like to admit."

Cameron fought his gag reflex. "Before now, we could touch what we worked. We touch the guitars. We touch the amps. We touch the girls. We touch the mics. With this, everything's such a mind game. What am I thinking? What are you thinking? What are they thinking? Are they enemies? Are they neutral? How do I hide what I feel? How do I hide what I'm thinking? How do I talk to everybody in every situation, and still stay safe? Your imagination gets the best of you. You can't touch anything! You get paranoid. *You* never even tell us if we're right or wrong. I've reached the point where I don't know what's real…"

The room fell silent.

Chuck smirked at Cameron. "I got that out of my system in the army. Doing a hundred pushups several times a day trains you, anchors you to be strong of body and mind. You're prepared, you're ready…you act instinctively. You don't react emotionally."

"You did one hundred pushups…" Something had dawned on Cameron. He dropped to the floor. Starting out at a rapid clip, he quickly realized that he would never be able to maintain that momentum and accomplish one hundred pushups. He slowed to a manageable pace.

Chuck watched, more than a bit stunned.

"What the hell are you doing?"

"Fifteen, sixteen, seventeen, eighteen…" Cameron panted. He was determined. Triumphantly, he counted off each pushup. At the count of thirty, every muscle in his arms began to burn.

Only a third of the way through…

He felt the muscles across his chest tighten. The ache in his arms worsened. He realized that he'd been holding his breath. Cameron exhaled, then controlled his breathing.

Breathe in when I go down; exhale as I push up.

Cameron forced himself to cease thinking about the remaining number of pushups, and to view each one as its own accomplishment. Still, he maintained his mental count.

"Sixty, sixty-one, sixty-two, sixty-three," he gasped. Satisfaction swept over him.

More than halfway through!

At that very moment, his arms began to buckle under the strain of his own weight. Each pushup required a gargantuan effort. His momentum slowed to an agonizing rate, but he pressed on.

"Eighty-eight, eighty-nine, ninety," he grunted, barely intelligible. He could barely remain fully stretched and prone, and he felt his knees touch the floor. Forcing himself to maintain straight legs made it almost impossible for him to continue.

Almost there!

Cameron ignored his screaming muscles and his scorched lungs.

"One hundred!"

"Do five more!" Chuck ordered, his voice sharp but intoning no anger. Cameron couldn't believe his ears. In agony, he continued, barely able to push himself up.

One hundred and two…

He struggled on, finally reaching his one hundred fifth pushup. Purely and simply, Cameron collapsed. Through his gasps, he heard Chuck clap, then laugh.

"All righty!" he chuckled. "That's enough. You're forgiven!"

Chuck offered his hand and helped Cameron to his feet.

"Remember this. You drew your own first blood! I *will* make you do this again if you screw up!"

Cameron sat on the edge of the bed. He resembled a wet rag, sweat drenching his shirt and dripping from his nose. He looked up into Chuck's smiling face.

"Now, I really *am* sorry about that army crack!" he gasped.

Chuck grabbed Cameron by the hair and raised the singer's face to his own.

"We will not speak of that again."

His smile was gone, his voice was hard, but he showed no trace of rage. Cameron nodded. Chuck released him.

"What's bothering you?" Chuck asked.

Cameron swallowed. A huge lump formed in his throat.

"Doug."

Can't cry…not now…

"What did you do with him?" Cameron entreated.

"We didn't just leave him there, if that's what you're asking." Chuck was stern. "We took care of him. We're not heartless."

"Why couldn't we be there? We didn't even send flowers. He was our friend. We were his family, for Christ's sake."

"We figured that out." Chuck sighed.

"How?"

"No one wanted his belongings," Chuck explained. "We contacted his only known relatives, the mother and an uncle. Neither of them wanted to be bothered. That's why we left Doug's stuff with you guys."

"He really didn't have a home 'til he started working for us," Cameron whispered plaintively. "Once, on Thanksgiving, we found him camped out in the back of the old truck."

"What was he doing there?"

"Hiding. He didn't have anyplace to go, and he was too ashamed to let us know."

Cameron couldn't fight his emotions any longer. He choked up.

"Why didn't you let us visit his grave? He deserved that, at least."

"There were more pressing demands. You guys helped us reel in a notorious outfit, an illegal-substances network with connections to organized crime in the US and Canada. We had to take you all out of harm's way. Remember, Clyde was seriously injured, and we had to get him competent medical attention. We moved you to Chicago, and that's why we're moving you cross-country."

"You made us forget him. Like he was insignificant."

"For that, I'm truly sorry." Chuck was remorseful, albeit reluctant to demonstrate it. "This work is rough. It's good for you to put this behind you. We won't talk about it anymore."

Cameron jumped from the bed and pointed at Chuck. "That! That right there! Why? Why do I have to ignore the death of my friend?"

Cameron struggled to keep his emotions in check. He didn't want to ignite another confrontation.

Chuck remained patiently calm. "It doesn't do us any good to dwell on it. We've got to look ahead, to the task at hand. If your emotions rule you at all, you're doomed."

Cameron walked to the end table and picked up Doug's Louis L'Amour novel. A paper fluttered from the back of the book. Cameron retrieved it from the floor and unfolded it. It was a pencil sketch of a smiling girl sitting seaside on a large rock.

Bambi…

He reveled in his memories of flirting with her at work, entertaining her at the shows, and their magical evening together on their first date.

Our only date…

He angered at the memories of how her brother was involved in running the operation foiled by the Roadhouse Sons, and at how Bambi had agreed to work with the US government to avoid going to prison. With melancholy and disgust, he remembered how her charges were dropped in exchange for her agreement to act as a plant in Spain's Communist Party, an organization to which she once belonged. Cameron recalled his shock when he realized that he'd made love with a Communist who'd worked to encourage resistance of the Eastern Block.

As though it were a movie.

He abandoned his thoughts of the past. He had one more unanswered question in the present. He held up the sketch for Chuck to see. Chuck shook his head ruefully.

"Have you heard anything about her?" Cameron asked, choking back tears.

"Nothing conclusive. The Communists aren't as organized as they were before, but the channel that she's working hasn't closed, as far as we know. The situation, we surmise, is evolving as we hoped."

"Is there any chance that I can contact her?" Cameron asked.

"No way."

Cameron folded the sketch and returned it to it's home in the back pages of the Louis L'Amour book.

No way...

Chuck reached for the L'Amour novel. Cameron passed the book to him. Chuck held it with respect, and raised it skyward for a moment.

"If it's any consolation to you, we showed Doug the same dignity we did Dwyer."

Chuck paged through the book. "You mind if I read this?" he smiled slyly. "I'm getting sick of the papers."

Cameron shrugged and started to fidget.

"What else is bothering you?"

"I'm fucking horny!" Cameron whispered, despite the static from the television.

"Man, I'm ready to claw the bark off a tree!"

Cameron gaped at Chuck, dumbfounded.

"You?"

"Don't be so surprised! You think you guys invented it?"

"If you don't mind my asking, how do you deal with it?"

"I try not to focus on it while I'm on assignment. That's easier sometimes than others."

"Tell me about it," moaned Cameron. "All the women we see, and I can't do a thing right now! How do you keep from thinking about that?"

"What do you guys usually do when you meet a girl? What's the first thing you look for?"

Cameron pondered Chuck's question.

"Well, I guess I look to see if she's wearing a ring."

"And if she is?"

"That kills the mood," Cameron admitted. Chuck nodded.

"So, if you have to, don't you sometimes picture a girl wearing a ring?"

"Yeah. I suppose I do."

"I learned that trick when I was stationed in Bangkok for so long," Chuck replied with a smile. "I can't tell you how many times the women will sidle up to you, married or not, and offer up their pickup line."

Cameron cocked his head. "What do they say?"

Chuck smiled and raised the pitch if his voice. "I love you, GI! No bullshi'!"

"No shit!"

"Another trick I learned there. I instinctively look for an Adam's apple. Trust me. Picture a woman with an Adam's apple and you'll droop like a weeping willow!"

Before Cameron could respond, a loud knock at the door heralded the return of the others. Chuck opened the door, and after a satisfactory debriefing of their excursion to the store, he was satisfied enough to suggest some time off.

"You can't keep a bow taut all the time. A lot of shit going on now, but I promise that when this is over and we get to Columbia, you'll have a little R&R before our next assignment."

"You fucking mean that?" Rich was elated.

Evan rolled his eyes. "Stop swearing all the time."

"Fuck you!" Clyde laughed at his own joke. Snapper smacked his arm.

"I propose a toast!" Rich popped the top on his beer can. "To R&R!"

The Roadhouse Sons raised their collective cans and proceeded to guzzle their brew.

"I'll do everything I can," Chuck assured them. "But no promises."

Never. Never any promises...

CHAPTER EIGHTEEN

"Rehearsing for Danger"

Cameron was in heaven. His fingers slid along the guitar strings, stirring with life, as though waiting for validation through the power of the amp. The weight of the guitar and its pressure against Cameron's side completed him. He was back in the arms of a long-lost lover.

Cameron hated the long breaks from playing. Those times rendered his soul adrift. The demands of his assignments couldn't possibly fill the abyss. He lived for nothing but his music, plain and simple.

He flipped upward the power switch on the amp and picked up the cord. He inserted the connection into his guitar's receiver. The resulting sound was the familiar and comforting thud-pop, crackle, and hum, and Cameron felt an emotional caress, as though from a soul mate who shared his exact sentiments. Cameron tuned the instrument. He didn't want to rush the process; he wanted to savor it, to cherish it. He couldn't wait to play, to create music and send it out into the universe, to be in a place in time that was no one's but his. To rush these moments and push them aside for discussions of set lists and endless performance retakes would intrude on the time that he was alone with the one mistress to whom he'd been devoted all these years. He was where he longed to be and doing exactly what he wanted to do.

Cameron placed his ear close to the neck of the guitar. He really didn't need the amp at this point. He plucked each string, turning its tuning peg slightly one way, then the other, coaxing the correct sound from each. After coarse turns of the pegs, there was always the fine-tuning, the ever-so-slight adjustment in tuning that rendered the instrument pitch-perfect. For as long as he could remember, this final part of the tuning process gave Cameron the quiver of anticipation; performing was just minutes away. He'd played the guitar for years, both professionally and as a student, but his amazement at his own perpetual anticipation to play never ceased. He looked forward to each and every performance, never knowing what would transpire. Each song that he played sounded different every time. Tunes they'd played forever were sometimes familiar friends, and other times complete strangers. Cameron could barely contain his excitement. He didn't mind that the Roadhouse Sons were knocking about in an abandoned garage. They were going to play!

One by one, each member of the band powered up their instruments. No doubt, they all experienced the same thrill that Cameron had as the energy from their respective amps surged through them. The boys tested their mics and Snapper adjusted the PA accordingly. Once the levels were set, Snapper looked up from the board and said, "Now let's get to work!"

The very air was alive with chords and voices. Each song was played with relish and to the apex of experience. Every song's climax was held, suspended and sustained, before gracefully surrendering to its denouement.

The band experimented with certain pieces, adjusting solos or eliminating repetitions. The Roadhouse Sons wanted this moment in time to stand as their best.

Cameron eyed his band mates' expressions. Each and every visage was the picture of pure bliss. The set list came easy, not because it was unchallenging, but because every note was heartfelt. Instinct alone guided each musician toward the music. They all just simply knew how it should be done.

No one had been idle during the long and excruciating hiatus. The boys had individually continued to practice and play, primarily as a means of maintaining their sanity. Having done so heightened their collective expertise. Simply put, the song sounded even better. The boys offered up their suggestions and demonstrated their new and revised visions for each piece. They chose a practical, rapid, and democratic manner by which to choose the new implementations. Each idea was played. If the change enhanced the piece, they adopted it. If not, it was quickly dropped. While employing this method of decision making, they managed to keep discussion at a minimum; chattering would only interfere with playing music, after all.

On occasion, Snapper accompanied the band with his harmonica, lending a blues feel to their songs. Blind Willy McTell's "*Statesboro Blues*" and The Doors' "*Roadhouse Blues*" sounded better when Snapper threw in his talent. Rich especially liked playing the blues selections. He had long been fascinated by the stories of Robert Johnson at the Crossroads, and swore that some day he'd go there and visit those dusty roads himself. Rich never needed a discussion about whether to play a blues song, and Snapper was his ally. In gratitude to their roadie, Rich made sure that the band played a special rendition of "*Red House*," Snapper's favorite song. Doing so gave Snapper his own solo opportunity, and he always maintained his position that, no matter what, "There was no experience like The Jimi Hendrix Experience!"

Never fully absent from the jam sessions, Chuck, in keeping with his custom, occasionally sat in on a song or two. Tonight, though, he kept a watchful eye on the place, glancing out the windows and casing the building's periphery. As a precaution, he had the band park and unload the truck *in* the garage, and he locked all of the doors and windows.

Despite the warm weather, Chuck wore a denim vest, which hid his pistol. The sudden blast of reality hit Cameron like a gust of Arctic air. His music-induced nirvana ruptured, Cameron played on nonetheless. He jealously guarded the escape provided by playing, and had long ago decided that distractions, no matter the context, would not rob him of his joy.

The band played most of the afternoon. As evening neared though, Chuck informed them that it was time to wrap it up.

"I don't want pack up and head home in the dark," he explained. "Too much opportunity for mischief."

"For us or them?" asked Rich, bursting into laughter at his own joke. No one laughed and no one argued. After the episode with Cameron and Chuck, the dangers the band faced were manifest, and the boys had collectively decided to try even harder to uphold the mission. At a very basic level, Cameron still hated the cold showers, but knew that whining accomplished nothing. There were no more complaints—about anything.

The first and second days of rehearsal were joyously uneventful. Nonetheless, Chuck decided to call a brief meeting.

"I wanted to do this here, well away from snoopy housekeepers," he said. "Things are going to get crazy from here on out, and I have to make certain that you guys are ready for anything. We're going to be stricter about our own security. I'm not talking about just double-checking locks and such, or only talking with the television or radio on. We've got to remember to be careful how we take our notes and keep our records."

Chuck explained that notes for their reports were to be kept at the barest minimum, citing only recall cues. The boys would have to memorize everything else.

"We figure they've already rifled through our rooms. They were pretty amateurish about it. They didn't take my gun. But we risk letting them know what we know. We need to secure our information."

"You mean codes?" asked Rich. He was confused. The band wasn't required to write many reports at all, and the ones they did have to write were recorded in the presence of Chuck and McIntyre. Until now, there was no need for notes; reports were compiled in a collaborative effort.

"No, not codes. That might work for you, but if something happened to you, we couldn't decipher your notes. I repeat. Keep your notes to the bare minimum and keep them out of sight."

"Ok, I think I get it," Evan replied. "You mean, for example, if we're going to make a report on the cleaning lady, we'd just write the words, *cleaning lady motel room*. We'd know what we meant. If we weren't around to explain, then you would at least know to check out the cleaning lady, right?"

Chuck nodded. "I'd find a less conspicuous way to phrase it, but yes, that's the crux of it. Don't write the words *cleaning lady*. You never want to give away what you know. Write the phrase *clean room*. A trained eye would know to investigate anyone in a position to clean the room. An untrained eye would think you were noting a chore for yourself. The other topic for discussion is concealment. You all have to start hiding items."

"I usually hide shit in my guitar case." Rich was the picture of boastful pride. He opened the case and revealed a false back to the lid. A small pouch was evident if one peeled back a corner of the plush shag.

Chuck shook his head. "That might work with your spare cash or your rubbers, but that's the first place a trained agent will look. That's where McIntyre and I found your weed, remember?" Chuck smiled broadly. Rich blushed, his face pink as a rose.

"Find a better place than *that*." Chuck continued. The boys laughed. Rich's face was now crimson.

"What about keeping important stuff on us, like in our wallets?" Clyde suggested.

"You wanna think about what would happen to you if you get caught? Incredulous!" Chuck looked at Clyde in a manner that was nothing short of parental loathing. Clyde was the first to break the gaze. He turned away sheepishly.

"I have an idea!" Cameron said with a smile. He pulled a book from his guitar case. For a paperback, its covers were a bit thick, almost twice the thickness of those on a telephone book. He raised the book for all to see.

"My fake book, my tablature book. What do you think? Would this work?"

"Man, we've got to do more than just hide shit in the sheet music!" Rich insisted. "Didn't you listen to the man? This is serious!"

"I know that!" Cameron was impatient. "Do you notice anything about this book? Anything at all?"

Chuck took the book from Cameron and examined it carefully, slowly thumbing through the pages, searching for anything out of the ordinary. Finally, he looked at Cameron and shrugged his shoulders. Cameron passed the fake book to the others. None of them found anything exceptional, nothing that differentiated the fake book from any other paperback.

"Watch this!" he said with a smile. Cameron chose a guitar pick from his case, then ran his fingertips over the edge of the back cover of the book, pausing midway. He waved the guitar pick with a dramatic flourish and wedged it between the cover's veneer and the matte paper comprising the cover's inner surface. After carefully sliding the pick downward an inch or two, he blew into the pocket created by separating the layers of paper. The pocket was approximately the size of postcard.

"I learned this living with an ex-girlfriend," Cameron said, beaming. "I had to hide my money from her so she wouldn't rob me blind. You just take a little Elmer's Glue and spread it on with a Q Tip and you've resealed it. Make sure your fingers are clean, grab a slightly damp tissue, and rub outward only on the shiny part because it won't soak up water. Make sure you don't have bubbles and wipe off the excess glue. Voila!" Cameron grinned at Chuck. "Would that work?"

"Like a charm!" Chuck said, after reexamining the book. "You're getting the hang of it all. That's one more thing off my list."

"What are the other things? Maybe I can help there, too!" Cameron was bursting with pride, especially after Rich pat him heartily on the back.

"Ha! Slow down, cowboy," Chuck smiled. "That'd be raising your pay grade. The next item on my agenda involves bringing you guys to the firing range. You've yet to be trained thoroughly in firearms."

Evan and Clyde shared an apprehensive glance. Neither one of them possessed a love of guns. Rich, on the other hand, was more than enthusiastic. "Why wait for a shooting range?" he said. "There's an old sand pit out past the edge of town. Why not use that?"

Chuck was exasperated. "I wouldn't draw any more attention to ourselves by violating local ordinances. As risky as it is not having you guys armed, it's a bigger risk to train you somewhere other than a range. It would raise too many questions, questions I don't want any of us to answer."

Cameron was apprehensive. The unexpected turn in conversation bothered him. He wasn't afraid of guns; he had owned and used many in his life and, until shortly before his recruitment, he actually carried a four-inch Colt Woodsman in his guitar case. What startled Cameron was Chuck's abrupt concern about the band's need to carry. They'd functioned well and unarmed until now. For Chuck to suddenly decide that the band should carry weapons meant that the current situation was much more serious than he'd indicated. He caught Chuck's eye, and cast a silent query.

Chuck sighed wearily. "For now, we keep our eyes open and stick together. We'll do this gig and get the hell out of here. We've got access to the police barracks in Columbia. I'll get you onto their range, and get you guys issued."

As the band members disassembled their equipment, each shared their experiences with firearms. Chuck pretended not to pay attention, but hung on their every word. To his relief, all of the Roadhouse Sons were well acquainted with firearms, and circumspect about proper use. He wouldn't be burdened with worry about mindless gangster cowboy posturing. Admittedly, that very image had bothered Chuck, especially since he and McIntyre had decided to upgrade the boys' credentials.

The boys continued loading the truck, chattering among themselves. Chuck watched them. He wondered once again if he'd made the right decision undertaking this mission. The state of affairs had progressed more rapidly, and in a different direction than Chuck had anticipated. Now the boys needed to be further trained in surveillance and information protection, and they needed to be armed at all times.

Chuck was reticent about continuing. Should he halt the mission and let the Roadhouse Sons return to their regular lives? They were not yet agents. None of them carried a badge and, therefore, were not actually protected in their service to the agency, despite their willingness to be subject to the caprice of danger. Incredibly, even though the boys knew the risks involved, they tried their best not to complain. Maybe Chuck didn't give them enough credit.

"Shake it off," he mumbled to himself. He lifted a Marshall amp and brought it to Snapper, who was loading the truck.

Suddenly, Cameron, who'd been breaking down mic stands, stopped dead in his tracks.

"Psst! Someone's outside the window!" he whispered. Chuck stilled himself, pretending to dust off an amp.

"Are you sure?" he asked.

Cameron coughed, nodding almost imperceptibly. "Two men just pulled away from the window over there," he said, his voice low. He quickly finished loading the mic stands and pulled cables and chords. To any casual observer, he was merely performing his usual tasks.

Chuck moved the amp further into the back of the truck. He slid the Marshall toward Snapper and Rich.

"Be ready to duck behind one of these when the lights go out," Chuck warned. The two men nodded, concerned. Chuck walked down the truck's loading ramp and continued on to the side of the garage bay, pausing to seemingly joke with Evan and Clyde, who were now on alert. From the outside, it appeared that Chuck was heading to the bathrooms on the other side of the garage. Still walking casually, Chuck reached for the knob of the bathroom door with his right hand, and used his left hand to quickly reach up and lower the interior lights switch. The garage was submerged into partial darkness, an inky, vaporous cast of the day's remaining light.

Knowing that visibility was also diminished by sundown reflecting off the windows, Chuck dropped to a crouch and crawled to Cameron, who was crouched behind the amp as instructed.

"See anything more?" Chuck whispered, drawing his gun.

"No," Cameron whispered. "Not a thing."

"Are you sure you saw something before?" Chuck asked.

Cameron had endured high stress levels and resultantly frayed nerves lately. It was indeed possible that his imagination was working overtime.

"I saw something, all right," he insisted. He grabbed Chuck's arm. "Ten o'clock!"

Chuck looked to the left. He saw a male silhouette move past the window, followed by yet another shadowy form. Everyone remained silent and motionless. Within thirty seconds, they all heard an odd, scraping sound.

"Someone's trying to open the bathroom window!" Evan hissed.

The attempt was unsuccessful. Whoever was trying to break into the garage moved to another window.

"Fans?" Snapper asked, unable to hide the fear in his voice. Before anyone could answer, they all heard loud pounding on the front door. For a moment, no one moved or spoke. Chuck waited a few seconds, then moved into position, facing the door, his gun poised and ready.

Cameron felt the onset of panic. The very idea of a shootout charged through his mind the images of Dwyer's limp, lifeless body, and the pile of rubble upon Doug. He held his breath, petrified that history was about to repeat itself.

Who'll be taken this time?

The two shadows moved to yet another window, continuing their circuit around the building. One of the intruders looked inside, pressing themselves against the window. Cameron squinted, peering through the darkness.

They have a guitar!

He conducted a silent inventory of the Roadhouse Sons' instruments; all were accounted for.

"Man, I think these guys are musicians! I don't think it's those other guys who were hassling us," he whispered.

Chuck maintained his stance. "Trojan horse, Trojan Strat. What's the difference?"

You've got a point there.

The silhouettes moved to yet another window and peeked into the garage again. Chuck moved to the other side of the building.

"You all keep on eye on them on that side. I'll check to see if there're more than two of them." Cameron, too, had wondered if the two men outside were simply decoys.

Chuck crouched low and moved along the wall to the far end of the room. He moved slowly into position and glanced out the window, his gun still drawn. Chuck moved on to the next window, then entered the bathroom. He emerged after a few moments. The two figures had continued moving from window to window as well, but without Chuck's sense of urgency. Cameron wondered if there was any real and present danger, until a rock crashed through a window.

Cameron, shaken off guard, waited a moment before reacting. The rock was on the floor near the broken window, suggesting that it hadn't been thrown, but used as a tool for access to the window latch. Cameron was about to move toward the window to stop the intruders from entering when, from the corner of his eye, he saw Chuck moving toward the window, too.

He obviously had the same idea!

Chuck reached the side of the window and waited. After several moments, a hand wrapped in cloth rose up from the outside and smashed the remainder of the broken windowpane, then carefully reached in to unfasten the latch. Without moving into view from the window, Chuck swung his hand upward, swatting at the intruder's hand.

What is he holding?

Chuck slammed a tire iron on the intruder's hand. Cameron flinched as the tire iron slammed into soft flesh. The intruder yelped and screamed and withdrew his hand. The protective cloth, a shirt, as it turned out, was caught on the jagged glass. Shouts and curses from outside abounded as one of the intruders managed to snatch the shirt, then Cameron and the others heard the sounds of people running away.

Chuck and the boys remained in place, very still, anticipating possible retaliation. Two minutes passed. The intruders were gone. Chuck moved along the wall and turned the lights on.

"Find a piece of board to put over that window," Chuck called out.

Clyde and Snapper found a partial sheet of plywood that covered the window quite well, and Chuck nailed it into place.

"When we get back to the hotel, I'll call Bob and let him know what happened," Chuck said.

"Aren't you going to call the police?" Evan asked. "Wouldn't that make more sense?"

"I'll call them after I call Bob. I want to make sure someone other than the authorities knows what happened."

"Who do you think those men were?" Rich asked.

"I have no idea," Chuck admitted. "They didn't try anything more after I slammed the one man, so my gut says they aren't people we've dealt with already."

"What if they were just a couple of musicians?" Cameron asked, slightly annoyed. "What if it was just a couple of guys that wanted to jam with us?"

"Why didn't they knock on the door, then?" asked Chuck. "Why sneak around? Why destroy property? Why attempt breaking and entering?"

"They still might have just been musicians," Clyde said. "They might have just wanted to try and use our shit."

"In that case, never mind," said Cameron. Chuck looked quizzically at Cameron.

"No one touches our stuff without our approval!" Cameron justified.

Chuck smiled. "All right, men! Finish loading up as fast as you can. Let's get the hell out of here!"

The band loaded the last of the equipment into the truck.

With a heavy sigh, Chuck pulled Cameron aside. "We've really got to be on guard now."

"Now?" Cameron gasped. "Don't you mean *still?*"

"No. Things just got serious," Chuck said, stolid and resolute. "Whoever they were, we inflicted injury upon them. Rest assured. They'll be in touch again."

Cameron froze.

Great. We drew first blood.

CHAPTER NINETEEN

"Push"

Jack Quinn—"Black Jack," as he was known—was the only member of the band whom Stanley respected. He didn't actually like Jack. When completely truthful with himself, Stanley admittedly couldn't stand any of them, but at least Quinn honestly believed in his own actions and the convictions that propelled them.

Arriving in the United States from Australia at a young age, Jack Quinn soon embarked on nothing short of a familial odyssey, shuffled from one relative to another, due to his family's extreme lack of stability. His heavy accent, foreign sensibilities, and slight build all conspired to withhold the complete acceptance of any group in which he associated himself. As a result, Jack was a loner with a lot of time on his hands to think. Spare moments were spent in solitude. The chance reading of an article on Paul Ricœur subsequently led Jack through quick studies of myriad philosophers, culminating in a higher interest in Nietzsche and the enthusiastic formation of Jack's own personal nihilist philosophy.

That journey, in and of itself, shaped his appearance. The birth of Black Jack Quinn was nigh. His wardrobe, from then on, was devoid of any colors except black or white.

"It's how I see the world," Quinn once explained to a reporter. "Color is an illusion and a deception. For you or against you is all there is. There's no room for anything else in my world."

His new attitude and élan opened the door to the world of the American punk scene, which in turn fostered in Quinn a heightened interest in music. He avidly followed many of the underground punk bands and, after getting his hands on a stolen guitar, he taught himself to play the songs he heard. His talent improved rapidly and exponentially, and Quinn soon became a hot commodity to the various bands bursting onto the scene of this budding genre's landscape.

Quinn's was the classic example of life imitating art. His personality often and completely conflicted with the members of the bands in which he played. As a result, he never stayed in any place, or with any group, for very long. Even in the case of Boney Jack, by the time the band signed with Stanley, Quinn was very nearly on the verge of leaving. Despite the fact that, for the first time in his life, he no longer had to worry about how he'd find his next meal, he seemed to suffer from an internal struggle, landing him far from a sense of security and accomplishment. The band's signing to top-level management apparently caused Quinn great difficulty in reconciling his antiestablishment attitudes about working for The Man and the blessing of commercial success.

For a lesser man, Black Jack Quinn's angst would have led to toil and duress, but not for Stanley, who recognized early on that the very same traits forging Quinn's philosophy of survival also made the young fellow a supreme opportunist. Stanley was quick to exploit that.

Several philosophical discussions with Quinn convinced Stanley that the punk guitarist was in fact not troubled at all by any inner struggle; he was, rather, comforted by conflict. Stanley ensured, therefore, that Quinn's struggle never abated.

At that very moment, though, he was in the desperate throes of solving a tangible mystery, one about which Quinn and he must converse. Stanley doubted that help was on the way. Despite his best efforts, he simply hadn't been able to spend any time alone with Quinn.

Stanley searched the usual haunts and finally discovered Quinn sequestered away in his suite. Stanley's shoulders sunk when he also discovered that Quinn, once again, was not alone. The band's lead singer, Boney Jack Preston was in tow and from the aroma that assaulted Stanley's nostrils when he entered the room, the two youths had obviously partaken of illegal substances. The smell was indication enough, but Stanley's suspicions were more than confirmed when he looked into the youths' eyes. All four of their eyes were very bloodshot and their comportments very relaxed. As annoyed as Stanley was at their state, he opted to ignore it. Admonishing their behaviors would render the two defensive, which, in turn, would only make Stanley's fact-finding mission more difficult. Instead, he decided to indulge their fantasy that their own indulgence of contraband escaped his notice.

Stanley had learned long ago to hide his negative sentiments toward the band, especially his irritation. Doing so in the current circumstance enabled him to endure what he most detested—the inebriation of others, and mindless small talk. Since Stanley could avoid neither of those anathemas, he'd ruefully sacrificed an hour of valuable time prodding the young men for information. Both of them, however, were incapable of following a direct line of questioning. Stanley's hopes of forcing them to focus and provide coherent testimony were dashed. Stanley's casual enquiries were met with wordy ramblings, and no information of any value could be squeezed from the intoxicated musicians. Stanley's efforts were in vain, and the situation was taxing him incredibly.

"You don't seem to be upset by this development, this forced Seattle exile." Stanley forced a smile. He could feel his blood pressure rising.

"Why should it bother us?" Quinn grumbled languidly. "We're used to being shit on by society. Now, they just bumped it up a notch." He was completely relaxed, his taut frame stretched out and his legs dangling over the chair arms. This insouciant posture infuriated Stanley.

Boney Jack laughed maniacally at Quinn's remark. Stanley was acutely concerned. Boney Jack appeared to be nearing a complete lack of control of his faculties. This only accelerated Stanley's exhaustion and lack of patience. He was about to unleash the full force of his ire on the pair, but realized that, no matter how momentarily satisfying that would be, to do so would ultimately prevent him from garnering the information he so desperately needed. He simply pressed on.

"I know you must be frustrated with having to stay here," Stanley said, his unctuous tone apologetic. His insipid bromide elicited no response from the drug-addled musicians. "I came to assure you that this will in no way affect your performances here," Stanley continued. "We'll be able to reschedule the other shows outside the city as soon as this situation is cleared up. I'm certain that we'll get this—"

Boney Jack erupted into a fit of uncontrolled laughter.

"Situation! Did you hear that? He called it a situation. Situation! A *situation!*"

Boney Jack screeched with mirth as he chanted the phrase. Stanley's annoyance dissipated, replaced by alarm at Boney Jack's behavior. The singer's speech held its familiar slur. There was, however, something different, something amiss. Stanley moved closer to the youth, visually examining him from head to toe. On the singer's arm were several marks resembling insect bites, their redness and inflammation accentuated by Boney Jack's pale skin. This discovery confirmed Stanley's suspicions. Boney Jack had added heroin to his roster of illegal substance abuse. The young man didn't notice Stanley's scrutiny, and babbled on.

"This isn't a situation, man!" the singer expounded. "Don't you know a political exile when you see one?" Stanley knew the youth was high as a kite; nonetheless, he was still disgusted by Boney Jack's euphoria despite the subject matter.

"Political exile? How did you arrive at that conclusion?" Stanley queried, bracing himself for the usual onslaught of drunken, disoriented reasoning.

Boney Jack bolted upright, his eyes bloodshot and blazing. "The government is out to silence all opposition!" he shouted. "They're going to make an example out of us! And turn us into martyrs!"

Stanley rolled his eyes. "Martyrs for what?" he sneered.

"Martyrs for the revolution!" Boney Jack thrust a defiant fist toward the heavens. Quinn erupted with laughter, causing Boney Jack to do the same.

Stanley could barely suppress his contempt. Ignoring the singer, he turned his attention to his guitarist, who appeared to be more lucid. Stanley glanced at Quinn's arms, which revealed nothing; Quinn always wore long-sleeved shirts. He was currently, par the usual when he drank, morose and withdrawn, which Stanley observed with great relief. With Quinn imbibing in his usual manner, Stanley had an iota of a chance to pull information from the youth. That is, if Boney Jack could be kept at bay.

"How are you doing with all of this, Quinn?" Stanley asked, feigning genuine concern. Quinn shrugged, but said nothing. Stanley was relieved that Quinn responded at all.

"I ain't got nothing more to say about this shit," Quinn mumbled, yawning and stretching his legs.

"Then would you mind if I talk about something other than the case? I was wondering if I could ask you about your visits with Mr. Collier?"

Quinn just sat in his chair. Stanley was about to repeat the question when the guitar player finally spoke.

"Who?" Quinn replied sleepily.

"Mr. *Collier*," Stanley insisted. "You remember. The agent from Los Angeles? He said he had bands with whom we could work."

Quinn ignored Stanley; instead, he just stared at his hands, occasionally running his fingers along the lines on his palms.

Boney Jack giggled spasmodically. "The guy with the shifty eyes," Boney Jack said, sotto voce. "The one that was going to make us famous, the most famous band in the world! We just couldn't say anything to anyone about it."

"He was full of shit!" Quinn slurred. "We're already fucking famous. I'm glad he's gone. Bullshit artist."

"How was he going to make you famous?" Stanley delved, laughing with forced camaraderie.

Boney Jack attempted to rise, but fell back into his chair. His expression was one of genuine shock. He just sat there with his head back, staring at the ceiling. Stanley's gut wrenched with panic. His distress waned when the singer suddenly began to laugh.

"We're already famous!" Boney Jack hissed, wild-eyed. Stanley fought the urge to shudder. Boney Jack's features were more wan and pale than usual. His sunken eyes even more so caused him to resemble that of a Dia de los Muertos calavera.

"Didn't you hear?" Boney Jack whispered, staring at Stanley with an evil grin. Stanley recoiled instantly, unable to hide his repugnance. The singer delighted in Stanley's reaction.

"Didn't you hear? I'm the Scourge of God!"

Stanley stared at him, dumbfounded. "You're what?" he stammered. Suddenly, though, he remembered Boney Jack's television interview on the local morning news. A local minister was leading a protest against the band and their music, branding them "agents of the Devil," and labeling the lead singer and his namesake band the "Scourges of God." Stanley hadn't paid much attention to it; that was the typical drama invoked by the band's critics. Stanley had heard it ad infinitum and ad nauseum, including from coattailers who tried to fashion obscene symbioses with the band in hopes of drawing attention to their various causes.

Boney Jack had seen the interview and Stanley realized that, far from being angered by the appellation, the singer deemed it a badge of honor, and one worthy of perpetuating.

"So, who needs Collier?" Despite the gargantuan effort to rise from his chair, the singer managed it and thrust a defiant fist into the air. "Why should the Scourge of God waste time with someone too scared to be seen in public?"

Boney Jack's booming declaration and pious stance reminded Stanley of a revivalist preacher. For just a moment, he wondered if Boney Jack was imitating the local preacher who'd bestowed him his new title.

"That fucker Collier was always afraid we'd been followed when we met him," Black Jack Quinn suddenly grumbled.

"Why was he worried about that?" Stanley felt sure that the revelation he so desperately sought was just moments away.

Quinn shrugged and yawned. "He said he'd been followed, but he thought he shook them. He always met us at odd times, and would never say what he wanted us for. Bastard never even wanted us to play. He just listened to our tapes and ran his mouth."

"What about?" As anxious as he was, Stanley resisted the urge to press aggressively for more information. The clandestine nature of the band's meetings with Collier, and Collier's fear that he was possibly being under surveillance, alarmed Stanley. He knew, though, that as addled as the two musicians may be, an impatient lack of finesse in his questioning could derail their train of thought, and the information could be lost in perpetuity.

"What did Collier run on about?" Stanley repeated.

"Nothing," Quinn snarled. "He never talked about anything, just food and TV and movies and fans." Stanley was perplexed.

"He didn't ever say why he wanted to speak with you?"

"Fuck, no!" Quinn stumbled over to the wet bar and grabbed an unopened bottle of whiskey. "He kept asking us to come see him, but all he ever did was waste our fucking time!"

Stanley just sat still, utterly nonplussed. Collier had purportedly established new connections for the band, and Stanley had managed to withhold that fact from the police. Collier had spent all of that time meeting with the band, and never established any plan concrete in nature.

Stanley couldn't let up, but could he trust the drunk musician's word? He needed more information, and he had to finally push for it. Time was of the essence.

"What did Collier discuss with you?"

Quinn's eyes were clearly out of focus. Stanley comforted himself with the hopeful notion that the guitar player was sufficiently inebriated to forget that the question was repeated a third time.

"Small talk," Quinn sneered. "Waste of time. Where were we staying, what we liked to eat, what we liked to watch on TV, what we liked to drink, were we followed...shit like that."

"Followed?" asked Stanley, throwing caution to the wind. "Why did he wonder if any of you or he were followed?"

Collier had the reputation of being a nervous type, but his peers knew that he was also circumspect, and instinctively able to avoid attracting attention. Why was he so suddenly and inordinately worried about being discovered, and enough so to mention this—to the band?

"Was he worried about reporters or groupies?" Stanley urged. Quinn swayed and gripped the edge of the wet bar to steady himself.

"I don't know, man. He said something about someone bothering him in LA. I heard him telling someone on the phone that he ditched whoever it was in Tacoma but thought they might have tracked him here. Probably someone he owed money to, or fucked over. Typical manager."

With growing anxiety, Stanley realized that Collier had felt so threatened that he employed great lengths to avoid those surveilling him, yet was uncharacteristically careless in mentioning his fears to the band. That could explain his unscheduled trip to Tacoma, but explained nothing else. A new question was raised by Collier's action. Who was on the receiving end of the mysterious phone call? In whom was Collier confiding?

Quinn staggered back to his chair and collapsed. He placed the whiskey bottle next to his feet and closed his eyes.

As if on cue, Boney Jack hissed demonically. "Mysterious men in dark cars!" He cackled at his own remark. Stanley couldn't decide if Boney Jack actually frightened him, or merely repulsed him.

"What does that mean?" Stanley queried.

The singer cackled uncontrollably and ignored Stanley, then suddenly stood up and fell upon him, grabbing from behind and loudly and unintelligibly prattled on in Stanley's ear.

With a piercing cry, Stanley spewed obscenities at Boney Jack, and disentangled himself from the inebriated singer, who collapsed on the floor. Boney Jack ranted and gurgled maniacally.

Stanley had reached his limit. "Just once, I'd like a conversation with you while you're *sober!*" He stormed from the room, slamming the door on the Scourge of God's uncontrollable, shrieking laughter.

CHAPTER TWENTY

"Off Limits"

Cameron approached the performance without his usual enthusiasm.

Instead of the joyful anticipation of homecoming, he was stepping into the belly of the beast. No reprisals had occurred as a result of the encounter at the garage several days prior, suggesting to the other band members that the harrowing debacle may have been an isolated incident. However, while Chuck didn't share this sentiment, he wouldn't elaborate on why he felt otherwise. That, more than anything else, made Cameron uneasy.

Another shoe's about to drop.

As promised, Chuck called Bob Larabee and divulged to him the entire incident.

"You better let me call the police," the old man suggested. "It'll be better for me to make the complaint. Otherwise, you might be accused of initiating it." Chuck didn't argue, and Cameron's disquiet over the situation increased.

He had no idea whether the police had investigated the incident. No one interviewed him, nor did anyone offer statements. He therefore suspected that the police had altogether ignored the episode or, perhaps, had actually tipped off whomever was harassing the band. Despite his misgivings, the band continued to rehearse at the garage without further interruptions.

Cameron wondered if he and the band had overreacted. Their antagonists could have been a rambunctious group of musicians simply wanting to jam with the Roadhouse Sons. However, purportedly spontaneous visits to "pick up a few things" by Bob Larabee and his cronies, revealed to Cameron that the building was under protective surveillance. Despite Bob's good intentions, Cameron felt no relief, and his apprehension increased tenfold. When the show date was finally upon him, Cameron felt nothing but dread.

The boys and Chuck piled into their various vehicles and followed Chuck's directions to the venue. Once there, everyone other than Cameron was thrilled to discover that they were going to perform in a typical roadhouse. He wasn't elated at all. He worried that the locals would greet them with a cool, if not icy, reception, and his anxiety wasn't unfounded. As the boys entered the roadhouse, no one spoke to them, other than to tell them where to set up their equipment. The staff's repeatedly unfriendly treatment of the boys didn't make things easier; the mere act of buying a drink initiated harsh rudeness and glares of disdain.

The venue's atmosphere exacerbated the situation. The jukebox played a Lynyrd Skynyrd song, and there were several posters advertising a cancelled wrestling show. A promotional picture of the Roadhouse Sons was taped over a wrestling poster, and the word "bullshit" was scribbled over the boys' faces.

This does not bode well.

The interior hall was a very large room. It was dimly lit, and neon beer signs shone like constellations in a honkytonk sky. Pool tables were positioned in a brightly lit area at the back of room, and there were several tables and chairs set up between the pool tables and the dance floor. The air was thick with the smell of smoke, booze, stale popcorn, and whatever swill was being served from the small kitchen behind the bar.

For the first time in his life, Cameron weighed the possibilities and repercussions of walking out the door. Knowing in his heart that to do so would make matters worse, he said a silent prayer to the music deities and helped the boys unload the truck.

Cameron was only mildly relieved to see that the band was to perform behind a barrier of chicken wire.

At least we can't be slammed with beer bottles.

He realized that projectiles could be the least of his problems.

Chicken wire isn't bulletproof glass…

He walked to the jukebox. Rich slid beside him.

"At least it's not playing '*There Stands the Glass*,'" Rich muttered. Cameron looked up to see his bass player sporting a silly grin. Despite his mood, Cameron couldn't help but smile in agreement; nothing would bother him more than that boozy lament.

Chuck approached the duo. "Everything all right?"

Cameron nodded, rolling his eyes.

"Just unload this stuff and set up your equipment," Chuck had told them when they arrived. "Don't talk to anyone. Don't interact with anyone. Just focus on this show. Got it?"

The boys reluctantly assured Chuck that they understood his edict, but Cameron bristled at the thought.

We're not just musicians. We're showmen. Especially me.

The Roadhouse Sons interacted with the crowd as a matter of nature. Guests of the band never doubted that the performance they witnessed was in their honor. For the audience as a whole, the band always made a point of inviting the crowd to be part of the show, unlike some of the other bands who, while arguably considered the best in the business, always made the audience members feel like they'd crashed a private party. Cameron hated the feel of those kinds of shows—despite his supreme respect for those musicians—and prided himself on the welcome and appreciation that his band bestowed upon the audience. The idea of being forced to behave like snobbish, aloof celebrities absolutely incensed him, and that demeanor was exactly what he was expected to impart.

On the other hand...

Cameron pondered the dilemma and delineated the facts of the situation. The band was to perform and keep to themselves. Despite the band's enthusiasm about performing in a roadhouse, it was a crappy, seedy venue. The band's reception by the locals and other denizens was so rude and unaccepting that the band would lose nothing by returning the behavior.

It's the perfect time to try something new...get out of hand...let everything go completely and irretrievably to fuckin' hell!

Cameron kept his epiphany to himself. He helped Snapper unload the Marshall stacks from the truck and began connecting cables. He deliberately avoided eye contact with the patrons, who were gathering to watch the band set up. Cameron mused at how fascinated people were with the bands set-up procedure.

We're monkeys in a zoo.

He double-checked the cables and extension cords at the power outlets, ensured that his equipment was functioning properly, and asked Snapper to assist the other band members with their monitor cabling. Cameron focused on the tasks at hand, seemingly paying no attention to his surroundings, but he remained acutely aware of the people gathering around the edge of the dance floor. In particular, he kept in his peripheral vision anyone walking toward the cage. Under the guise of seeking an extra cable, he moved closer to the exit.

Never know how fast we'll have to get away.

Two men approached the area near the chicken wire at the stage. Cameron didn't recognize them. They weren't anyone he'd seen during his arrest or at the American Legion. The men said nothing. They just stood there, watching the band set up. Finally, one of them pressed his face against the chicken wire and waved to garner Cameron's attention.

"Hey, buddy!" whispered the man, sotto voce. Cameron pretended to ignore the man, who more loudly repeated his question. Cameron had no choice but to acknowledge him.

"Yeah?"

"With your hair so long, I was wondering if you squat to pee!" The man and his friend burst into laughter and sauntered away.

Cameron groaned.

It's gonna be like this all night…

Cameron slammed the cables to the floor. He went outside to the truck, where he saw Chuck who'd, judging from his expression, overheard the exchange. So had the Roadhouse Sons.

"I don't need to say don't let them get to you," Chuck said. "But—"

"But don't let them get to us," Evan finished.

Chuck grinned and nodded. Cameron glared at them. Chuck gave Cameron a paternal pat on the back.

"I have a few rules for tonight," Chuck continued. "First off, all drink orders go through me. You don't deal with the waitresses, and you certainly don't let anyone in the crowd buy you a drink."

The boys grumbled and sputtered in protest. Chuck raised both hands.

"This is not up for negotiation! This venue is risky. We don't want to take any chances on anyone slipping you a mickey. Remember Burlington? I do!"

"So much for the iota of fun we'd have in this shithole," Clyde muttered.

No interaction. No booze. No nothing. Why bother?

"I'm not regulating how much you can drink, just how you acquire it. Are we ready for sound check?" With a nod of his head, Chuck beckoned the band inside.

The boys reluctantly conceded and readied for their performance. Cameron seethed.

The sound check was no better than load-in. Cameron's two "fans" made catcalls and repeatedly disparaged the band's musical prowess. Cameron ignored them and indulged in his fantasies of revenge.

I'd love to put that guy's face through an amp!

The situation worsened when the two men incited other onlookers to blow kisses at the boys. The air was thick with tension and, as show time approached, each of the band members was in fight-or-flight mode. Chuck bought one stiff drink for each of them. It didn't help. Alcohol wasn't going to temper the adrenaline coursing through their collective veins.

Cameron watched with detached interest as the hall filled with patrons. Some, however, were more attractive than he expected. He nodded politely to several female patrons and waitresses who wandered by and finally bestowed upon him an appreciative glance.

Off limits...

As Cameron had recently revealed to Chuck, he longed for some amorous entanglements, and was ready to rip down the chicken wire with his bare hands. But the desire for affection soon turned to disgust, as some of the more rambunctious patrons, encouraged by their giggling girlfriends, tossed peanuts and popcorn through the gaps in the wire. Instinctively, Cameron turned to tell Doug to take care of it. He lost his breath when he remembered that their former roadie was no longer there.

He'd never tolerate this crap.

Cameron's emotions welled.

Maintain...showing your heart on your sleeve in this crowd would be deadly.

He stormed through the back door.

Just have a cigarette...

After several minutes, the boys joined Cameron. Discontent filled the air, thicker than the cigarette smoke.

Rich, ever the happiest to gripe first, offered his take on their circumstances.

"If we hadn't agreed to do this to help Bob out, I'd say load all this shit back into the truck."

No one argued, but all of the boys admitted that it was out of the question to dishonor the image of the members of the American Legion.

"They did get us this gig," Snapper said quietly.

"It'll be pulling teeth to get through it," Clyde smirked.

"What song do you want to open with?" Evan asked, twirling his drumstick between his fingers like a miniature baton.

"I have no fucking idea," grumbled Rich. "I can't figure this place out. They've got Jim Reeves *and* Lynyrd Skynyrd on the jukebox. And some old blues tunes. Haven't heard much of our type of music."

"Yes, you have!" Cameron smiled. "You just didn't notice. They like Skynyrd? OK, we give them Skynyrd." Cameron sang, "With a girl named Linda Lou—"

"'Gimme Three Steps'!" Rich yelled. "Yeah!"

"Everything else we take from our last set list. Fuck 'em!"

The Roadhouse Sons stepped over the threshold and back onto the stage. Chicken wire notwithstanding, Cameron stepped up to the mic and introduced the band. His speech was met with a disappointing mixture of polite applause from some patrons, catcalls from others, and aggravated silence from the rest. This neither surprised nor bothered Cameron; he'd played tough rooms before and, despite his earlier misgivings, now welcomed the challenge. The previous tensions and related grumblings subsided as he looked out over the crowd and the band struck their first chords.

The staff had dimmed the lights. Cameron couldn't discern individual faces, but the hall was filled by a mass of silhouettes.

At least lots of people came out...

No one was on the dance floor yet, but that didn't surprise Cameron, either. No one ever danced the first dance. The boys played easily, caressing from their instruments every beat, every note, and every syllable of the lyrics. Cameron sang, albeit with slightly less fervor than usual. Forced indifference cramped his style.

Love me or hate me, I'm a pro either way.

He stepped aside as the boys indulged in brief, impromptu solos. The gig offered them the opportunity to relax. At the very least, they were enjoying their own music despite the lack of joy in the circumstances. When the song concluded, the boys were greeted with increased enthusiasm and louder applause. Enlivened by the audience's minimally cordial response, the band continued on, playing songs by The Doors, The Allman Brothers Band, and The Rolling Stones. The boys relaxed and the audience responded accordingly. The dance floor crowded as more patrons vied for space to let their hair down. Chuck supplied the boys with a steady supply of libations, having conspired with the club owners to bring the band a washtub filled with ice and bottled beer.

For Cameron, maintaining detachment from the audience was pure anathema. He cheated, occasionally calling out to the dancing patrons, but allowed himself no conversations, despite the various faces pressed against the chicken wire, demanding his attention. Upon realizing that they were being ignored, the patrons would scuttle away, sheepish from their efforts in futility.

"'Turn the Page.' Bob Seger," Cameron mouthed over his shoulder.

I need that song...

Cameron's rendition of the piece was the complete embodiment of the frustration and angst in the original composition. When he sang the line, "Is that a woman or a man?" someone in the crowd shouted "Yeah!" Cameron couldn't see who it was, but figured it was the man who'd insulted him earlier. Cameron was able to shrug it off, an easy feat, as the audience continually clapped louder and longer, and the catcalls diminished almost entirely.

As the band's set progressed, the crowd's enthusiasm was contagious. The boys were so enthralled with performing that they didn't at first notice Chuck standing off to the side, pointing to his watch to signal the end of the first set. Despite his exhaustion and thirst, Cameron was reluctant to stop, but nodded his acknowledgment to Chuck. His shirt was soaked with sweat and he knew he'd have to change into another one. He stepped up to the mic.

"Thank you! We're gonna take a short break and we'll be back in about ten minutes!"

He handed his guitar to Snapper and stepped outside. The fresh air was a welcome change from the hot lights of the stage and the cigarette smoke invading the hall. Cameron leaned against the wall and closed his eyes. He was soothed; the day's earlier anxieties were becoming distant memories.

Playing my music. Back in my world.

He reveled in the feeling of relief, ever grateful for the dissipating strain. As the tension eased from his body, he marveled at just how cramped his shoulder and back muscles had become. He rolled his head around releasing the compression in his neck. He heard someone approaching from behind, but with eyes closed and head rotating, he continued his self-massage.

"I'll be back inside in a minute. Check the tuning on my guitar, all right?"

"Hey there." Cameron heard a sweet, melodic voice.

He reeled around, admonishing himself for not remembering to never leave his back exposed.

That was not his roadie. He was acutely aware that a woman had sidled up next to him, just inches away. His very nerve endings could feel her.

The vision before him was a perfect match to the sound that had just graced his ears.

Holy...

The glow of the stage door lamp cast just enough light upon her.

She's as tall as I am!

Her wavy brown hair fell past her shoulders, and she had feathered bangs, which beautifully framed her face. Her brown eyes matched her hair, and her endearing smile was alit with lovely dimples. She wore a form-fitting white blouse and denim jeans stretched over her curvaceous hips. A heart-shaped pendant, like an arrow, pointed directly to her cleavage. She wore no makeup that he could see, but the look in her eye revealed that she was anything but a wholesome girl next door. Despite her obvious experience, Cameron respected her confidence.

"My name's Chastity," she smiled. "I really like your music."

"Thank you." Cameron smiled sincerely. "I really like the irony."

"The Doors are my favorite band," she continued, ignoring his jest. She leaned on the wall, situating herself next to him. She turned to face him head on, and feigning shyness, ran a fingernail down his chest. Cameron was mortified that he still donned his sweaty tee shirt.

I should get my other shirt.

As he stepped toward the truck, Chastity spoke. Cameron froze.

"I saw them, you know," she said, leaning into him. Her face was just inches from his.

If my sweat bothers her, she sure isn't showing it.

"The Doors?" he asked, smiling gingerly. He swallowed hard.

Keep your cool!

Cameron knew that his answer wasn't the most profound, but he doubted that she was there for an erudite conversation.

"Yeah..." Chastity ran her fingernail up to his chin. Cameron fought the shudder he felt rising from his core. "But not with Jim Morrison. I saw the band they did afterwards."

"The Butts Band?" Cameron asked. His smile widened, not only at the humorous moniker that Robby Krieger and John Densmore bestowed upon the former Doors, but at how apropos it was to Chastity's curves.

"Mmmm," she cooed, nodding. "I like the Butts."

"I'm a breast man, myself," Cameron cooed in response. Chastity's gold heart glistened as it arose and descended with her breathing. She drew a deep and deliberate breath, then slowly exhaled. Cameron raised an eyebrow in appreciation.

"Can I make a request?"

Cameron said nothing. He didn't want to appear eager. She continued to caress his neck and cheek with her fingertips. Cameron slipped his arm around her waist. He could smell her perfume, a floral fragrance that he couldn't place, but one that he definitely liked. She slipped her free arm around his neck and continued fluttering her fingers over his lips and eyes.

"Do you know anything by Grand...Ffffffunk?"

Chastity hung on the F sound so pointedly and forced the K with such finality that Cameron almost laughed at her blatancy.

Geez Louise, I could have her right here!

Chastity kissed Cameron on the lips with such intensity that he was compelled to pull away.

Can't get riled up now...gotta perform.

His lips stuck to hers. Despite the taste of synthetic strawberry from her lip gloss, he couldn't help but conjure an image of lying nude with her in a field under the summer sun.

Suddenly, Cameron heard the sound of footsteps approaching. Snapper and the others were leaving the stage area. They were about to join him when they saw he wasn't alone. Quickly, they retreated to the other side of the truck. Chastity, undaunted by the interruption, kissed Cameron's neck. Cameron was about to return her kiss when they were interrupted again, this time by Chuck.

"Hey, there!" Chuck said. His voice was loud and jovial and, to Cameron, downright annoying.

"Thought you might want this," Chuck said, handing him a beer. Chuck carried a small bucket filled with bottles.

Interrupting me on purpose... I wouldn't put it past you.

"Would you like one?" Cameron smiled at Chastity. She helped herself to one of the bottles. Chuck smiled and offered her his hand. He politely asked her name and engaged in small talk. Just as quickly as he'd appeared, he dropped her hand and veered toward the others.

Chastity caught Cameron's eye, raised the bottle to her lips, and slowly inserted the entire neck of the bottle into her mouth. She removed it and took a demure sip of beer. Cameron squeezed her hip and was about to whisper into her ear when Chuck came barreling around the side of the truck, yelling at full volume.

"Break's over! Let's go! Show time!"

I hate you.

Cameron was mad with lust, and frustrated that he didn't have the chance to divulge the scenarios deluging through his mind. Chuck bounded through the doorway and back onstage. The rest of the band straggled by, one by one. The boys employed a nonchalant manner of disregard; if they didn't look directly at Cameron, they weren't violating his privacy.

Cameron gave Chastity a quick kiss on the lips.

"Duty calls," he whispered. She pouted and tugged on his shirt, giving him a final kiss before letting him go. She walked away, turning only once to smile and wave before disappearing into the darkness.

Cameron stretched, shaking off his delirium.

Settle down, boy!

He guzzled the rest of his beer and returned to his place on stage. The boys greeted him with smiles, winks, and various hand gestures.

Damn it! I still didn't change my shirt!

Loud applause resounded as Snapper worked the lights, signaling the return of the band. Cameron reviewed the set list. They'd chosen two songs by Grand Funk. He grappled with himself over playing them early on. He decided against it. He'd been on the circuit long enough to avoid being creatively swayed by a groupie. The song list continued as planned.

The crowd was much more responsive than they were earlier in the evening. Cameron couldn't decide if he'd relaxed, or if the audience had.

Doesn't matter. They're dancing and getting into it.

He looked out over the crowd and saw Chastity's white blouse swaying around the dance floor. She danced among a group of girls who were as enthusiastic about the band as she was.

Maybe Chuck won't make us wait 'til Columbia...

Cameron quivered with anticipation, but knew that his standard moves disguised it. He turned to see Clyde gyrating lasciviously toward the crowd. Several young women vied appreciatively for Clyde's attention. The sight never ceased to amuse Cameron; Clyde loved every second of it and played up to the girls in comic proportions. Rich, their occasional curmudgeon, was more animated than usual, and Evan pounded out his licks with great enthusiasm.

This isn't so bad after all.

As Cameron approached the mic, he saw Chuck speaking with someone he didn't recognize. It was obvious, though, that Chuck knew the fellow. After a few moments, the two men separated. As the band concluded their song, Snapper appeared at Cameron's elbow with a note that read: *Need to make an announcement. Take a short break.*

"OK, folks!" Cameron said. "We're going to take a short break. I think someone's got an announcement to make. Isn't that right, Chuck?"

Chuck made his way to the entrance of the stage and, bypassing the chicken wire, stepped up to the microphone. Cameron, grateful for the round of applause he received, introduced Chuck as the band's manager.

"Thank you, everybody!" Chuck said, his manner still jovial. "I hope you're all having a great time. I know you were probably counting on a wrestling show—"

The rear of the hall erupted into an unruly series of loud whistles and cheers. Chuck, undaunted, paused briefly to allow the raucous din to subside. He proceeded with his speech, reminding the audience that they were assembled not only for a good time, but for a good cause. He introduced the man with whom Cameron had seen him speaking just moments ago.

"Hello, folks!" the man said. The squeal of feedback from the microphone interrupted him. Cameron stepped forward and touched the man's shoulders, moving him a few steps backward from the mic. The man shuffled uncomfortably, as though expecting the microphone to take on a life of its own.

"Many of you know me. My name's Brody Aldrich. I'm with the local American Legion."

Brody spoke in the staccato manner employed by an exceedingly self-conscious person. He explained that the Legion was holding another fundraiser to support the war effort, and he encouraged the audience to buy war bonds. Brody briefly described his service in Vietnam, reiterating to the crowd the importance of the Legion's substantive mission, and thanked the attendees for their continued support. He stated, with incredible sincerity, that he hoped everyone was having a good time, and discussed the details of the Legion's raffle. Brody cited that the first- and second-place winners would receive a side of beef.

"Yeah! Beef!" shouted someone from the back.

Brody blushed, and continued.

"Tip your waitresses and tip your glasses!" he said, proud of his bon mot.

Knowing that he'd reached the apex of his oratorical impact, he walked away from the microphone. Happy to receive a substantial round of applause, Brody beckoned Cameron to the mic.

Cameron enthusiastically shook Brody's hand and called for another round of applause. The crowd eagerly obliged. Cameron consulted the set list. The next song couldn't have been more perfect. It appealed to patriotic fervor and to Chastity's request. Cameron turned from the mic and called out to the Roadhouse Sons.

"'American Band'!"

He felt the thrill of anticipation as Evan marked time with his drumsticks, starting the riff that signaled the countdown to the guitars. Cameron felt as though he would burst. The others felt it, too. Passion washed over each of them. They were buoyed along, propelled in a manner that none of them had ever before experienced with this piece. The dance floor filled so quickly that Cameron wondered if the boys should play the song again.

Chastity moved toward the front, her white blouse a will-o'-the-wisp, flashing ethereally through the crowd. She made her way to the stage and positioned herself, chicken wire notwithstanding, right in front of the band. Cameron watched as she grabbed the wire, twisting and arching her back seductively. He enjoyed it immensely, though had to admit to himself that she was indeed quite brazen.

Look at everyone. Don't single her out…

If nothing else, Cameron was a consummate professional. Still, though, he was a professional who welcomed perks. He engaged in just enough eye contact with Chastity to keep their mutual interest alive. She rewarded him with suggestive smiles, lip licking, flashes of her ample cleavage, and wiggles of her delicious posterior.

God bless Grand Funk!

The Roadhouse Sons concluded the song to thunderous applause. With barely a second to rest, the band immediately launched into Jimi Hendrix's *"Red House."* Snapper snuck out from behind the lights to contribute his skills on the harmonica. Just as Cameron had hoped, the dance floor filled with lively ladies anxious to demonstrate their best vamp moves. Chastity upheld the front, surrounded by several of her sycophantic female friends.

As the set progressed, Cameron realized that the clock was working against them. It was almost time to end the gig; no one wanted to be out after curfew. Reluctantly, Cameron called the last song of the evening, one that he felt was highly appropriate. He strummed the opening chords of Grand Funk Railroad's *"Some Kind of Wonderful."* He searched the dance floor for Chastity and ruminated on the usual and likely scenarios. She would innocently linger about as the band disassembled their gear. Suddenly, she'd discover that she was stranded without a ride home, or realize that her gas rations were in jeopardy. Somehow, she'd conjure an excuse that would explain why he must justify to Chuck that there was no other choice but to bring her back to the motel.

She followed me home, Chuck. Can I keep her?

Fortunately, Evan was the lead singer on the piece. Cameron provided only harmony and the onus of selling the song to the masses was not upon him. As the song ended, Cameron searched for the vision that was Chastity. He saw her curvy silhouette walking across the dance floor, away from the stage.

She's got her arm around some other guy!

With a sunken heart, he saw that his unwitting competitor had an arm around her waist, too. The man's hand was in a plaster cast.

Cameron was bitter. Bitter and enraged, and more so than when he arrived.

Are you surprised? She's just another cock tease groupie. Get over it.

He unplugged his guitar from the amp and threw the cable onto the floor. He stored his guitar in its case and secured the latches. Evan, Clyde, and Rich, intent on disassembling their gear and packing the truck, didn't notice Cameron's distress. Snapper did, but he knew better than to hover if Cameron's jaw was clenching.

The load-out proceeded at its regular pace, but to Cameron, it felt like an eternity. He heard the laughter of several patrons still hanging about, and for a moment was sure that he heard Chastity. He didn't look for her. If it was Chastity, he'd be damned if he was going to give her something else to laugh at.

Snapper stored each piece of equipment in its designated spot in the truck, ensuring that no shifting of the cargo would occur during transit. Cameron enjoyed watching this part of the process. It was clear-cut and direct; unlike performing, there was nothing left to caprice. Each amp, each drum, each mic stand, each guitar all fit perfectly into its place.

Chuck came outside to help. He'd collected the band's fee and was gathering the last of the guitar cases when Cameron walked away and headed toward the stage.

"Hey!" Chuck hissed. "Come 'ere."

Cameron walked back to his manager. Chuck gave Cameron his guitar case and sympathetically shook his head.

"Groupies haven't been the same since Miss Pamela and the GTOs quit."

"Oh! I suppose you knew Miss Pamela?" Cameron sneered.

Chuck smiled wryly. "We've enjoyed each other's company on occasion. Somewhere, I think I still have that velvet shirt she made me."

Cameron gasped and his jaw dropped.

"You're full of fucking surprises, aren't you?"

"No pun intended," Chuck grinned, and broke into hearty laughter. He loved it when he actually shocked the boys. It was a rare occurrence, but beauteous to him.

"Next, I suppose you're going to tell me you knew Cynthia."

"That didn't work out. Let's just say plaster can be very cold, and leave it at that, all right?"

Cameron shook his head in stunned amazement. "One of these days, you are coming clean. I have got to hear this story!"

Chuck laughed even louder. "If the Vietcong couldn't get it out of me, what are your chances?" He headed toward the cab of the truck. Cameron followed like an adoring fan.

"They probably tried torturing you. Come on! Tell me! I'll just keep annoying you 'til you do." Chuck guffawed.

"Go do the idiot check and make sure we've got everything."

Cameron returned to the stage area and quickly examined every square foot. Nothing was left behind. The boys didn't bring any lights. The spotlights used during the performance were part of the house's lighting system. They were powered on, fully blazing.

Shit! Turn those off. What a waste.

Cameron suddenly noticed that there were patrons still lingering in the hall, but they'd stopped talking and laughing. He became acutely aware that he was standing in full view of the people who, due to the bright spotlights in his eyes, could see him better than he could see them. He moved about, conducting a final check of the stage area, and turned to leave. The spotlights were suddenly powered off. Cameron was plunged into darkness. It happened so fast that he was momentarily blinded and, he realized with great apprehension, completely vulnerable.

Cameron couldn't see. He rubbed his eyes, opening and closing them tightly. His vision was returning. He happened to look over his shoulder and espied the silhouettes of men gathered at the bar. All of them were facing in his direction. It appeared that they were moving toward the stage.

Are my eyes playing tricks…?

Cameron stumbled. Regaining his balance, he fled from the stage and returned to the truck.

No way I'm staying in there alone.

"All clear?" asked Chuck.

"All clear!" Cameron replied. With Cameron's nod, Snapper pulled the truck door down and locked it. The boys were already in the van waiting for the truck to pull up behind them. The small caravan proceeded from the Cattleman's Club. No one looked back. Had they glanced for just a moment, they would have noticed several shadowy figures in a car, watching them leave. Those persons were not alone, however. They, too, were being watched.

No one had noticed the figure clinging to the underside of the Roadhouse Sons' truck.

CHAPTER TWENTY-ONE

"An Icy Chill"

"You're lying," Stanley said. He looked Simms directly in the eye as he spoke, his voice devoid of emotion or warmth. Simms was oddly defiant, not his customarily acquiescent self. Stanley, though quite curious about it, was experienced enough to know that Simms' behavior was no cause for concern. Simms demeanor of late was increasingly resistant. The change was subtle, but indeed noticeable, and Stanley wondered how and if Simms' comportment would shift in the days to come.

"I'm telling you the truth!" Simms voice cracked. He pounded his fist on the desk. "Collier never mentioned anything about anyone following him from Los Angeles or Tacoma, or anywhere for that matter! I cannot, for the life of me, believe that you would give any credence to the drunken ramblings of those two cretins! Especially over *me*! This is incredible!"

Stanley puffed his chest and straightened his jacket lapels. He raised his head and glared down his nose at the man seated in front of him. Simms instinctively recoiled and sunk into the back of his leather chair. Simms' display of trepidation pleased Stanley to no end, and the latter intended to capitalize on it.

"Concerns about my rationality or competence are ill placed," Stanley sniffed menacingly. He leaned into his colleague's face. "Especially if you expect me to believe that Collier would mention something of this nature only to us."

Simms gripped the arms of his chair. "But he must have, if the musicians are telling the truth. He certainly said nothing to me!"

"Despite the perceptions of him in the music world, Collier was no fool," Stanley said, imperiously towering over Simms. "He had been involved in this business nearly as long as I have. In fact, I was one of his mentors when he first came to the West Coast. If he had something of prime importance to reveal, such as being followed or threatened, he would have done so, and with someone he could trust to manage the situation. Obviously, I should have been contacted. But I wasn't, was I? Can you explain that?"

"I don't believe—"

"You don't believe what?" Stanley barked. His eyes flashed umber as he lunged toward his assistant. Simms flinched. Stanley felt a rush of satisfaction. "You don't believe that I could manage this? You don't believe that Collier would have come to me? What? What don't you believe?"

"I don't believe he was being followed in the first place."

Stanley was stunned. Mustering his vitriol, he sneered at Simms. "Why?"

"For the very reason you just mentioned!" Simms was so nervous that spittle dribbled unnoticed from his mouth. "He said nothing to you, and he said nothing to me. We only have their word that he said anything at all!" With complete derision, Simms pointed his thumb over his shoulder.

"We have the telephone numbers," Stanley pointed out. "From Seattle, as well as Tacoma. How do you explain Collier's presence in Tacoma?"

Simms hesitated before answering. Stanley maintained his posture, his face just inches from Simms'.

"I have no idea," Simms replied, finally.

"You called all of those numbers, correct?" Stanley demanded.

"Yes."

"Well?" Stanley barked. "Where were they?"

"How do you mean?"

Stanley slammed his hand on the table. "Did the numbers belong to hotels or to private residences?" he shouted.

Simms couldn't respond, unable to form a complete sentence. "I…uh…"

"Did anyone answer the phone?" Stanley enunciated each syllable in the manner of those impatient with the infirm or elderly.

Simms shook his head.

Stanley eyed his subordinate, snatching and holding his gaze. The two men stared at each other for several moments. To Simms', it was an eternity.

"This does not bode well," Stanley said at last.

His voice was calm and his response measured. While there was no overt implication of danger, Simms knew that Stanley's mercurial temper could cause him to erupt into another rage at any time. However, there was no further outburst, nor were any more words uttered. Instead, Stanley, with great calm, walked to the window. As Stanley stood there, taking in the Seattle skyline, Simms' discomfort grew. The silence was palpable unbearable.

"That does not bode well at all," Stanley said, softly. "You do realize the implications here, yes?" His composure and restraint inexplicably terrified Simms, whose face paled so suddenly that Stanley chuckled.

Stanley cocked his head and spoke in a singsong. "Mr. Collier's been keeping secrets from us…" His eyes locked onto Simms'.

Simms' chest tightened. "What does that mean?"

"It means that Mr. Collier was staying with someone else when he was supposed to be here."

Simms' eyes widened.

"Secrets are not good kept to one's self," Stanley said, his voice even. "Something is very suspicious. Think about all possible consequences of keeping secrets. Especially if they are allowed to remain secret to *us!*" his cold and calculated tone sent shivers up Simms' spine.

"I want every one of Collier's steps retraced," Stanley commanded.

Stanley was scared, Simms knew, and was trying desperately, and unsuccessfully, to conceal it.

"We purchased his travel vouchers and accommodations, correct?"

Simms nodded.

"Very fortunate for us. We have a plausible reason to question any changes made to his itinerary. We must locate the source of that Tacoma listing."

"We could be making a mountain out of a mole hill."

Simms enraged Stanley when he waxed glib and flippant, and Simms always spoke with insouciance when the situation was most dire. At that moment, Stanley felt as though he could pummel Simms, repeatedly and without remorse.

"He was at a location unbeknownst to us," Stanley said, coolly. "That is no mole hill."

"He may have been visiting one of his women." Simms attempted to restore the gravity to his demeanor. "He was forever scoring conquests. That number could easily belong to one of them!"

"It just as easily could not," Stanley retorted. "Until we know for certain, we must assume the worst."

"And if it turns out that I'm right, you'll feel very foolish" Simms derided.

Stanley's fury raged within. How dare Simms mock him! He assured himself that, at some point, he'd inquire as to whether Simms could be transferred. That, though, was a musing for another time.

"Oh, I won't. I assure you," replied Stanley, one eyebrow cocked. He smiled, his mouth tense and his tone steely. With pronounced deliberation, he walked back to his desk.

"We will impart measures to determine what Collier's contacts may or may not know. Until we ascertain those facts and assess the damage, we won't relax for a moment."

Stanley slid the phone toward Simms.

"Now, find out where he was."

Chapter Twenty-Two

"Alarms"

Through the darkness and the fog of sleep still clouding his mind, Cameron struggled to open his eyes. He could hear noises in the distance, but was unable to discern them or their source. For a moment, he thought it was the rumble of thunder. As he roused, though, he realized that Chuck was stumbling through the darkness toward the door. Once the door opened, Cameron heard a cacophonous commotion outside.

The band truck!

Now fully awake, he pulled on his jeans. Fumbling with his belt, he dashed out the door. He hurried down the stairs and into the parking lot, quickly regretting that he hadn't bothered to wear shoes as small pebbles stabbed into the tender soles of his feet. Ignoring the pain, he followed Chuck's shadowy figure dashing to the truck. Still too dark to see clearly, Cameron tried to identify the voices he heard as the ethereal forms of several men fighting danced macabre near the vehicle. He was unable to determine not only the identity of the attackers, but the defenders as well. He could see that the cab door was open, but thought it odd that the cab light wasn't on. Three men were bent on trying to get to the truck while being fought off by two others.

Cameron assumed that his fellow Roadhouse Sons were trying to fight off the assailants, but suddenly his band mates ran up to him, seemingly out of nowhere. Without stopping to figure it out, Cameron dove into the fight, fists swinging at any form he didn't remotely recognize. He felt his knuckles make contact with someone's jaw. He followed that up with a swift kick to their ribs, and watched as the shadowy form crumpled to the ground, the wind sufficiently knocked out of whomever it was. Jumping over the prone figure, Cameron ran alongside Rich, who had pushed another attacker against the side of the truck, and was pummeling them with fast and furious one-two punches. Evan and Clyde jumped two other figures, while Snapper tackled the legs of yet another, causing him and the assailant to fall face first into the gravel.

Cameron, meanwhile, was handling the retaliation of his attacker, who'd sailed a fist toward Cameron's face, but struck so wide that Cameron was able to dive into the man's ribs, slamming the man into the side of the truck. During all of this mayhem, Chuck silently and expertly delivered a roundhouse kick to one of the shadow figures, then brought a forearm across the back of the man's neck, forcing the attacker, who grunted in abject pain, down to the dirt. Cameron, having espied this in a moment of unlikely calm, noted that Chuck's stealth and style were markedly different from the others; everyone else shouted as they fought.

At least we know which ones are ours.

Amidst the bellowing and commotion, Cameron heard someone scream in agony. Almost immediately, the lights of the parking lot were turned on. Suddenly, there ensued a mad scrambling of bodies diving into darkness. Cameron could have sworn that he saw someone slide under the truck.

"Guys! Against the truck!" he heard Chuck shout and, wearily, the band followed his command, shivering in the cold. By now, all of the outside lights of the hotel were on and Cameron caught sight of three men scampering across the parking lot to the end of the building. One of the men was leaning against another for support. The man providing support turned to look back, giving Cameron a good look at Buzz Cut. He didn't recognize the other two, but he thought one of them had his hand wrapped in a bandage. However, when he gave his statement to Chuck later on, he couldn't be certain.

"Are you guys all right?" Chuck asked. Cameron caught the sound of Chuck's heavy breathing. The band members nodded and Cameron counted heads to be certain that everyone was there.

Clyde, Rich, Evan, Snapper, Chuck, and… Who the fuck is he?

Chuck was helping someone sit on the step to the truck's cab. Other than the man's sandy brown hair, Cameron couldn't distinguish any other features about him. One of the man's eyes was swollen shut, and his lower face was covered with blood due to a nasty nosebleed.

"Are you all right?" Chuck asked, tilting the man's face up toward his own. "Can you hear me?"

The man nodded, slightly, but said nothing; he was breathing through his mouth. It was then that Cameron recognized the man was Brody Aldrich.

What the hell is he doing here?

"Don't tip your head back," Chuck said, putting his hand on top of the man's head. "That's an old wives' tale. You'll choke that way. Let's get you upstairs."

Turning to face the rest of them, Chuck looked them over closely, his eyes resting on Snapper.

"Are you okay?" Chuck asked. Cameron noticed that Chuck's tone didn't match the look of concern on his face. Following Chuck's gaze, he noticed Snapper, slightly stooped, pressing his hand against his stomach. He wouldn't look at Chuck.

"Yeah, I'm all right," Snapper insisted. "I just got a shot in the nuts, that's all. I'll be fine."

Saying nothing, Snapper turned and headed back to the room. Chuck helped Brody to his feet, and motioned for the rest of them to follow.

"Shut that door and make sure the truck is locked up good this time," Chuck snapped. He didn't wait for a response and quickly followed Snapper to the room. Cameron, closest to the truck, did as Chuck instructed. He clambered into the cab to check the lock on the driver's side when, having not even tried the lock, he noticed something unusual. The plastic casing of the cab light was on the dashboard. The light bulb was sitting inside it.

That wasn't there when we got out.

Had one of the others come out later to retrieve something, only to discover the bulb was burned out, then tried to replace it? He would ask, but suspected the answer to be negative. The thought unsettled him. Shutting the door, he double-checked it and confirmed that it was indeed locked. He yanked on the driver's side door handle. It, too, was locked tight, and yet he'd seen the passenger's side door wide open when he arrived on the scene.

What the fuck is going on?

Proceeding as though someone had broken into the truck, Cameron examined the doors and windows for any signs of jimmying. The driver's side was in the lee of the lights, so the darkness made it difficult for him to see. Abandoning that investigation, he went around to the passenger's side where he was able to get a better look at the doors and the window. Again, he noticed no obvious scratches or marks, nor were the wing windows open. He stooped to inspect the area under the truck, but saw nothing. His apprehension increased. Cameron was anxious for a logical explanation for how the door could have been opened, but simply couldn't fathom one.

Chuck'll take a look at it in the morning. He'll see something I can't. He's got to.

As Cameron headed back across the parking lot, the small stones stabbed into the bottom of his feet like hot needles. At the walkway, he rubbed each foot against the opposite leg and hurried up the stairs. The others were gathered in his room and Chuck was applying a wet cloth to Brody's nose.

"Can you breathe?" Chuck asked.

Brody nodded and Chuck carefully removed the cloth.

"Thankfully, the hotel electricity's still on." Removing the lampshade, Chuck brought the bedside lamp up to Brody's face.

"It doesn't look broken. That's good. Someone just landed a good punch. It'll be sore, but you'll be fine. The bleeding seems to have stopped, too. That's good. You need a cold compress, though."

"Says you," Brody muttered. He turned toward the wall mirror. Dabbing gingerly at his face, he wiped away the dried blood.

Chuck sent Clyde and Evan to the ice machine. "Let me know what you see out there. I want to know if the cops are on the way or not," he ordered.

Cameron realized Chuck's instructions were more for Brody's benefit than theirs. He had a gut feeling that the cops wouldn't be there, but one could never tell.

Never hurts to be sure.

Surely, Buzz Cut had some involvement with the goings-on; one of his men had been hurt. There was a very real possibility that they would cause trouble. It was what Cameron would expect in a normal situation—experience had taught him that was how things happened—but this was not a normal situation.

"What's the matter with you?" Chuck said, turning to Snapper.

The roadie stood in the corner, rubbing his hand over his belly.

"Nothing!" Snapper insisted. "Like I said, I just took a ball shot, that's all."

"You don't rub your belly with that," Chuck said. "You rub your crotch."

Before Snapper could move, Chuck lunged toward him and grabbed his wrist. Cameron saw something drop to the floor. With a quick twist, Chuck bent Snapper's arm upward, preventing the roadie from retrieving the object. Chuck picked it up. He gave his wrist a flick. The object opened up to reveal a small blade.

"That's what I fucking thought!" Chuck snarled, slipping the switchblade into his pocket.

Cameron watched as Chuck, with the slightest movement and effort, repositioned Snapper's arm backward. The roadie withered.

"You and I will talk later," Chuck said, leaning menacingly into Snapper's face.

He won't discuss this in front of strangers!

Cameron glanced at Brody, who appeared to be completely unaware of what was going on; he gingerly dabbed at his face. Just then, Clyde and Evan returned with a bucket of ice.

"The cops are in the hotel office!" Evan said breathlessly. "They're talking to the manager!"

Chuck didn't seem to hear. He stuffed a fistful of ice into a hand towel and carefully applied it to Brody's swollen eye.

"How many are there?" he asked, finally.

"Just one," said Evan. "I think it's Beecham, but I couldn't tell for sure. They only had one light on inside and all I could see were silhouettes."

"Then how do you know there was a cop inside?" Chuck asked, pointedly. "Did you see a car out front?"

"Basic outline," Evan replied in short, clipped tones, shaking his head. "Recognized the build, saw the outline of his gun and caught the glint from his badge."

"But no car out front," Chuck muttered.

Cameron was about to interject when a figure appeared in the doorway. Having expected the police, Cameron was shocked to see two men he didn't recognize. The first fellow was roughly Chuck's age and clean shaven with carefully parted dark hair, and while the man was not wearing a tie, Cameron saw that he was wearing slacks and a pressed shirt. The second man had a swarthy complexion, dark eyes, and short dark hair. He, too, was dressed in shirt and slacks but was wearing a tie. The first man, directing his attention to only Chuck, spoke in a clear, commanding tone.

"Is everything all right?" he asked.

"Everything is fine...at the moment," Chuck nodded, eyes locked on Brody.

In his own time and with calm comportment, Chuck described the earlier events. The man removed a notepad and pen from his shirt pocket and took notes. Chuck's remarks were unembellished and pointed. The man dutifully noted everything that Chuck said, then turned to each of the band members. Cameron was curious as to why Chuck was allowing the inquiry from this stranger. Then it dawned on him. Suddenly, yet another figure appeared in the doorway, but this time it was someone Cameron recognized.

"What in the Sam Hill is going on here?" Officer Beecham demanded, pushing his way into the room. "Trouble seems to follow you folks wherever you go, and this time it's gone too far! I've got reports of you starting a fight here in the parking lot and I've got a couple of injured parties that are willing to press charges."

"You can add me to that list," Brody muttered, raising his hand wearily.

Officer Beecham shook a finger at him.

"See?" the officer snapped. "Another one! I gave you fellows plenty of room to prove to me you weren't trouble and you've blown it now! I've got a report that you jumped three men as they were coming home from the dance tonight—"

"They didn't jump anybody," Brody interrupted with an angry outburst. "I followed the Pecham boys from the dance when I overheard them say they were going to fix those longhairs good! I came to warn these fellows and I saw the Pecham boys trying to break into the Roadhouse Sons' truck. These guys must have already known something was up 'cause as soon as one of the Pecham boys tried climbing into the cab, the door flew open and one of these guys jumped out and knocked the guy to the ground. The other two who were trying to get into the truck jumped into the fight, but this fellow managed to knock 'em away. I came over to help him and one of the Pecham boys caught me on my blind side and gave me this black eye. One of the other ones pushed my face into the side of the truck."

Brody pulled the cold pack away from his swollen eye and turned his face toward Officer Beecham.

"That was when I heard more of these guys come running down the stairs to help their buddy," Brody continued, "because once the fight wasn't going their way, the Pecham boys decided to skedaddle, as usual."

"Well, that's not the way it got reported to me," Officer Beecham snapped, puffing out his chest.

"I can corroborate this man's account," the other stranger said, calmly.

"Just who are you?" Beecham sneered, glancing over his shoulder at the man.

With a smile, the man reached for what Cameron thought would be a billfold, but when the man opened it, there was no mistaking the reflection of a badge.

"I am Special Agent Michael Navarre of the Federal Bureau of Investigation," the man replied. "This is my partner, Special Agent Ed Farhat. I believe you and I spoke on the phone today."

Cameron thrilled at the color draining from Beecham's face.

"I can't see how this involves the Feds," Beecham replied, his force and vigor completely diminished. Special Agent Navarre's smile, though, remained; his partner said nothing.

"We're staying in the room next to this one," Navarre explained. "We saw everything unfold exactly as this man described. In fact, I had just completed collecting statements from all involved when you arrived. Would you like a copy of my report, or would you prefer to collect statements yourself?"

Officer Beecham hesitated before answering. He begrudgingly conceded that a copy of Navarre's report would save having to collect the information again, especially when all of the others had nothing to add to either account. But then the officer recovered himself.

"I still have the report of one of the Pecham boys being attacked with a deadly weapon," Beecham insisted. "No one's explained that yet!"

"Nobody had any damned weapon, and if anyone was attacked, one of those idiots probably did it themselves," Brody snapped. "None of them could shit right if gravity didn't help them! Besides, even if they did get hurt, whoever did it could claim self defense, since the Pecham boys were the ones that started this shit in the first place!"

Chuck quickly concurred with Brody's statement. Though Beecham wasn't mollified, he ceased to press the issue.

"I saw no one draw any type of a weapon," Navarre said, his demeanor calm.

"You couldn't have seen anything," Beecham insisted. "All of the lights in the parking lot were off!" Beecham immediately flushed crimson.

"How would you know?" Cameron shouted. "You weren't even there!"

"Uh...that's what the Pecham boys told me," the police officer insisted, attempting to regain his composure. "Assault with a deadly weapon is a very, very serious charge and I am not going to ignore it, and if you think I am, you don't know how hard this dog is going to fight!"

Check…

Cameron felt nauseous.

"That is a serious charge," agreed Navarre. "Since you weren't present, you've received second-hand information. I was an eyewitness. The lights did, in fact, come on before the altercation broke up. I saw no weapons drawn or used. I did see one of the other men assault an undercover federal agent in the line of duty. That, too, is a serious charge, and we can provide a clear description of the person involved, and therefore press charges. That makes my dog bigger than your dog."

Checkmate.

"Who's an undercover agent?" Beecham demanded. Though obviously shaken, he was by no means ready to give up the fight.

"That would be me," Chuck said, producing his badge. "Special Agent Charles Lamont, also with the FBI."

Direct hit!

Cameron gleefully watched Beecham's shoulders sag. Clearly defeated, Beecham struck an entirely different tone with the two agents. Since Navarre had already taken the statements of everyone involved, there would be no need for anyone but Navarre and Farhat to go to the police station. In an effort to curry favor with everyone, Beecham tried to convince Brody to go to the emergency room, but the man refused.

"I'll have them drop me off at my house on the way to the station," Brody grumbled, pointing at Navarre and Farhat. "I've had enough excitement for one night, and I'm none too happy knowing I'll have a headache tomorrow without the benefit of getting drunk tonight."

As the special agents assisted Brody to their car, Beecham turned to Chuck and the band. He said nothing at first, then mumbled his adieu and skulked out.

Totally deflated!

Beecham seemed genuinely afraid of his newly discovered lack of power. In that moment, Cameron knew for certain that the police officer was involved with everything under their investigation. He was about to speak when Chuck halted him with an upheld hand. Chuck carefully looked around outside, then closed the door.

"Listen up," he said, sternly. "They'll be shutting the power off any minute, so we need to move fast. Evan—you, Clyde, and Rich go to your room, get packed and return here. We'll pack up, too. Bring pillows and blankets from your room. You'll be staying in this room tonight. Sleep in your clothes. We're out of here as soon as it's light."

"What the fuck for?" Cameron asked. For a second, he wondered how Chuck would react to this trace of insubordination. To his relief, Chuck didn't ire.

"Everything just got hotter," he sighed. "I'd hoped to be able to stay undercover entirely, but that got blown to hell. No point in whining about it. I know those guys. They'll take advantage of throwing Beecham off guard and press it home until he squeals like a pig. In the meantime, with no cover, we have no reason to stay here. That means we head to Columbia. We're just doing it a bit earlier than I had intended. In the meantime, I don't want us separated until it's time to get out of here. You won't get much sleep, but it'll be better than nothing."

"If our cover's blown, does that ruin everything?" Evan asked.

Chuck shook his head. "No," he explained. "It just means that we've jumped out and yelled surprise on the count of two instead of the count of three. We've got plenty of evidence to nail these guys, and now we can add assault to the list."

"And burglary!" added Rich. "Don't forget that. They broke into the truck! Remember, the cab door was open."

"Yeah," Cameron said. "The cab light had been removed and was on the dash. They must have done that. Remember, Brody said he saw someone trying to crawl into the cab."

Chuck listened, cogitating. He shook his head dismissively and told the others to retrieve their belongings. Snapper and Cameron began to pack. Suddenly, out of nowhere, Chuck slammed the roadie against the wall.

"When were you going to let me in on your little toy?" Chuck growled. "Belt knives are only borderline legal at best. Having them altered like switchblades makes them even more questionable."

Snapper swallowed hard. He began to tremble.

"Look, I have every right to defend myself!" he stammered. "I can't carry a gun and I'm not as big as you, *or* as intimidating. It's not a switchblade! It doesn't work on a spring. It's a jackknife! I just made it open smoother than usual. That's all, and no one can prove otherwise!"

Chuck retrieved the knife from his pocket and examined it closely.

"Did you wipe this off?" he demanded. "You better tell me the truth because I'll know if you're lying."

"No, sir," Snapper insisted, vehemently shaking his head. "I never even used it! I took it out but didn't open it. After everything died down, I was trying to put it back into my belt buckle, but something must've gotten jammed and it wouldn't go in."

Chuck offered no response, but kept Snapper pinned to the wall.

The roadie was sweating profusely. "Look, check it out!" he insisted. "It's not even sharpened. I couldn't cut butter with it! I just have it for a warning, for show."

Chuck examined the blade once again, then closed it. He released his grip on Snapper.

"You do have that right," he grumbled. "I don't see anything on the blade and I can run my thumb along the edge and not feel a thing. You're lucky they didn't say what kind of injury those jokers got, because if they'd said a stab wound or any kind of cut, I'd have had to turn you in. That wouldn't have been pleasant, would it?"

Snapper shook his head. Chuck shoved the small knife into the roadie's hand. He turned his back and grabbed his duffel.

"I like cowboys in the movies," he muttered, stuffing his clothes into his bag. "I do *not* like them on my team! The next one who pulls that shit is going to be hung out to dry, and don't think I don't mean it!"

Cameron and Snapper packed in silence. When they were finished and the others had returned, Cameron ventured a question.

"Who do you think was in the truck?" he asked. "Do you think they were able to jimmy the door? The light bulb was on the dash."

Chuck shook his head. "I honestly have no idea," he sputtered. He went into the bathroom and closed the door.

He's trying to figure something out.

Cameron felt a cold chill run down his spine. As if to underscore Cameron's apprehension, the hotel's power went out.

All was black.

CHAPTER TWENTY-THREE

"Wild and Free"

I feel like I'm waiting outside the principal's office.

Cameron's mood had become black and festering, a feeling that he hated. The day had started off poorly. Chuck's tossing and turning the previous night had kept them all awake, and anxious to roll as many miles behind them as fast as possible, he'd roused them up at the first inkling of daylight—without coffee or breakfast. Then, adding insult to injury, he made them load the van. When Chuck returned to the room to make a phone call, Cameron was tempted to venture to the diner, but Chuck returned before Cameron could act, so they hit the road hungry. The truck's gas tank was nearly full; therefore Chuck declared that there was no need to stop anywhere. As vexed as the Roadhouse Sons were, Chuck's tone convinced them not to argue. Cameron didn't mind the idea of a non-stop trip, until he discovered that he was out of cigarettes.

His only consolation was watching Chuck wake up the hotel manager at check out. Cameron remembered Evan telling them that the hotel manager was talking with Officer Beecham after the altercation in the parking lot, so he knew that the manager hadn't had any more sleep than the rest of them. Chuck raised enough hell over their stay that the flustered, groggy proprietor granted them a generous discount on their bill.

The accounting gods will be pleased.

The initial part of the trip passed in silence. Since Snapper usually drove, Cameron tried to sleep, but was only able to do so fitfully. No one bothered to turn on the radio; an uneasy silence permeated the van. Finally, Cameron could no longer tolerate it.

"Did we totally fuck everything up?" he asked.

Chuck, his arms crossed over his chest, shook his head. "No," he yawned. "I already told you that they'd assigned someone to take over for McIntyre and me. We were just waiting for them to arrive. Navarre and Farhat were the ones. We would have handed everything over today and gone our merry little way this afternoon. As it turned out, it might have been better this way."

"How do you figure *that*?" gasped Snapper.

"Because our good friend, Officer Beecham, was no doubt about to spring a trap on us. Charging us with assault would be the perfect excuse for getting us off the street and hopefully keep us from telling anyone about what was going on. I'm pretty sure that was why they were always trying to provoke a fight with you guys. I wouldn't have been surprised if there hadn't been some complications or an accident while we were in custody."

"You think he planned on killing us?" asked Cameron.

Chuck shrugged. "I doubt it would have gone that far, but perhaps there would be some reason to keep us locked up indefinitely, or charge us with some other infraction. With someone in the County Attorney's office working in cahoots with him, he'd at least try and ship us off to prison, or lose us in the system. As it was, things blew up in his own face faster than he could react."

"Like...?" wondered Snapper.

"Like having two special agents suddenly get involved in your investigation," Chuck said. "Not to mention one of the people he was after turning out to be an undercover agent. I'm sure that put him in a bind!"

"I'd have thought you'd be going out of your mind about that! We might've blown your cover, for crying out loud!" Cameron was incensed.

"I'm not Batman, for God's sake," grumbled Chuck. "I don't have to keep a secret identity if I'm not going to be there anymore! And besides, *you* didn't reveal anything! *I* did, and I did it on my own. For once, you guys didn't have anything to do with that fracas last night. Beecham's friends started it, hoping to catch a few annoying flies. What they ended up with was a whole hornet's nest. Having two federal agents show up caught him off guard. Having one of the people he was hoping to arrest turn out to be a third federal agent pulled the rug right out from under him. To make things even worse, Navarre and Farhat had already hijacked his investigation and collected official statements before he could twist things to his advantage. His plans were ruined right before his eyes."

"You really think he had a solid plan?" Cameron pressed.

Chuck nodded. "He was already in the manager's office when all of this went down, but his patrol car was nowhere to be seen. He had to have been waiting there for everything to unfold. He needed probable cause to arrest us. The best laid plans of mice and men... While Beecham and his friends are trying to figure out how to deal with this, I'm sure Navarre and Farhat will press their advantage and spring their other investigation on them. I would!"

"So, everything wasn't a big, damn mess then," Cameron repeated. "Then why are we running away?"

"How do you mean?" asked Chuck, visibly confused.

"Leaving at the crack of dawn, not stopping anywhere, for anything," Cameron pointed out. "Looks like running away to me!"

"Not running away," explained Chuck. "We're running *to*. I talked to McIntyre yesterday before the show, and she said that we needed to get to Columbia as soon as possible because the USO had a sudden opening for us, and we needed to get things set up with them *today*. I figured we would be able to get a good night's sleep after last night's show, so we could get a nice, fresh start this morning. Didn't work out that way, though."

"I'll say it didn't," Cameron sulked. He looked out the window, his expression sullen and surly.

"You will each have to provide oral reports about last night," Chuck said, to the mutual groans of Cameron and Snapper. "It won't be too bad. You'll just have to give your statements. They'll type them up for you and you sign them. Then you're done. But don't get used to it. It's only because we're pressed for time that they arranged for other people to compose the statements for you."

"How'd you pull that?" Cameron asked.

"Good old Henry Clay." Chuck yawned. "He's the head of the USO and retired a few years ago from the bureau. Since a lot of agents have enlisted, much of the old guard's been called back. Henry's holding down two posts right now. He's regional director for the USO, and acting chief of the Columbia office. He's allowed to work out of the USO office. He's arranged his priorities around us and, therefore, nothing interferes with our availability."

When the Roadhouse Sons arrived in Columbia, Chuck's revelation proved true. Agents quickly ushered them into windowless offices and, far from being comforted, Cameron was ill at ease, despite the fact that he knew he wasn't being charged with anything. He'd made statements to an agent before; he couldn't help but feel nervous. Special admission to the agents' small cafeteria, being addressed as Mr. Walsh, and being wished a pleasant day after signing his typed statement only made the experience more surreal. However, there was no time for reflection. As soon as they were finished, Chuck ushered them into the lobby where McIntyre awaited them.

"Hello, fellas!" she said, cheerily. "You guys look like something the cat dragged in." The band grumbled a tepid response. McIntyre chuckled. "We'll walk over to Henry's office. It's only a few blocks, and the fresh air will do you some good. I hope."

McIntyre stepped out into the morning sun, the band straggling after her. She and Chuck bantered small talk as they headed down the street and the band members fell in line single file behind them.

"Can you guys break ranks, for heaven's sake?" she said. "You make me feel like a mother duck!"

After walking several blocks, they came to a brick building with large windows on its ground floor. They entered the lobby, which was flooded with natural light. Lines of gold lettering indicated the businesses located there, including several law and investment firms, and a real estate office. McIntyre led them through the vacant lobby, through the back door, and out into a small, open quadrant. There was a building to their right and one directly ahead, toward which McIntyre led them. The area to the left opened onto the street.

They entered the small, unassuming three-story structure, which was dwarfed by the other building on the quad. Cameron read the entrance sign.

United Service Organizations.

Below the insignia was a sign that read: "Deliveries to side entrance." Contrary to the eerie quiet in the previous building, this one was alive with the sound of telephones ringing, people talking, and the buzz of intense activity. With her usual sense of purpose, McIntyre led them down a hall and to a flight of stairs at its end. Once on the second-floor landing, she led them through a door into another hallway, half the length of the previous one.

Much quieter here…

The middle of the hallway opened to a reception area. A woman was seated behind a desk. Behind her was a wall with a door in the middle, unadorned with any indication of who worked inside.

"Hello, Barb," McIntyre said with a smile. "Is Henry available? I wanted him to meet the band."

The woman returned a smile that lit up her face. She had sparkling eyes, and short dark hair, with just a touch of gray.

Pretty eyes. Can't make out the color.

Barb spoke in a very soft voice, telling them to have a seat. She rose to see if Henry Clay was ready to meet them. Her disappearance through the unmarked door gave Cameron more flashbacks to high school. Finally, she returned and beckoned them to follow her.

McIntyre, Chuck, and the band stepped into a short hallway. There were two doors on each side, as well as another door at the far end. That door was open, but like all the others, had no distinctive markings of identification. They walked to that door and stepped inside what appeared to be the entire end of the second floor. Seated behind a desk was an older man sporting auburn hair with gray at the temples. Though he was sitting down, Cameron discerned that he wasn't a tall man, perhaps five feet five inches. His skin was very pale, suggesting that the man spent much of his time indoors. He had sharp and vigilant dark eyes that scrutinized them as they entered his office. The man said nary a word. Cameron's sense of being examined, yet not judged, again raised the sensation of having entered the surreal.

"Have a seat, gentlemen. And, of course, lady." The man's voice was firm, yet slightly high-pitched. His tone was authoritative but pleasant. The man's hands were rested palms down on his desk, and he sat bolt upright in his chair. The only part of him that moved were his eyes. He didn't smile, but didn't deliberately evoke apprehension. Cameron felt more at ease, but remained on guard.

This guy's used to getting things done...

"Fellows, I'd like you to meet Henry Clay," said Chuck. McIntyre proceeded to introduce Clay to each of the band members, who took turns shaking the man's hand. "Henry, you've got yourself a nice set-up here, I see. Better than the Fed?"

Henry Clay finally smiled. "Yes," he admitted. "Most of the things that demand my attention are here. They just called me out of mothballs to babysit. A good team there with a lot of experienced people. They know where to find me."

"You're not back at the ranch?" Chuck asked, surprised. The older man shook his head.

"Not much need," Henry explained, his tone reflective. "The government seized the beef herd right after rationing went into effect. They needed them for the war effort. My son manages it for us while we're here. We try to get down there once in a while, but with the USO and the Bureau, the opportunity doesn't present itself often."

Henry made every effort to sound upbeat, but Cameron could tell that it was a chore. In a varied array on the desk were several framed photographs, some with Henry and a woman whom Cameron assumed was Henry's wife. There were also family photos, a photo of a middle-aged man, and several photos of men who appeared to be Cameron's age.

"Are those your sons?" Cameron asked, trying to break the ice. Henry became slightly more animated, and held one of the photos.

"That one is," he replied, pointing to the photo of the middle-aged man. "These are my grandsons. They went out for the war effort, too."

"They enlisted?" Rich asked.

Henry sighed. "They signed up last month. Two of them went into the air force; the third went into the army, the US Army Corps of Engineers. The two pilots are stationed in Seattle, Washington. Which brings me to you fellows."

"What have we got to do with Seattle?" asked Cameron. He winced as he felt Chuck's gaze; he'd likely breached hierarchy protocol with his query.

"That's the opening I have for you," Henry explained, unaffronted. "Have you folks ever heard of a band called Boney Jack?"

"The punk band," Evan asked. "Yeah, we've heard of them. They're not bad. They're real big on the West Coast."

"They're a real big pain in the neck," Henry said, his irritation evident. "They've worked several of our tours in the past and had quite a following with the troops and the crowds at our events. All that's changed suddenly, and I have to confess, I'm not the least bit sorry that it has."

"What happened?" Cameron asked. Chuck eyed him disapprovingly. "If you don't mind my asking, that is," Cameron added hastily.

"The USO does not allow anyone with a criminal record to be involved in any of our tours or our shows, or in any other capacity," Henry said. "Boney Jack, the artist *and* the band, has been arrested for disturbing the peace, for disorderly conduct, and probably for anything else possible. That means they're off the tour, and as much as that is a huge relief, it leaves me with a huge problem. We've got a big concert scheduled for the Seattle military installations and refugee centers, and we need someone right away."

"We can handle that!" laughed Rich.

"Not so fast," said Evan. "They're a punk band. We can't just step into their spot just like that. People are expecting a certain sound."

The band proceeded to discuss and debate the pros and cons of Henry's proposal. Henry eyed the band members carefully, but didn't involve himself in their conversation. After several minutes of observation, Chuck agreed to let the band make the final decision. The band concluded that since they were well-known in the Northeast but little known outside of the area, especially in the Pacific Northwest, they would take the offer.

"We can make our sound more edgy," suggested Cameron. "We obviously can't pass ourselves off as Boney Jack, but we can give them a show that won't disappoint."

The others agreed emphatically, and suggested myriad approaches to the situation. Henry, realizing that they could go on indefinitely, brought the meeting to a close.

"That's settled then," he averred authoritatively. The band nodded in reply.

"What's our ETA?" Chuck asked with a smile, leaning back in his chair. "I can tell these boys are ready to start rehearsing."

"That's why I needed you fellows here right away," Henry replied, sheepishly. "The first concert is set for three days from now."

"Three days!" cried Snapper. The rest of the band was slack-jawed and speechless.

Henry shrugged and offered an understanding, albeit wan, smile. "If I had more time, I'd give it to you," he replied. "Unfortunately, I don't. However, it's only a thirty-hour drive, if you leave straight from here."

"Yeah, *if* we were able to use the interstate," Snapper said irritably. "Which we're not able to do! So one of the three days is already out the window!"

"That's where I can be of great help to you," Henry smiled. He opened one of several folders on his desk. "These are the special USO passes, which identify you as officially involved in the war effort. They allow you to travel on the interstate, allow you to increase your gas rations by fifty percent, and allow you a speed limit of fifty-five miles per hour. If you leave in the morning, you should be able to make it in time."

Henry's purportedly helpful news was met with muted grumbling and grouchy comments about the pressing schedule. Nonetheless, everyone in the room knew that any refusal from the band had never been an option in the first place. While the band devised their strategy, Henry pulled two more files from the pile on his desk. He opened one, and addressed Chuck and McIntyre.

Henry nodded toward the guys. "Before I start, let me inform you both that I am well aware of the history of your team, and will not ask them to leave the room. It's quite evident from your reports, and theirs, that they have a thorough grasp of the situation and have proved themselves capable. Therefore, in the interest of your new assignment, they should be part of this briefing. Do either of you have any objections?"

"We have none," McIntyre said. Chuck nodded in agreement.

"Initially, your assignment was to continue your deployment, predominantly as eyes and ears. The Northwest is a hotbed of activity right now, with the naval base and the submarines in constant activity, as are the air force base and the army personnel stationed there. The additional complications of the refugee camps and the constant swelling of the population with people entering on behalf of the war effort exacerbates the situation, as does the close proximity to the Alaskan Front. You can understand why we need you posted there."

"I don't understand at all," said Clyde. "How and why is that our concern?"

Cameron had noticed that, recently, Clyde was returning to a state of constant irritability, refuting his usually calm, easygoing demeanor.

Maybe it's just fatigue…

"With this concentration of war effort activity, we are certain that there are networks and operatives working the military bases and refugee camps, not to mention the community at large."

"So, that's what we're supposed to be working on," Evan realized. "The black propaganda we keep hearing about."

"Correction," said Henry. "That's what you were going to work on. You will be doing more."

"Like what?" Chuck asked, nonplussed.

The very sound of Chuck's obvious surprise made Cameron's gut wrench.

Henry removed an eight-by-ten black-and-white photograph from the folder and handed it to Chuck. Cameron noted the newspaper clippings attached to it. He wondered if they were reviews, or part of the band's promotional package.

"This is John Collier," Henry divulged. "He was a talent agent working in Los Angeles and San Francisco since 1971. We have evidence that he was also a Soviet agent working with a network on the West Coast, one that we've been trying to crack for years."

Cameron spoke first. "You said he *was*. Did he defect?" Cameron held his breath. He'd interrupted with an honest question, but knew that he'd again revealed his inexperience. He berated himself for the very nature of his question, and for trying to appear savvy in the midst of three heralded agents.

Henry smiled knowingly. "No," he said. "Once an agent defects, there is no further mention of them other than by those assigned to debriefing. In this case, unfortunately, Collier is dead."

"It says here that he committed suicide." Chuck tapped at one of the clippings. "He jumped from a window in his hotel room."

"That is the official cause of death. But the police don't believe it. Neither do we. The hotel room was completely ransacked, far more than it would have been during a mere burglary. Details were kept from the media, but we know that parts of the carpet were torn up, and the mattresses and cushions slit. We're confident that Collier was thrown from that window by whomever ransacked his room."

"Henry, what does that have to do with us?" Chuck asked.

"Collier had been in contact with us shortly before he died. He indicated that he wanted to defect, and that he had an item of vital interest and importance to the war effort."

"Did he indicate what the item was?" asked McIntyre, her eyes glued to Collier's file.

"No," sighed Henry. "No one took him seriously. The information was never passed on to their superiors. We receive dozens of eccentric claims every day, and even in the best of times, they're not a priority because so many are boys crying wolf. With decreased manpower, they're even less so. It wasn't until after Collier's death that anything became known to us. When his name arose here, the Seattle police requested a records search. By then it was obviously too late. We've pored over Collier's submitted reports and it's clear that he suspected that someone was on to him before he died."

"Do you think the KGB did this, to try and make it look like suicide?" asked Cameron.

"No. The KGB is too crafty to do anything that would draw such attention to their organization. Had it been the KGB, Collier would have simply disappeared into thin air."

"Do you think it was a drug deal gone bad, or someone he owed money to?" To Cameron, his inquiry referenced plausible theories, but Henry negated them once again.

"Collier wasn't a drug rogue. No agent or agency anywhere would become involved with such activity. The rule is to never commit any action that renders agent or agency subject to blackmail, coercion or duress, thereby leaving agent or agency vulnerable to exploitation. No. I'm afraid whoever did this is someone who, thus far, has successfully evaded our radar."

"Any theories?" asked Chuck.

"I would hazard a guess that it wasn't any intelligence agency, for the reasons I've cited. Collier's name was submitted for a visitor's pass to attend a benefit show at the army base. We suspect that Collier was trying to inform us of a network within the refugee camp and bases, and that he had a contact. We need to find out who that contact was."

"Why do you think he was going to meet a contact there?" Cameron asked. "He was a talent agent, after all. It would make sense that he'd be there with his performers. None of the acts he represented were or are scheduled to be in any of the shows," Henry replied. "He had no legitimate reason to be there."

"Could he have been scouting new talent?" asked Rich. "They're always doing that. That's what bands count on to make it."

Henry shook his head once again. "No, we thought of that already. All of the bands booked have their own representation, and with more established representation than Collier could provide. One of those agents was the one to submit his name, in fact."

"Who was that?" Chuck asked.

"A man by the name of John Stanley."

"Of Philly Records?" Clyde gasped.

"You've heard of him?" Henry asked, cocking an eyebrow at the guitarist.

"Yeah, of course I have! He's signed some of the biggest names in music. He sold his recording studios a few years ago for a big profit and he's been working in promotion about ten years. He does concerts all over the world!"

"Those are our findings, as well," Henry agreed.

"Then that would make sense that he would be bringing this Collier guy to the show!" Clyde was practically shouting.

Henry awaited an explanation.

"He's probably looking to bring in an associate or something," Clyde explained. "From what I remember hearing, Stanley bought out his other two partners quite a while ago. He had a big operation before the war, and he's still got offices all over. It's gotta be too much for one person to run. He could have been introducing Collier to his West Coast operations."

"Stanley was trying to bring a Soviet agent into a military installation." Henry's tone was cold. "How would that have helped him?"

"You said yourself that you guys didn't know Collier was a Commie agent until after the fact," Clyde said, impatiently. "If you guys don't know this stuff, how is anyone else supposed to magically know it?"

The room fell silent. Cameron shivered.

Chuck'll give us holy hell later.

An eternity passed. At last, Chuck cleared his throat.

"Henry, do you think this Stanley should be given a closer look?"

"A closer look, indeed," Henry said, closing the file. "Stanley is the manager for Boney Jack."

McIntyre and Chuck eyed each other.

"He's been booking shows and personal appearances at the bases and refugee centers for some time. He'll assist you fellows as you take Boney Jack's place. Between your concerts and your work on the Collier case, you Roadhouse Sons will be busy, no question about that." With a smile, Henry added, "I'll bet you boys are hungry, and you look tired. We have a cafeteria downstairs and a small dormitory on the third floor for crew use after curfew. You can sleep up there."

Henry went to the door and called Barb.

"Can you take these fellows down to the cafeteria and get them something to eat? They're famished."

Henry turned his attention to the band.

"I know we have hot dogs, at least. Items for the servicemen come through here, so there's real coffee and real cream in the cafeteria. You're part of the war effort now, gentlemen. We'll do our best to take care of you. Please excuse me now, though. I need to talk to this gentleman and lady."

Henry opened the door. The Roadhouse Sons filed out of the room. Cameron was the last in line and, realizing that the door didn't close all the way, he lagged behind to listen.

"I received the message about your request." Henry spoke in an uncharacteristically low, hushed tone. "I don't understand why you want that file, but I requisitioned it for you nonetheless. I was told the file was permanently closed when he died."

Cameron's stomach churned. This time, he couldn't hold back. He grabbed Barb's wastebasket and vomited.

CHAPTER TWENTY-FOUR

"Icy Fingers"

Stanley carefully slipped the receiver into its cradle. He didn't dare hang up the phone hastily, in case whoever was on the other end was still there. Any action interpreted as belligerent or brazen could foster the accusation of insubordination. Such were the subtle signs they sought, for which retribution was always swift and unrelenting. That was a reality of the paranoid ethos under which Stanley had worked for years. In his private thoughts, he chafed at his situation. He never expressed those thoughts aloud, not even in total privacy. There was no way to tell who might be listening for even the mildest hint of carelessness on his part, and the opportunity to exploit it. After all, wasn't that exactly what he'd done?

Stanley poured himself another drink from his precious decanter. The brown liquid shimmered in the sunlight through the glass, but the vision provided him no comfort. He knew that as time rolled on he was turning to drink more and more for relief from the tentacles of stress constricting his very being.

He examined his reflection in the liquid, but the flickering image of his own face mocked his efforts. Closing his eyes, Stanley swallowed a mouthful, hoping to lose himself in its warmth, willing the sweet relief and relaxation to emerge from its depths. But that comfort eluded him as well, the disappointment all too familiar now.

Ruefully, he raised the glass once again to his lips, then paused. His access to liquor was abundant, but not unlimited—yet another assault on his invincibility. Setting the glass on the table, he turned to look out the window. His resistance had collapsed; he struggled to keep at bay the feeling of abject fear.

"Who was he with?" they had asked. "Why did you not inform us of the situation of Collier's death when it occurred?"

They never yelled. No matter how severe the circumstances, they always maintained the same unruffled tone. The deep timbre of their voices reverberated through Stanley, carrying with it implied, but ever unspoken, peril. They knew Collier was involved in something; that was clear. Stanley was certain that Simms had wasted no time in bringing the situation to their attention.

Stanley felt himself choking with rage at his subordinate's duplicity. He visualized scenarios in which he could repay Simms' treachery. Lost in his revenge fantasies, he experienced a revelation.

They'd only spoken of Collier's death, a fact they could have gleaned from news reports. They also only asked questions about possible suspects. Anyone with even mild curiosity about the situation would have done the same. It suddenly dawned on Stanley that they had asked nothing of Collier's presence in Tacoma, a fact of which they were obviously unaware.

Relief washed over him. Stanley found comfort in the fact that they had yet to uncover any evidence of Collier's suspected deceit, or of Stanley's own potential culpability. If they had, there would have been no discussion.

The very reminder of no impunity caused Stanley's mouth to go dry. His temporary relief was instantaneously ripped away. With trembling hand, he sought refuge in his glass; the harshness of the alcohol burned his parched throat, a jeering reminder of its inability to provide true solace.

He cursed the costs, on all counts, of their support in this enterprise, and even more, the fact that he couldn't function without it. Stanley knew it was useless to indulge his thoughts any further. As far as he could tell, they hadn't yet discovered the mystery of Collier's passage through Tacoma, or its disastrous implications.

Stanley guzzled the rest of his liquor. Although alone, he spoke aloud.

"They will. It's only a matter of time."

CHAPTER TWENTY-FIVE

"Mistaken Identity"

Cameron just wanted a quiet place to rest, to sleep, to die. It didn't matter where. The ride from Missouri was just as long and as tiring as he had feared it would be. Mechanical troubles—a broken hose on the van, and a flat tire on the truck—intensified the aggravation, but those things paled in comparison to the smaller annoyances collected on the way.

There were periodic stops by law enforcement, complete with the requisite inquiries as to whether they were legally authorized to use the highway. There was the constant struggle to sleep while someone else drove. For Cameron, that was the true test. A chronically light sleeper, Cameron could never get truly comfortable in the truck. To compound his torture, both Chuck and Snapper easily employed various schemes to keep themselves amused and awake. To Cameron's consternation, the method they finally settled upon was to sing Bobby Sherman's *"Seattle"* whenever the city was mentioned. At first, they were content to simply sing the words. As the game progressed, however, they chose to simulate the various musical instruments, including the trumpet solos, and not content with merely hammering them out on the dashboard, they started to blare them. The combination of sleep deprivation and excessive irritation caused Cameron to demand that during his off time they allow him to sleep in the van instead.

This option provided no relief either. As if travel games in the truck weren't already vexatious, in the van, Evan and Rich had decided upon playing poker as their means of respite. Lacking chips, they'd attribute monetary values to different shapes and colors of guitar picks, and rattled with fatigue, they constantly forgot the assigned denominations. The rules of the game were forgotten in their entirety as the two each argued the case for their respective picks. After an hour of such nonsense, Cameron resolved to run away at the first rest stop. It was then that an incident with Clyde made matters worse.

While the other two were engaged in a Mad Hatter's poker game, in an effort to stay awake himself, Clyde switched the dial on the radio from station to station, as well as from one waveband to another. This resulted in a muddled dissonance, ranging from frenzied radio preachers to country music, accented with jazz and talk shows. It was when Clyde settled on the news station that Cameron became concerned. Along with items of local interest, there were accounts of the war. This time, however, reports about the Alaskan Front were replaced by reports of efforts by the US Pacific Fleet and allies under the ANZUS Treaty, Australia and New Zealand, to relieve the siege of the Hawaiian Islands. NATO forces were resuming their push toward Vienna, and the tentative peace between Taiwan and mainland China still held, despite reports of more purportedly accidental shelling of the islands of Quemoy and Matsu by Chinese military. Inevitable references to the 1960 presidential election occurred, referring to the instance when both Nixon and Kennedy stated that they would be willing to use nuclear weapons if China attacked those islands again. This reminiscent media commotion further caused the threat of force into the fore of every US citizen's thoughts.

Another formidable top news story consisted of reports that the East Germans were considering declaring Berlin an open city. Negotiators, though, in Geneva were holding out for the possibility of a withdrawal of East German forces from Berlin, followed by a limited release of NATO POWs. Such a move would cause a potential chink in the Warsaw Pact efforts in Europe, and on possible opportunities for the US and its NATO allies.

Cameron pondered the news just in, and wondered if it meant that the war was finally turning in their favor.

If we can keep from being nuked, that is.

Thoughts of an early victory buoyed Cameron's waves of exhaustion until he heard a strange thumping noise. Fearing that the van had a flat tire, he sat up in alarm, only to see that Clyde was pounding the steering wheel with his fist and fighting back tears. A quick glance at the Mad Hatters found them lost in a debate on the game value of the yellow guitar picks compared to the green ones.

Oblivious to everything else...

"Man, what's the matter?"

Don't embarrass him.

Clyde shook his head, attempting with all of his might to restrain his tears.

"Nothing. Nothing at all. Our guys are going to be drinking coffee in Vienna any day now, and upset a rice bowl over a little bit of shelling in China. I'm heading to play a guitar in Seattle while people are starving in Honolulu, and the Germans'll be drinking beer in a free Berlin before you know it, so nothing's wrong at all! Even if it was, I don't want to talk about it!"

With that, Clyde slammed his fist even harder on the wheel. A sense of isolation and fear gripped Cameron. He slid into the passenger's seat and sat in silence. Clyde visibly shuddered, his attempts to suppress his anger and tears all but impossible.

"Would you like me to drive for a while?" Cameron offered.

Clyde shook his head emphatically. "No! I can't do jack but play a guitar and drive this friggin' van, and if what everyone says is true, those two things right now are as vital as fighting, so I'm *going* to do this, and you're not taking it away from me!"

Cameron's assurances of pure intentions fell on deaf ears. Clyde was fuming. Realizing the futility of his efforts, Cameron slid out of the passenger's seat and resumed his place in the rear. He settled in and once again attempted slumber, but to no avail. Clearly, the stress that Clyde had experienced back in Missouri had not faded, but remained, and with a vengeance. Adding insult to injury was complete weariness, which surely compounded Clyde's anxiety.

Cameron lay on the floor of the van drifting in and out of fitful half sleep. He awoke when the band arrived at their scheduled stop. He crawled out of the van and stumbled across the parking lot to a small sundries shop. He knew that there was nothing he could do for Clyde. He needed sleep; they all did. But sleep, unfortunately, was an ever-elusive pleasure.

The band presented to the shop manager passes for each of their vehicles, proving their authorization to travel. They assembled around a table and swarmed the menus.

We look like a collection of the walking wounded.

"Where you folks headed to?" a buxom brunette waitress asked, hot coffee in tow.

"We're going to Seattle—" Chuck said, only to be interrupted by Snapper, who burst into sudden song. Chuck burst into laughter. The others stared in shock. Cameron seized the roadie's arm.

"Your death will be slow and painful," he growled.

For a moment, Snapper thought Cameron was joking and took a deep breath to continue his solo. However, as the guitarist's grip painfully constricted the roadie's arm, Snapper knew that Cameron was dead serious. Snapper squelched his singing, but not until a quick glance at Chuck caused them both to erupt into fits of laughter.

"Pitiful," hissed Cameron. He turned his attention to Clyde. "You all right?"

Clyde nodded, his composure regained. He smiled and turned to Evan, with whom he made small talk and told jokes. The two examined their menus, prompting Cameron to do the same. With the interstate highway system open only to essential war-time traffic, the rest stops supplied many items now restricted from civilian consumption. The strain of their travel and the idea of coveted culinary ecstasy caused Cameron to ignore Chuck's warnings about consuming rich foods, especially after their perpetually meager, plain diet. He gleefully devoured a large order of biscuits and gravy, washed down with real orange juice, and real coffee with real cream. A few hours later, though, his indulgence hit him hard. He was stricken with sudden diarrhea and vomiting, and the constant need to stop either beside the road or at any available rest area caused the last leg of the band's journey to go from an estimated four hours to nearly eight. Cameron received no sympathy from the others, even despite what should have been their joyous arrival in Seattle.

Throughout the course of their drive from Missouri, Chuck maintained contact with McIntyre via a secret telephone number specific to the band. In order to ensure that McIntyre was available for their calls, he provided to her coded references for their en route stops, as well as estimated times of arrival. Cameron's gastrointestinal distress caused complications with this arrangement, which in turn drove McIntyre into an uncharacteristically foul mood; she had plenty of security concerns festering in Seattle and the band's tardy arrival exacerbated the situation. On top of it all, the band's frenzy at being told that they had a mandatory early morning call time set the situation totally afoul.

"There's nothing that can be done about it!" Chuck snapped. "We're assuming the schedule of the other band, and they're scheduled for a visit to the refugee center and military hospital this afternoon. The security arrangements are too complicated to cancel at the last minute. There isn't another group available to take over."

"At least in a hospital Cameron can grab a bedpan and not hold us up anymore," Rich groused.

Cameron snarled and shoved his middle finger at Rich.

Chuck, increasingly impatient, ordered everyone back to the vehicles. Cameron rode in the truck this time, the muscles in his abdomen and legs constantly on the verge of cramping, and causing him shortness of breath.

Probably have food poisoning, too…

Chuck had written down their destination address provided by McIntyre, which she'd informed him was also the home of the *Seattle Times*. This set-up allowed McIntyre and the agent posing as her secretary to form acquaintances with various receptionists in the building, thusly allowing them to monitor any gossip shared, including the backstories of what was published in the paper. It also allowed free rein over information about various individuals who worked or conducted business in the building, or with the newspaper. On a less esoteric note, it helped the band to locate with ease what was to become their central office.

Arriving at the building only slightly later than planned, the Roadhouse Sons were guided first to the restroom for Cameron's sake, then to the haven of Concert Entertainment. Once inside the office, Chuck and the band found McIntyre and her "secretary" in the outer office with a man whom none of them recognized.

"Chuck, I'd like you to meet Jack Stanley," McIntyre said, her customary cheerful smile painted on her face. Chuck, though, detected her irritation. "Mr. Stanley is the manager of Boney Jack, the band we're replacing. Mr. Stanley, this is Chuck Lamont. Mr. Lamont is the road manager for the Roadhouse Sons."

"Pleased to meet you, Chuck," said Stanley. The man stood up and was easily as tall as Chuck, and wore a freshly pressed shantung suit, eager smile, and enthusiastic handshake. Something about the man, a rather priggish quality, annoyed Chuck, who instantly understood McIntyre's irritation. "I'd like to thank you for helping us out with our little *inconvenience*, shall we say. I doubt it's been too much trouble for you? I mean, it was a good thing that you were available to assume our bookings on such short notice."

"Please don't worry about it, Jack." Chuck smiled, returning Stanley's firm grip with one even firmer. "Supporting the USO is never any trouble whatsoever. We're always happy to do our civic duty." The other man registered no response to Chuck's parry.

"Mr. Stanley was filling me in on the events that the band has scheduled," McIntyre said, diffusing the growing tension between the two men.

"*Has?*" asked Evan. "Don't you mean *had?* I thought we were taking over for them."

"You're correct in both regards, Mr.....?" replied Stanley.

"Dixon," Chuck said. "Allow me to introduce the Roadhouse Sons. Evan is our drummer. This is Rich Webster; he's the bass player. Over there is Snapper, our roadie, and this is Clyde Poulin, our rhythm guitarist. And here, a bit under the weather, is our lead guitarist and vocalist, Cameron Walsh."

Cameron, who'd stumbled into the room and slumped into the nearest chair, begrudgingly rose to his feet. Unlike the others, who'd all politely greeted Stanley, he didn't acknowledge the introduction. Instead, Cameron slumped back into his chair and rested his head in his hands.

Somewhere, anywhere else but here!

"Rough night, eh, Cam?" Stanley guffawed with a knowing wink. While his tone was familiar, Chuck, McIntyre, and the band noted a tinge of scorn. Cameron raised his head slightly and glared at the man.

"Cameron ate a bit of bad food on the trip out here," Chuck explained to McIntyre. Cameron lowered his head and moaned. "He'll be fine."

"I hope so," she replied, her concern evident. "Your first stop today is the naval hospital by one p.m. for set up. You've got a show this afternoon, followed by a visit to the Bremerton Refugee Center afterwards."

"What time is it now?" Cameron asked with a sigh.

"Almost ten thirty," McIntyre said.

Cameron stared at her, horrified. "You're kidding me, right?" he pleaded.

McIntyre shook her head ruefully and pointed to the ersatz art deco clock on the wall. Cameron's heart sank.

"It's not as bad as all that," Stanley said, jauntily. "You can take the Seattle Ferry, vehicles and all. That will take you right to Bremerton." He turned to Chuck. "Since Puget Sound is closed to non-military and non-essential traffic, you'll need special passes to travel on the ferry. I was fortunate enough to obtain one for my clients, and will be happy to pass it on to you."

Cameron visibly gagged.

A ferry!

"That's very generous of you," Chuck smiled, "However, those passes aren't legally transferable. I'm certain Miss McIntyre has already worked with the USO and obtained all of the necessary passes and permits we'll need. Isn't that correct?"

McIntyre nodded with a smile and retrieved the folder offered by her agent-cum-secretary.

"They're all here," McIntyre confirmed, and passed the folder to Chuck. "Ferry passes, travel passes for the interstate, and the passes to the bases, including driving, parking, and personal passes for you and the boys."

"My goodness, you are thorough," Stanley averred, his face pinched. "Would you, by any chance, consider working for me?"

"Thanks, no. I have all I can handle with this band," McIntyre laughed.

Stanley shrugged dramatically with faux disappointment, his face now emblazoned with a charming smile.

"In that case, let me give you the name of my liaison at the naval base."

"Again, thank you," said McIntyre, firmly. "Each base has already assigned us our liaisons."

"Well, let me at least tell you the names of *some* of the people with whom we've established relationships," Stanley insisted. "There are people who are looking forward to seeing us every time we visit, and I know there is no way that their names could have been noted."

A ferry travels on water…water has waves…waves go up and down…

Cameron dry heaved and raced to the bathroom. Stanley, nonplussed, offered parting pleasantries and excused himself. McIntyre, one eyebrow raised, eyed Chuck and returned to her inner office. When Cameron returned, Chuck was waiting to direct him back to the band truck, despite his pleas for mercy.

The trip across the sound was exactly as Cameron had feared. Under usual circumstances, he was never seasick. In fact, he enjoyed spending vacations with his family on Lake Erie fishing for salmon. Today, though, he knew before he stepped foot upon the deck that the trip would be different than the others, and he was right. Halfway across the sound, he was folded over the railing, retching. Chuck brought him a can of chicken soup, which Snapper had heated on the truck manifold before embarking. Cameron tried waving him off, but Chuck would not listen.

"You're dry heaving," Chuck insisted. "If you don't put something in your stomach, you'll have real trouble! Just drink some of the broth."

Reluctantly, Cameron accepted the soup. He debated even trying. The thought of the can near that greasy engine caused a wave of nausea to wash over him. Chuck sniggered.

"Try reading something other than that Louis L'Amour book," Chuck said. "Maybe try reading Truman Capote once in awhile."

"What the hell does that have to do with anything?" Cameron gagged and grabbed the rail with his free hand.

Without missing a beat, Chuck continued. "Well, in *Other Voices, Other Rooms*, one of his characters had to deal with motion sickness," Chuck explained. "And so he'd eat a pickled egg when he thought he'd puke. Keep something from coming up by forcing something down was his advice."

"Did it work?"

"I have no idea," said Chuck with a grin. "I never finished the book."

Cameron was about to raise the soup to his lips when a sudden swell caused the contents to splash all over the front of him. With a shout, Cameron dropped the can and saw to his horror that his white dungarees and tan shirt were ruined.

"Damn it!" he bellowed, pinching the steaming shirt away from his chest.

"Oh, shit! I am *so* sorry," gasped Chuck. "Are you all right?"

"Yeah, I'm fucking *fine*!" snarled Cameron. "I've got to get to a gig in less than an hour and I don't have any more clothes!"

"Damn!" Chuck whistled, shaking his head. "Don't worry. We'll get you into something. Just get below deck to the van and get out of those clothes."

Cameron did as he was told. While he was disrobing, Chuck knocked on the van door and handed him a bundle of clothes.

"They're *black*!" Cameron said, examining them. "I never wear black!"

"Can't be helped, man," Chuck said, apologetically. "That was all we could find that was clean and would fit you. If it helps, just pretend they're dark blue."

Cameron, clearly disgusted, snatched the clothes from Chuck and quickly dressed.

Stress, exertion, and the perpetual tossing of the waves brought on another attack of nausea, sending Cameron back to the rail. As he began to feel his legs weaken, Cameron saw the wisdom in Chuck's warning, and returned to the van to eat something. The only food remotely palatable to him if unheated was canned Beefaroni. Cameron found the can opener, then forced the pasta into his mouth and rested. He fell into a light sleep. He'd barely shut his eyes, it seemed, when they arrived at Bremerton Naval Base.

I didn't even feel the ferry dock...

They were met by a petty officer who conducted them through security and brought them to the stage.

Nice setup! At least there's that.

With the assistance of shore patrol personnel, Cameron and the others performed the sound check, then headed backstage. They were surprised at the comfortable couch and the delicious edibles awaiting them. Clyde, Rich, and Snapper dug in to rarities such as Ritz crackers with block cheddar cheese, Coca-Cola, and Cheez-Its, while Evan ate Cheerios with milk and drank brewed coffee. Cameron gingerly nursed a cup of tea and resolved to ignore his bothersome condition, though he admittedly hoped that his body wouldn't get the better of him.

Suddenly, they heard their name announced.

"Holy mother of God!" cried Rich. "Is it time already?"

The Roadhouse Sons made their way back to the stage area. Cameron and the boys looked out over what had been an empty field. The grass was filled with men and women seated on blankets, as well as in wheelchairs and on stretchers. Many in the audience wore bandages.

From beholding that sight alone, Cameron promised himself to give the audience his best performance ever. Throughout the first set, he knew that his band mates had made the same decision. Even Clyde seemed thrilled. Finally, the Roadhouse Sons were doing something real, to them, for the almighty cause.

Their performance was heartfelt and they were greeted with sincere and enthusiastic applause. As previously instructed, Cameron and the others made their way through the crowd to greet as many patients as possible. Snapper, with the assistance of their assigned shore patrol personnel, and a very quiet Chuck, performed tear-down and load-out. The band returned backstage.

"If they missed Boney Jack, they sure didn't show it," said Rich. The others didn't know how to respond. This was the band's first exposure to the direct reality of war. Cameron made a cup of tea. He, like everyone else, had nothing to say. The exertion of his performance had taken a toll on him, physically and mentally. He could feel himself shake.

There was a knock on the doorjamb. Their escort arrived to take them to the refugee hospital. Cameron hesitated as he realized what would be involved.

These are the ones too bad off to come to the show.

He wondered in earnest if he was up for the visit. Slightly nauseated, he drew a deep breath, then exhaled and followed the others. They were shown to a car and driven to the front of one of several large, unrefined buildings that were obviously constructed in haste to accommodate the swarm of evacuees from the Alaskan Front. The boys were greeted by a team of doctors and nurses, as well as naval and USO personnel, all of whom explained the patients' conditions and counseled the band on how to manage what they were about to encounter.

"Most of the patients are fine, or as fine as they can be under the circumstances," a man, Doctor Freidman, explained. "Those with physical injuries are healing, for the most part. We've been able to help others with emotional anxieties as best as our resources allow. One group, however, is dealing with challenges both physical and emotional. You don't need to worry. We won't expose you to anyone too unstable. Try to remember that many of these people are still in some form of shock over what has happened to them."

"Did any of these people go through the latest attack on Anchorage?" Clyde asked. Doctor Freidman nodded.

"I'm afraid so. Many in these wards are recent arrivals, in fact."

Cameron glanced at Chuck.

"We're not expecting you to talk to each patient individually," the doctor continued. "Many of them don't respond to outside contact, but there are quite a few who do. Stop and say hello to them. Make small talk. Don't force it if they don't respond to you, but take a moment if they do. They might show you something quite ordinary to you, but to them it is something special that connects them with familiarity of the homes and lives they had to leave behind. It's all right to indulge. The professionals help them adjust. Right now, they just need to know that someone cares. You're celebrities, and just taking the time to come see them is a real boost for their morale. They also may be moved to give you something as a sign of appreciation. In such a case, please don't refuse it. Accept it and give it to your accompanying nurse or orderly. We can return it to them later."

Doctor Freidman paused and removed his spectacles. Evan and Clyde peered toward him.

"One very important note. No matter how much you may be tempted, don't give the patients anything other than your autographs or pictures. No gifts of any kind, please. Those can be stolen and can lead to a great deal of trouble for everyone. It's important that we're able to maintain peace and calm here. Now, shall we begin?"

Doctor Freidman led them through the front door and into the makeshift lobby. They made their way into a building, which reminded Cameron of his boyhood days away at camp. The building was divided into various wards, all configured in the same manner. Rows of single beds were positioned along each wall, and there was a wide aisle in the center. The Roadhouse Sons, their demeanor awkward, maneuvered through the rooms and down the aisles, pausing briefly at each bedside. As they'd been advised, some patients asked them for autographs. Snapper was pleased when he was asked, too, and heartily signed a steno pad. He turned to the next bed to offer his signature and, also as they'd been advised, that patient paid him no attention whatsoever.

Evan, Clyde, and Snapper were then led to a brightly painted ward filled with young children. As the band members navigated the room, some of the youngsters asked the boys if they'd seen members of the children's families, or if the boys had seen their pets.

One young girl asked Clyde if he had seen her mother. Clyde sat at he edge of the child's bed.

"I didn't tell her I was going outside to play," she whispered, fighting back sobs. "Then there were loud noises and lots of fire and I got lost and couldn't find my way home. I didn't see her when they put me on the ship. She won't know how to find me!"

Utterly helpless and at a loss for words, Clyde looked up at the nurse, who shook her head sadly.

"You just rest, honey." The nurse spoke in soothing tones and leaned down to tuck the bedclothes around the little girl. "We're trying to find your mom for you, but you just rest now, OK?"

Clyde watched as the nurse moved on to the next bed, pausing for him to catch up. Before he left, Clyde leaned in toward the little girl and gently bopped her on the nose with his finger.

"I've got a little sister," he said, beaming his most charming smile. "You look just like her, you know."

The little girl looked at him quizzically at first, then her face burst with a smile. Clyde smoothed her blanket and gave her a kiss on the forehead. The little girl swooned and closed her eyes, her smile still upon her lips. Clyde moved to the next bed.

"You don't have a sister," whispered Rich.

"Shut up if you know what's good for you!" Clyde hissed.

Meanwhile, Cameron had accompanied another group of doctors and nurses into a ward filled with severely wounded adults. He visited every bed, pausing briefly at each one. Many of the patients acknowledged his presence; some did not. He didn't try to force interaction; he was as cheerful and pleasant as possible to each person, despite his own physical and emotional toil. Finally, he had to stop and rest.

"Are you all right?" the orderly asked. Cameron nodded halfheartedly.

"Why?" Cameron asked. "Do I look that bad?"

"Your face is as white as a sheet and those dark circles under your eyes remind me of a raccoon," the orderly grinned. "I guess that's why they asked you guys to fill in for Boney Jack. You look just like him!"

Is that a compliment or an insult?

Cameron silently resumed his tour through the ward, his sheepish orderly in tow. As he made his way down the aisle, Cameron saw young man prone in a bed, muttering and seemingly oblivious to his surroundings. He responded to nothing anyone said, or to any activity in the room, until Cameron arrived. Cameron hesitated, then leaned over and greeted the young man.

"Hey, man, how are you?"

As though a switch had been thrown, the young man became suddenly animated.

"It's you!" he cried, his voice cracking with emotion. "I thought you weren't coming. I almost gave up!"

Cameron felt panic in his gut. "It's okay, brother!" Cameron reassured him.

Where the hell is my guide?

The orderly had already moved to another bed. Frantic, Cameron turned his attention back to the young man.

"I've got something for you," the young man whispered, reaching into his pajama top. He withdrew a worn out, dog-eared postcard and shoved it into Cameron's hands.

"This is yours," the young man rasped, clutching Cameron's arm. "I've been waiting to give it to you. Don't lose it! You can't lose it!"

The young man, completely agitated and irrational, clutched onto Cameron and tried to get out of bed, crashing a lamp to the floor as he did so. Orderlies and nurses responded, including the one accompanying Cameron. Two people grabbed him and escorted him away, while the others tried to calm the hysterical youth. Cameron was ushered into the hallway. There, he found his band mates seated, waiting for whatever was next. He sat as well, for what seemed like an eternity.

Suddenly, a nurse emerged from the room. Cameron jumped from his seat and handed her the post card.

She shook her head. "You might as well keep it," she sighed.

"Doctor Freidman told us to hand over anything they gave us and you'd return it later."

"Keep it. I can promise you he won't ask for it."

"Why?"

"He just died."

CHAPTER TWENTY-SIX

"Savoring"

Simms watched with gleeful satisfaction as Stanley hurried into his private office. Watching the color drain from his superior's face was always worth the daily aggravation and humiliation. Simms had come to savor even the tiniest bit of tasty karmic retribution, and this guiltless pleasure was becoming increasingly addictive of late. He was careful not to gloat, but Stanley's angst offered such instant gratification to Simms that it was almost impossible to deny the relishing of it.

Stanley's snippy timbre yanked Simms from his revelry. He was about to make an excuse for his woolgathering when he realized that his superior's voice was squawking at him through the receiver still in his hand! He couldn't say one word, or his eavesdropping would be revealed. There was nothing he could do. To hang up now would reveal that he had not followed the required protocol of placing the call on hold until Stanley could take it himself. Simms was not usually foolhardy enough to risk that, but holding his breath, he convinced himself that, in order to satisfy his curiosity, the risk was necessary. He felt immense satisfaction knowing that the other party was immune to Stanley's treacly charm. He raised the receiver to his ear, then thought better of it, and lowered it noiselessly to the desk. That way, no one could hear him breathing.

"Don't pretend you're surprised at this call," the other voice snapped. "Have you read today's paper?"

"Yes, I have," replied Stanley, detachedly. "All of them, in fact. But I'm afraid I noticed nothing of any grave concern. To what particular article are you referring?"

"Glibness is hardly advisable…" The other voice was menacing, which caused Stanley great anxiety. Simms, in turn, received such pleasure at Stanley's fretting that he could barely contain himself.

"I'm referring to the list of deceased refugees," the voice continued. The irritation was palpable. "We just learned that your contact was among them."

"I didn't have a contact among the refugees," Stanley insisted, his tone tinged with panic. "I have contacts among the staff, but that's all. I've never, ever been in contact with the refugees!"

"Tim Woodhouse, our courier from Anchorage, the man from whom you were supposed to receive a package…a package we're very anxious to get our hands on," the voice insisted impatiently. Simms felt a shiver run down his spine. He could only imagine Stanley's state.

Stanley said nothing. After several moments of intense silence, he finally spoke.

"I have no way of getting to the bases."

Did Simms detect a delicious note of pleading? Stanley was clearly alarmed by the caller.

Stanley continued. "That possibility is completely unavailable to me right now. You know that! I planned to work with the band who've assumed our tour dates on the bases, but the military rescinded *my* clearance, as well. I explained that to you when—"

"You just said that you have contacts among the staff. Why didn't you make use of them to renew your clearance?" The voice was completely and resolutely unsympathetic.

"You don't understand," Stanley said, his voice becoming a moan. "I only use them to help me acquire supplies and drugs from the pharmacies. For anything other than that, they'd be useless! They're mercenaries who work for whomever offers to pay them. It would be suicide to entrust anything more to them than being a supplier."

"Yet you saw no risk in involving them with our operation, even that far?"

Simms all but felt Stanley's sudden gasp.

"Can you make use of them to locate Woodhouse's effects?"

Simms heard Stanley's sickening, hard gulp.

"That's a possibility." Stanley was breathless. "But I can't guarantee anything."

"You had better." The voice was ominous. "Failure is not an option."

"That…is out of my hands," Stanley said, plaintively.

Simms no longer drew satisfaction from his superior's suffering. If Stanley was indeed that frightened, then the situation must be truly dangerous, which meant Simms couldn't expect to escape the fallout either.

Stanley continued. "When something happens to the refugees, their belongings are disposed of," he stammered. "What little they may have with them is usually so threadbare, not even the staff will take it, I've heard. Their things are usually disposed of or destroyed, as I say, especially if there's no next of kin to claim them. Whatever they might have had would be long gone by now!"

"For your sake, that better not be the case."

The threat was clear and unveiled. Simms regretted his impulse to eavesdrop. Suddenly, he was faced with a much more serious concern. Standing in the doorway, and sporting a sadistic grin, was Boney Jack. Simms felt the grip of sheer panic. He hadn't replaced the receiver and there was no way that he could do it now without betraying himself. What if the musician said something, or slammed the door? Simms' eavesdropping would be exposed for sure. Of all the messes that Boney Jack—singer and band—had thrust upon him, the situation at hand would surely subject him to the most serious consequences ever placed upon Simms.

In each of the previous instances, Boney Jack had been the instigator. Simms was constantly subject to such caprice and was always held accountable for having not prevented the chaos. With the telephone off the hook, Simms could claim no such innocence. The look on the musician's face suggested to Simms that Boney Jack was fully aware of Simms' predicament, and about to take full advantage of the situation. Then again, how would Boney Jack know that Simms was doing anything out of the ordinary? Simms knew that displaying even an iota of fear would be the worst thing to do. The musician would sense it immediately.

With his hand raised palm outward, Simms indicated he would be with Boney Jack momentarily. Perhaps playing to the singer's ego would placate him for a moment, hopefully long enough for Simms to conjure a better course of action. Though his mind raced, he caught bits of the private conversation.

"Do I need to remind you of how much you owe us for your success?" the voice asked.

"Of course not. You know perfectly well that you don't."

"It would be unfortunate to have all of your hard work and success go…up in smoke." The blatant analogy churned Simms' gut.

"I've always been very careful to repay you and not cause you concern, haven't I?" Stanley's tone was flat and lifeless.

"We're not discussing your past. This is your future. The cost is greater; the risk is greater; the *consequences* are greater. Your contacts at the hospital must investigate and report what happened to Woodhouse's effects. Immediately!"

Stanley attempted a response, but Simms was unable to hear what he said. The line went dead. Boney Jack had pressed his finger onto the telephone's cradle button and cut off the call.

Boney Jack laughed. "Off the hook. Now on the hook! Naughty, naughty!"

Simms slammed the receiver down, hoping to pinch the musician's finger, but his nemesis was too quick for him.

"I'm bored, Chrissy," Boney Jack hissed, leaning into Simms' face. Simms fought a gag reflex at the smell of stale liquor, cigarette smoke, and body odor from someone who'd clearly spent the last several days without a bath.

"I've been grounded long enough, little man," the musician rasped. His eyes were slits. He leaned in even closer. "I'm the Scourge of God, damn it! I'm not going to stay in a squalid hotel room any more!"

Simms put his handkerchief over his mouth and nose and leaned away. To his utter relief, Boney Jack didn't try to move closer, but cast a fiery glare at Simms from the other side of the desk.

"You're free to go anywhere in Seattle," Simms maintained, breathing as shallowly as possible as he spoke. "If you want to go somewhere, just go!"

Boney Jack pounded his fist onto the desk, his pallid face flushed with anger.

"How?" he demanded. "Fly? Walk? I want a car and I want it now!"

"That's impossible and you know it!" Simms countered. Boney Jack's sudden complexion and spiky hair reminded Simms of an amaranth. "All of your gas and travel rations were confiscated as part of the terms of your release. Anywhere you wish to go will have to be by a cab or on foot!"

"Little people like you ride in taxis," spat Boney Jack. He circled the desk, slowly at first then increased his speed. "And little people like you walk. I demand a chariot!"

The door at the other end of the office slapped open.

"What is the meaning of this commotion?" shouted Stanley. "They could hear you two on the other end of the phone!"

"Your ward is suffering from cabin fever and ennui," Simms said, wiping his face and escaping to the sideboard. "I was explaining to him the only options available for relieving his condition, and he did not find them acceptable. I'm sorry if that disturbed you."

Simms dabbed at his forehead. He searched Stanley's face for an indication that he'd been aware of Simms' eavesdropping. As usual, Stanley betrayed no sign of such a possibility.

"Then for God's sake, get him a car and let him go out!" Stanley stomped his foot as he shouted.

"That's not possible," Simms reminded him meekly. "That would violate their terms of release.

Stanley quivered with rage. "Then give him *my* car and driver!" he screamed. "They're only supposed to stay in the city, not their rooms! Don't presume to be a lawyer in addition to your other lines of purported expertise. I don't think I could handle dealing with that nonsense as well!" With that, Stanley stormed into his office and slammed the door behind him.

Boney Jack cackled. Pure and utter rage swelled in Simms. He couldn't allow such a public undermining to betray his thoughts or feelings. Boney Jack leaned into Simms' face, his eyes sparkling with delight.

"I want my chariot," he hissed, flicking his serpentine tongue. "He just offered me his, and said you had to get it for me. So make sure you do it quickly, and make certain I have something to quench my divine thirst. The Scourge of God rides forth!"

Turning with a mighty sweep of his arms, Boney Jack began his exit, but not without sending the entire contents of Simms' desk cascading to the floor. Hands clenched and trembling with rage, Simms picked up the telephone receiver to call for the car. He heard voices on the line. Glancing down at the phone, he realized that, by mistake, he'd punched the button for Stanley's private line.

"You're out of your fucking mind. There's no way they kept that stuff," a dull, thick male voice said. Simms didn't recognize it. The voice reminded him of the how the band members spoke when they were under the influence of some substance or other. He wondered if one of them had called Stanley. Then he remembered. The phone didn't ring. Stanley must have placed a call.

"Never mind your ridiculous assertions," Stanley snarled. "Find out what happened to his belongings!"

"Do you have any idea how many croak out here a day?" the voice asked. Simms knew that the person on the other line was the contact at the refugee center mentioned by Stanley earlier.

"I don't care if they all die in a single night," Stanley snapped. "Find out what happened to his things! If the military can keep track of how many times a private shits, then they'll have a paper trail for you to follow!"

"If I can get access to it." The contact yawned. "This is a big hassle and I could get into a lot of trouble for poking around in those offices. This could cost a little bit more than usual."

"You could get into a lot of trouble if you don't poke around in those offices. The ones who want his belongings are not at all accustomed to being told that they can't have what they want. It will be very bad news for you, indeed, if you disappoint me."

"Are you mixed up with the mob or something?" the contact whispered. "You should've told me!"

"You just listen to me, and you'll only have to deal with me." Stanley was ice. "If you don't come through, swimming in Puget Sound with cement shoes will be the least of your worries."

"Fine," the other man replied, obviously shaken. "I'll be in touch as soon as I know anything."

"You'd better," Stanley advised. He hung up.

Simms smiled and punched the button for the outside line. He would call for the car later. He had a more important call to make. After all, Stanley wasn't the only one with contacts at the bases.

CHAPTER TWENTY-SEVEN

"Head Games"

Upon their arrival in Seattle, the Roadhouse Sons were delighted to find themselves situated in a small, comfortable suite at one of the hotels designated by the war effort for housing entertainers. Though far from luxurious, there was a kitchen and dining area with a sitting room and half bath—with continual hot water—located on the first floor, along with three bedrooms, a second sitting room, and a full bath located on the second floor. The band had to sleep two to a room, but at least they were able to sleep in real beds with comfortable mattresses, and not in the van or the truck. No one complained, especially since both sitting rooms were equipped with color televisions.

The USO ensured that the suite was supplied with regular deliveries of rare commodities, such as peanut butter, cheese, coffee and milk, and in the same amount that was issued to a regular household. Such goods were supplied in addition to what they could purchase with their own rations. As an added bonus, the hotel was classified as an Essential Zone; it also housed offices for government and military personnel, which thereby rendered it exempt from the brownouts and blackouts in other parts of the city.

Despite these luxuries, Cameron was still quite shaken and distracted by the death of the young man in the hospital. At first, he ventured to speak about it with Chuck and his fellow band mates, but upon Chuck's insistence, he tried not to dwell on what had transpired. The fact that there simply wasn't much time to mourn made it easier for him.

Their first day in Seattle was a harbinger of things to come. The Roadhouse Sons found themselves on a tour of the Puget Sound area, from Lakewood and Tacoma to Olympia, Bremerton, Navy Yard City, and myriad military bases and hospitals. On days when there were no performances, there were appearances on television stations, radio shows, and interviews with newspapers and magazines. Before they knew it, the months of May and June flew past. And while there was little time to relax, the open-air shows where they performed gave them the benefits of the ocean breeze and breathtaking views of Mt. Rainier. Those assets of nature contributed greatly toward relieving the boys' exhaustion.

Not everything was so pleasant, however. Despite the respite from any specific case-related work, to the band members' consternation, the issue of the constant bizarre and antisocial behavior by Boney Jack hung over their heads like the Sword of Damocles.

"We really don't have any comment," Cameron explained to yet another reporter. "We've heard their music, but we've never had any contact with them. We filled the slot in their tour schedule. That's all. If another band had created an opening, we'd have filled theirs instead. I've never met any of them, so I really don't think it's a good idea to say anything about them personally. We kind of dig some of their stuff, so I guess they can't be all bad."

Nevertheless, the specter of Boney Jack was a perpetual issue that defied eradication. More and more, newspapers expended a great deal of resources and effort to cast the Roadhouse Sons as the antithesis of Boney Jack, which did not go unnoticed by certain opportunists with esoteric agendas. To no one's surprise, Jack Stanley became more persistent, almost aggressive, in his attempts to negotiate a deal with the Roadhouse Sons to engage in a public relations tour with Boney Jack. Chuck and McIntyre had toyed with the idea, but didn't propose it seriously to the Roadhouse Sons. Not only were the Roadhouse Sons reticent to fuel the media's fire to create a feud between the bands, the boys faced the reality that, again, there simply wasn't any time, and lack of time was a perpetually sore subject.

"Man, you promised us some R&R way back in Missouri!" bemoaned Cameron. "All we got was a case of Montezuma's revenge!"

"Correction!" replied Chuck, eyes glued to the beloved *Sackett*. "I promised you I'd *try* to schedule some R&R in Missouri, and *you* were the only one that got sick, and you got sick in Oregon. Please pay attention to details. They're very important."

"Detail this!" snapped Cameron, flipping his middle finger. Brazen disrespect for Chuck's authority would usually place the perpetrator in serious trouble. But this time, Chuck indulged Cameron. He placed his book on the table, folded his hands and sighed.

"I know," he soothed. "We're *all* wound tight like a spring, but there is nothing I can do about it at the moment, and I really mean *nothing*."

"Well, you better figure something out!" Cameron stood squarely in front of Chuck. "Because I am about to fucking snap, and I am not alone in this, in case you haven't noticed."

Chuck folded his hands behind his head. "Yes, I have noticed," he replied, heaving another sigh. "In case you haven't noticed, I'm not far behind you. But right now, you have so many appearances, performances, and obligations strung together like beads that there's not enough room for a dinner out, much less a period of much-deserved debauchery."

"Beads!" snorted Cameron. "They might as well be rosary beads, for crying out loud!"

"Those might come in handy."

"Great!" Cameron plopped into an overstuffed chair. "You're not content with trying to make us choir boys, you want to make us monks! Is that it?"

"Not worth the effort to make you get haircuts," Chuck yawned. "I mean you might want to fortify yourself with some divine intervention for your appointment tomorrow morning."

Cameron's gut flinched. "And why is that?"

"Because you guys get to share the spotlight with Boney Jack tomorrow morning at a press conference."

"Are you fucking kidding me?" Cameron jumped to his feet. He ran fingers through his long brown hair and began to pace. He was muttering under his breath.

Just what I fucking need.

"I'm not happy about it either, if that's any consolation," Chuck cajoled. He picked up *Sackett*. "But I didn't have anything to do with it. We already had the press conference scheduled. The press just changed the format on us. The newspapers put it together to drum up publicity for the upcoming show."

"I thought we worked with the USO and didn't need to worry about all that!" Cameron made no effort to hide his profound irritation.

"We do," Chuck confirmed, ignoring Cameron's petulance. "However, Boney Jack doesn't any longer, and *they* need to sell tickets. Considering how much work their lawyers are doing, they are going to have to sell a lot of tickets and their management isn't making any secret about it, either. So, promoters are trying to milk the whole situation for all it's worth, and many of them are trying to push the battle of the bands idea."

Cameron stopped dead in his tracks. "You don't mean we have to play with them, do you?"

Chuck shook his head.

"No, you don't."

Don't patronize me.

Chuck continued. "No matter what absurd ideas anyone has about hiring the Roadhouse Sons, your performances are locked up tight for pretty much the entire summer."

Cameron was about to protest once again when Chuck held up his hand.

"Before you flip out on me, yes, I did schedule some time off!"

Cameron breathed a sigh of relief, but was surprised at himself that his eagerness to escape for even a few days only made the anticipation of it worse.

"When? Man, I'm serious. I'm ready to snap any minute."

"Can you at least hang on until tomorrow night?" Irritation crept into Chuck's voice.

"Tomorrow night?" cried Cameron. "We get the night off? You're not fucking with me, are you?"

"You have a full day scheduled tomorrow, and I do mean a full day. You've got that press conference in the morning, an interview at noon, and then a show for the military families tomorrow afternoon at Fort Lewis." Chuck paused for a moment, and snickered.

"What's so funny?" asked Cameron, both concerned and alarmed at his manager's attitude.

Chuck shook his head. "I was just thinking about how you're going to go the whole spectrum tomorrow."

"Why?" Cameron demanded.

"Because tomorrow you'll go from Boney Jack in the morning to Up With People in the afternoon. You can't get much more polar opposite than that!"

Cameron buried his head in his hands. "You've got to be kidding me! White bread, whole milk, and lots of shiny teeth. Snapper will be happy at least."

"Why's that?" Chuck asked, confused.

"Milk and cookies back stage," Cameron said with a derisive sneer. "He loves that shit."

"Knock it off!" Chuck snapped. "Up With People are good kids and have a tough job, so you might want to think about changing your attitude about them!"

"Why should I do that? They're a bubble gum act with a lot of happy kids straight out of a *Sid & Marty Krofft* show. I'll tell you right now, the first sign of a puppet and I'm out of there, and you're not stopping me!"

Chuck leaned in toward Cameron, who knew by the set of his manager's jaw that the man was not amused.

"They're opening for you tomorrow," Chuck said, sternly. "And I'll say it again. You seriously rethink your attitude about them. I'm dead serious about that."

"Again, why?" Cameron defiantly thrust his face into Chuck's. His responses were now instinctive. The band had nothing in common with Boney Jack or Up With People and that, coupled with intense burnout, rendered discretion impossible. The sound of laughter from the sitting room upstairs beckoned him, but he had to hold his ground.

"Because they're doing the same job you're doing! They're entertaining troops and patients in hospitals, as well as families of servicemen on active duty. And they're kids, just barely out of high school in many cases. Some of them are away from their homes and families for the first time in their lives, and performing in military bases on the edge of a war zone. You guys have the benefit of road years under your belt, so you've acquired a defense against the realities of the big, wide world. They haven't!"

Chuck paused. The muted sounds of the upstairs television thumped away mindlessly.

"Yeah, they smile, they show a lot of teeth, and they keep an upbeat attitude and act like they're all on a sugar rush. But don't think for a minute they don't work as hard as you do, and that they aren't just as equally frightened when they see someone sitting in the audience with an arm or a leg missing, or a bloody bandage where a limb used to be. Think of what those kids go through when they have to visit a hospital ward filled with little children who don't know where their families are or what's going to happen to them. You do that at their age. Try to keep *going*, never mind smiling, just like they do. Then you can make fun of them."

"Hey, I'm sorry…" Cameron was weary. Remorse washed over him.

"We're getting set up for a big pre-Fourth of July Celebration and Up With People're going to knock themselves out to kick it off. And if when they're done you don't make them feel welcome like the most patriotic act since Kate Smith sang "*God Bless America*," I will personally kick each and every one of your asses!"

"I said I was sorry! I won't make fun of them anymore."

They sat in silence. Cameron shifting uneasily while Chuck stared at the floor, drumming his fingers together. Cameron was about to speak, but noticed the gnashing of Chuck's jaw. To say anything now would make matters much worse. The silence became oppressive. For a moment, Cameron pondered turning on the radio, but thought better of it; Chuck abhorred ambient noise. He wasn't sure that Chuck was finished with their conversation, so leaving the room was also out of the question. Finally, in desperation, he picked up *Sackett* and began reading.

You can't say anything about this. It's mine.

Cameron had only read a few paragraphs when Chuck noticed that he had the book.

"Don't lose my place," Chuck said. "I was at my favorite part."

"Don't worry," Cameron replied. "I see where you marked the page."

"What are you talking about?" Chuck asked. "I didn't mark it."

"You must have," Cameron insisted. "See? This letter's underlined."

Chuck held out his hand. Cameron gave him the book. Chuck examined the page and, confused, flipped through the rest of the book.

"There's a whole bunch of letters underlined," he mused. "I don't know why I didn't notice them before. Did you?"

"Yeah," Cameron said, stretching. "I thought you did it to keep from bending the corner of the pages."

"No, I didn't do it. I bet Doug did it."

"Doug!" Cameron laughed. "You're kidding, right? If Dougie ever read anything other than a comic book or *Playboy*, I'd be pretty damned surprised. I don't even know why that book was in his stuff."

"How do you explain these?" Chuck continued flipping through the book.

"I don't know!" Cameron was vexed. "Doug probably got it from someone else, or it got mixed up in his stuff by mistake. Is there a name in the front?"

"Nothing but a stamp saying it's the property of Lyndon Institute Library, which means it's stolen!"

Chuck tossed the book back to Cameron. "I'm going for a walk before curfew."

With a brief wave of a hand, Cameron vaguely acknowledged Chuck's departure. He studied the pages of the book.

It could be nothing...

The random nature of the markings bothered him; it was impossible for him to concentrate on the words, as opposed to the letters. As he scanned the pages, he noticed more underlined letters.

Like buying a new car. Suddenly, they're everywhere.

He noticed something else. In addition to underlined letters, there were other letters with diagonal lines drawn through them, suggesting that the markings were not at all accidental. Cameron also discovered hyphens in the margins. He could stand it no longer. He grabbed some onion paper and a pen, turned to the front of the book, and meticulously examined each page. He copied each and every marking on each and every page. When he was finished, he found himself staring at a collection of letters that made absolutely no sense to him.

Uegebkofftmfftkombfmutuepkokuhutgemefatueadpkdeikikdkmrrndkurkpat Suetatngftknputsemdkpurktfekfutsemdepurdktfnktmrfkdpsuettatfkmsueecgk efkdrdasaftkdodkiombfmututoatefmtoateftfottmofiufthuofadmttpefdw- kradktlasatk

Cameron felt incredibly foolish. What if they really were just random, insignificant markings made by some ordinary person? There were no clear breaks indicating where words or sentences would be.

Wait...only certain letters have slashes through them...

He examined *Sackett* again. There was no obvious indication as to why some letters were selected over others; sometimes they fell in the middle of a word, and other times at the beginning or the end. Also, there seemed to be no pattern regarding the selection of the letter itself. Sometimes a letter would appear without any markings whatsoever, and other times not. The more Cameron contemplated the situation, the more he was convinced that there had to be some sort of coded message.

Quit playing spook. Ask Chuck about it when he gets back.

Cameron sat on the sofa, closed his eyes and waited.

Chuck arrived moments later. Cameron beckoned him to the couch and showed Chuck the markings. Chuck examined them carefully, then studied Cameron's paper.

"Cryptography isn't my forte, but I admit it does look like something."

"Do you think it's anything important?" Cameron asked, heady with the excitement

This could be valuable!

"I honestly have no idea," Chuck admitted. He gave Cameron the paper.

"But, I mean, we should show this to someone, right? It could be something important, don't you think?"

"Hard to tell. Look, I know you're bored and going stir crazy, and here's something that seems pretty cool, but I'll tell you right now to forget it. Look, this was all marked up before we got it so we know it doesn't have anything to do with us. It came from a high school library! It's probably a code for hooking up at a party, or something."

"But—" Chuck waved his hand, silencing Cameron.

"Drop it! I'm telling you! Don't ask me to pass it on, either. There's a war on, and we've all got better things to do than find out who is going out with who, or whatever this may or may not be about. If you want to play with this on your own time, feel free. That's all I have to say about it!"

"You were the one that was curious about it, first," Cameron cried.

"Correction! I said I thought it was weird. I always think stuff I don't know is weird. It comes with the job, but I also know when not to waste precious time. Don't bug me about it if you decide to pursue this. Got it?"

"Yeah, man, I got it," Cameron muttered. He briefly studied his paper and dropped it into his guitar case. As he did so, something else caught his attention. The beat-up postcard from the young man at the refugee center was in his guitar case, too.

I forgot about that.

Cameron kneeled down and stared at the card. It was creased and torn; it's design a typical style found in any truck stop or tourist trap. There was nothing unusual or distinctive about it. A picture of a grizzly bear attempting to catch a salmon graced the front while the back was divided, with one area for a message and the other for an address. It was addressed to Boney Jack, and bore a message. The handwriting was a quick scribble. One corner was torn off and another was adhered with transparent tape that was beginning to peel away from the card.

Cameron recollected his time at the hospital and the disturbed young man who insisted that Cameron take the postcard. The youth had warned Cameron not to lose it.

Then, right there, he died. Heart attack, they said.

The young man had mistaken Cameron for Boney Jack. Later, Cameron had debated forwarding the postcard to Boney Jack in order to fulfill a dying fan's last wish, but rejected the idea. From what he knew of him, Boney Jack was a punk rocker absolute narcissist without a shred of sentiment. He wouldn't have cared at all, and would likely have destroyed the card just to show how much. The young man's tragedy would've become more dismal. Cameron sighed and placed the postcard in his guitar case.

"Are you fretting over that postcard again, now?" Chuck demanded. His voice was so sudden and clipped that Cameron jumped up and almost fell.

"I swear! Dogs worry bones less than you worry matters!"

"Well, excuse me!" snapped Cameron. While he understood Chuck's ability to remain unsentimental at all times, Cameron was never completely comfortable with the attribute.

"I feel bad for some guy who died thinking he'd met a big rock star when he'd only met me. I didn't realize that would get on your delicate nerves so friggin' much! What the hell is wrong with you, anyway?"

"Wrong with me?" Chuck was incredulous.

"Yeah, you!" Cameron faced him. "You don't connect with anyone or anything, and if anyone around you does, you get pissed! Well, fuck you! I feel bad when some kid who didn't know where he was or who he was talking to dies. He was a refugee and they didn't even know his name at first. His last wish was to give that stupid card to his idol and he died not doing it."

"We've already discussed this," Chuck insisted. "I'm not doing it again. You can't afford to have sentimental connections in this business."

"I'm a musician!" Cameron retorted. "I'm *all* sentiment!"

"You're more than that now and you know it!"

Cameron stormed into the kitchen. He refrained from dignifying Chuck's insult with a response; they'd argued about the stage versus reality too many times, and he was sick of it. To insinuate that being a musician was less worthy than his other occupation enraged him. He opened the refrigerator, took a beer, and returned to the living room.

Chuck was examining the postcard. His breathing was regular and his demeanor lighter.

If you're big enough, so am I.

"Now, if you were going to play spy master and find out what Boris was trying to tell Natasha, this would be a fun place to start," Chuck said, smiling and waving the card.

While Cameron recognized Chuck's attempt to diffuse the tension, he still felt insulted. Nevertheless, he decided to play along.

"Why's that?" he said, gulping a mouthful of beer.

"First off, you've got a picture of a bear trying to catch a salmon. That could be your first clue."

Cameron shrugged and shook his head. "Clue about what?"

"The bear is a Russian symbol. Salmon are pink, which is a shade of red," Chuck explained, nodding vehemently with mock assertion. "So, this is obviously a Commie signal of some sort. Probably a message for Fearless Leader."

Cameron rolled his eyes.

Keeping the peace isn't worth this bullshit.

"Take a look at the back." Chuck fostered a faux Russian accent. "Have you read the message? We're so sorry, Uncle Albert, that you haven't heard a thing all day but the Kettle is on the boil and I believe it's going to rain. So lift your feet up or a gypsy couldn't get a cup of tea."

Cameron rolled his eyes at Chuck's ruse. "Yeah. It almost sounds like it's from that Paul McCartney song, but the lyrics are all mixed up."

"That could be a cloooooo," whispered Chuck, with dramatic sotto voce. Cameron laughed.

At least this is better than arguing.

"Let's seeeeee. If the young lad was going to give the card to Boney Jack, why would he call him Uncle Albert?" mused Chuck, fanning his fingers over his lips. "If he was going to give it to a musician, why would he mangle the lyrics of a perfectly good song? That's hardly the way to impress someone in *your* profession, isn't it?"

Cameron acknowledged the dig with a terse grin.

No need to aggravate an old situation. This time, anyway.

"That does make sense to me...sort of," Cameron explained, to Chuck's surprise. "They told me at the hospital that he'd been out of it ever since he arrived. He got there with the last batch of refugees from Anchorage. Who knows when he wrote it? He might have done it before the attack or after, or even after he left Alaska. He could've written it at the hospital. He could have been addled when he decided to do it and mixed everything up. Or, maybe he found a card someone else had addressed and wrote the message himself later."

"Those are very good theories, but they don't hold up. Even though the message itself is a scramble, the address is perfect," Chuck said with a smile. "And the handwriting is the same in both cases."

"He addressed it first, then wrote the message?"

"Too farfetched," Chuck laughed. He studied the card again, this time with it right up to his face. "No. That couldn't be it. You know something? I am more curious about this. This is all just a little too strange."

Thank you, God!

They huddled over the card. Neither of them spoke. Chuck flipped the card from front to back, front to back, then halted his gaze on the picture.

"You know, it mentions lifting your feet up, and the picture does have the bear raising a paw," Chuck muttered, oblivious to Cameron's presence.

"That's the corner with tape on it," Cameron pointed out. "Could that be significant?"

"Nah, too obvious," Chuck averred. "A good spy would never do something like that. Hiding something in plain sight is the same as leaving it out in the open, no matter what the novels say. Nope. The tape is just to hold the corner on. Here, you can see where it was torn off."

"But why save that corner when there was another one missing?" Cameron countered.

Chuck furrowed his brow. "You've got something there," he admitted. "Do you have a knife on you?"

Cameron retrieved a paring knife from the kitchen. Chuck slid the point of the knife along the edge of the postcard where the tape started, then slowly peeled it off, removing a layer of the card with it. With an eyebrow raised and a glance at Cameron, he examined the bits of cardboard in front of him. He poked at what resembled an iota of paper fiber and was about to tease Cameron more when the color drained from his face.

"Sweet Jesus," Chuck gasped. At first, Cameron thought Chuck cut himself.

He's not bleeding.

"What's the matter?" Cameron was unnerved. Chuck had never had such an expression on his face.

He's messing with me!

He was about to concede to Chuck's jibes until his manager carefully set one of the pieces on the table and got on his knees to examine it even closer.

"What is the matter?" Cameron insisted.

"Keep your voice down!" Chuck whispered. He pointed with the edge of the knife to the corner segment. Cameron saw a minute black dot, which Chuck carefully poked at with the tip of the knife.

"This is a lot of effort for a joke." Chuck met Cameron's gaze, his eyes wide and alert, his shoulder muscles tense.

"This isn't a joke," Chuck whispered. "I think it's a microdot."

"You made your point. Ha, ha, ha. My imagination got the best of me!" Cameron raised his hands in surrender. "Once again, I made a big deal out of nothing. It won't happen again. I promise!"

"I said keep your voice down!" Chuck rasped. "I think you just got lucky."

You're not getting me this time.

"I finally get lucky and it's here with you," Cameron derided. "I make mountains out of molehills. I get it! Don't spoil it by getting us all pissy with each other again."

"I'm serious!" Chuck was not smiling, nor did his eyes possess their usual impish gleam. They were cold as ice.

"How do you know it's a microdot?"

Chuck eyed the second-floor landing to ensure that they were alone. With great care, he opened a magazine to a predominately light page and placed it back on the table. He moved the point of the paring knife over the magazine and, with a nod of his head, beckoned Cameron to examine the point of the knife. Almost imperceptible to the naked eye was a small black speck.

"Jesus! It's the same size as a period in this magazine!" Cameron exclaimed. The speck resembled an innocuous particle from the postcard fibers.

"This is completely uncharacteristic to this material!" Chuck clucked his tongue. "There are no other similar specks in this postcard. For a second I thought it was just a speck of dirt, but when I picked it off so easily, I knew it was a singular element. If it was part of the postcard material, it would be ingrained in the pulp, not nestled in between the layers."

I'm still not convinced.

Cameron smirked to himself.

Chuck glared at him. "Get me a tissue!" he snapped. Cameron retrieved a tissue from the bathroom. Chuck carefully pressed the point of the knife against the middle of the tissue. The small, black dot was more evident against a pure white background. With great care, Chuck folded the tissue into quarters so that he wouldn't lose the precious cargo.

"Get me your pitch pipe!" Chuck ordered.

"Why?" Cameron was nonplussed.

"I need the case. Go get it! And bring me a brown paper bag, not too big!"

Cameron did as he was told. Chuck removed the pitch pipe, tossed it onto the table, and nestled the tissue into the center of the sponge foam and closed the case. He put the case in his right front hip pocket. He then carefully swept the remainder of the postcard into the brown paper bag, and brushed his hands in the bag.

"Get me some tape. Do it!"

Cameron rummaged through his guitar case and found a spool of black cabling tape. He held it toward Chuck.

"That'll do."

Chuck folded over the top of the brown paper bag three times and taped any possible opening around the flap created. Without saying a word, he went to the phone.

"Who are you calling?" asked Cameron.

"McIntyre," Chuck mumbled. He dialed McIntyre's number and for several moments tapped his feet and eyed the ceiling.

"Hey there," he said, affably. "Can you meet me at the office? We have to review some details for the admiral's cotillion."

Chuck listened, interspersing an occasional staccato "Uh-huh, uh-huh" into the conversation.

"No. The office would be much better for discussing that gig. Yes, I know it's close to curfew, but how about you send a car for us and we meet you at the office?"

Chuck smiled and terminated the call. He hurried up the stairs.

"Wait here," he ordered Cameron. Cameron listened to the conversation on the second floor. He heard Chuck speak, then heard the boys' responses, but couldn't discern what was said. Within moments, everyone was downstairs.

"McIntyre's sending a car to pick us up," Chuck said, grabbing his jacket from the closet. He felt for the pitch pipe case in his pants pocket, and shot a glance to Cameron.

It's still there.

"But it's almost curfew," Rich insisted. "Won't that attract attention?"

"In any other circumstance, perhaps. We've been here for a while. You know that's why we picked this area for our base. We're in a zone amidst offices with personnel who keep odd hours. Cars come and go at all hours, so if we operate during restricted times, nothing seems unusual."

Cameron felt a minor wave of nausea. A chill ran down his spine.

The added tension was trying Cameron's patience even more, and despite Chuck's attempts at small talk, only caused him duress. Suddenly, the phone rang and Cameron felt as though he'd jumped out of his skin.

"Come on," Chuck ordered. "Our car's here."

Cameron donned his leather jacket and, on impulse, grabbed the sheet of paper containing the coded message from his guitar case.

"I don't have to tell you to be quiet about this…" said Chuck, as they locked the door of the suite.

Cameron shook his head. In the hotel lobby, two men awaited them at the front door.

They sent two agents…

The band filed into a large van. Chuck gave the strange men no instructions or directions. The man in the front passenger's seat turned on the radio, and tuned into a station seemingly broadcasting nothing but static. Finally, the sound of an announcer came through, but the man spoke in such a pulsing manner that Cameron felt dizzy. The wave of nausea returned.

I feel like I'm back on the ferry.

In an effort to fend off vomiting, Cameron redirected his attention to Chuck's conversation with the driver.

They drove through the streets of Seattle, most all of which were nearly deserted. The reduced street lighting cast an ominous pall over the city. Cameron discerned that the driver was deliberately using a circuitous route to discourage anyone who might be following them.

Good chance to take in the city…

The Roadhouse Sons, despite having no knowledge of their current situation, exalted in the inadvertent tour of Seattle. They drove past the waterfront and the semi-lit Edgewater Inn. Cameron smiled at the myths and magic surrounding the establishment.

The iconic shrine to the rock-and-roll lifestyle!

Evan whispered to Clyde. "Edgewater Inn!"

"Vanilla Fudge! Led Zeppelin!" Clyde whispered back.

Cameron began to hum the tune to Frank Zappa's *"The Mud Shark."* Someone in his midst was humming the harmony. Cameron looked around the van. The agent on the passenger side shot him a knowing grin. Cameron smiled back and softly sang the lyrics. The agent driving joined in. Chuck burst into laughter to the point of tears.

"How come you guys didn't stay at the Edgewater?" the driver asked.

Chuck rolled his eyes. "I've got enough on my mind without having to worry about these clowns waving their wangs out the windows."

The driver chuckled. "It would be a lot more fun for us if you were there, though!"

You're preaching to the choir.

Ice broken, the remainder of the ride was filled with shared stories of various carnal encounters experienced in their respective journeys. Several minutes later, they arrived at an underground parking garage. The driver pulled up to an elevator. Yet another agent greeted them. They filed out of the van and into the elevator. The agents in the car drove away. No one bid adieus.

The doors to the elevator closed. They rode in silence for several floors. The elevator stopped and opened into a hallway. There, McIntyre and three other male agents await them. One of the agents appeared to be the others' superior; he stood a foot or so in front of the other two. One of the other men held a clipboard. McIntyre led them to a conference room. The room was furnished sparsely with a large wood veneer table and surrounding chairs. In the middle of the table was a tray with a large pitcher of water and several glasses.

McIntyre closed the doors. Chuck passed custody of the brown paper bag and pitch pipe case containing the microdot to McIntyre, who refused it and pointed to one of the agents. Chuck handed the items to the man.

"My exemplars are on file here. The one receptacle's unconventional, but it was the best I could do."

The agent accepted both items and proceeded, in everyone's presence, to complete, in triplicate, a form on the clipboard. The agent handed a copy to McIntyre, then left, clipboard and evidence in hand. McIntyre nodded to Chuck and the agent superior, who addressed Cameron first.

"This young fellow insisted that you give the postcard to Boney Jack?"

"No!" Cameron clarified. "He thought I *was* Boney Jack, and wanted to make sure I wouldn't lose it."

"He offered no explanations as to why?"

"No."

Say little…

"The refugee was delirious at the time and died almost immediately thereafter," Chuck stated.

The agent superior cleared his throat. "We're experiencing a marked increase in activity in the last sixty days. Prior to the attack on Anchorage, we were approached by an individual claiming to be an agent, and who sought to defect. In exchange, he offered information on a purported Soviet spy ring based in Seattle. We receive innumerable such calls on a daily basis. At times, it's near impossible to sort the attention seekers from actual persons of concern. This refugee's case ended up in a stack of files with many others. We were finally able to examine it this week."

"The defector…was he legit?" Chuck asked.

"He's dead. The fellow was quite literally scraped off of a Seattle sidewalk approximately ninety days ago. Upon his death, we had no reason to consider him a person of interest. His death was ruled a suicide, and not surprisingly so, in light of the stress level people encounter due to the war. That applies especially to citizens residing so close to the action here, and experiencing more of the constant threat of Soviet attack."

"What makes you curious now?" Cameron asked.

"The fellow who jumped to his death was a man named John Collier. Police reports indicate that he was a small-time record producer from Los Angeles. For the most part, his records show nothing of significance, but he was a named party in an investigation approximately three years ago."

"What was that about?" Cameron asked.

The agent superior poured himself a glass of water and held it up, inviting the others, all of whom declined. He cleared his throat again and continued.

"It was a narcotics investigation. We learned of a drug ring operating from his studio. Our investigation revealed that he wasn't a guilty party, so no case was brought against him."

"Why the sudden interest now?" Cameron asked.

"Apparently, Collier was in Seattle attempting to sign a deal with Boney Jack's management company."

"I get it now!" Cameron acknowledged. "So, when the band who fills in for Boney Jack says they have something you might be interested in…"

"We're interested. Someone who claimed to be a spy committed a purported suicide. Someone peripherally involved with that person's interests discovered an object of interest."

"I think it's too much of a coincidence to ignore," Cameron declared.

McIntyre opened her briefcase and removed a black folio, from which she withdrew a manila folder. She handed it to the agent superior.

"Roadhouse Sons' reports thus far, including regarding the young refugee. Also, their schedule to date, with performance and appearance dates and locations, along with the daily itineraries."

He turned to Chuck and the band. "You'll file additional reporting documentation."

"For what?" Cameron protested, images of detailed reports inducing a state of panic in him. "Except for the hospital visits, we don't have contact with anyone. We show up, play, then leave."

Until that moment, the third agent hadn't spoken. He'd stood at the opposite end of the table the whole time. He pushed his eyeglasses up the bridge of his nose, took two steps forward, and spoke in a hushed tone.

"Interviews, press conferences, autograph seekers, et cetera."

Cameron eyed the man for a moment.

Okie-dokie, E.F. Hutton…

"We don't really have anything to do with those people. We don't talk or interact all that much," Cameron averred. "Especially when the gig is over. We go on our merry way."

The man took two steps back and resumed his previous position. The agent superior studied Cameron carefully. For a fleeting moment, the musician was convinced that he was in real trouble.

"You've not processed a crime scene yet. You shouldn't question *any* method of gathering intelligence."

Cameron was incensed, but managed his tongue, and briefly explained his experience with McIntyre when they discovered Dwyer's body.

"Did you collect the evidence?"

Cameron admitted that he had not. McIntyre had reported Dwyer's demise and a team of crime scene technicians had collected the evidence. The agent superior comported the air of a college professor.

"When you're more familiar with that process, you'll learn that items deemed inconsequential to most are of great significance to the trained eye. For example, in one homicide case, the entire prosecution rested on one piece of evidence, a matchbook cover. The most seemingly innocuous item could solve a case."

Cameron acquiesced without further protest or comment.

The paper!

"In that case, look at this this!" he said, removing the onion paper from his pocket.

"I though we decided—" Chuck stopped himself.

"Please…" Cameron's face implored Chuck, who then explained to McIntyre and the agents the coincidental discovery of the markings in the *Sackett* book. Cameron divulged how they discovered what he still felt was a special code.

The agent superior accepted the paper and examined it.

"I won't accept this as official evidence yet, but I will send it to Cryptography and have it examined."

He placed the paper in the Roadhouse Sons folder and rose from his seat. Cameron looked at McIntyre. She winked at him.

We're done…

McIntyre escorted the agents out to the hallway.

Cameron leaned in toward Chuck and whispered into his ear.

"When do they want these reports?" Cameron asked.

The agent superior paused in the doorway, his back to them.

"Yesterday."

CHAPTER TWENTY-EIGHT

"Misstep"

Simms knew that he was powerless to help himself. This was the end. He attempted to push himself up from the desk, but the pain made it impossible. He clawed for the phone and, unable to grasp the handset, he watched it tumble from his fingers, taking with it his last hope of survival. Soon, the telltale signal that the phone was off the hook would resound. He hated that sound; there was nothing he could do about it now. He wanted to laugh, but couldn't utter a syllable. Had he been thinking clearly, he would have avoided using the phone altogether. The self-recrimination he felt was petty and foolish, a waste of his effort. What reason did he have for saving effort or energy now? He could feel himself weaken. The wound in his neck prevented him from speaking, and blood poured from him, staining his collar with a stunning crimson. He knew he would be dead soon.

Simms was not surprised at all to discover that someone else was involved in this; that someone else had interests, and therefore sources, at the hospital. He was surprised, though, to learn that his killer was among them. If only he'd been more vigilant, he wouldn't have been blindsided.

His right arm slid from the desktop and limply swayed at his side, as useless to him as his hindsight. He caught sight of his calculator and felt a faint glimmer of anticipation. He was alive enough to know that there was no way for him to call for help, nor was there any possibility that it would reach him in time. There was a way for him to reveal who took his life, if he could only move his left arm, and raise his right arm, just one more time. Only the fingers of his left hand responded to his brain's command. The calculator, just barely within reach, was Simms' last hope. He could feel it against the tip of his finger. Simms was able to move it close enough to grasp, and with gargantuan effort, flopped his right arm back onto the desk.

Blood continued to ooze from him, and the desk was now covered. Pain and weakness prevented him from moving his head. Through the haze of impending death, he pictured the surface of the calculator. There were twenty-five buttons on its face; the numbers occupied nine spaces on the left side of the keypad. Running his fingertip along the edge, he determined the location of the numbers. He knew that the number "5" was located in the center of the numerical keys. He punched it. But, where was the number "2" key located? He needed the number "2." Was it above, or below the "5" key?

Simms' vision blurred. His arm tingled. At death's door, he knew he had to act. The calculator had the same numerical button placement as a telephone, didn't it? The "2" key was directly above the "5," or was it? Was he wrong? Was the calculator laid out the opposite of a telephone?

There was no time for second-guessing. Ashen from the lack of blood, and numb all over, Simms feebly pressed the button once, then twice. He moved his finger back to "5," attempting in near futility to recall the location of the "7" key. Simms couldn't remember what the number looked like anymore. He knew, somehow, that it was significant. He pressed what must have been "7." His finger flopped from the dial pad. Had he pressed the wrong key? Did it really matter? Yes. His brain screamed. He sensed the crimson all around him. He had to notify someone about *something*, using specific keys he'd selected. What was it that he had to convey? He couldn't remember. He was too weak, yet aware with utter certainty that his last moments on earth were upon him.

Simms wondered if he'd turned on the calculator, and knew it was an odd concern. He mused at his mental meanderings, and tried to emit his last laugh, but merely sputtered blood. Unable to focus his attention on anything anymore, Simms surrendered and succumbed to the inevitable.

I'm so cold, he thought.

Then, everything went black.

CHAPTER TWENTY-NINE

"Full Spectrum, Full Impact"

He was in hell, no question about it; on the lowest rung of the hell ladder and these were the devils poured over and hand selected by an irate Almighty to torment him for all eternity.

Friggin' press conferences!

Sharing the dais with the members of Boney Jack—at least the ones who had decided to show up—could only be chalked up to punishment for his multitudinous sins, which ironically did not produce one iota of remorse upon introspective review.

If that's the reason I'm here, I should have enjoyed myself more!

Cameron wished that someone would permanently silence the punk rocker. For the last five minutes, Boney Jack had hijacked the microphone from the drummer midsentence, harangued the press, and continually jeered at the Roadhouse Sons. Cameras were flashing, and reporters with toothy grins were eagerly scribbling down the pseudo-blasphemous drivel spewed by the self-appointed Scourge of God, complete with his spittle showering upon them. Cameron didn't understand one iota of Boney Jack's yammering, nor did the speaker himself, who obviously didn't care if anyone failed to grasp the nuances of his diatribe.

He probably forgets everything the minute it dribbles from his mouth.

It was obvious to Cameron that attention and publicity were like a drug to Boney Jack, who drew protean strength from the flash of the bulbs and the scribbling of the reporters. The gaunt and ghoulish young man had no intention of giving them up. In fact, he was milking the crowd for everything it was worth.

A baleful glance from Cameron to Chuck and McIntyre produced no reaction. To Cameron's dismay, they were as engaged in the spectacle as intently as anyone else.

"What do you have to say in response, Mr. Walsh?" a reporter asked when Boney Jack finally ceased his vitriol to take a breath. Cameron, having sought refuge in his own thoughts, was caught off guard, but quickly recovered.

You got sick of him too, eh?

Cameron looked toward Boney Jack and shook his head. Boney Jack rose from his chair.

"Tell me something," Cameron cooed, his tone calm and measured. "Does your ass ever get jealous of the crap that comes out of your mouth?"

Boney Jack froze. He'd clearly anticipated the customary verbal sparring or incensed rebuttal that followed his rambling tirades. Instead, the punk rocker was treated to an outburst of laughter from the press as well as his own manager, Jack Stanley. Cameron smiled as he turned his attention back to the reporters, who were now focused entirely on him.

"So, does that mean the Roadhouse Sons don't like punk rock?" asked one reporter.

Oh, Jesus. Gimme a break…

"I'm not saying that at all," he replied with a warm smile. "In fact, I have a few tapes of the Sex Pistols that some friends in England sent to me and I've nearly worn them out. You have to appreciate music that defines not only a band, but the genre itself, and who can forget the Grundy incident?"

A few reporters chuckled at Cameron's reference to the 1976 scandalous live appearance of the Sex Pistols on the London talk show where host, Bill Grundy, had provoked the band members into swearing and other inappropriate behavior. Cameron was amused at the hushed whispers in the audience as the reporters tried to explain the reference to each other.

He was an experienced musician, an old hand at doing interviews and conducting himself as a professional representative of his band. He didn't need to engage in histrionics or outrageous behavior to make an impact on the press. Cameron did it through his music, his abilities, as well as his charm and personality. The sight of Boney Jack deflating as the attention of the room shifted from him to Cameron painted a clear picture of Boney Jack's ineptitude. Cameron knew how to work that to his advantage, and did so with full intention.

"Perhaps little Jack here wanted to create a Seattle incident," Cameron laughed. "I really don't know why anyone over the age of three would act like that in public."

The members of the press snickered. Boney Jack sputtered a few meek syllables, but Jack Stanley quickly intercepted the microphone. At first, Cameron was expecting him to come to his singer's rescue and restore the momentum of the press conference. Instead, Stanley jovially spoke appropriate platitudes and ended the conference, thanking the press for attending. Boney Jack stared at Stanley in abject disbelief.

He's stunned and silent! Thank God!

Stanley turned away from Boney Jack and feigned distraction by repeatedly checking his watch. Boney Jack stood still as a statue.

I swear, his lower lip is quivering. Score!

Cameron strode toward his band mates. Evan and Chuck slapped him on the back. Clyde hugged him and Rich and Snapper clapped and congratulated him, then left with McIntyre to set up for the afternoon performance. Several reporters had stayed behind to meet Cameron, and shook his hand, asking for additional photographs of him and the band. There was no mistaking the favorable response by the press to Cameron's frank and refreshing demeanor compared to the bullying antics of Boney Jack and his annoying faux rebel compadres. Cameron had only spent two hours in Boney Jack's company and was anxious to be rid of him.

As he and the Roadhouse Sons bid adieu to the remaining reporters and headed toward the door, they heard a loud crash. Everyone in the room halted in their tracks, startled by the clatter.

What the...?

Boney Jack was kicking chairs and flipping tables. One photographer, attempting one more photo op of the famous bad boy, barely escaped the flying furniture.

"I am the Scourge of God!" Boney Jack screamed, his ashen face red with rage. "I will not be ignored!"

The room fell silent as everyone witnessed the tantrum.

"No one makes a fool out of me!" he bellowed, stomping back to the dais and pointing a quivering finger at Cameron. "You haven't heard the last of this!"

With that, the punk rocker toppled the dais, stomped back down the length of the room, and exited through a door in the back. Immediately, the remaining press correspondents turned to Cameron. Before they could utter any questions about his take on the matter, Cameron shook his head, smiled mischievously, and shrugged.

"Thank you for coming today. We have to leave now and prepare for this afternoon's performance."

With that, Cameron and Evan nodded politely and left the room.

"Keep your eye on him!" Evan grabbed Cameron's arm and whispered in his ear. "That guy is fucking dangerous!"

Cameron shrugged again. "What's he gonna do? We'll probably never even deal with him again."

"I don't know…" Evan conceded. "But he just had his image blown to hell and he'll probably try anything to get it back."

"That, my friend, is his manager's problem, not ours," Cameron smiled. "We've got to get ready for the other extreme now."

Evan's brow furrowed.

"We get to babysit the Up With People kids," Cameron laughed. "So remember. Watch your language and behave. Chuck tells me they're all at impressionable ages."

They ran to the elevator to catch up with the boys. However, a mob of reporters awaited them, eager for another quote or photograph. Cameron and Evan felt like salmon trying to swim upstream. Over the heads of the crowd, they saw Chuck, clearly irritated. He was engaged in a heated discussion with Stanley. Chuck waved Stanley away and pushed through the sea of press correspondents, finally reaching the elevator.

"What was his problem?" Cameron asked.

"He can't take no for an answer," Chuck grumbled. "If someone had just blown apart my artist's image after all my time and effort, I'd be throwing a conniption. Not him, though. He wants to capitalize on it with a tour!"

"You're kidding!" Evan gasped. "He just can't let that idea go, can he?"

"I'm afraid not," Chuck snapped. "This elevator's slow as molasses. Follow me."

He led the band down the stairwell, through a storage room door, and outside, where the van was waiting for them.

Peace at last…

The van was chock-full of chatter and jokes about the press conference, and praise for Cameron's comportment. Despite the accolades, Cameron wished that they'd focus on something else. No sooner had he wished it than the van pulled up to the base, and the topic of conversation switched to the upcoming performance.

McIntyre, Rich, Clyde, and Snapper greeted them and led them to the stage for sound check, after which they headed to their dressing room. Cameron stole away to a private corner while the others reenacted the press conference, complete with hoots and howls of laughter. While they carried on, the sudden burst of music and loud applause filtered to the dressing room.

"That must be the Frosted Mini-Wheats kids," Cameron chuckled. Chuck glared at him.

"I'd like to teach the world to sing…" Cameron trilled.

"I mean it!" Chuck spat.

Oh, relax, for Christ's sake!

Cameron settled into a chair and listened. He couldn't hear the song well, but could discern that the beat was solid, the timing was good, and the execution spot-on.

"Do they have a recording?" he asked Chuck.

"Nope. Live," Chuck replied, giving him a knowing look. "They have their own band, equipment, everything. Even lights on huge trusses, but they used the ones provided here this time. It's really quite an operation. You should go check it out."

I have no intention of visiting Romper Room.

As the performance continued, though, Cameron's curiosity piqued. He arose from his chair, nonchalantly left the room, and quickly made his way toward backstage. From there, he had a great view of the performers. Also backstage was a group of adults whom he could only assume were Up With People personnel. Onstage, approximately one hundred and fifty brightly clad youths navigated the stage in a complex, synchronized choreography. As an announcer explained some of the dancers' routines, Cameron heard someone sidle up behind him.

"Hey! That's their Super Bowl routine!" Snapper said with a grin.

"Which Super Bowl?" Cameron asked. He'd never been much of a sports fan, but he'd watched a little football in his day.

"I think it was in seventy-six," Snapper explained. "Yeah! Super Bowl Ten. I remember these kids did the National Anthem and a Bicentennial tribute."

Cameron looked at Snapper as though he was an alien being. On one hand, he was incredibly surprised that Snapper even knew about this group. On the other hand, he was so impressed with the performance before him that had no frame of reference about how the youths' tours were planned, or any other aspect of their enterprise.

"These same kids?" Cameron asked, incredulously.

"Well, this same group," Snapper clarified. "I doubt it was the exact same kids. Besides, that show filled an entire football field, and this one is much smaller. Didn't you watch it?"

"No. The only thing I remember about that game is the Steelers played the Cowboys, were the odds-on favorite, and when Glen Edwards caught the ball he guaranteed the Steelers a victory and me three hundred bucks."

"Philistine," Snapper chuckled. He leaned in closer. "I never forgave Staubach for that play."

Onstage, the announcer began an elucidation of the history of American dance and music, beginning with the Charleston and the Virginia reels. As he did so, the band, singers, and dancers moved from one musical selection to the next, each song and movement segueing seamlessly. To the audience, the fluid motions and crisp vocals seemed effortless. However, as a performer, Cameron knew the amount of rehearsal, practice, and discipline that went in to making it seem that way.

Very impressed...had no idea...

The medley was flawless and allowed the audience enough time to identify the melody and enjoy their reminiscences before transitioning to the next song. John Denver's "*Take Me Home, Country Roads*" transformed to Woody Guthrie's "*This Land is Your Land*" like a refreshing breeze. From his own experience, Cameron knew that switching between songs, let alone musical genres, was no simple feat. The boys were enraptured by the performance and murmured their approval. At each transition, the audience went wild with applause.

These kids are good!

The program shifted from a celebration of American music to an armed forces tribute. The singers and dancers parted, creating a wide aisle down the middle of the stage to make way for a trio of young women in dark pencil skirt suits. The band vamped.

Suddenly, in perfect syncopation, the girls turned to face the audience. Those in the audience who could, stood up and cheered. The girls' costumes were perfect replicas of the WAAC uniforms of World War II, and reminded Cameron of old photographs of the Andrews Sisters during their tours with Bob Hope. The trio sashayed downstage matter-of-factly as three young men placed microphone stands for each of them. Their performance began with the high-spirited *"Don't Sit Under the Apple Tree"* and whisked to a sentimental rendition of *"I'll Be With You In Apple Blossom Time,"* which then burst like a firecracker into the song Cameron knew was coming—*"Boogie Woogie Bugle Boy."*

To loud applause and continued cheers, the three young girls receded with graceful precision into the ensemble, who moved forward to strains of the opening score of *"This is My Country."* A hushed and respectful silence befell the audience. Movements onstage were much more restrained, almost reverent.

There's no rushing through that song...

Every syllable of each word was clearly defined, its emphasis direct. The final note was held long, rising to a climax, which led the group into their finale, *"America the Beautiful."*

Many in the audience dabbed away their tears. Cameron felt a great deal of admiration for Up With People for evoking such positive emotional influence on their audience. As the song concluded, there was a pause, a calm followed by a storm of thunderous applause, both in the audience and backstage. Cameron clapped as loudly as anyone. He was happy to do so.

They sure as hell earned it!

The youths enjoyed several well-deserved bows before exiting the stage. Cameron and the boys waved and congratulated the younger performers as they passed by. Several in the group smiled and nodded back, while others were engrossed in their own conversations and didn't seem to notice the Roadhouse Sons. As the stage emptied, Cameron, Rich, and Clyde snuck out through the emergency exit to smoke. Evan remained onstage to set up his drum kit, and Snapper methodically began performing his last-minute inspections while the crew for Up With People removed their equipment from the stage.

Clyde was nearing the punch line of a dirty joke when Cameron and Rich stepped out of the building. They stopped dead on their heels when they came face to face with three young men and two young women from Up With People. They were having a smoke, as well. He prayed that none of them had heard Clyde's raunch. Much to his chagrin, his prayers went unanswered.

"I thought you guys left," Cameron said sheepishly.

"Don't worry about it, man," said one of the youths as he passed his cigarette to one of the young women. "We've heard and said worse."

"Really?" Cameron laughed. "I had a whole different picture of you guys!"

"Most people do," smiled one of the young women. "Most people think we're a bunch of goody-goodies."

"If we want to smoke, we have to separate ourselves from the rest of the cast," the second young woman said. Cameron offered to share his cigarettes.

"Here, have a smoke. I'm Cameron, and this is our bass player, Rich, and our lead guitarist, Clyde."

Introductions continued. The three young men were Leon, Cody, and Curtis, and the two young women were Lynn and Penny. Leon, Curtis, and Penny were from Nebraska, New Jersey, and West Virginia, respectively, and all blue-eyed blonds. Cody and Lynn were both from New Mexico.

Clyde flirted with the girls. "Penny and Lynn, you look like you're sisters." They laughed, wise to such pick-up line maneuvers; they looked nothing alike.

Cody and Lynn, however, did. Both were dark in complexion, with upturned button noses, dark eyes, and chestnut hair.

"Watch it," Cody said. "She's like a sister to me!"

The rockers asked questions about how the five became involved with Up With People, and were surprised to learn about the myriad auditions they'd endured, and that they called themselves "Uppies" for short. The youths told Clyde, Rich, and Cameron about the host families with whom they stayed at every destination, how they all took turns participating in advance public relations for their cast, and how, in addition to their performances, they performed community service and volunteer work in many of the locations on their one-year tour.

"That's what we're doing here at the base hospital," Curtis explained. "We're taking shifts helping out with the orderlies and some of the nursing staff."

"You mean like changing bandages and giving shots?" Clyde exclaimed.

Curtis shook his head. "No, nothing medical. We help out with serving meals and bringing the mail or gift baskets to the patients."

"We girls help out with the children's wards and the nurseries," Penny added. "We read stories and play games with them, that sort of thing."

The young people shared more stories; the rockers were surprised to learn that, for most of them, Up With People, like college much of the time, marked the first time they'd ever been away from home. For two of them, it was a chance for a new life.

"Home was awful," Lynn admitted. "This was a chance to get the hell out, have a roof over my head, and eat. I knocked myself out auditioning and made damn sure I landed a spot in this cast." Leon admitted to a similar motivation.

"You know, you guys did a tremendous job out there," Cameron said.

"You did a great fucking job!" Rich gushed. He immediately blushed at his selection of verbiage. The Uppies laughed.

"Don't worry about it," Cody insisted, with a grin. "Believe it or not, we swear once in a while, too!"

"I don't believe it!" Clyde smiled. The Uppies laughed even louder.

"Well, we might not be big rock stars like you," Penny chuckled, "but despite what you think, there aren't too many haloes in this bunch. You should see us cuss when we're breaking down the stage at one o'clock in the morning and have to load the truck then board a bus for the next town in time to perform at a nine a.m. high school assembly."

"But don't tell our cast director that," Curtis said in a conspiratorial whisper. "She'd have a heart attack."

"Yeah, that and if she knew everything that goes on aboard the buses," said Penny.

"She'd keel over if she knew that *we* know everything that goes on aboard the buses," Lynn giggled. "Lots of cast romances that aren't as secret as the star-crossed lovers think!" The Uppies exchanged esoteric glances. The Roadhouse Sons exchanged glances of their own.

Out of seemingly nowhere appeared Chuck.

"I've been looking all over for you guys. Stage is set. Let's go!"

Clyde laughed and kissed the young ladies' hands. All of the men shook hands and exchanged wished each other good luck.

"You really did do an incredible job," Cameron repeated. They all wished each other well on their respective journeys.

Cameron, Clyde, and Rich walked to the backstage area and met up with Snapper, Evan, McIntyre, and Chuck. The boys nodded to each other and entered the stage. Attendants offered them their instruments and they strapped themselves in. Everyone approached their designated microphones and Cameron looked out over the audience.

"Wow," he said, with a sincere smile. "That's going to be one tough act to follow!"

A thundering ovation from the audience confirmed it. Cameron hesitated for a millisecond, then turned to the band.

"They're nice kids, but now it's our turn. Let's wipe the floor with 'em!"

CHAPTER THIRTY

"Come Undone"

A lesser person would panic. Jack Stanley did not consider himself a lesser person. Yes, the situation was serious, too serious to be ignored or handled in less than a meticulous manner. However, panicking would lead to mistakes. He could afford no mistakes, least of all such amateur ones like those made by the others.

The most egregious mishap was letting Simms live long enough after his attack to knock the telephone receiver off the hook. That drew the attention of the switchboard operator who, in turn, alerted security when calls to the office went unanswered. The security officer then discovered the body and notified higher authorities. A trained killer would have done the job correctly; death would have been immediate.

Another crucial mistake was making no attempt to disguise the intruder's search to resemble a robbery. Although the mild disarray was too slight for crime scene technicians to notice in an unfamiliar site, Stanley discerned that a search had taken place due to disorder so uncharacteristic of Simms; several drawers had been rummaged, leaving Stanley to conclude that the perpetrator had to have been looking for something specific. Stanley had no idea what that could be, but he knew he had to act hastily. Whoever had killed Simms may have been inexperienced, but the Seattle police were not.

This was the second time the police had to investigate a murder that peripherally involved Stanley, and this time was much more serious than the last. The police had a lead linking Simms to Collier, and there was no possibility that they would miss the connection this time and, unfortunately for Stanley, upon arrival at his office, he wasn't permitted to enter. A homicide detective awaited him at the door.

"The coroner states that the time of death occurred between ten o'clock a.m. and noon," the detective said. "Can you account for your whereabouts during that time?"

"I most certainly can." Stanley was the picture of calm. He remained unagitated during the previous interrogation regarding Collier, and he had willed himself to nerves of steel for the current inquiry.

"I didn't come into the office this morning. Simms was here and we conferred over the phone about the day's agenda. My primary concern was a press conference this morning at the Hilton. That was at nine o'clock. I left my apartment for the hotel by eight fifteen to make certain that everything was in order and to prevent delays. The press conference lasted until roughly eleven a.m."

"Is there anyone who can corroborate that?"

"There certainly is," Stanley snipped. "My driver for one, and the entire Seattle press corps, for another."

The detective wrote in his small steno pad and, with rapid-fire delivery, repeated his questions. Stanley knew that the detective was trying to trip him up. Anxious to get away long enough to commence damage control, Stanley maintained his composure against the barrage of questions. He knew that adamantly repeating the same words over and over inevitably revealed prevarication, so he carefully responded to each repetition, modifying his answer just enough to match the detective's comportment. He was simultaneously scanning the room, memorizing the details of the crime scene.

Through the open door, he could see Simms' desk. Simms was face down on it and a pool of blood had collected, soaking the papers around him and running onto the floor. Simms' arms were spread out like wings, one by the telephone and the other resting on his calculator. From the shadows cast to the floor by the outdoors via the window, he could see that two of Simms' desk drawers were slightly opened, something that Simms would never have done. His meticulous sense of, and desire for, order perpetually compelled him to close all drawers always, unless he was retrieving something.

Stanley surveyed the rest of the room. He didn't notice anything else out of the ordinary, though it was difficult to be certain while sequestered in the doorway. The flashes from the crime scene photographer's camera disrupted his focus; he was already dividing his attention between his own cursory review and the detective's questioning.

"Were you making any kind of a deposit?" the detective asked so suddenly that Stanley was pulled from his mental inventory and caught off guard.

"I beg your pardon?"

"Was the victim preparing a deposit of some kind for you?"

"I have no idea what you mean." Stanley was flummoxed.

"The victim appeared to have been entering numbers on his calculator," the detective stated tersely. "But we couldn't find any deposit slip or money, and we're trying to determine if robbery could have been a motive."

Stanley seized the opportunity to proffer a red herring, and possibly buy himself valuable time.

"That could very well be," he averred. "You see, sometimes fans will send in money in order to cover postage for an autographed picture, in hopes that they'll receive a personal response from one of their favorite musicians. We do try to discourage it, but the fans do it anyway."

The detective paused a moment and stared straight into Stanley's eyes.

"Do you collect a lot of money that way?" The detective's tone revealed to Stanley that the man found his statement to be dubious at best, and if not dubious, then reprehensible.

"I am really not sure," Stanley laughed. "Simms handles, or rather handled, all of the fan mail, and took care of that sort of thing."

"Just give me a ballpark figure," the detective insisted. "Would you say it was perhaps ten or twenty dollars? Maybe a hundred, even?"

"Really, Detective..." Stanley stayed his course. "I honestly have no idea, but if you insist on an answer I would have to say less than one hundred dollars per month. If it provided more revenue than that, I would have taken steps to cease it immediately! We want to make money selling tickets and records, not operating bunko schemes," he sniffed.

"But not in the thousands?" The detective wasn't entirely convinced of no malfeasance.

Stanley was dumbfounded. "Certainly not!" he exclaimed. "How unthinkable! Why, if that was the case, no one would trust our staff for a minute. We wouldn't even be able to sell our tapes on the roadside. How could you think such a thing?"

"Your late associate punched a large number into that calculator. We have no evidence or explanation indicating why."

Stanley was rattled. "I've no idea why he did that," he puffed. "A large number would indicate only a range of ticket revenue for appearances or concerts. Checks of that amount go directly to our accountant, and are not handled here by either Mr. Simms or me."

"Then you have no idea of what he could have been doing?"

"None whatsoever," Stanley said, flatly. "Unless it was something personal, also for which I'd have no explanation whatsoever."

"Did the victim have that kind of money?"

"Not that I am aware of!" Stanley was irritated. He tidied his jacket and swept his lapels, stalling for time. A serendipitous idea crossed his mind, and he pounced on the opportunity. "Perhaps I could be of help if you told me the number that Simms punched."

"Five two two five seven," he replied without consulting his notes, and maintaining his steady gaze. "Do you have any idea what that number means?"

"Certainly not," Stanley gasped. He was shocked, pure and simple. "That's over fifty-two thousand dollars! I would certainly know if Simms was handling an amount such as that, and he'd be dismissed. As I said, large revenues are handled by the accountant. He must have omitted a decimal point. That is the only explanation I can offer, unless…"

"Unless what?"

Stanley hesitated. He knew better than to appear overly eager; he'd arouse even more suspicion. He feigned maudlin.

"Unless his fingers were simply twitching as he lay dying. In which case, the numbers mean nothing."

The detective stood in front of Stanley with such a look of consternation that Stanley felt he was doomed. He wondered if the detective's expression was donned when the man was pondering possibilities. Stanley hoped so; the look was indeed unnerving.

"Mr. Stanley, I don't need to remind you that this case is similar to the Collier case." The detective's voice was crisp and clipped. His gaze did not waver.

"No, Detective. You don't," Stanley replied. His voice was calm, his demeanor professional, but he chafed at the detective's air of superiority. "I have considered that very fact."

"This is quite a coincidence. The first homicide I investigated indicated that Collier was scheduled to have a meeting with the deceased individual we are now preparing to remove from your office. Both of them, coincidentally, were either employees of, or business associates of, yours."

The two men faced off.

"I am aware of those facts, Detective." Stanley's voice was low and cold.

"I don't like coincidences, Mr. Stanley. I don't like them, and I don't believe in them. I advise you to remain within city limits."

"Detective, as you are no doubt aware, I am currently confined to the city proper, or have you forgotten the terms of my clients' release on bail?"

For a mere instant, the detective's eyes wavered from Stanley's, the latter of whom, with inner glee, realized that the detective had, albeit temporarily, forgotten the bail terms.

"Then consider this a friendly reminder to obey those conditions," he countered.

Stanley wanted to laugh in the man's face. Instead, he pressed his advantage.

"Am I being charged with a crime, Detective?" Stanley demanded. "If so, I suggest you do so immediately. In the meantime, I wish to call my attorney! At once! And I refuse to answer any more questions until he is present. If I am not being charged in connection with this tragedy, your attitude is callous and unnecessary. Do I have to remind you that Mr. Simms was a valued employee of mine, and for quite some time?"

The officer cleared his throat and benignly stepped away from Stanley, who knew that he'd gained temporary control. He was determined to keep it.

"You are not being charged with a crime, Mr. Stanley. I am merely recommending that you remain where you can be reached without difficulty."

"As you wish," Stanley replied. There was no hint of challenge or argument in his response. Stanley relished his victory. Now he could work on devising a plan of action for any remaining damage control.

In a gesture of dismissal, Stanley flipped his attorney's business card at the detective, who immediately shifted his attention to the crime scene. Stanley turned to leave, careful not to rush, but to walk in the usual steady gait of a busy man.

Stanley assessed the unfortunate turn of events. He cursed the situation. His closest business associate had just been murdered in the office next door to his. He needed to set in motion his strategy to take control, and that included making certain telephone calls from his office; its close proximity to the crime scene investigation rendered that all but impossible. What if he was overheard? He needed to find a place where he wouldn't be disturbed. The only guarantee of that was in his apartment, twenty minutes away.

"Twenty minutes' delay," Stanley muttered, once out of hearing range. He had no choice; he had to go home.

Stanley hurried outside on to the street corner and waved down a taxi, all the while cursing his driver, who fastidiously adhered to his own car's maintenance schedule. He gave directions to the taxi driver and promised a bonus if the man made haste. A few minutes later, after several short cuts and running several yellow lights, Stanley was walking through his apartment door.

He explained to his maid that there had been an unfortunate death in his family, and requested time alone. As soon as he heard the maid close the front door, Stanley hurried into his private office and locked the door. He pushed a chair against it, wedging the chair back under the doorknob.

He had an extremely important telephone call to make; he could only hope that no one else had already done so. If they had, things were already irretrievably beyond his control.

He inhaled deeply. He dialed the memorized number, knowing that he wouldn't be talking to his usual contacts. This situation was beyond their scope. Stanley dreaded making the call, one he'd made only two other times in his life. His hand trembled. He froze mid-dial. The mystery numbers of Simms' calculator entry matched what he was dialing. Out of context, they made no sense when the detective asked him about them. Now, the panic that he'd resisted all morning raged through him. The phone rang once…twice…a third time…

"Clayton's Men's Wear." A brusque female answered.

"Good morning." Stanley was shaking. "Emma says she would like to speak to Arthur."

"Yes. We've been expecting your call."

CHAPTER THIRTY-ONE

"Crossing Paths"

Cameron could hardly believe it. Freedom had been so close—within his very grasp, in fact—until Chuck brought everything to an abrupt halt.

"Don't forget to turn in that report," he reminded Cameron as they prepared to return their hotel suite.

"What are you talking about?" Cameron snapped. "I did that at the office."

"No. You gave your statement," Chuck corrected. "You still need to complete your report."

The musician slumped against the wall in despair. Chuck eyed him suspiciously.

"Don't tell me you haven't finished it yet," he warned. Cameron shifted uncomfortably under Chuck's withering glare.

"Well, no...not exactly," Cameron mumbled. Chuck's irritation was obvious. "I mean, I haven't started it yet."

Chuck's face flushed crimson. His jaw was clenched. Cameron flinched involuntarily.

"Now don't get pissed at me," Cameron insisted. "They only told me to write it last night. We've been busy all day!"

"I wrote mine last night!" Chuck growled. Cameron got the message. No explanation or excuses would be tolerated.

"All right, man! Calm down!" he urged. "I'll do it as soon as I get back to the hotel tonight."

"Correction! You'll do it as soon as we get back today." In the blink of an eye, Cameron's opportunity for his long-awaited leave disappeared.

Protesting was useless, so there he sat, composing pages and pages when, at last, the final page of his report was complete. He described in detail the events leading up to the discovery of the microdot. He included the message in Doug's book; he didn't dare run the risk of assuming that it would be ignored or overlooked. To ensure the security of the report until it could be surrendered to McIntyre and the agent superior's team, Cameron allowed himself the added precaution of hand writing the entire account onto sheets of his onion paper.

He carefully peeled apart the back cover of the fake book and slid in the original set of papers. Confident that the papers were flattened and would go unnoticed of someone handled the book, he sealed the cover's perimeters with glue and wiped away the excess. He blew on the edges of the cover until they were no longer tacky to the touch. He didn't know if Chuck would bring it to the office, or if McIntyre and company would send a courier. Regardless, Cameron certainly wasn't going to leave the book laying about for anyone to find.

He felt pleased and relieved to have the onus of the report out of the way, and was even more relieved when he discovered that it wasn't even six o'clock in the evening.

Still have all night…

Cameron picked up the newspaper. Earlier that day, some of the solders at the base had clued him into the late-night establishments. He perused the list of bars and clubs and found one that seemed promising.

The Paradise Club on Second Avenue…

He smiled when he saw the closing time.

Eleven o'clock! Plenty of time for a few drinks. Listen to some good music. If the stars are in the proper position, I might make a nice acquaintance!

Cameron hurried upstairs to take a quick shower and change. On his way out, he remembered that he needed to report to Chuck his whereabouts, in case of an emergency. He hated feeling like a schoolboy by having to account for his actions, but reluctantly acknowledged the wisdom of it. In this case, complied by leaving a note.

"At the Paradise. Cameron," he spoke as he jotted the note for Chuck. Just as he was about to close the door behind him, the phone rang.

Shit.

Cameron pondered ignoring it; this ring was not one of the band's prearranged signals. Nonetheless, he couldn't allow himself to leave. Grumbling a mile a minute, he closed the door and answered the call.

"Hello?"

"Hello. I am looking for Mr. Charles Lamont," said a woman's voice. Her demeanor was professional and direct.

"I'm sorry. Mr. Lamont isn't here," Cameron replied with the same direct comportment. "This is his answering service. Would you like to leave a message?"

"Do you know when he'll return?"

Cameron struggled to formulate a response. Chuck didn't like the band members to divulge any information about him, and he didn't like anyone speaking on his behalf.

"No. He didn't give a time," Cameron ventured. This wasn't a lie. Chuck hadn't told him when he'd return. "However, if you leave your name and number, I can have him get in touch with you when he comes back."

"This is Philly Records," the woman said. Cameron fought the urge to slam down the phone.

Jack Stanley! I'm so sick of that man and his asshole band!

"I'm calling on behalf of Mr. Stanley," the woman continued, as though reading his thoughts.

"I'll tell him you called," Cameron hoped that his tone indicated clearly that he was through talking with the woman. She disregarded him and spouted off a telephone number. Cameron begrudgingly wrote it down, along with the time of the call. He was reasonably certain that Chuck would toss it into the trash as soon as he read it, but that wasn't his choice to make. Cameron hurried out the door, pausing only place a toothpick in the upper right corner of the door, a protocol required by Chuck, and adhered to by whomever was the last person to leave the apartment. If the toothpick fell to the floor, it was a clear indicator of an unauthorized entry. Ensuring that the toothpick was in place and that the door closed properly, Cameron locked the door and sauntered down the hallway.

* * * * * * * *

Jack Stanley contemplated the message he'd received from his new secretary, an irritating woman on temporary assignment to his office. His frustration grew. He just had to find a way to speak with Cameron Walsh. His plan was built upon hopes of scheduling a meeting with Chuck Lamont and thereby gain access to the musician. His hopes were cast asunder. He was about to pour himself another drink when, suddenly, an idea struck him. He buzzed the secretary on the intercom.

"Miss Laughton, could you please try that number again and ask to leave a message for Cameron Walsh?" He waited.

"Mr. Stanley, I'm afraid I can't get through," Miss Laughton's voiced said. "I've tried the number twice and the call goes straight to an answering machine. Do you wish for me to leave a message?"

Stanley pressed the speech button. "No, that won't be necessary, Miss Laughton. Thank you, and that will be all for today. You may go home with a full day's pay. I'm going to make some calls to Mr. Simms' family to offer help with the funeral arrangements, and I would prefer to do that in complete privacy. I will see you in the morning."

Stanley barely discerned the woman's remarks and farewell as he uttered vague pleasantries. He paid little attention to Miss Laughton; he was preoccupied with major concerns of his own. The call he'd made that morning had, as expected, proved ominous. The connections between the circumstances surrounding both Simms and Collier's deaths were proving to be enormously frightful for him.

"There can be no doubt that Collier was murdered," they'd said.

"By whom?" Stanley had asked.

"Mr. Collier was apparently seeking other employment. It seems that the murderer was one of his new associates."

A chill ran down Stanley's spine.

"How long had he been considering work with another company?" Stanley had inquired. His mouth had gone dry.

"That is of no consequence to you. That is an internal affair. Mr. Collier was involved in handling certain items of merchandise for us. A particular piece was of great importance to us, one we had ordered and which we were quite anxious to receive. Mr. Collier, though, attempted to reroute it."

"I am aware of that situation," Stanley had said, hiding his surprise and chafing at the reminder of the infernal package that never arrived from Anchorage.

"You were supposed to retrieve it for us," they'd said, coldly, flatly, reminding Stanley of his failure.

He had gasped, and then coughed violently. When he regained his composure, he'd tried to be glib. "One can't be responsible for the pony express, can one?"

"Especially if the carrier doesn't work for us."

"The courier quit the company as well?" he'd stammered, his legs weakening, causing him to flop into a chair.

"It would appear that they never worked for us to begin with. Mr. Collier had been quite clever about working independently. Unfortunately, he didn't realize how long we've been in business and how successful we are. One does not become a successful global entity by allowing employees such as he and Mr. Simms to be their own boss, or steal our customers."

Despite the fact that they couldn't see him, Stanley had nodded, clearly flummoxed. "You mean Simms quit, too?" His head was pounding.

"He was thinking about it. However, they were not careful about choosing business associates. But that is our worry, not yours. You have other concerns."

Stanley had furrowed his brow.

"Our merchandise. We've finally located it. You must retrieve it."

"You found it?" Stanley had cried. "That's incredible! Where is it?"

"Mr. Collier and Mr. Simms had arranged for it to be passed to your protégé, Mr. Preston, at which point they would gain custody of it and utilize it themselves. However, their courier met with a series of misfortunes and accidentally passed it to someone else. He died before he realized his mistake."

Their meaning and intent had dawned on Stanley, slowly, then with thundering impact.

"The man who died at the military hospital?"

"The very same," they'd said. "He couldn't tell one musician from the other, and gave his fan mail to the wrong one." Stanley had felt a glimmer of hope.

"Was it given to someone from the Roadhouse Sons?" he'd asked. The chuckle on the other end of the line had confirmed his inquiry. "But how did you know this? I've been trying to find out since that happened!"

"Mr. Simms' inside source possessed more loyalty than Simms did. When the confusion was discovered, they notified us immediately."

"But what about my source?" Stanley had insisted. "Why wasn't I notified? I could have taken care of this right away."

"Perhaps you should hire a better assistant." They'd literally sneered through the telephone at him. Stanley had offered no reply.

"The item was a microdot and it ended up in the hands of Cameron Walsh," they'd finally revealed.

"But how was I to have positioned myself to avoid that?" Stanley had asked. "Our contact is minimal and incredibly strained, thanks to Boney Jack."

"We've rectified that situation, thanks to our contact at the *Seattle Ledger.*"

They provided to Stanley the hotel address and suite number for the Roadhouse Sons. They'd also told him that intelligence had discovered that the band had reported difficulty with their television set, and a repairman was scheduled to come to look at it.

"We are quite anxious to retrieve the item. Perhaps you could accompany the repairman," they'd suggested.

Stanley had assured them that he would go to the hotel, and ended the telephone call. It was then that Stanley had told his secretary to call the Roadhouse Sons. With Chuck Lamont away from the hotel, he needed to act fast.

Stanley hurried to his bedroom and changed his clothes. He donned a worn pair of khaki pants and a blue chambray shirt, into the pocket of which he placed a small toolkit and a pair of latex gloves. He grabbed a canvas bag and stuffed into it a green-and-gray reversible windbreaker, a pair of sunglasses, a baseball cap, and a pair of black-rimmed reading glasses. He exchanged his dress shoes for a pair of canvas sneakers, then opened his jewelry box. Removing his rings, he slipped on a wedding band and changed his expensive wristwatch for one less remarkable. Stanley lifted a drawer from his nightstand and rummaged through cards hidden in a false bottom. He found a nondescript ID badge referencing a nonexistent repair company. Inlaid was an ill-focused photograph, which mildly resembled him, benignly accurate but not discernible as definitely Stanley, should anyone be asked. Stanley hurried out of his apartment and used the service elevator. He exited via the rear of the building.

From there, he quickly walked one block, then hailed a taxi. He requested a location three blocks short of the actual address, offering a distractingly ample tip to the driver. Stanley walked with purpose, but attracted no attention. He stepped into a coffee shop and found the restroom. Once inside a cubicle, he donned his hat and jacket and filled his bag with paper towels so that it would appear as though it contained tools. He left the restroom and resumed his journey. As he stood at a corner awaiting the traffic light change, he retrieved the black-rimmed glasses and put them on.

Stanley arrived at the Roadhouse Sons' building, entered, and blended in with a small group of people, walking with them toward the elevator. He waited while they all embarked, then slipped into a vacant elevator. He reached the band's floor and casually made his way down the hall to their door. Despite the fact that no one else was present, he remained vigilant.

He rang the doorbell and waited a few moments before ringing it again. There was no answer. He rang the bell a third time. Satisfied that there was no one at home, Stanley removed the gloves and the toolkit from his breast pocket and began to pick the lock. He was familiar with buildings like these. Since wartime rendered electricity scarce and costly, homeowners and landlords were disconnecting alarm systems and hiring security guards who were happy to work for a pittance.

With the door unlocked, Stanley hesitated before entering and ran his hand over the top of the door. He felt nothing. As he entered the suite though, he noticed a toothpick on the floor, just inside. He made a mental note to replace it when he left.

He suddenly felt as though he'd been hit in the head with a pan. The gargantuan nature of his task almost floored him. How on earth was he expected to find a postcard in an entire suite, and with the added pressure of having no idea when any occupants would return? His strategy had to be methodical. The postcard was given to a musician. He'd been around musicians since he was in high school and he knew how their minds worked. Provided that he hadn't discarded the postcard, Cameron Walsh would very likely store it in his room. A cursory search of the downstairs revealed no bedrooms. Stanley moved swiftly to the upstairs.

The first room was in a state of complete disarray. An envelope in the wastebasket was addressed to Evan Dixon. There were two beds in the room. If one bed was Evan's, then Stanley knew that the other one had to belong to another of the Roadhouse Sons, but who? The end of a guitar case stuck out from under the second bed. Carefully sliding it into the open, Stanley saw the Clyde Poulin's name painted on the case. He slid it back into its previous position and scurried down the hallway.

The second room wasn't very neat, and had a similar setup. There were three guitar cases with tags indicating that they belonged to Rich Webster. Again, there was no clue as to the identity of the other occupant. Stanley hurried to the next room in order to avoid wasting time.

The third room was in slightly better condition. The beds were made and, in each of the corners near the beds, a guitar case leaned against the wall. One, while obviously worn, had no identification whatsoever. The other sported a plethora of gaffer's tapes and stickers, including a faded one that read "Cameron." Stanley began a systematic search of the room. He searched through the drawers of the dresser, careful not to disturb its contents. Finding nothing, he carefully examined the contents of the wastebasket. Again, he found nothing. Turning his attention to the guitar case, Stanley placed it on the bed and gingerly opened it. He lifted the guitar by its neck, and peered into the bottom of the case, but found nothing there, either. He smiled as he replaced the guitar, and ran his fingers along the inside lid of the case.

Boney Jack's bassist, Jack Ralston, would occasionally hide contraband in his guitar case and Stanley inevitably found it every time. Fool that Ralston was, he never realized that it was always the first place to be searched. Stanley smiled in satisfaction as he found the small catch, which revealed the case's false backing. His smile faded as he discovered that this hidden compartment was also empty of clues. Stanley replaced the guitar case where he'd found it and smoothed the case's imprint from the bedspread. As he stood up, he noticed a stack of books on the floor by the head of the bed. He looked closer and found a small, dog-eared paperback Western and two tablature books. There was nothing particularly noteworthy about the paperback, and a postcard would be obvious if it was inserted therein. On the other hand, a postcard could easily be placed undiscovered into one of the tab books.

Stanley flipped through the pages of the first tab book and found nothing but scraps of paper with song references written upon them. He picked up the second tab book. Somehow, it felt different in his hand, yet he found nothing hidden amidst the pages.

"Why does this feel odd?" Stanley whispered to himself.

He closed his eyes and ran his hands over the entire book. The back cover of the book felt firmer, as if something had been placed within it to fortify it, perhaps. To his naked eye, though, it looked perfectly normal.

Stanley decided to flip through the pages again, this time starting from the back of the book. That was when he noticed something unusual. The very edge of the back cover was shiny, while the rest of the book was rather worn and the back cover itself was stiffer than the front cover. He pondered the quandary for a moment. He removed the small toolkit from his pocket, selected a miniature razor blade, and worked the tip of it into the corner of the back cover. With the proficiency of a surgeon, he gently slid the blade down the length of the book cover. A layer lifted, and once his fingers could fit inside, he delicately removed two sheets of onion paper, upon which appeared to be a handwritten letter.

There in Stanley's hands was an account of Cameron's visit to the hospital. Stanley's pulse quickened. Cameron had written of his encounter with Tim Woodhouse and the latter's insistence that Cameron take the postcard. Stanley's blood ran cold as he read of the discovery of a microdot hidden inside the layers of the card, and the subsequent surrendering of both the postcard and the microdot to federal authorities. Stanley pondered absconding with the onion papers and vacating the premises, but he realized that if he did so, his presence there would be revealed.

Replacing the folded papers exactly as he had found them, Stanley used the bottle of glue on the nightstand to reseal the book cover. He wiped off the excess glue and restacked the books in their original order. He turned off the light and hurried downstairs. As he was leaving, he noticed Cameron's note. Stanley knew the location of the Paradise Club; it was one of Boney Jack Preston's favorite haunts. The very thought of running into that band there, especially in light of his mission, rendered Stanley even more anxious. Pausing briefly at the door, he turned back and snatched the message pad from the table. He tore off the top sheet with Cameron's message, as well as the three sheets below it, to ensure that no one would be able to see writing impressions.

He hurried from the apartment, retrieving the toothpick and placing it on the top of the door in the middle. He closed the door and used his tools to lock it. He ran toward the elevator but could already hear one of the cars moving as he pushed the call button. To avoid discovery, especially by any of the Roadhouse Sons, Stanley used the emergency stairs. As he descended, he removed his hat, ID badge, and glasses and stuffed them into the canvas bag. He donned his windbreaker and continued to the parking garage on the ground floor. With sunglasses on, he stepped into the garage and made his way to the sidewalk.

He heard a mild a commotion in another part of the garage and was grateful for the diversion. He casually increased his pace. Walking around the block to the rear of the building, Stanley continued up the street, careful to discern that he was not followed. On the next block, he hailed a cab and gave the address of a street corner near his apartment. He realized that even the slightest delay could be costly, but he couldn't chance reporting his findings from a public phone.

Distracted, Stanley benignly humored the taxi driver's attempts at repartee.

There was too much on his mind...

CHAPTER THIRTY-TWO

"Red Herrings"

Chuck was barely able to contain his roadie, who managed to wriggle out of even the tightest grip Chuck could manage and no amount of soothing could calm Snapper.

"Look at it!" Snapper screamed, pointing at the band truck. He was quivering with rage. "*Look at it!*"

Chuck sighed. He saw it. He knew very well what Snapper and the others were so upset about. Despite the supposed security of the apartment building and its garage, someone had managed forced entry and vandalized the band truck. All four of the rear tires were slashed. Eggs were smashed on the windshield, and the sides of the truck had been sprayed with black spray paint. With deliberate intent, the culprit had altered the design on the side. Instead of the stylized, weather-beaten sign proclaiming the Roadhouse Sons, there was now an adornment of lines suggesting that the band's logo had been draped with toilet paper, on a portion of which was a wicked sun smirking—complete with fangs.

"How the sweet fuck could this have happened?" Snapper demanded, his voice cracking.

"Snapper, calm down! I'll get to the bottom of this. Calm down, or I'll have to restrain you again!"

"How can I calm down? I'm responsible for this band's equipment. And that truck! That truck, right there! See it? You can't miss it! It's the one with no tires, no windshield, and shit marked all over the side!"

In his excitement and anger, Snapper's stance verged on physical threat to Chuck, who had no choice but to grab him by the back of his shirt and shove him up against the wall.

"That is enough!" Chuck barked. "I said I'd find out what happened!" Chuck's grip on Snapper remained fierce. "I don't need to worry about you running off and doing something stupid! Now, quit your screaming and make yourself useful. Check the spare tire and clean up this graffiti!"

Reluctantly, Snapper fell silent, his eyes still ablaze with anger. Chuck stormed off to find a security guard. Snapper, still trembling with anger, fished out the keys to unlock the back. Rich ran to his side. Until now, he hadn't dared to be within ten feet of Chuck and Snapper.

"Man! Look at that shit!"

"If they touched a thing in here, I'll hunt them down and kill them!" Snapper hissed.

To his and Rich's relief, the contents of the truck were untouched. Snapper and Rich proceeded to thoroughly check every single piece of equipment. Once they were satisfied that each element was intact, Snapper removed the spare tire from the back.

"Bright side is we only need to find three tires, now," he groused as he closed the rear of the truck.

"How in hell are we going to come up with three tires?"

"Start pooling our tire rations and try to find someplace that can fix all this," suggested Snapper.

Rich pondered the situation for a moment. "But even with all of our rations combined, and Chuck's, we won't have enough to replace all of these."

"Well, we'll have to give it a try," muttered Snapper. He stomped away.

"Where are you going?" cried Rich.

"I'm hoping to hell that this useless garage at least has a janitor's closet with some cleaning supplies." He pointed at the truck. "That mess isn't going to fix itself!"

Rich guarded the truck, perching himself upon the back bumper. He lit a cigarette and twirled it between his thumb and forefinger. Despite that he appeared nonchalant, anyone who knew the bassist would discern that his concentration was focused on rectifying the situation and locating the parties responsible for it. There was no doubt in Rich's mind that the recent press conference with the Boney Jack band, and all of the orchestrated conflict, were the catalyst for the malicious retaliation.

While he didn't think that the punk band members themselves would've done the damage, Rich did suspect that, at the very least, the vicious act was performed by one of Boney Jack's devotees. They likely found the Roadhouse Sons' location after seeing the truck drive through the city. Both box and cab were adorned with the familiar Ryder yellow, and the box had the distinctive Roadhouse Sons wooden sign logo on the side.

Experiences with jealous boyfriends, husbands, and fathers of the Sons' female admirers, as well as rival bands, had sold the boys on the benefits of anonymity. While Chuck understood their desires, he reminded them that their logo connected them to the high-morale USO tours.

"Anonymity and secrecy can breed suspicion," he'd said. As a result, the Roadhouse Sons emblazonment was proudly posted on the side of the truck.

Rich examined the graffiti. The more he looked at it, the more it actually grew on him. He thought it was, perhaps, a good idea to keep it.

"I'll mention it. After Snapper calms down," he chuckled to himself, watching Snapper storm about the garage, with Chuck, equally grim, close behind.

Snapper had managed to acquire a bucket of warm water, rags, and a scrub brush. Without one word, the roadie climbed up onto the running board and began to scrub the windows. Rich considered breaking the silence, but was apprehensive about the storm that might ensue.

"While you were sitting here, did it occur to you to check the van?" snapped Chuck.

Rich drew a final drag from his cigarette and threw it to the ground, snuffing it out with his boot heel. "No," he said, exhaling slowly. "Clyde and Evan are in the van and they're not back yet. There was no reason to be concerned about it, just like there is no reason to take things out on me."

"I don't like your attitude," Chuck grumbled.

Rich shrugged. "Fire me then," he replied, his voice quiet. "I didn't have anything to do with this. I'm not responsible for the security in this garage, and if you're going to treat me like I am, you can either fire me or kiss my ass because I am *not* playing that game."

Chuck glared at the bass player. He considered a reprimand for such overt insubordination, then acquiesced at the futility of it.

"You're right. I'm sorry. I just needed to grouse, I guess."

"That's fine," Rich said, with no trace of sarcasm. "I'd've probably done the same thing. But, in the meantime, what do we do now? Did you find a place that can fix these tires?"

"That was the easy part," Chuck smiled. "Technically, as part of the USO tour, we're part of the war effort and are therefore entitled to assistance from the government. I made a call to the base and requisitioned some tires. They're sending a truck over in the morning. When they get here, we might have to arrange for a tow truck to change them, but at least we'll have them."

"Any gigs scheduled that we need to get to tomorrow?"

"No gigs. Just an appearance tomorrow morning," Chuck replied, the relief in his voice evident. "Snapper can stay here with the truck while the band takes care of that. Are you all right with that, Snapper?"

"I'm not all right with anything!" the roadie yelled. "This shit is damn near baked on! I'll have to get it off with a paint scraper!"

"That'll scratch the glass," Rich responded, grabbing a rag. "Let's give this a try first." He climbed onto the opposite running board and scrubbed at the dried eggs.

Chuck was pensive. For several moments, he just stood there, watching them in silence.

"Tell me… What would you guys've done if you couldn't call for some surplus tires?"

"That's easy," said Rich. "We'd have figured something else out."

"Like what?" Chuck pressed.

"For starters, probably do what we did the last time something like this happened." Rich's eyes remained on the windshield. "We had a blowout once and had to load everything essential into someone's car and head to the next gig, and pray like hell we made it on time. Otherwise, we'd've been fired and then wouldn't have the money to get the truck fixed. This isn't new for us, Chuck. We're just farther from home than usual, with a bigger truck and more shit to move, that's all. But we've got a van now that holds more stuff, so I guess it all works out."

Chuck was impressed. When challenged, the boys didn't panic or make excuses; they simply dealt with difficult situations, logically and practically. They always faced challenges head-on.

From the front of the truck, Snapper's voice was less irate and he even laughed once or twice. Chuck guessed that must mean the dried eggs were coming off the glass.

"Are you calling the police about this?" Rich asked, quietly.

Chuck nodded. "I already did. Didn't have a choice, really. The big dogs don't handle this sort of thing. I'm going upstairs, though, to notify McIntyre. I just wanted to make certain there was nothing else to worry about here."

"We've got this under control," Rich said. He lit another cigarette. "Snapper and I can get some more soap and water if we need it. We'll wait here for the cops and ring you when they get here."

"I just wanted to be certain no one else was around here to start any more trouble."

Chuck took several steps away, then hesitating, turned back to look at Rich and Snapper.

Rich laughed. "We can handle it if they do! We're big boys! Besides, if they're stupid enough to hang around a roadie after vandalizing his truck, then they deserve a pummeling."

"I don't need any more shit to worry about." Chuck, impatient, shook his head and turned away.

"Then don't," Rich replied, drawing long on his cigarette. "We're not going to go looking for any trouble, and I seriously doubt that whoever did this is still around. Unless it was that useless lump of a security guard. We've got this under control. Go make your phone call."

Chuck traversed the side of the building and sauntered through the lobby, taking the elevator to his floor. At the door of the boys' suite, he paused and glanced to his left and to his right. He was alone in the hallway. He unlocked the door and opened it slowly. He casually slid his hand along the upper edge. He froze. The toothpick, always set in the upper right, wasn't there. He ran his fingertips over the top of the door one more time and felt it—in the middle.

Fending off panic, he stood in the doorway, assessing the interior. Everything was as he left it, except for one anomaly glowing from the staircase.

"I could've sworn I turned off my bedroom light when I left..." he whispered to himself.

He called out for Cameron, hoping on the off chance that the singer was still home. He heard no reply. Chuck mounted the stairs, about to enter his room. He paused for a moment in the doorway. Something was different; he could feel it. He wasn't sure exactly what prompted his alarm. He visually scoured his room once more, then moved toward his telephone. He placated his concern by persuading himself that he was enduring a simple case of nerves, but the ill-placed toothpick set off an unquenchable alarm.

Chuck dialed McIntyre's office number. He glanced at the nearby notepad to see if Cameron had left any indication of his whereabouts. There was no note. Leaving the premises without informing its occupants as to one's location was a serious breach of protocol, and totally out of character for Cameron. Just then, the receptionist answered McIntyre's telephone. Chuck requested McIntyre.

"Hey there, orange blossom," he said cheerily.

McIntyre's equally cheerful response clued him in that she'd received his coded message, and that there was trouble looming.

"Well, hello there, big guy! I was just about to call you," she replied.

"How would you like to go out on the town tonight?" Chuck said, feigning attraction. "We've got rats and I don't feel like hanging around here."

"Wild horses couldn't drag me away from an invitation like that," McIntyre giggled.

"Great! I'll be waiting in the car. Say…wear that orange blossom perfume for me, would you?"

McIntyre coquettishly agreed and ended the call. The mention of orange blossom was Chuck's coded method of informing her of a dangerous situation, and mentioning rats was notification that the apartment had been compromised. Waiting in the car meant that he would meet her in the garage. Her reference to wild horses indicated to Chuck that she was leaving as soon as she terminated the call. The promise to wear the perfume provided indication that she would notify their superiors and commence emergency procedures.

With his peripheral vision, Chuck spotted a copy of the day's paper on the coffee table. The paper displayed the curfew notices for the week. He grabbed it and left the suite, returning to the garage. Snapper and Rich were finished scrubbing away the last of the smashed eggs from the band truck. Rich was, arms flailing with enthusiasm, pondering their night, while Snapper nodded vehemently.

"Hey! Did Cameron mention where he was going tonight?" Both Snapper and Rich shook their heads.

"You mean he's not upstairs? The way he was bitching about that report, I figured he'd be here all night," Rich said. "Why?"

"He wasn't in the apartment, and he didn't leave a note."

Snapper and Rich, perplexed, stared numbly at Chuck.

Chuck handed Rich the newspaper. "I found the newspaper you guys were checking out for nightlife. I wondered if he'd mentioned any destinations to you."

Rich examined the club notices.

"We talked about going out, but Cameron was in his room working and didn't speak up."

"Which reminds me. Why the heck are you guys still here and not out? The truck's clean," Chuck asked.

Rich lit a cigarette and drew upon it deeply. "We were headed out, remember? But Snapper left his coat and extra cigarettes in the truck and we came back to get them and saw all this and, shit, you know the rest."

Chuck nodded. "Were you guys all going somewhere together?"

"No. Snapper and I wanted to go to a blues club, and Clyde wanted to go to a hard rock place. Evan decided to go with him."

"How'd you know which was which?" Chuck asked, examining the notice. The advertisements made no mention of the type of entertainment offered by the clubs.

"We were talking to one of the soldiers at the base," said Snapper. "We told him we were looking for some cool places to go and asked if he could recommend any. He mentioned half a dozen or so. Some of them weren't in the ad, though. They operate on different days, I guess."

Chuck eyed him warily. "Can you remember them?" he asked.

Snapper shrugged and looked at the paper. "Yeah, that's one. It *is* in the ad. That's the Buckaroo Tavern. The Jade Pagoda, that's another. The Night Lite's one, and that one, the Paradise Club, sounds familiar."

Rich pointed to another name. "Ed's Kort Haus. One soldier said that's a great place to play pool."

"Were any of these the ones you were going to?" asked Chuck.

"No," Rich said. "We wanted to listen to music, too, not just hang out and drink."

"Though we wanted to do that, too," Snapper chimed in.

Chuck frowned. "This at least gives us something to work on."

Just then, McIntyre drove up and screeched into the parking spot next to them.

"Hop in, guys!" McIntyre yelled, ramming open the passenger's side door. "*Hurry! Get in!*"

Instinctively, Rich spoke aloud. "This can't be good news."

Snapper stared at Rich.

"You're right..."

CHAPTER THIRTY-THREE

"Outplayed"

Stanley hurriedly punched the numbers into the telephone keypad. He'd briskly scampered back to his hotel, and the exertion left him gulping for air. He couldn't afford to give the impression of panicking; that would be a weakness not unnoticed, more likely appreciated, by the ones he was calling. He had to control himself.

The phone rang once, then twice. Stanley wished against hope that no one would answer; then he wouldn't have to deliver the bad news. There was no way of telling exactly how they'd take it, but he knew it wouldn't be favorably. His hopes rose as the other line rang a fourth time. He was tempted to break protocol and hang up before the tenth ring when, alas, the click on the other end sank him into despair.

"Emma misses Arthur terribly." He spoke quickly as soon as he heard the familiar deep breathing on the other end. "Emma would desperately like to speak to him."

A male voice responded. "I see." The delivery was measured, ominous, and cold, and the sound made Stanley's skin crawl. "Perhaps Emma is becoming homesick. This is the second time this week that she's called. Arthur had not heard from her in years before now."

"Times change," insisted Stanley, nervously.

"Perhaps it is people who change. Arthur doesn't like to be in relationships with people who aren't independent."

"I assure you, if Emma was to be independent now, Arthur would be even less pleased. It seems that someone accidentally received a special item that was intended for him."

"He is aware of that."

"Is he also aware that it was given to someone *else*?"

Stanley held his breath. The silence on the other end was stultifying, and reminded him of the calm before a storm. He could only hope that the impending tempest wouldn't consume him.

The voice responded, calm and with absolutely no sense of urgency. "Arthur would rather talk to Emma face to face. Have Emma meet Arthur at the small café near Pike Place Market. I believe Emma likes flowers. Arthur will bring a small bouquet for her. From White's Florist."

As if to punctuate the conversation, the man on the other end hung up, abruptly and with no closing salutation.

Stanley had no time to waste. The mention of a small bouquet was a verbal code, indicating that they were leaving immediately for the rendezvous site. He'd recognize his party by the white Styrofoam coffee cup they'd be holding. Under the circumstances, Stanley felt fortunate that he'd changed his clothes earlier; his usual attire would've attracted far too much attention at the Marketplace. What he'd worn to search the Roadhouse Sons' suite was suitably inconspicuous. He hurried from his apartment.

Stanley was on his last raw nerve. Even the closing of the door sounded ominous.

* * * * * * * *

Cameron opened the door to the Paradise Club. The sounds and smells washed over him like a familiar wave. He paused for a moment and drank it in, paid the cover charge, and wandered into the main floor of the club.

An all-girl band was onstage. The poster by the door listed them as Lunatique. It was obvious that they, like the Sons, were a cover band. The lead singer was finessing the lyrics to *"Magic Man"* by Heart. Cameron navigated his way to the stage and caught the singer's eye.

"Seemed like he knew me...he looked right through me...yeah," she purred, staring at Cameron. She was a tall, striking woman with rich, wavy auburn hair that cascaded over her shoulders in loose curls. She moved as though each and every word caressed her smooth, white skin. During the guitar solos, she closed her eyes and formed her mouth into a silent moan, all of which further heightened her ersatz eroticism. The stage lights, instead of pulsing to the beat, slowly changed from purple to green to pink to blue, and the smoke in the room cast a dreamlike quality upon the entire club.

Cameron winked and smiled at the singer and made his way to a side table where he could have a view of the room and the stage. He'd barely seated himself when a waitress was upon him, quietly asking for his drink order, then fading into the smoky gloom. The band played several more songs by Heart. Cameron studied the singer. Each song was performed in equally as seductive a fashion, and while she didn't single out any one patron, she managed to convey to every man in the room that each song was implicitly between each of them and her.

The waitress returned with Cameron's drink. As he offered her a tip, he happened to notice activity at a table in the opposite corner of the room. A small group of men were gathered in hushed but animated conversation, and repeatedly glancing furtively his way. In the dim light, Cameron didn't recognize any of them. He didn't know anyone in Seattle, nor would he recognize anyone outside of the army bases.

Just some soldiers out on the town, or someone who recognizes me from a newspaper article or interview…

He decided to keep an eye on them. After several moments, the men left the table and entered the hallway toward the exit. Cameron relaxed a bit, surprised with himself that he felt relief.

The show continued. The band alternated various classic blues tunes from genre legend Big Bill Broonzy, and completed their set with Eric Clapton's *"Double Trouble."*

Cameron concentrated on the band. Including the vocalist, they were a five-piece ensemble, with a guitarist, bassist, drummer, and keyboard player. During the Broonzy numbers, the bass player played harmonica. She resumed playing bass for the Clapton song. Cameron noticed that the other musicians, while not quite as animated as the singer, were also adept at attracting the audience. The girls were generous with each other, as well. Each of their peers were allowed their respective showcase moments when the others would step back and allow them their time to shine. Cameron appreciated such professionalism; it showed that the band knew the virtue of showmanship.

He summoned the waitress and asked her to send the singer a drink, with his compliments. When the set ended, Cameron headed toward the stage when suddenly a hand pressed down on his shoulder. The next sensation he felt was a sharp knife in his back.

Looks like there's a change of plans…

"Someone wants to see you," a voice whispered in Cameron's ear. The overpowering reek of cigarettes and booze stung his nose. Instinctively, he tried to pull away, but the grip on his shoulder tightened and the point of the knife pushed a little deeper into his back. Cameron wished he'd taken that drink to the stage himself. At least then he would have something to throw back into the man's face. He thought it best to remain calm. In a crowded club, innocent people could get hurt.

"Then let's not keep them waiting," Cameron said. "Lead on."

Cameron was discreetly manhandled through the maze of people and led toward the back of the room and to the hallway.

They didn't leave after all.

Cameron knew his assailant must be one of the men he'd seen in the corner. The man moved him through the crowd in the hallway, acting as though he was drunk, and cracked inane jokes, all the while patting Cameron on the shoulder. The hallway continued past the entrance and led to the restrooms. Several people watched the spectacle of a sober buddy leading his drunken companion to the bathroom, and offered Cameron sympathetic looks, which he returned with a weak and wan smile.

At the entrance to the men's room, another man was leaning against the door, informing patrons that one of the stalls was currently out of order. The crowd was outraged when he then admitted Cameron and his captor. The man closed the bathroom door, separating Cameron and his abductors from the commotion. Cameron forgot everything around him when he saw Boney Jack propped up in the far corner of the stall.

The punk rocker seemed paler than usual; the circles under his eyes were even darker, yet his eyes blazed hot.

"Hello, funny man," Boney Jack slurred. "You're not talking so big now, are you? No one makes a fool out of me and gets away with it."

"Are you still bitching about that press conference?" Cameron snapped, trying to buy enough time to devise an escape plan. "You made a fool out of yourself running your mouth, and you know it! I just didn't let you pretend anymore. You've always been a joke, for Christ's sake! Don't you ever read your own interviews?"

"I'm the Scourge of God," Boney Jack hissed, straightening up to his full height, swaying as he did so. "Do you hear me? I'm the Scourge of God! I'll make you payyyy!"

Brays like a fuckin' donkey...

Without warning, the door banged open. The crony who'd been guarding it fell backwards onto the bathroom floor. A man dressed in black stepped over him. Cameron seized the opportunity and kicked his attacker's wrist. The knife spun away, and its owner rose to retrieve it. The man in black expertly delivered the knifeman a sharp punch to the kidney, followed by a karate chop to the back of the head, causing the thug to collapse in a heap. The knife clattered and skittered across the floor into another stall. Boney Jack, who moments ago had been proclaiming his Scourgedom, sank into the corner and shrieked like a schoolgirl.

Before Cameron could react further, the man in black grabbed Cameron's arm.

"*Let's go!*" he shouted. Cameron, for the first time during the entire altercation, was finally able to get a look at his rescuer, and found himself staring into the last face he ever expected to see.

"Doug?"

CHAPTER THIRTY-FOUR

"The Storm Breaks"

McIntyre turned on the car radio. She turned the channel knob back and forth until she found static. She looked at Chuck in the passenger's seat. He'd called her, and she'd arrived at the band's suite as fast as she could, where Chuck revealed the evening's events. Rich and Snapper listened in stunned silence at Chuck's assessment that an unauthorized individual had invaded their living quarters.

Every member of the band knew the protocol if they were to be the last one to leave the premises. Firstly, they were required to inform one of their peers of their intended whereabouts. Secondly, they were to leave the chosen marker in a designated area atop the door and search for and remove it upon their return, regardless of who had placed it. If an intrusion occurred, the perpetrator would have no knowledge of the procedure, and their presence would be obvious. The Roadhouse Sons had always adhered to the protocol, despite the fact that they were convinced of merely humoring Chuck by doing so.

McIntyre drove on, listening intently to Chuck's entire account. She didn't interrupt him, nor had her expression changed since the onset of his statement, despite its revelation. McIntyre was known for her remarkable ability to quickly devise a course of action. Her talent rested in her self-discipline of refraining from formulating conclusions until she received every possible iota of information.

As Chuck finished his statement, Rich felt chilled to the bone; he realized that McIntyre was driving downtown in close proximity to the government offices immune to curfews. Rich's sense of foreboding loomed over him, palpable and constricting.

"Is there anything else?" McIntyre asked.

"No," said Chuck. "Not on our end, anyhow. But I take it you've got something?"

McIntyre nodded. "A shitload," she muttered.

Her uncharacteristic use of profanity alarmed Rich and Snapper. They exchanged furtive glances.

"There's been another murder."

"Who now?" Chuck was obviously surprised.

McIntyre relayed the circumstances surrounding Simms' death.

"Apparently, there was some connection between Collier and Simms." She shook her mane of wavy blonde hair.

"A possible contact?" Chuck asked.

"Wha…?" Snapper's inquiry was cut short by Rich's firm grip on his arm.

"The higher-ups think so," McIntyre said. "However, his name hadn't shown up on anyone's radar, and they didn't make any connections until you and Cameron brought in your little Cracker Jack prize last night. By then, Simms was already dead."

"How did that lead us to any connection?" Chuck asked.

"The connection was Simms' employment with Stanley and Boney Jack. The next tidbit of information is a bit more surprising. It seems that Simms was seeking what Woodhouse handed over."

"Why would he have been looking for that postcard?" Snapper asked.

McIntyre glared at him in the rearview mirror, another uncharacteristic behavior for her.

Rich felt as though he was having an anxiety attack.

"He obviously wanted the information stored in it." McIntyre's tone was clipped, and daunting. Snapper blushed and sank into the seat.

"Do they know what was in it?" Rich spoke cautiously; McIntyre's wrath wasn't anything he wished to experience. He considered her a bit unpredictable.

"No," she replied. "They've developed the microfilm so far, and it's contents are written in Russian and encrypted, but that's all we have thus far. It's too soon to tell if it's an internal communiqué, or if it's intended for us."

"Was Simms the designated recipient?" Chuck asked.

McIntyre sighed. "He doesn't appear to have been. But, why would anyone want to send that precious cargo to a member of a punk band, especially the lead singer? It doesn't make any sense."

"There's no denying that Boney Jack comes across as a loose cannon," Chuck agreed. "But what if it's all just an act, carefully contrived and executed?"

"With all of the attention he draws to himself?" McIntyre exclaimed. "Not to mention to his entire band and management? That's entirely reckless. Do you think for one moment that the Soviets would risk such lack of control?"

"It was just a suggestion," Chuck cooed.

They drove in silence. After several minutes, Chuck spoke.

"Have they found any more information on Simms, by the way?"

"No!" McIntyre's frustration was obvious. "They're still checking that lead. Like I said, he hadn't shown up on anyone's radar before. Ever. When he finally does, he's murdered, just like his contact."

"So who do you think the killer is?" asked Rich.

McIntyre and Chuck glanced at him as though they were parents quieting the children in the back seat.

Rich ignored their reaction and pressed his inquiry. "Two people with connections to the Russians are murdered. It's like someone is feeling around in the dark and they don't know what they're looking for. I might be way out in left field, but I don't think they were the main focus of any of this."

"Neither do I." With the car paused at a stoplight, McIntyre turned around, full body, to look at Rich.

Snapper viewed her actions as an invitation to the discussion. "What do we do now?"

"We don't do anything, until instructed otherwise. At this moment, the case is handled above our heads. It's out of our jurisdiction."

"Then what are they going to do?" asked Rich.

"Need-to-know basis," Chuck answered.

The topic was closed, Rich could tell, but he wasn't ready to cease his questioning.

"So, Chuck...the idea that this murder had something to do with whoever broke into our pad...is it a possibility or a coincidence?"

"You know how I feel about coincidences."

"Yeah...I've inherited that from you, it seems. So, like Snapper said...what do we do now, about the break-in, I mean?"

"For that, we have a response." McIntyre was finally relaxing. A plan of action was always her best comfort. "I notified our superiors, and we don't act until advised to do so. Next..." She looked at Chuck. "I take you in now and you file your complete report, then maybe they'll tell us what to do."

Rich and Snapper eyed each other and sulked. Snapper mouthed the words, "Fucking reports!" and Rich clucked his tongue, shaking his head in disgust.

Chuck sagged into the seat and grumbled.

"Withered and weary...so friggin' weary..."

* * * * * * * *

"Come on!" shouted Doug. He grabbed Cameron's arm and yanked him from the men's bathroom. Doug was inexplicably clutching his abdomen, but nonetheless shoved his way through the front door.

"Hey, Sexton!" the doorman shouted. "Get back here, or you're fired!"

Doug ignored the man and lunged across the parking lot, stumbling occasionally and still clutching his side, Cameron still in tow.

"Slow down a little! You're killing me!" Cameron cried. His lungs were burning, and the resulting confusion from seeing Doug suddenly materialize from thin air numbed his psyche.

He had so many questions. He didn't know where to begin. Myriad profanities spewed at them by the angry doorman were a clear revelation to Cameron that the time for questions wasn't upon them.

He'll tell me soon enough...I hope...

Doug dragged him into a narrow, dark alley. He slammed himself against the side of a building, treating Cameron in the same manner. He motioned to Cameron to walk behind him. He slowly backed down the alley several more feet, into complete darkness. Cameron began to whisper, but Doug hushed him with a light tap to his arm.

A group of spectators had followed Boney Jack and his two attendants out of the club and into the parking lot. Doug and Cameron could hear the small crowd much better than they could see them. After three or so minutes, Doug pulled Cameron in a rush fuarther down the alley. They wound their way through a series of alleys and darkened streets, alternately running and speed walking, and all the while ducking out of sight whenever they heard the sound of approaching cars.

"Doug! Is it really you?" Cameron wheezed. "Man! We thought you were dead!"

"Not now! We've got to get you out of here, and fast! Those guys are crazy! They'll be looking for us. Follow me. I've got an idea."

"Man, what the hell happened to you, and who's Sexton?" Cameron asked. He was desperately inhaling, attempting to draw cool air into his lungs.

Doug turned suddenly and shoved his face into Cameron's. "Not now!"

They stepped into another darkened street.

Pike Street...Market...

For no relevant reason, visions of the fishmongers tossing deliberate near misses of their daily catch toward amused spectators flashed through Cameron's mind. In the distance, he could see the Pike Place Market lights.

Seafood businesses were open until curfew. Fish wasn't originally rationed; it didn't dry and can as well as beef or chicken, but deprivations by the Soviets in the Pacific and the Gulf of Alaska hampered supply. The government, therefore, allowed citizens to take advantage of fishing boat arrivals, and the coastal residents were supplied with as much fresh fish as possible.

A boat must have just unloaded, judging by the crowd.

Doug hauled Cameron down the street, snapping him from his reverie. Doug still clutched his abdomen, and was also favoring his right foot.

Twisted ankle?

Suddenly a car careened around the corner and screeched to a halt in front of them.

"Shit!" cried Doug. "Move it!"

They ran toward the crowd at the market, the car rapidly gaining on them. Cameron feared that it would plunge straight into the throng until he saw the posts silhouetted against the harsh lights of Pike Place.

Barriers!

Cameron gasped with relief. Doug yanked him around the first barrier and pushed through the crowd. They ran, breathless, and heard a thud, crash, and screams, followed by the screech of tires again.

They ran the barriers!

Angry shouts and threats ensued from the crowd. Doug and Cameron knew that the vehicle had caught up with them, yet their pursuer's driver had no choice but to stop the car due to a swarm of angry people. Doug and Cameron took advantage of the delay and plunged themselves into the crowd, Doug pausing just long enough to whisper into the ear of a fishmonger. The man was reciting a lyrical poem and, without missing a beat or a syllable, acknowledged Doug's request and nodded to him. Doug then grabbed Cameron's arm just as they heard the sound of running footsteps and the crowd swell yet again with shouts and expletives.

Shit! They're on foot now!

"Sock eye, sock eye, sock in the eye," sang the fishmonger poet to his crony behind the display case. The fishmonger's pal tossed a large salmon to him. Happily reciting his poem, the fishmonger caught the salmon, held it by the tail, and proceeded to spin like a discus thrower, smacking it into the face of Doug and Cameron's assailants.

"Ohhhhhhhh!" the fishmonger yelled, as the man stumbled, dizzy. Several people in the crowd cheered.

"Whoops!" the fishmonger laughed as he kicked the man's legs out from under him.

As the perpetrator attempted to struggle to his feet and stagger away, another thug entered the scene. Without warning, the crowd heard a piercing shout. Doug and Cameron turned to see who, or what, it was. There stood Boney Jack, having emerged into the circle of light, like a ghoul stepping out of hell itself.

The second thug caught sight of Doug and Cameron.

"Come on!" yelled Doug. He grabbed Cameron's sleeve and ran farther along the colonnade toward a stand displaying a scant selection of cut flowers.

Cameron's breath came in sharp gasps; he was lightheaded. He slipped on ice from the fish stands, and nearly tripped over an old blind man playing guitar. Cameron accidentally slammed into Doug, who dragged him down a ramp to one of the market's lower levels. The thug had left his buddy behind at the fishmonger's stand and was in hot pursuit of Doug and Cameron.

The old man continued to play the blues. He let out a loud, plaintive cry as he belted and held a high E note. Cameron turned to steal a glance, and beheld a beautiful sight. The old man, still singing, leaned back, extended his legs, and tripped the thug, sending him face first onto the ground.

Yes!

Cameron, lungs ablaze, kept apace of Doug. They entered a darkened passage and proceeded to yet another lower level of the Market. They passed a couple snuggling in the darkness.

"Sorry..." Cameron muttered as they hurried past.

Doug led him to a stairway and, to Cameron's surprise, led him back up to street level, but farther away from their point of origin. To his great relief, Cameron espied Boney Jack and his entourage running into the darkness.

There's no way Boney Jack saw us...

"This way!" Doug wheezed, staggering across the street. They arrived at an odd little out-building. Doug rushed Cameron around the side of the structure, where a road-weary Suzuki GT500 motorcycle awaited them. Doug retrieved a set of keys from his pocket and motioned for Cameron to get on.

Doug coughed and held his abdomen. He gently rubbed his sides. For the first time during his entire interaction with Doug, Cameron noticed Doug's requisite black trucker cap.

That's where it went...stolen from on top of the stereo...Jesus!

"Where are you staying?" Doug turned around his cap, the bill of it now in the back. Cameron told him the address of the band's suite.

"I know where that is. Hang on!"

Cameron dutifully climbed onto the rear of the Suzuki and grabbed the sissy bar. Doug started the engine.

They lurched forward and sped into darkness.

CHAPTER THIRTY-FIVE

"Revelations"

Stanley arrived at Pike Place Market and casually perused the various booths and respective merchandise. In more pleasant times, the Market housed a variety of small dealers, ranging in offerings from local produce, textiles, used books, and 45s and LPs, to original artworks. These days selections were limited. Gone were the myriad rows of produce and flowers; the variety was scant and paltry. In many respects, the area resembled a low-income flea market, but the merchants struggled mightily to uphold their pride and appearances.

Stanley crossed Pike Street and entered a coffee shop. A handful of customers lingered, caressing their ceramic cups for warmth. He approached the counter and requested one small serving of black coffee to go, and proffered payment. In turn, he was handed a white Styrofoam cup, aromatic with a fresh roasted brew. He left the shop and crossed Pike Street again, returning to the Market.

Stanley walked among the stalls, in search of an individual with a similar cup. As he wandered down one side of the Market and turned to head back to his point of origin, he noticed a woman leaning against a corner of the opposite building and reading a newspaper. She wore slightly faded denim jeans and a peasant blouse, which draped past her waist to mid-thigh. Her hair was black and cut feathered; it fell forward onto her face as she read, but she didn't push it out of her eyes. She sipped from a white Styrofoam cup.

Stanley stopped at one of the flower stands and pointed to a white carnation.

The elderly proprietress winked at him. "In China, we have peony!"

Stanley thanked her and pointed again to the carnation, offering two one-dollar bills. The old woman's eyes twinkled with appreciation and she quickly handed to him the most robust white carnation she had. Stanley nodded, smiling tersely, and walked away.

He ambled nonchalantly toward the woman reading the paper. As he approached, she looked up and smiled.

"Flowers are hard to come by. That must be for someone special."

"It is. Someone with whom I was hoping to talk...face to face..." Stanley cooed. "Rather than over the phone."

"Smart man," the woman murmured coquettishly. "I think a lot of things can be discussed over a cup of coffee rather than over the phone, don't you?"

"Oh, yes!" Stanley agreed, leaning toward her. He kissed her cheek.

"Come with me," she whispered in his ear. "I know a place where two lovers can talk in private."

The woman disposed of the newspaper in a nearby rack. Stanley slipped his arm around her waist. She leaned against his shoulder and slid her arm through his. They headed toward the fish market. She navigated him through the crowds.

"Let's go down the ramp to one of the lower levels. There're shops there that aren't busy, and they're only open in daylight to conserve electricity. It's really private."

Stanley complied. While the niggling bureaucracy made life difficult for the shop owners there, the lower level provided a perfectly secluded environment. She veered him into the shadows.

"We can talk now," she said, softly. "We can keep an eye on the hallway and the ramp from here."

"We have serious trouble," Stanley stated. His voice was calm and dignified, his demeanor unhurried. Nothing he said, nor the manner in which he said it, could reveal any inner turmoil or anxiety.

"We...a very dangerous word. You should use it with care."

Stanley sighed. Such talk, complete with veiled threats, bored him. "I'm aware of its implications. There is no other appropriate word. *Our* little bundle ended up in the wrong hands."

"Whose?" She pressed her body against his. To the casual observer, they were two lovers enjoying the privacy of the darkened alley.

"Cameron Walsh. That idiot fool at the hospital thought Walsh was Boney Jack and gave it to him by mistake. Apparently, Walsh discovered *our* little surprise and showed it to his friends."

The woman caressed his chest, but said nothing. Stanley knew he'd just delivered bad, and unexpected, news.

"Do you know to whom he showed it?" she cooed.

Stanley drew her closer to him and leaned in as though to kiss her neck. He whispered in her ear. "We think the FBI," he said softly. Tension ran through her entire body, and he felt every nerve of it. He was relieved when, at last, she relaxed. She rubbed the tip of her nose on his and giggled.

"It seems that the FBI is not the only point of concern."

"What do you mean?" Stanley laughed ribaldly, rubbing his nose against hers. "Who else would be involved? The Chinese?"

"We haven't been able to determine that." She gave him a long, lingering kiss. "We believe whomever it was also killed Collier."

"Did they kill Simms, as well?" He rammed his mouth upon hers.

"Hey! Easy, now!" She pulled her face from his and smiled. "No. Simms was handled by one of our own operatives."

"One of ours?" Stanley pushed her away. "Why wasn't I informed of that?"

"Oh, darling," she cooed, in a stage whisper. "You get so nervous sometimes." She placed her hands on his buttocks and nestled his hips into hers, laughing at him. He felt the revolver tucked into her waistband. "We had evidence that there was a double agent working in your network. We couldn't take chances. Everything was under surveillance."

"I am entitled to know who killed Simms!" he growled.

"Darling, don't be jealous," she teased. She kissed him on the cheek. "That isn't for me to say. We realized that you weren't the one we were looking for. However, your associate was. Apparently, he and his accomplice, Collier, had been planning on making a gift of our efforts for some time. Unfortunately, someone else got to them before we did."

"Your operative did some damned sloppy work," Stanley sneered. "In his final death throes, Simms was still able to leave a numerical clue on his calculator."

She betrayed no surprise at Stanley's assertion. He knew she would never reveal whether Simms' death was planned, or an unfortunate and coincidental necessity. He also knew better than to pursue the subject.

"Is that why they used a courier instead of mail?" He desperately wanted to lead the conversation into an arena that he knew she'd discuss. "So Woodhouse could give it to their American contact?"

She shook her head, whispering. "No. That was an unfortunate circumstance of war. Anchorage was bombed before it could be mailed so, alternately, he was instructed to keep it on his person until he could give it to you. That should have worked, but he was wounded more severely than anyone realized and he gave it to the other musician by mistake. It seems Collier knew of the alternative plan and tried to intercept it. However, someone got to Collier before he was able to."

"The Americans?"

For reasons unbeknownst to Stanley, she was suddenly annoyed. "That wouldn't make sense! If he was about to deliver sensitive information to them, why would they off him? Even if they didn't take him seriously, they would have waited to see what he was holding. That also rules out the British and the other NATO allies. China hasn't been involved in any of these operations, as far as we can tell. We don't know with whom Collier and Simms were dealing."

Stanley was shocked. "An unknown force is infiltrating one of our networks, and you have no idea who's behind it? This is beyond belief! Walsh also stated that he'd discovered a possible code in a book owned by a former friend."

"Was there any indication of what it was?" she asked. Stanley shook his head.

"Then I doubt there is any importance to it," she said.

Before Stanley could respond, a cacophony of commotion sounded from the level above them. Stanley and the woman moved farther into the shadows. They heard shouting and gasps, followed by laughter and profanity. The shadowy figures of two men came rushing down the corridor. Stanley tightened his embrace on the woman, actually reaching for her gun. He needn't have bothered; the two men rushed past, and Stanley and his female cohort were unnoticed. The first man, Stanley noted, walked with a bit of difficulty, but managed to move with surprising agility. Stanley turned to the woman for a moment, then looked away from her. To his astonishment, the second man's face was fully visible and he couldn't believe the coincidence. He instantly recognized Cameron Walsh.

"Excuse us!" Cameron panted, holding up one hand as though to ward off espying an intimate moment.

Stanley and his female companion, ensconced in the shadows, were concealed perfectly from passersby; Cameron didn't realize to whom he spoke. However, Stanley had not only a clear view of Cameron and the man with whom he was running, but of the three angry men who suddenly appeared in the corridor, as well.

Rage accosted Stanley's very being when he saw that Boney Jack, obviously inebriated, and two other ne'er-do-wells skulked past the entrance to the lower level. For a moment, Stanley wondered if his drunken star would attempt the descent down the corridor into darkness, but Boney Jack and his companions staggered back the way they'd come.

Stanley's ersatz lover yanked on his waistband. "I don't need to inform you that someone has become more trouble than they're worth," she whispered. Stanley made no argument. There was no need. He had come to that conclusion a long time ago.

"Go home," she insisted. "Wait for instructions." With that, she gave him a lingering kiss, then disappeared into the darkness. Stanley pulled his cap low and moved away in the opposite direction. To the objective observer, two clandestine lovers had completed their rendezvous.

* * * * * * * *

At last, Cameron and Doug arrived at the Roadhouse Sons' living quarters. Doug was obviously in pain; he'd struggled to keep the Suzuki balanced.

"Park in the back of the building," Cameron said. "All these spots are spoken for. Your bike'll attract attention if you park it here."

Doug was apprehensive.

"It's OK," Cameron explained. "That security guard never moves out of his box until it's time to leave."

Cameron guided Doug to the rear of the building. Doug glanced about and, satisfied that his motorcycle would be safe, parked it and followed Cameron through the rear door to the back stairs. As they ascended, Doug stopped several times to catch his breath, clutching his side all the while.

"Are you hurt?" Cameron asked. He tried to move Doug's hand but Doug smacked his arm.

"I'm fine!"

I know better...

They continued up the stairs, pausing at the second-floor landing. Cameron opened the door and checked up and down the hallway. It was empty. He motioned to Doug, who followed him to the elevator. They rode in silence. The elevator chimed.

"Follow me," Cameron said.

They hurried down to the boys' suite. Cameron slowly opened the door and slid his hand across the top edge. He grabbed the toothpick.

"Chuck still doing that shit?" Doug muttered.

Cameron smiled and nodded. He stood at the doorway and listened.

"Good! No one's home," he said, beckoning Doug inside. He led Doug into the kitchen. Doug sat at the table, grunting as he landed.

"Let me see your fucking shirt!" Cameron demanded.

Doug realized the futility of protesting. Slowly, he pulled his hand away from his side. His shirt was soaked with blood.

"Lift up your shirt. Now!" Cameron was stern.

Doug did as he was told, wincing as the garment pulled away from his skin. There on his right side was a five inch-long laceration.

Cameron whistled. "Motherfucker, that's gotta hurt…"

"It looks worse than it feels." Doug spoke through clenched teeth. "It just hurts like a bastard every time I move fast. Is it still bleeding?"

"Uh-uh…I don't know how you could even walk."

Doug nodded, relieved. "I didn't think it was still bleeding, thank God. Do you have anything for me to fix this up with?"

Cameron hurried to the bathroom. He rummaged through the medicine cabinet and the linen closet. He discovered a first aid kit and a small bottle of witch hazel, and ran back to the kitchen. Doug was at the sink, carefully bathing his wound.

"Fucker ripped my best shirt," he grumbled. Refusing Cameron's offers of assistance, he pointed to the first aid kit. Cameron opened it.

"Wash your hands, then give me those cotton balls, that witch hazel shit, and a couple of those big gauze pads. Oh, and the tape."

Again, Cameron did as he was told. Doug used cotton balls to dab the wound with witch hazel. Assured that the wound was clean, he covered it with two gauze pads and taped them to his skin. He plopped back down in his seat at the table. Cameron followed suit. For several moments, they sat there, saying nothing.

"OK, man! I need a fucking explanation!" Cameron yelled.

Doug held his forefinger to his lips.

"I thought you were dead!" Cameron's eyes were tearing up.

"According to those asshole friends of yours, I am," said Doug.

"What the hell are you talking about?" asked Cameron. "You better start from the beginning."

"Fine, then!" Doug gasped. "I need some water."

Cameron retrieved a plastic cup from the cabinet and filled it with tap water. Doug guzzled it, and fiddled with the empty cup.

"Remember that fire at the civic center in Burlington?"

"How could I forget it? I've had nightmares ever since!"

"Remember how I went back in to look for that old guy, Everett?" Cameron nodded. "Well, when I went in there, I didn't see him, but I did see one of the other guys who had tried to jump us. I went after him."

"I went in after you, trying to find *you*!" Cameron was crying. "That was a damned stupid thing to do!"

"Pot, kettle, black!" sneered Cameron. "Please do continue."

"The guy ran out the front of the building and, like I say, I went out after him. We ran right into a bunch of state troopers and Burlington cops. They grabbed us both and hauled us in. Over and over I tried telling them to contact you and Chuck, but no one would listen."

"Why didn't you call?" asked Cameron. "You're allowed one phone call."

"I tried, but I never got the chance. After they brought me in, they handed me over to a couple of suits who started asking me questions about Gus and the Mustang."

"Not that shit again..." gasped Cameron.

When the Roadhouse Sons were first recruited, it was discovered that Doug was a very close friend of one Gus Kalbe, a specialist in radar development. Gus was recruited by the navy to engineer and monitor a top-secret radar jamming device system installed aboard the Mustang, a specialized Arctic Ocean patrol submarine. The system would immobilize Soviet radar and communications, thus preventing any advance warning to the Russians of attack on their soil. The device was, instead, used against the United States, enabling the Soviet invasion of Alaska and the Canadian northwest. The Mustang was destroyed at the very beginning of the conflict. There were no survivors. Doug never fully recovered emotionally from Gus Kalbe's death, and harbored great bitterness toward the authorities responsible.

"Yeah, that shit again!" Doug spat. "This time, they hauled me down to D.C. and put me in a cell. They questioned me for weeks, wanting to know about Gus and the people we hung out with. I even had to be questioned *with* that asshole, D'Lorenzo!"

"Oh, that must've been something!"

Special Agent D'Lorenzo, along with McIntyre, had recruited the Roadhouse Sons and, as it turned out, had also convinced Gus Kalbe to work on the Mustang project—a reprehensible action that Doug held responsible for Kalbe's death, and which earned for D'Lorenzo Doug's perpetual and undying hatred.

"Oh, it was!" Doug snarled. "They must've known it, too, because they had me in manacles and at the far end of the table whenever he and I had to be in the same room together."

"I'll bet D'Lorenzo wouldn't have agreed to go in there unless you were kept the hell away from him!"

"No kidding! The big pussy! They kept me there for almost a month, and kept telling me they'd pass my information along to Chuck and McIntyre, who never, ever got a hold of me. Finally, they just released me and told me I was free to go. No one told me how to get in touch with any of you and I had no idea where you'd gone. By that time, I had other shit to worry about."

"Like what?"

"Like the fact that I was dead."

Cameron's eyes teared up. He wondered when and how they were going to broach the subject of Doug's purported demise.

"They fucking declared me dead!" Doug shouted, throwing his cup into the sink. "I found that out when I went to get my ration book replaced. They busted me and accused me of trying to defraud the government and tossed me in jail for another month!"

"Man, just calm down! Tell me the rest." Cameron was not in the mood to manage Doug's temper.

"Yeah! Calm down," Doug jeered. "Fuck me over six ways to Sunday and I have to calm down. Well, don't worry, that's what I did! As if I had a choice. My family wouldn't let me come home, I had no idea where you guys were, and I didn't have a job. I had *no* fucking money and didn't have any rations, either."

"What did you do? You're here and you don't look too bad…"

"I figured it out," Doug muttered. He checked his wound dressing, saying nothing.

"Well? What did you do?" Cameron repeated.

"Back before I started working for you guys, I had another job. Nothing big or anything, but it was something that I knew I could get back to and didn't need papers for it."

"What was it?"

"I was a pro wrestler," Doug said. "I did some work in Montreal for the Vachons in their Grand Prix promotions. Just undercard stuff, but I knew I could go back to it."

Cameron chuckled. "I'm not surprised. You loved watching it. You'd buy those wrestling magazines. The other guys teased, but it never seemed to bother you."

"I got some work," Doug sighed. "I couldn't get into Canada, obviously, but the Vachons got me hooked up in upstate New York and I went there. It was easy to work under the table because some of the promoters didn't like to attract too much attention, either. I changed my name to Don Sexton and wrestled under a hood so no one would recognize me. They called me the Crimson Mask and put me on a lot of the undercards. I made enough to eat and was able to share rooms with the other guys. As I got bookings with different promoters, I was able to work my way cross-country. That's how I found you guys."

"Missouri!" Cameron smacked the table. "We replaced a wrestling show that got cancelled. You were on that show? Why the fuck didn't you let us know?"

"I didn't dare." Doug's voice was almost a whisper. "I didn't know how much shit I'd stir up, so I just stayed in the back of the bar and watched. You guys still sound great…"

"That's too bad," Cameron sighed. "We sure could have used you! You're not going to believe this, but a bunch of guys—"

"Tried to break into the band truck after the show," Doug interrupted. "I know. I overheard them planning shit at the bar and snuck out before you guys finished your last set and stowed away."

"What do you mean, stowed away?" Cameron insisted. "We didn't see you!"

"I was in town ahead of the wrestling show because I was also supposed to be on the ring crew. So, I was staying in their storeroom and saw some heavy-duty rope back there. I took some of it and made a cradle underneath the box and rode home with you. I waited 'til everyone went to bed, then climbed into the cab and waited to see if those assholes would show up. They did."

"Wait! How could you have climbed into the cab? We had that thing locked up tight!"

With a mischievous smile, Doug drew his key ring from his jeans pocket and shook it. "How quickly you forget!" he laughed. "I've still got my set!"

"You toad!" Cameron laughed. He went to the refrigerator and retrieved two beers. "I *knew* you weren't dead! Chuck kept telling me to let it go, but I fucking *knew* you had to be alive, since you left me that sign and all."

"Sign?" Doug was sincerely perplexed.

"The orange! You left an orange when you took your stupid hat back!" He pointed at the Doug's worn black cap. "Chuck found your hat after the fire and gave it to me. I left it on my stereo, and when I went back that night, it was gone and there was an orange in its place. Then I knew you were OK."

"I didn't leave any orange!" Doug insisted. "I didn't even notice my hat was missing. All my stuff was taken when they booked me that night. I got stuffed into a jumpsuit and didn't get any clothes back 'til they released me in D.C. My hat was with the rest of my stuff."

Cameron stared, dumbfounded. The comfort of an explanation he'd embraced for over a year suddenly evaporated, creating in its stead additional questions and a menacing sense of the dreaded unknown. Before Cameron could respond, the front door flew open. In the doorway stood Chuck. Cameron had never seen him so surprised.

Oh, shit...

CHAPTER THIRTY-SIX

"Three Steps Forward, Two Steps Back"

"It's closer!" McIntyre rebuffed Chuck's chiding.

She talked over her shoulder to Rich and Snapper, who were flummoxed and sulking in the back seat. "I left that site as our contact location for updates or directives. My offices are less remote from your suite and from the club district. It's less difficult to search for Cameron in a hurry if we had to leave from there."

Upon arrival at her office, McIntyre's secretary handed her a small stack of message slips. A quick check of the names revealed that she and Chuck had return calls to make. They left Rich and Snapper in the reception area and entered McIntyre's office.

"Secure location, secure line…" Chuck muttered.

He picked up the receiver, dialed, and upon clearing the call through to the correct superior, dutifully reported the suspected break-in at the boys' suite, as well as the vandalism of the band truck. His superiors reached the same conclusion as he and McIntyre—the incidents were most likely unrelated.

"We have the how, where, and when. Do you know what they were looking for? That will give us the why. Did they plant any surveillance devices?" the voice on they other end persisted. Chuck replied negatively to each question.

"It will take time for us to assemble a team to dispatch there tonight," he was told. "We're working on it. We're stretched tight on specialized manpower. They're serving double duty with the local law enforcement, not to mention assisting the military."

"McIntyre and I will conduct the search," Chuck offered. "We'll report what, if anything, we find and, depending, we'll decide on further action. Personally, I think it was just a recon mission. I'd be surprised if there was anything there."

"You're probably right, but we'll take no chances. Conduct a detailed search of anything and everything. Whatever you do, be careful."

"What should we do about Cameron?" Chuck asked.

"Is there concern about Cameron's safety?"

"Not at this juncture," Chuck replied. He reviewed the details of Cameron's clothing and appearance, and the musician's likely whereabouts, including the clubs about which Cameron had inquired form reading the newspaper.

"We *can* dispatch local police patrols…"

Chuck sighed with relief. "Good. We'll worry about the security breach."

He handed the receiver to McIntyre, who, awaiting her turn to speak, had glued herself to Chuck's side.

"Are there any updates on the Christopher Simms death investigation?" she inquired. "We're still treating this as a homicide, right? Every death is a homicide until proven otherwise." Chuck looked at her quizzically. She mugged back at him and waved him away.

"Nothing much," her superior replied. "Thus far, we've checked his records back to college enrollment. He attended the University of Miami in '66, but we have nothing prior to that. The transcripts he'd submitted when he enrolled there were fakes."

McIntyre gasped. "No one bothered to check them!"

"There was no reason to at that time. The high school he listed was a legitimate institution. It now turns out that no one named Christopher Simms ever attended. At the university, he majored in business, was an average student, and never participated in any radical movements. He held two jobs before going to work for Philly Records in '75, and those checked out. There was nothing in his record to suggest anything out of the ordinary about him whatsoever, so his transcripts weren't further checked."

"Despite the fact that he seems to have sprung out of the earth in 1966," McIntyre muttered.

"Exactly. Not the way our agency would conduct things now, I agree."

McIntyre clucked her tongue. Chuck didn't need to hear the other side of the conversation; he could tell that she was frustrated.

"Do you have any more on the murder itself?" She looked at Chuck and mouthed the words, "It's like pulling teeth sometimes." Chuck smirked and rolled his eyes.

Her superior responded after a moment of silence. McIntyre wondered if it was possible to read lips through the phone line.

"The police report stated that the cause of death was a stab to the throat that nicked the internal jugular. The weapon was a small to medium, perhaps round-tipped, device...a dull screwdriver perhaps. The path of the puncture wound suggests that the killer was facing him from above, which leads us to think that the assailant was standing and leaning across Simms' desk."

"Then it must have been someone he knew." McIntyre's enthusiasm heightened. "It had to be someone whom he'd allow in close proximity. He must have known them very well. Has anyone compiled a list of any close friends or colleagues?"

"Negative. He was purportedly a workaholic, and not by choice, considering his job title at Philly Records."

"He was Jack Stanley's assistant!" McIntyre averred.

"Not according to their employee records. As of '77, he was officially listed as manager of Boney Jack," her superior revealed.

"Which is a polite way of saying he was a full-time babysitter. So, to be clear, there are absolutely no leads on any close associates or connections?"

"None whatsoever. Any obvious living associate, including Jack Stanley, the Boney Jack Band, you, Chuck, and the Roadhouse Sons, were all at that press conference."

"That's incorrect. Regarding Boney Jack, Stanley was there, the eponymous lead singer was there, Caesare the drummer was there, as was one of the guitar players, Russ Gibson. The bass player wasn't there, the other guitar player wasn't there, and Simms wasn't there. Remember, I was there, too. Those three were absent."

"Do you know which guitar player wasn't there?"

"Sure. I overheard Stanley having a fit about Jack Quinn and Jack Ralston being absent, as well as about Simms not being there."

Another several moments of silence ensued.

"Stanley wasn't suspicious about their absence?"

McIntyre clucked her tongue again. Chuck mouthed the words, "What the hell?"

She shook her head and continued speaking into the receiver. "Stanley seemed convinced that Simms was ironing out some other problem caused by the punkers. I have a question. Did their drummer, Caesare, and Russ, the other guitarist, *say* that they were at the press conference?"

"People saw them, including the press. Jack Quinn *did* say he was there, but Ralston didn't, and they each have a witness to back up their respective alibis."

"What *were* their alibis?" McIntyre asked.

"Quinn claims that he was there, and a woman from the hotel staff who helped set up the room vouches for that. Ralston claims that he was ill and stayed in. The maid from housekeeping claims that she saw him asleep in bed while she was cleaning his suite."

McIntyre turned to Chuck, her eyebrows high. "I have an idea," she said to her superior. "The press conference was covered by all of the newspapers and a plethora of magazines. We should contact each of the publications and acquire copies featuring the band PR, and especially ones with published photos. That should prove if Quinn was there or not."

"What about his alibi?"

McIntyre chuckled, her demeanor albeit grim. "I've observed musicians in captivity for some time now. They endear themselves to young ladies desiring attachment to them. I doubt musicians are any different in the wild. We should find out whether that housekeeper was really on the job, or snuggled in a broom closet with Quinn."

Chuck was anxious for the phone call to be over, but no such luck. McIntyre pressed on.

"A little pressure on her could reveal whether he's lying or telling a half-truth," she suggested.

"One's as bad as the other in a murder investigation," came the reply. "When asked the nature of his illness and if he sought medical attention, Ralston claims that he didn't call a doctor because he felt that his illness was caused by something he ate. He reiterated that he'd been in the suite all day. And no one saw him leave the hotel. Research so far with the taxi companies servicing the hotel don't reveal a match in hailed fare, but it's a large hotel serving masses of people."

"Fortunately, Boney Jack aren't able to go anywhere anytime soon," McIntyre reminded her superior. "Court-ordered confinement to the City of Seattle proper, remember?"

"Barbara," said the voice, eerily calm. "If someone was willing and able to commit a murder, they won't be intimidated by a court order."

"True... Is there anything new on Collier's connection to all of this?"

"A virtual carbon copy of Simms' situation. Different dates and locations but, prior to entering University of Southern California, we have nothing. No student with his name was ever enrolled in his cited high school. There is no record of his birth, either, under the name and date provided by him. What we do know is that he dropped out of college in his sophomore year, and worked in bands and clubs. Other than the occasional traffic violation, there is nothing noteworthy about him, and nothing linking him to Simms until he approached Philly Records in '78. He wanted them to spearhead the careers of several bands whom he managed."

"Are you thinking what I'm thinking?" McIntyre asked.

"Sleeper agents," surmised her superior. "Apparently so. Two men, with no prior contact and no activities remotely suggesting involvement in espionage, suddenly in contact, both attempting to pass to us alleged Soviet intelligence. And both men ultimately deceased, entrenched in mysterious circumstances."

"Sleeper agents are like cockroaches," McIntyre sighed. "For every one we see, there're a hundred in the walls. Were they both part of the same network, or did one recruit the other?"

For the first time, the voice revealed fatigue. "Admittedly, we're slogging through that research now."

"Has the record company connection been checked?" McIntyre inquired.

"Nothing worth further inquiry. The company was started by Vic Arnold in the late '50s when he bought a small label. He handled mostly rhythm and blues acts, then took on some '60s British bands. The resulting success prompted Arnold to form a few acts of his own. In '61, he hired Jack Stanley as a songwriter. Stanley eventually became a producer and later on became Arnold's partner. When Arnold retired in '72, Stanley bought Arnold's interest in the company."

"I take it you've researched both of them?" McIntyre's question was rhetorical.

"Arnold served under Eisenhower in World War II and achieved the rank of major. He was assigned to the Allied Control Council Berlin-Schöneberg, Germany, where he served under Patton and McNarney and, as I said, Ike, until being discharged in 1947. Arnold was a theatrical agent before the war and again forged a career in theater and entertainment after he returned to the States. He was a lifelong Republican, liked Ike, supported Nixon, and passed away in '77."

"If Arnold was ACC Berlin-Schöneberg, he had contact with Russians. Is that problematic?"

"Under the ACC, we were allies with the Russians at the time. Regardless, we and military intelligence verified and reverified. No issues have surfaced. According to Arnold's file, he was as pure as the driven snow, so there's no reason to believe that his association to Collier indicts Collier in any way."

"What about Stanley then?" McIntyre was willful and determined. Chuck had often likened her to a pit bull attempting to bite and shake loose a fire hydrant.

"Unlike Simms and Collier, Stanley's dossier is pristine," the voice said. "He was born in Hamilton, Ontario, in '39, attended public schools, and graduated from University of Toronto in '61. He held odd jobs in Windsor, Ontario, until, as I said, he was hired by Philly Records as a songwriter in December of that year. He became a US citizen in '73. You're apprised of the rest."

"Anything out of the ordinary?" she pressed. Chuck motioned for McIntyre to hang up the receiver. "Cameron!" he mouthed. She smacked Chuck's arm.

"Other than a problem with his taxes in '72," her superior said, "nothing. It appears that he became a US citizen to avoid paying business tax in both the US and Canada. The '72 dispute was paid and settled, and the file was closed."

McIntyre pondered the information; she couldn't discern exactly why, but found it to be unsettling.

"But where did Stanley get the money to buy out his partner? He wasn't there long enough to accrue that kind of money! Ten years isn't enough to save that much, especially on a salary at a small record label."

"His father's estate," replied McIntyre's superior. "When Stanley was twelve, his father died in a work-related accident at a fertilizer plant. Funds resulting from a double-indemnity clause in the life insurance policy, combined with a settlement from the employer, was set up as a trust against which Stanley was able to borrow."

"Ah, I see... Before I hang up on you, how can I ever thank you for this wealth of information?" McIntyre said, faux sweetly. "Is there anything else?"

She welcomed the laugh she heard on the other end.

"Yes. As I told Chuck, be very careful. We have the pieces of a mighty puzzle, but no idea yet how to assemble it."

* * * * * * * *

Stanley requested that the cab driver drop him off a block from the hotel. He walked the rest of the way. To have the doorman see him exit a taxi rather than his usual vehicle would raise too many questions. Going out for a walk, for some fresh air—incognito, for all intents and purposes—would appear reasonable, especially considering all of the negative publicity of late.

Unfortunately, his desire to perambulate undetected evaporated. A car careened toward the front of the building and abruptly stopped, the vehicle disgorging Boney Jack and one of his devotees.

The musician attempted to stand upright, instead staggering and swaying more than was usual, his arm draping wearily over his unwitting crony's shoulder. Stanley espied the look of disgust and irritation on the doorman's face. Stanley had only mere moments to avert a confrontation.

Hurrying up the sidewalk, he called out, "That's all right, I'll take him from here!" Stanley pulled off his cap to reveal his face.

The doorman was not appeased. "This is a respectable establishment, Mr. Stanley. We won't indulge this type of behavior, especially right here for all the world to see!"

"Yes, I understand," placated Stanley. He offered a wan smile, dug into his pocket and handed to the doorman a ten-dollar bill. "I'll bring him upstairs out of sight immediately."

Stanley discreetly slipped Boney Jack's arm around his neck and gestured threateningly at the doorman, causing him to release his grip on the musician.

"Take your leave!" Stanley barked. The youth ran toward the sidewalk, looked back once, and ran.

Stanley led the staggering musician into the lobby. Boney Jack mumbled, incoherently at first, then with more conviction.

"The Scourge of God, I am!" he slurred, saliva dripping from the corner of his mouth. "The Scourge of God!"

"Jack! Now is not the time!" Stanley urged, attempting to maneuver him toward the elevator without attracting more attention.

Boney Jack suddenly recognized Stanley. "You!" he muttered in drunken amazement. "How did you get here so fast?"

Stanley ignored him and struggled to push the button to summon the elevator. The small crowd gathered there edged away in revulsion.

"You're mad at me!" Boney Jack slurred, bending down into Stanley's face. "You saw what I did, didn't you?"

Stanley panicked. Had Boney Jack seen him at Pike Street Market?

"Saw you there," Boney Jack repeated.

Stanley scrambled for a cover story until the musician spoke again.

"You saw what I did to the truck, didn't you?" Boney Jack laughed.

Stanley had no idea what he was talking about. "What truck?" Stanley asked, impatient.

"Fucking Roadhouse fucking Sons!" Boney Jack hissed. His vitriol alarmed those around him.

"Eggs, everywhere!" Boney Jack laughed and pointed at Stanley. "You were in the garage. I saw you there." He began to cough, shaking violently.

The implication of Boney Jack's statement hit Stanley like a ton of bricks. Boney Jack had seen him exiting the Roadhouse Sons' living quarters!

The elevator doors opened. The violence of Boney Jack's coughing increased.

"I think he's going to be sick!" Stanley cried. He dragged the musician into the elevator. As Stanley had hoped, the prospect of a vomiting drunk horrified the other passengers, who decided to step aside and wait for the next car.

Stanley propped Boney Jack into the corner and shook him.

"What did you see?" he demanded.

Boney Jack's head flopped like a rag doll as he laughed, then convulsed again, coughing unrelentingly. "Eggs and paint all over! Those motherfuckers!" he wheezed. "Saw you. You saw me! That's why you're mad at me again." Boney Jack was suddenly very serious. "Why are you always mad at me?" He attempted to pull himself upright. "I'm the Scourge of God!"

Stanley realized that despite Boney Jack's inane babbling, he'd indeed seen Stanley at the garage. If Boney Jack had seen Stanley, it was likely that his two friends had seen him, as well. Before Stanley could decide what next to do, Boney Jack plopped forward upon him, pushing him against the wall. At that very moment, the elevator doors opened to Boney Jack's floor. Stanley struggled, dragging the debilitated musician to the door of the Boney Jack band's suite. He fumbled through the musician's pockets, found the room key, and opened the door, shoving Boney Jack in ahead of him.

The light from the wet bar illuminated the room. Its reflections from the mirrors on the opposing walls gave the room a soothing half-light, enabling Stanley to navigate toward Boney Jack's bedroom. He gently positioned the musician on the bed. As Boney Jack sank into the mattress, he relaxed. Stanley noticed that the young man's breathing was more regular. He worried that the musician was about to fall asleep.

"Wake up, damn you!" he snapped, slapping the musician's face. "Don't you fall asleep on me now! What did you see?"

Boney Jack started, then stared at Stanley, obviously perplexed.

"How did you get here so fast?" he whispered. "Did you see what I did?"

"Did you see what *I* did?" Stanley demanded, shaking him. Boney Jack began to laugh.

"Those assholes!" he smiled. "Did you see what I did to them? Eggs, eggs everywhere…"

Stanley was losing patience. He had to know what the musician saw, but the idiot was incoherent. "Pull yourself out of your drunken stupor! Did your friends see me?" Stanley demanded.

"Made fun of me…" Boney Jack slurred, his demeanor suddenly serious. "They laughed at me…at *me*! The Scourge of God!"

"Will you stop this nonsense?" Stanley shouted, his frustration getting the better of him. "What did you see at the garage?"

"Revenge!" the musician hissed, raising himself up on his elbows, his eyes widening in dramatic affect. Another coughing fit ensued. Stanley slapped him on the back.

Boney Jack was suddenly lucid. "You *saw* me," he mumbled to Stanley. "You saw me in the garage."

Stanley, encouraged by Boney Jack's seeming flash of coherency, attempted to capitalize on it. "What did you see me doing?" he inquired, casually, carefully.

"You were against the wall. You were going outside. You were going to tell on me." Boney Jack pushed himself up, his weight on his elbows. He swayed and began to roll over on his side. He coughed, his body convulsing.

"What did your friends see?" Stanley pressed. He had to know if there were any more witnesses.

Boney Jack returned to a prone position. "The bastards saw eggs!" he laughed. "They saw eggs everywhere. All over the windshield! All over! The truck is painted! Hahaha! They fucked those bastards!"

"Did they see me?" Stanley demanded.

Boney Jack began to wheeze. "They were painting the truck," he gasped. "They were doing what I told them to do. They obey the Scourge of God!" He coughed as though he was severely parched.

Stanley heaved a sigh of relief. No one but Boney Jack had seen him.

"I only have to deal with one witness," Stanley said aloud, but Boney Jack paid him no attention.

As Stanley pondered his next course of action, Boney Jack's body shook with spasms into yet another coughing fit. Stanley looked about. The light from the other room shone upon the ever-present array of vodka bottles. Stanley grabbed one and stuffed the bottleneck into the musician's mouth.

"Here! Drink this," Stanley snapped. "Moisten your throat!"

Boney Jack instinctively gulped down the burning liquid. He began to cough again, this time uncontrollably.

"Drunken fool! You've inhaled some vodka by mistake," Stanley sputtered.

Boney Jack was attempting to spit out the vodka and suddenly dropped the bottle. Stanley jumped back to avoid the splash, just as Boney Jack convulsed so severely that he began to gag, eyes widening as he realized he was about to vomit. Boney Jack attempted to push himself up, but Stanley pushed the singer down and placed his hand over the young man's mouth while simultaneously pinching Boney Jack's nostrils closed with his other hand.

Boney Jack struggled, exhibiting an amazing amount of strength for one so inebriated. Stanley felt a sudden, unexpected glimmer of respect for Boney Jack. The self-appointed Scourge of God was certainly putting up an incredible fight for his life, vain though it was. Stanley was sober, alert, and in a position of perfect leverage. Boney Jack was none of that. Stanley loved the terror he saw in Boney Jack's eyes right before the singer's struggling ceased; was there a plea for mercy? Stanley held Boney Jack's nostrils closed and kept his mouth covered. The worst situation imaginable was that the job was not complete, and Stanley would witness Boney Jack surging upright still alive! After several moments, Stanley could smell that the young man's bowels had released, his assurance that Boney Jack was indeed deceased. Nonetheless, Stanley felt the man's pulse; there was none. Stanley stood up slowly. He looked down at the body on the bed. There was vomit around the edges of the mouth; the eyes stared blankly at the ceiling.

"And thus ends the Scourge of God!"

Stanley chuckled, eyeing the vomit on his hands. He went into the bathroom to wash. He was careful to wipe his hands and the sink with toilet paper so he could flush the evidence. He wasn't particularly concerned about the presence of his fingerprints in the room. He was—or had been—Boney Jack's manager. There was no reason why Stanley's fingerprints, or any other physical evidence, wouldn't be there. Nearly a dozen people had seen Stanley carrying away his inebriated client. Stanley would simply aver that he'd put the singer to bed and that the man was fine when Stanley left him. He'd maintain that Boney Jack, while asleep, must have choked on his own vomit.

"Attila the *Hun* was known as the Scourge of God! He struck terror in the hearts of all Europe," Stanley spat at the corpse. "My grandfather told me many stories about Attila the Hun. We Hungarians consider him our cultural hero. What's that? You didn't know I was Hungarian? Why, yes, I am! And since there is no longer any reason for affectations or aliases, my real name is Janik. Ha! Janik Senyo…Jack Stanley, for short."

Stanley wiped his hands and entered the bathroom. He flushed the toilet paper and returned to the corpse. He laughed aloud, a giddy, maniacal laugh filled with triumph.

"Do you know how Attila the Hun died? He choked on his own blood! Yes! On his wedding night, in the midst of his camp and surrounded by his warriors. *He* died like a man."

Stanley stared at the figure prone before him, the arms hanging limp to the sides, the legs at awkward angles, all akimbo from the struggle.

Contempt surged in Stanley's chest. "You were nothing but a spoiled rich boy who couldn't deal with the fact that his family had money, except by mocking everything you were afraid to be without. And how did you meet your end? Choked on your own vomit, lying in your own shit, and soaked with your own piss. The very embodiment of the decadent West."

Stanley walked to the door and switched on the light. He thoroughly examined the room one last time to ensure that he'd left behind nothing incriminating. He switched the light off and stood still, listening for sounds other than his own breathing.

"I am Janik Senyo," Stanley hissed into the darkness.

He was about to spit toward the corpse and thought better of it.

Janik Senyo left the room and closed the door behind him, leaving the limp body of the late Jonathan Victor Preston III to be found in the morning by the housekeeper.

CHAPTER THIRTY-SEVEN

"A Way Out"

"Keep your hands where I can see them!"

Chuck barked his order while pulling his gun from his holster. Doug slowly raised his arms, a leveled gaze of righteous hatred thrust upon his former manager.

"Are you out of your mind?" screamed Cameron. "What the hell has he done?"

"Stand up! Slowly!" Chuck bellowed. He ignored Cameron's question and advanced cautiously. McIntyre, Rich, and Snapper eased their way into the apartment, hedging behind Chuck.

When Rich realized the identity of who stood before him, his knees buckled. Snapper caught Rich mid-falter; he, too, was completely taken aback. He hadn't seen Doug in eons, only to be told that he was dead, this man whose place he'd taken. McIntyre, however, drew her pistol. She'd seen ghosts before, and knew better than to trust them. Snapper backed Rich against the wall and they remained there, stunned into silence.

Cameron jumped between Doug and the armed agents. "Have you both gone crazy?" he demanded. "This is *Doug*, for Christ's sake! Put the guns away!"

Chuck spoke, his voice an eerie calm. "I'm only going to say this once. Step out of the way, Cameron. Now."

"I *won't!*" Cameron insisted. "This is Doug! Really! In the flesh!"

"Do as he says, Cameron," McIntyre advised. "He's not kidding, and neither am I." McIntyre, still pointing her gun at the errant roadie, had positioned herself at Chuck's side.

Cameron was horrified.

They're dead serious.

For a millisecond, he considered defying their orders. He looked at his friend and hesitated. All of the years they'd known each other, everything they'd lived through, flooded to the forefront of Cameron's memory. He knew that whatever Chuck and McIntyre thought to be true was wrong.

It's got to be…

Cameron spread his arms like wings and remained in position, shielding Doug.

"I'm not moving!"

"I will arrest you for interfering with a criminal investigation and for obstruction of justice." Chuck's face flushed crimson. He was angry, and made no efforts to disguise it.

"Do it, then! I'm not letting you touch him!" Cameron knew he'd likely made a serious mistake in refuting Chuck.

"You're interfering with a federal investigation!" Chuck warned. "Step aside or you'll be in deep, I guarantee you!"

"What investigation?" Cameron was astonished.

No fucking way!

"At the very least, suspicion of espionage." Chuck aimed his gun at Doug's head. "He is suspected of operating on behalf of the Soviet Union, and is likely the one who broke in earlier."

"It's true, Cameron," McIntyre said quietly. Her pistol was pointed at Doug's chest.

Cameron felt as though a bag of hammers had walloped him in the head.

Impossible!

"That's bullshit!" he screamed. He backed into Doug, arms still spread, protecting him, body on body.

"*Move*, Cameron! That is an order!" Chuck moved his aim from Doug's head to Cameron's.

Rich and Snapper, still backed against the wall, gasped. Cameron's knees weakened. He felt nauseated, but despite his malaise, stayed glued to Doug.

"Cover me!" Chuck said to McIntyre. "Doug! Turn around slowly, move into the kitchen and put your hands on the table where I can see them. Spread your legs to shoulder width."

Doug did as he was told. Cameron gagged.

I'm going to throw up…

Chuck holstered his gun. He sidled past Cameron and stood behind Doug. McIntyre's pistol was aimed at the back of Doug's head.

Chuck seethed at Cameron. "You want proof?" Chuck spat. "The burden of proof is not on me!" He whispered into Doug's ear. "Are you armed?"

Doug shook his head. Chuck began pat-down procedure on the roadie. He placed his left foot between Doug's legs, aligned it with Doug's left foot, and planted his right foot six inches back. Chuck frisked the upper portion of Doug's torso, then moved his hands down both sides of Doug's body. Every half foot or so, he pulled Doug's clothing away and squeezed. He ran his hands down Doug's chest, back, sides again, then his arms. Chuck missed no part of Doug's physique; he included armpits, the nape of Doug's neck, and the full circumference of his waist. Chuck then squatted down and performed similar inspections of Doug's legs, his knees, feet, abdomen, and crotch. Again, Chuck missed nothing. He felt the back of Doug's knees and ran his fingers around the interior periphery of his shoes.

"Lift up your feet, one at a time. I'm checking the soles of your footwear. Don't try anything stupid. There's a pistol aimed at the back of your head."

Satisfied that Doug was unarmed, Chuck stepped away from him.

"Cameron and you, sit!"

Chuck pointed to the table. Cameron and Doug complied.

"What about us?" Snapper was still supporting Rich, whose face was ashen.

"You too," Chuck said, "Get in here."

They did as they were told. McIntyre moved into the kitchen and remained standing, weapon drawn, positioning herself to cover the room.

"So, let's hear about your little adventure."

Chuck's tone was ice cold. Cameron shuddered; Chuck spoke so mechanically, so suddenly devoid of human emotion. With hands resting flat on the table, Doug reiterated to Chuck almost exactly what he'd earlier told Cameron.

He didn't tell the part about hiding in the truck…and he still has a key…

Chuck and the others listened. No one said a word until Rich, ever inquisitive, attempted to ask a question, but was quickly hushed with a glare from McIntyre's.

"Do you know a man named Brian McAllister?" Chuck asked.

Doug nodded, but was clearly puzzled. "Yeah. He lived up the street from me back in Gorham. What does he have to do with anything?"

"How well did you know him?"

"Pretty well, I guess. I did some work for him a couple of times, and he'd sometimes hang out with me and my friends and play cards. We weren't close buddies or anything."

"Did you ever spend time with him without any of your friends around?"

"I don't know..." Doug was still confused. "I suppose so. He'd offer me a beer after I did work for him. I didn't go out with him on a regular basis. He wasn't really my type of person."

"How do you mean?"

Doug shifted in his seat. He stared at his hands, silent for a moment. "I don't know," he muttered. "We just didn't have anything in common. There was no reason to be around each other much outside of work."

Chuck drew a slow, deep breath. "Did you ever talk to him about the Mustang?"

Doug rubbed his face and groaned, animal-like.

"Hands on the table!" Chuck yelled.

Doug slammed his hands down. "*That* shit again!" he growled. "No! I did not talk to him about the Mustang, or about anything related to it! Why? Because I didn't know Gus was involved with that until just before he died! Not even when *your* friend, D'Lorenzo, and his buddy convinced him to reenlist in the navy and work on it!"

The reference to D'Lorenzo, tossed out as bait, as an accusation, was ignored completely.

"Did you ever talk to McAllister about your friend, Gus Kalbe?"

Doug was annoyed. "Yeah, I suppose. We talked about a lot of things. McAllister asked about all my roommates, not just Gus. Like I said, we'd hang out occasionally. Gorham didn't have a lot of people our age. We were about the same age, so..."

"Did he ask you questions about Gus, *specifically?*"

"Like I said, he asked questions about all of my roommates. Once in a while, he'd ask specifics."

"Did you talk about Gus serving in the navy?"

"Yeah, we talked about that. We also talked about Rick being jailed for hanging a dummy off the Portland Street Bridge one night and getting the police and ambulance called out. We talked about Lloyd getting stuck working at his family's sawmill 'til he could move to California. We talked about me and about my family. We talked about a lot of stuff. Jesus! I can't remember all of it."

"Did he offer you additional work after you were more familiar with him?"

"Yeah. He thought it would be easier for me to make a few bucks staying in Gorham than traveling all over, looking for work."

"What were you traveling for?" Cameron interrupted. Chuck didn't protest the interruption, nor did McIntyre, who remained poised with gun drawn.

Doug's defenses dropped considerably as he spoke directly to Cameron. "Around the time I had started working for you guys, the fall of '76, I'd go back to Gorham between gigs, remember? I did odd jobs for McAllister to pocket some extra cash. I think it was around Thanksgiving of that same year I met that dick, D'Lorenzo. Yeah, it was! We didn't have a lot of gigs until just before Christmas, so I had some weekends off and stayed home. Gus met D'Lorenzo's friend, Campbell I think his name was, at work and they'd come over to go snowmobiling."

"Was there ever any time when you were all together with McAllister?" Chuck probed.

"Yeah!" Doug exclaimed, hit by a flood of memory. "There were a few times that we all got together to play cards!"

"McAllister, too," Chuck averred.

Doug nodded. "Once or twice. If there were any times they got together without me, I don't know about 'em. That was when things started picking up with the band and they were hiring me more."

"When did you last see McAllister?" Chuck's tone was terse and demanding. Doug recoiled.

"I don't know." Doug eyed Chuck, and responded with deliberation; Chuck's turn-on-a-dime demeanor rendered Doug cautious, then not so much. "I remember coming home one weekend in January or February and they said he'd moved. I was bummed because I was hoping to start shoveling roofs and driveways for some extra cash, and I was pretty sure he'd hire me."

"Did they say why he left?"

"No." Doug started to laugh. "But we had a hell of a lot of fun imagining why. We figured a jealous husband or boyfriend, or maybe both, caught on to him. He was the biggest pussy hound I've ever met. Get a load of this! He preferred married women! He was always taking off for a weekend to Montreal or Portland or someplace where they wouldn't get a reputation, he told us. What a gigolo...he never went out with the same woman too long, that's for sure."

Chuck turned to face McIntyre. She, still vigilant, nodded but said nothing. Chuck turned to face Doug, his stare intent.

"What if I told you that Brian McAllister's real name was Alexi Russinovich, that he was a Soviet operative, and that he had learned your friend, Gus Kalbe, had been a student of the man who first proposed the Mustang system, *and* that all of his rendezvous infidelities were not romantic getaways, but were meetings with his KGB superiors?"

"No…fucking…way!" Doug gasped. He was dumbfounded.

"What if I told you that your name appeared repeatedly in his reports, citing you as a possible willing observer of Gus Kalbe and his activities?"

Doug said nothing, his eyes wide as saucers and his mouth agape.

"What if I told you that McAllister was planning on using an ice fishing trip to Lake Willoughby with your friend, Gus Kalbe, as a ruse for recruitment to the KGB?"

"That would never fucking happen!" Doug snarled. "Gus would never do it!"

"It's in the reports McAllister gave to his contacts. Unfortunately for him, he didn't realize in time that we had already caught his contact and converted him to double agent. We already knew everything McAllister knew."

Doug stared at Chuck, agog. No one spoke. The silence was broken only by the hum of the refrigerator. McIntyre had said nothing during the entire interrogation. She remained impassive as ever, her gun aloft, aimed at Doug's head. Rich and Snapper sat mute, casting worried glances to each other and to Cameron, both not daring to make a sound.

Cameron wracked his mind, desperate to break the silence.

Scream!

To his immense relief, after long last, Chuck spoke, his gaze steady on Doug.

"Cameron, get the book."

Cameron, caught off-guard, stared at Chuck.

"Get the book."

Sackett…

Cameron ran from the kitchen and returned, the dog-eared paperback clutched in his hands. He presented the book to Chuck, who carefully thumbed through the pages, opened it to a specific passage, then slid the book across the table to Doug.

"Look familiar? This was found among your effects. The name of your high school is on the inside front cover. It couldn't possibly belong to anyone else. Read this portion," Chuck ordered, pointing at the designated paragraph.

"This isn't mine," Doug said in a quiet voice. "This belonged to Gus. He found it at a yard sale before he shipped out. He was going to take it with him to read on the submarine, but at the last minute he was told to leave all personal effects behind, except the clothes he wore. They sent back all but the clothes on his back after he got on board. Gus *gave* me that, and sent this hat home to his folks, with a note asking me to keep them both 'til he got back."

Chuck pointed to the book again. "Read that aloud."

Doug stared at the book, then at Chuck. "I'm not reading anything," he snapped, pushing the book toward Chuck.

"That was an order." Chuck shoved the book toward Doug once more. "I've asked twice. I won't ask a third time."

There was no avoiding the situation, Doug knew. He raised the book to eye level, holding it as though it was a vial of infectious bacteria. Cameron, eyebrows furrowed, exchanged glances with Rich and Snapper as Doug carefully studied the passage. He shifted in his chair, fidgeted, and finally began to read.

"Sh-sh-shame was up-up on m-me here. I was a gro-oh-oh-own man and could-could-couldn't rehhhhh-red eeen-enough to get the-the sennnn-sense out of a let-terrrr." "

He can barely read...

Cameron felt embarrassment and sadness for Doug, who obviously embodied the very words he was struggling so hard to read. Each word read aloud was isolated from its predecessors and successors, separated as though there were individual elements. There was no lyrical flow suggesting any comprehension of the author's vision, or even of the verbiage itself. Cameron was familiar with the passage, and he remembered that the word Doug read as "up on" was actually "upon" and "red," pronounced by Doug as past tense, was supposed to be "read" in present tense.

Doug continued. "M-m-my eyes could," Doug paused, his face twisting as he struggled to make sense of the word before him, attempting to read ahead silently.

"Sheen...sheee-yen?"

"Cheyenne," Cameron blurted.

"Don't help him!" Chuck bellowed, his eyes steely and focused on Doug.

Doug's face flushed. He was humiliated. He looked to Chuck, his eyes pleading for mercy. Chuck shook his head, his stare unrelenting. Doug's face reddened to a deep crimson.

He's pissed now...

The book flew across the table, hitting Chuck in the chest.

"What the fuck?" Doug demanded. His voice caught and he coughed.

Is he going to cry?

Saying nothing, and having not reacted at all, Chuck slid the book across the table, reopened it and pointed to another passage.

"No!" Doug leapt to his feet and flung the book at Chuck. His body trembled and his voice wavered. "I'm not a Commie spy! Arrest me or shoot me! Either way, go straight to hell! But you're *not* fucking with me anymore!"

"He's right!" Cameron roared. He stood up and slammed the chair backward against the counter. "What the hell is the point?"

"I'm helping him," Chuck said, his voice a maddening calm.

"By humiliating him?" Cameron turned to McIntyre. She remained steadfast and unflinching. Cameron stepped toward her. Her gaze remained on Doug.

"The Soviets allegedly ceased recruitment. Now we have confirmation, and now we know why."

"Twenty minutes ago you both had your guns drawn!" Cameron yelled. "You were ready to shoot him because you thought he was a Commie spy! Now you say you've just proved he isn't? Then put away your fucking guns!"

Chuck stared at Cameron, his eyes flinty and unfeeling. Cameron imitated McIntyre and stood his ground, resolute and detached.

Snapper and Rich exchanged glances, petrified to move an inch during the standoff. After what seemed to Cameron like an eternity, Chuck motioned to McIntyre to store away her firearm. She did so and sat at the table as though she'd been there the whole time.

Man, she pisses ice cubes...

McIntyre tapped the table, indicating that Cameron should sit. Chuck retrieved the book and mindlessly flipped through the pages.

Chuck coughed, and addressed Doug. "Even though you didn't mention being in the truck back in Missouri, I deduced that you were. I staged a surveillance of my own that night."

Doug was taken aback.

Cameron prayed that the situation would remain calm. "How could you know?" he ventured.

"The door locks weren't picked," Chuck explained. "That coupled with the fact that after the fire in Burlington we never found your set of keys. That was a long shot, true, but then I found the final clue in the cab—a powdery substance, orange dust."

Doug braced himself for a new accusation. He crossed his arms and glared at Chuck. "Go on!" he growled.

Chuck smiled and pointed at Doug for emphasis. "That orange dust was definitive. There's only one person in this group who's never been able to resist Cheetos, and that is you. I doubt the rest of us have even seen them since we left Vermont."

Doug fell slack-jawed.

"It was obvious that you tried to wipe it away. That's when I realized that you were still alive. I requested your file, and it was then that I learned about McAllister. I'd also read McAllister's reports, and the reason he vehemently suggested that the KGB disassociate. He stated that you were practically illiterate. I contacted your high school and retrieved your transcripts, meager as they are."

Doug turned away, ashamed. "What did you find in those?"

"You dropped out of school in the tenth grade. Based on your test scores, you'd barely reached a fourth grade reading and comprehension level. That explains to me why you always weighed in with oral commentary during report training with McIntyre and company."

Doug closed his eyes as though willing away the entire room and everyone in it. Cameron's heart ached for Doug, for how difficult it must have been to carry such a load in silence, for how it felt to maneuver through life, praying that his illiteracy remain undetected.

"That's bullshit!" Cameron protested. "He can drive and read road signs and he was always reading magazines and comic books and wrestling magazines and posters! And what about this book?" Cameron snatched the paperback from the table and waved it like a banner.

Chuck sighed. "In comic books, he can look at the pictures and discern the story and plot from those. His guidance counselor described him as functionally literate, meaning could read enough to get by, but he would never be a Rhodes Scholar."

Cameron turned to Doug. Doug was wiping tears from his eyes, his secret now out in the open. Rich and Snapper cast their eyes downward, as though to give Doug privacy.

That's why he was always so defensive...everything was a threat...

"You didn't need to say it like that..." Cameron grumbled. He tossed the book onto the table.

"Yes I did." Chuck insisted.

Doug stared off into the distance, avoiding eye contact with anyone. An awkward silence palled the room. He hung his head in shame and melancholy.

Doug finally spoke. "Can I go now?"

"No!" said Chuck. He leaned forward, communicating only with Doug.

"You said your part, now I'll say mine. I believe that the Soviets wanted to recruit you, use you to pass information. You were Kalbe's best friend and roommate. To the Soviets, you were an easy mark, until McAllister discovered your limitations."

Cameron knew the vigor in Doug's soul was evaporating. He hated Chuck for it. Doug raised his eyes and waited for Chuck to continue.

"There was no dispute of your utter fealty to family and friends. McAllister advised that you'd be—"

"Not worth the effort," Doug finished.

"Too difficult to recruit, *or* control," Chuck soothed.

They got that right.

"Let's move on." McIntyre spoke softly, reassuringly. "How did you find us here?"

"The day after your show, I asked the bartender when you guys were playing next. The guy with the black eye, the one that was fighting off those guys the night before, said you were headed up to Columbia. So I went there to ask around. At first, nobody had any information, and I needed money. I contacted a couple of wrestling promoters who told me they were booking shows for USO tours. I asked about rock bands, and eventually saw a USO schedule with you guys on it. So I came to Seattle."

"You didn't have any money or rations. How did you get here?" McIntyre pressed. She knew Chuck welcomed a respite from the interrogation.

"I got booked for some matches myself and rode across the country with other wrestlers. I had to toss in extra cash for expenses because I didn't have any gas rations. That was rough at times, but I managed." Doug very pointedly spoke to Chuck, his accusation apparent.

"That was not our doing," Chuck countered. "There was confusion in Burlington concerning your remains. When you were transported to Washington, they were pretty sure, without the benefit of dental records, that the body recovered from the fire was yours, and issued a death certificate accordingly. Your subsequent attempt to acquire a ration book commenced an investigation involving another branch of the government. You were suddenly cited as a person of interest, which surprised me, since you were already declared deceased. By all means—"

"Wait a minute! You knew I was accused of trying to fake a ration book and you didn't do anything?" cried Doug.

I guess all the fight isn't out of him after all.

"Until Missouri, I had no indication that you were alive. Until I saw you standing here tonight, I still grappled with it. We fucked up."

"Chuck…" McIntyre warned.

"I'm sorry. I will try and straighten this out for you." Chuck extended his hands to Doug.

"Jesus, Chuck…" McIntyre sighed.

Doug was livid. He kicked his chair aside and pounded the kitchen counter. "Remember how Dwyer and you drilled it into us not to trust anyone? Well, I don't. That includes *you!*"

"Fair enough, but all of this could have been avoided if you'd listened to me in Burlington and not gone back into that building."

"What about this nightmare tonight?" Doug resembled a rabid dog.

"Handled differently. Entirely. You wouldn't be taken into custody for attempting to flee the scene of a federal investigation. It would be an internal inquiry. McIntyre, the band, and I would have known your whereabouts and activities, and we would've avoided all of this."

Doug sighed and returned to his seat at the table.

"How did you find Cameron?" Chuck asked.

Doug hesitated, regaining his composure. "I told you I wrestled my way from Missouri to Seattle. Once I got here, I couldn't wrestle anymore because the man that promotes the shows in Seattle won't book anyone that doesn't have the right papers or who seems suspicious. I had to find other work. It was hard. I dug through trashcans a few nights to eat, but there are plenty of places that'll hire without asking questions. I got a job as a bouncer at a couple of clubs, including the Paradise Club, and found a room to let nearby. The landlord let me trade rent for odd jobs. I bought a motorcycle to get around on, and kept tabs on where the band was playing, and waited for your gig here in Seattle. I have to be careful around secure areas since I don't have a real ID. Anyhow, tonight Cameron showed up at the club and those guys were trying to rip him apart in the bathroom. I got him out of there and brought him back here."

Chuck cast a baleful glance toward Cameron. "You'll have to file a full report on that."

"Fuck!"

"Cameron!" McIntyre admonished.

Chuck turned to Doug and resumed his inquiry. "How did you know to come here?"

"I kind of know the neighborhood, and Cameron gave me directions to this building."

"You've never been to this building before?"

Doug shook his head. Chuck drew and exhaled two deep breaths and stared at the ceiling. Eyes still heavenward, he pointed at Doug.

"What's the protocol for leaving the base of operations?"

Without missing a beat, Doug launched into his response. "The last person to leave the base of operations shall indicate so in writing, then place a marker in the upper right-hand corner of the door directly above the doorknob to indicate that the base of operations is unoccupied. Said marker shall be retrieved upon return to indicate that the base of operations is occupied. Said marker, if misplaced, can also indicate that the premises has been compromised."

"I'm glad you said that," Chuck sighed, leaning back in his chair.

"Why?"

"Because, while working with you can be like dancing with a porcupine sometimes, Doug, you do know your procedures. If you'd been here, I doubt the breach in security would have been so obvious. That eliminates you as a suspect."

"Suspect in what?" Cameron queried.

Chuck revealed his discovery earlier that evening, including divulging that the marker was misplaced and that Cameron had failed to indicate in writing his intended whereabouts.

"Is that why you just glared at me? I did write down where I was," Cameron insisted. "And I did put a toothpick in the right-hand corner of the door, at the top. I'll get the pad."

He left the room to retrieve the notepad.

"There's no paper on this pad. I know—"

Cameron was about to vie for his honor when the phone rang. He answered it. Chuck scowled; since when did Cameron answer the phone?

"Hello? Yeah, it's me. Who? Oh, yeah. Hi. What? When? Ok, man, listen, just calm down. Have you called the cops? Ok, then, listen. Let me talk to my manager and I'll give you a call right back. What's your number?"

Snapper, feeling that it was finally safe to speak, couldn't quell his curiosity. "What was that all about?" he asked.

"That was Jack Ralston, the bass player from Boney Jack," Cameron said. "He's wigged out and didn't know who else to call."

McIntyre eyed Chuck.

"What's the matter?" Rich spoke, too, grateful for Snapper's lead.

Cameron looked Chuck square in the eye.

"They just found Jack Stanley in his office. A gunshot wound to the head. Apparently, he committed suicide."

CHAPTER THIRTY-EIGHT

"Betrayed and Retrieved"

Jack Stanley returned to his suite. He poured a stiff drink to steady his nerves. The telephone rang twice, then nothing. It rang once more. Again, nothing. Stanley knew the person calling was his contact. When the telephone rang again, he allowed it three rings before answering. That was the code, his signal to speak freely.

"Jake is very hungry," the male voice said, rife with menacing undertone. A rush of anxiety washed over Stanley. That code, that signal was notification that he should leave. The signal wasn't really unexpected. Stanley had learned it long ago, but to finally hear it as a command was a shock.

"Would Jake like reservations made for him?" Stanley's cool, calm demeanor belied his apprehension.

"No. Jake is very, *very* hungry. Jake ordered delivery. Meet him at the office for dinner."

The caller hung up. Stanley belted down his drink and left his suite. He looked at his watch. Curfew would be enforced in mere minutes. Luckily, he had to simply ride an elevator to the temporary office he'd been forced to use since Simms' death. He surmised that he'd be able to implement instructions as soon as he received them, and without attracting attention on the streets.

Stanley stepped out of the elevator. He thought about the information concerning Simms, but put that out of his mind. There was no time to think about Simms; that man was beyond anyone's reach or concern. Stanley had his own situation to worry about. He unlocked his office door. As he reached for the light switch, he felt cold steel, the muzzle of a gun pressed against his left temple.

"Jake is very hungry."

The muted, raspy whisper raked Stanley's ears. He'd just heard the password, but couldn't quell the grip of fear. His gut wrenched.

How could he have been so careless? Just because he'd entered his own office, there was no guarantee of safety.

"Jake ordered delivery."

Stanley's reply calmed him to a minor degree. He'd just responded in code. Much to his alarm, though, the man didn't tell him to switch on the light. The ensuing command startled Stanley.

"Shut the door! No sudden movement!"

Stanley did so, careful to keep the gun pressed against his head to ensure the stranger that there was no attempt to resist.

The office was dark. The shades of the large picture window behind his desk weren't drawn and the room's furnishings stood in silhouette. The muted Seattle skyline was visible through the window. Stanley could barely make out the lights of a ship sailing through Puget Sound. The sparkling stellar image of the city's lights was a comfort to him, albeit exceedingly short-lived.

"Recent developments are attracting attention," the man rasped. "We cease our operations tonight."

"I understand…" Stanley's mouth grew arid as a desert. The role he played in the sudden turn of events implied deeds that were irrefutable, and for which he had no choice but to remain accountable. He panicked.

"What is to be done?" Stanley swallowed so hard he emitted an audible gulp.

"Your instructions await you. There. On the desk."

Stanley hesitated; the gun was still mashed against his temple. He wondered for a millisecond if the situation was less dire than he suspected, if there was still a chance for redemption. The man increased the pressure of the gun against Stanley's head.

"Move!"

Stanley did so. He heard the rustle of plastic as the other man moved with him, nudging him across the carpet.

"Sit down in the chair directly in front of you."

Stanley moved into one of the chairs facing the desk. There before him was a clear view of Seattle, now looming like an omen of ill portent. An end table rested between him and the man. From the corner of his eye, Stanley could see light reflected from an object, but he couldn't discern what it was, and dared not to look.

"On the table beside you is a gun. Pick it up and aim it at your right temple."

The man increased the pressure of his weapon against Stanley's skull. Stanley knew his fate. He thought of the Boney Jack's struggle for life when the drunken fool knew his end was near. Stanley's instinct was to resist, to formulate a plan of escape. To do so was pointless, a mere effort in futility. When he felt another gun pressed against the base of his skull, he choked, petrified and unable to breathe.

"You have left us no choice. The punk music scheme has drawn too much attention to you and your network. You are more trouble than you're worth. Pick up the gun."

Stanley did as he was instructed. His heart pounded and his breathing was so shallow; he knew he could faint. He loathed how foolish he was to end up in this situation. He knew that he'd become too comfortable. And careless, as a result. He was about to pay the price.

Stanley picked up the revolver. He felt the worn rubber grip on the handle. The gun was his own, the one he hid in his desk. Of course, there would be only one set of fingerprints on it—his own. How clever that he would meet his demise by his own hand and with his own gun. He trembled as he placed the muzzle of the revolver against his right temple.

He waited, focusing his attention on the beautiful beacons in the distance. He felt the stranger remove the second gun from the base of his skull. Something brushed his right hand. A sharp blow crashed him on the right side of his head. Then…nothing.

The man watched Stanley's body slump over the side of the chair. The gunshot rang and buzzed in the man's ears. The wisps of gun smoke reflected the scant light as they floated and wisped in midair. He knew that Stanley wasn't pretending to be dead. He stood over Stanley and released the deceased man's hand, allowing Stanley's arm, and the gun he'd held, to fall naturally.

He grinned. Stanley would've been mortified to be discovered in that position, soaked in blood and stinking of shit, in *old* clothes. Perhaps the excellently forged suicide note on the desk would've assuaged the dead man's vanity; Stanley, confessing—pontificating in his prosaic verbosity—the unbearable duress, the mental anguish and strain he'd suffered due to the actions of his band, not to mention the crushing guilt he felt for murdering Chris Simms in a fit of rage.

The man ceased his musings. He had to hurry. He was holding both of his guns in his left hand. He took one of them in his right hand and flipped the safety then lifted the back of his windbreaker just enough to tuck the gun into the rear waistband of his pants. He repeated the steps with the other gun. He checked the tautness of the wristbands of his cellophane gloves and leaned toward the window to check as much as possible that they were clean. He carefully removed his oversized windbreaker, allowing it to turn inside out as he did. He took two steps backward and gently spread the windbreaker on the floor near his feet. He was careful not to drag it, to avoid smearing any blood there. He removed his surgical booties and rain pants and placed them on the windbreaker. He followed suit with his plastic safety glasses and the bandana covering his mouth. He rolled the windbreaker and its contents into a tight bundle. He removed a plain brown paper bag from the pocket of his jacket and stuffed the bundle into it. Still wearing his gloves, he left the office and closed the door. He checked to make sure that the hallway was unoccupied. He removed his gloves, stuffed them into his front jeans pockets, and headed to the emergency stairs. The offices were usually deserted at this time of night. If anyone had heard the gunshot, it would take them several minutes to report it to the front desk, and for the police to arrive and investigate. While that provided him the opportunity to escape, there was no excuse for carelessness. His superiors were just as quick to reward excellence as they were to punish negligence.

He opened the door to the stairwell and sauntered onward at his usual pace. There was no need to hurry. There was nothing suspicious at all about Jack Ralston being seen, once again, late at night, meandering about the building with a brown liquor store bag tucked under his arm.

Jack Ralston was satisfied with his job well done. He'd simply followed instructions. In the event of any questioning, he had his orders. He'd say that he'd been drinking heavily and tried to call Stanley to discuss the band's ongoing legal troubles and, unable to reach Stanley in his suite, Ralston called the garage to see if Stanley had taken his car out. Since he was told that Stanley hadn't left the building, Ralston looked for him in his office; Stanley was often there working late at night and was known to occasionally ignore late-night telephone calls. Hence, it would be logical for Ralston to visit Stanley there. He discovered the body and called the police. Totally shaken, he also used the office phone in an attempt to contact his band members whom, he'd hoped, had returned from their respective nights on the town. No one from Boney Jack was available. Desperate to speak to someone, he contacted Cameron Walsh. The calls to the police, and all subsequent calls, Ralston was instructed, were to be made from Stanley's office, therefore allowing a cover for any inadvertent general contamination of the crime scene, and would account for any possible physical evidence Ralston may have left behind.

The plan, thus far, had been executed seamlessly. Upon receiving his instructions, though, Ralston was nagged by just one element of the plan.

"Why Walsh?" he'd asked. Other than the occasional meeting and press junket, he'd never had much interaction with him, or with the Roadhouse Sons. He had nothing against Cameron Walsh, per se, but there was nothing really concrete that suggested a connection between them.

The answer Ralston had received still unsettled him. "We know for a fact that Walsh and his manager are working for the FBI," they'd told him. "Walsh intercepted important correspondence intended for us. At this time, we have no gauge as to what information was gleaned, or on how to determine who else is working with them. Simms' and Collier's circumstances are too suspicious and won't be ignored. We feel that Walsh and his mates will be eager to befriend you, a purportedly bereft fellow musician."

Ralston strolled to his suite, unlocked the door, and sidled in. He locked the door behind him, ran to the kitchen, and stuffed the brown paper bag deep into the trash. He grabbed another paper bag from the floor and disposed of the cellophane gloves in the same manner. All of his stash blended perfectly with the other sacks and bottles in the trash bin. He headed to the bathroom, washed his hands, thoroughly checked his garments, shoes and the soles thereof, urinated and washed his hands again.

Ralston reentered the kitchen. Nothing was out of place; everything appeared to be normal. If he couldn't see anything irregular, neither would the housekeeping staff the next morning. He grabbed a half-empty bottle of Jack Daniels from the counter, gulped a hearty swig, and left the apartment, noisily closing and locking the door behind him. He headed to the elevator, booze bottle in tow and humming some nonsensical tune, and pushed the button to call the car. The elevator arrived within moments. Ralston entered the car and pushed the button to Stanley's office floor.

He reached Stanley's office, opened the door, switched on the light, and screamed.

* * * * * * * *

"Why would he call you?" Chuck was suspicious.

"He was babbling," Cameron responded. "Something about not being able to find anyone else, and needing to talk to someone. He thought of us and got our number from Stanley's Rolodex."

Snapper and Rich were dumbfounded, first at the news about Stanley. Despite the fact that they never liked him much, the thought of him committing suicide was pure shock. They were even more nonplussed that Jack Ralston called any of the Roadhouse Sons, especially after such a tragedy.

"Smells funny to me," Snapper murmured to Rich.

"What exactly did he say?" McIntyre asked. "You weren't on the phone with him for very long."

"He told me that he found Stanley in his office, slumped over in a chair with a bullet hole in his head!" Cameron was having a difficult time wrapping his mind around the tale. "He found a suicide note. He called the cops, tried to get in touch with the other guys in his band, and couldn't get ahold of them. He started to get scared and paranoid and thought of us, so he took a chance and called." Cameron turned his attention to Chuck.

"He wants me to come over right away. He says he can't deal with this alone."

"What else did he say?" McIntyre asked.

"That's all he said."

"Why'd you tell him you'd talk to Chuck?" Rich asked, incredulously. "Someone was freaking out and you blew him off?"

Cameron shot him a dirty look. "Listen, I'm not Dial-a-Prayer!" he snapped. "I don't know the guy that well! I figure Chuck and McIntyre know how to handle it."

Chuck was introspective. He and McIntyre looked at each other for what felt to the boys like an hour.

"Cameron, where did he say he was calling from?" he asked, cautiously.

"He said he was in Stanley's office waiting for the police."

"He's at the crime scene?" McIntyre yelled. She turned to Chuck. "He's *contaminating* the crime scene!"

Chuck threw his head back and growled under his breath. He looked at Cameron, his eyes pure fury. "Cameron, did he say if the police are there?"

"They're not yet. He said he's waiting for them."

Both Chuck and McIntyre moaned, disgusted.

"What's the big deal?" Doug demanded. "We're not at the crime scene. We didn't do anything. We're not connected!"

Chuck buried his face in his hands. "True, but you don't understand. He's contaminating the crime scene and therefore compromising a proper investigation. That's anathema to McIntyre and me, and I'd think it would be to you all by now. Cameron, did he sound like he was sober?"

"Hard to tell. He's really upset."

McIntyre clucked her tongue. "He could be destroying or tampering with evidence."

"But why would cops need anything?" Doug asked. "Didn't he just say Stanley probably offed himself?"

"Doug!" McIntyre sniped. "Every death is considered a homicide until proven otherwise, remember?"

"It is. Even I know that," concurred Snapper.

Doug looked away, sulking.

"Wait..." Chuck was contemplative. "We have a little unfinished business with our new arrival here. Look," he said to Doug. "As far as the powers that be are concerned, you are not now, nor were you ever, considered a Communist spy, or any threat thereof. I believe that and I'm sure McIntyre does, too—"

"Not quite." McIntyre eyed him. She was resolute. "I'll agree that McAllister wasn't able to convert him and that he never betrayed his country, but if you want to bring Doug back into the fold, my answer is negative."

Everyone in the room froze, shocked at McIntyre's pronouncement. It certainly wasn't the response that Cameron expected. He'd assumed that his crew was back together and that they'd continue on their merry way.

Other than McIntyre, Doug was the only one who didn't look like someone kicked them in the solar plexus. He just sat, stoic and relaxed, staring at McIntyre.

The expected rejection...the other shoe dropped...

"Well, then," Doug said, quietly. He rose to his feet. "No point in me hanging around here, is there?"

Chuck gestured for Doug to remain seated. "Not so fast!" he turned to McIntyre. "Why?"

"I'm not saying he's a bad guy. He's not," she expounded. "But let's face it. The reason the Soviets didn't want to touch him wasn't just his illiteracy. He's obstinate and independent. Dwyer reported on several occasions that they butted heads. I remember those times vividly. Remember how Doug and D'Lorenzo constantly bickered and quarreled? Always practically coming to blows. And surely you haven't forgotten that last night in Burlington! Two people intimately involved with this case are murdered, and I know that you don't believe Stanley committed suicide, so his death makes three. Chuck, we cannot afford to have a loose cannon on our hands."

The room was cast into awkward silence.

"Can I say something?" Doug ventured, his voice uncharacteristically quiet.

"Yes." McIntyre nodded her approval.

"I'm not going to argue with anything you just said. It wouldn't do any good because I can't deny a word of it. Though I don't know why in hell McAllister thought about recruiting me, I didn't really have any beef with him. As for Dwyer, though, I did not get along with him. But I had a good reason. I didn't feel safe following his orders. He wasn't gonna look out for us, and I wasn't gonna go down without a fight."

"Why didn't you feel safe?" Chuck asked.

"Because of D'Lorenzo being involved. He was one of the people who talked Gus Kalbe into reenlisting and taking that job on the Mustang. Gus didn't want to, you know, not for one minute, but they worked him and worked him. He finally gave in. They even tried to get all of his friends and family to talk him into it. Gus said he'd do it just so they'd finally leave him and his family alone. When the Mustang was destroyed, some of those same guys came back to Gorham. We were mad as hell when we found out they were feds. And they treated the townies like dirt, like the Mustang thing was *our* fault. They followed us to the funeral home and took down our license plates. They asked questions when we left the cemetery and they wouldn't leave Mr. and Mrs. Kalbe alone, either. Two old people who just lost both their boys and they were hit with questions like they were criminals. Right in their own home! Mr. Kalbe had a stroke because of it! D'Lorenzo was in on all that and I hate him for it, I'll always hate him for it! When Dwyer made it clear to me that he knew and trusted D'Lorenzo and that nothing could change that, I knew I couldn't trust Dwyer, either. We were just meat to him!"

Doug was trembling, and held up a shaky hand, pointing at Chuck.

"When you got here after Dwyer died, I figured you were just like him. But you and I came to an understanding and I started to trust you. That night in Burlington, though, you told me to leave that old man behind…stuck in the fire! I knew you were just like Dwyer after all. No guilt about letting people die. You broke faith with me. I had no reason to keep faith with you. But now I'm back and I see that you really aren't like him."

"How?"

Doug nodded toward Cameron and Rich. "Because I see what you've done with them. You've been good to them, good for them. I always did my best to take care of them. These guys were better to me than my own family. When I couldn't find them after I got the hell out of Washington; I lost it. I thought something had happened to them, and I wasn't around to prevent it. I got drunk for a week. There was nothing to live for. I started hitching cross-country. Maybe I was hoping something would happen to me. There's a lot of wide open space, someone could get lost and never be missed."

Doug paused and rubbed his eyes. He sighed heavily and ran his fingers through his hair.

McIntyre was studying him, eyeing him. "Go on," she said.

Doug turned to Cameron. "Something good happened. I ended up in Gaston, Missouri, and found you guys again."

"We thought you were dead, Doug. You didn't even talk to *me*!" For the first time since Doug's return, Cameron was angry—at him.

"I saw that you guys were all right…and how Chuck kept you safe, kept an eye on things all night."

"After you died, I couldn't see straight. You should've talked to me…*me*!"

Doug hung his head ruefully. "I couldn't. I fucked up. I didn't think you'd welcome me back."

"No shit!" Cameron hollered. "Then why did you travel across the country to find us? And save me from those goons the other night?"

"Why did I save you from those goons? In Missouri, you were safe. Tonight, you weren't!"

Chuck and McIntyre exchanged furtive glances.

Cameron slammed his fist on the table. "How long were you going to let us think you were dead? Was that part of your plan, too? Messing with our fucking minds?"

"Hey, Cameron. Relax, will you? He's here now…" Rich said.

"No, that wasn't what I meant to do," Doug insisted. "I thought it was best if I stayed away." Doug pointed to Snapper. "I see you didn't really miss me..."

Snapper threw his hands up. "I'm not touching that with a ten foot pole."

"What the do you expect us to do?" Cameron shouted, leaning across the table. "Wear arm bands and drape the drum kit in black? You got a lotta nerve, buddy. You're alive and didn't tell us? And you're pissed because we had to replace you? Aren't you something! We're not dealing with jealous boyfriends and rival bands anymore. We're in deep now..." Cameron gestured toward McIntyre and Chuck. He sat down, his head in his hands. "Listen. These two aren't the only ones who don't have time to worry about you, pal. Neither do I anymore."

Once again, the pall of silence fell upon the room.

Doug looked at Cameron, who refused to return his gaze. No one dared speak. Doug rose to leave.

"Sit down," Cameron ordered. "No one said you could leave."

"Cameron, this is our job now," Chuck interceded. Cameron glared at him, while Doug stood in the center of the room, waiting.

Chuck approached Doug and stood face to face with him.

"Doug, I'll lay it out for you. You're obviously resourceful. You made it solo all the way across the country without being detected. You found us without any help. You detected the threat in Missouri... You have the potential to be one good, solid agent. To be frank, though, you're a real pain in the ass. If we bring you back in, you have to be in...one hundred percent."

Doug nodded.

"We're serious, Doug," McIntyre interjected. "There are no more chances. If you're in, I'll buy it. But I will tell you now, with everyone here as my witnesses, if I ever have to draw my firearm on you again, I'll fire it."

"The band still needs to take a vote!" Cameron shouted.

Chuck laughed and waved him off.

"No! Dwyer and I set up these terms in the beginning, and you and I agreed to them, as well. Anything affecting this band is decided by all of us, not just you guys."

"OK, then," said Chuck. "Let's take a vote. I vote yes."

"Me, too," said Snapper.

"I'm not sure," said McIntyre.

"Neither am I," said Rich.

All eyes were on Cameron. "Neither am I. You've got to earn our trust again. You let us think you were dead because you didn't trust us to understand. You don't do that to family."

Cameron stormed into the living room.

Chuck looked to everyone else. "That's two affirmatives and three undecided," he sighed. "We're missing two band members. We'll have to wait it out."

Suddenly the door opened. Clyde and Evan burst in, laughing and joking with each other, ebullient from their night on the town. They froze, dead in their tracks. There stood a ghost—Doug, alive and well and standing in Seattle.

Evan's jaw dropped. He looked at Cameron, who'd just reentered the room. Cameron turned away; he wanted none of it.

Clyde shook his head violently. "Am I dreaming?"

"Ask him yourself," Cameron snapped. "Chuck, what are we going to do about Jack Ralston?"

"What do you think?" Chuck asked McIntyre.

"All three dead now. Collier. Simms. Stanley. One way or another, this is going to require our attention. It would be easier if we were in it from the start."

Clyde and Evan sat at the table. Doug just stood there, figuring that the longer he was present, the more likely he'd gain favor and not have to leave at all.

"You're right." Chuck yawned. He was weary. "Cameron, you better call Ralston back and tell him we're on our way."

"But he asked for just me," Cameron said. "Don't you think having you there would raise questions?"

"No. I'm your manager and Stanley's been trying to work with me on a mutual deal. I was with you when you got the call. It disturbed me, so I came along, too."

"And McIntyre?" Cameron asked.

"That's easy," smiled Chuck. "She's the one with the car. We can't go anywhere without her."

"Will someone please tell us what's going on?" implored Evan.

"Jack Stanley shot himself," Chuck said. "Ralston found the body, can't get ahold of his own band members, and he's wigging out. He wants Cameron to come over and talk with him."

"Why Cameron?" Evan asked.

"He wants to talk to another musician, probably," Chuck replied.

"Or...someone who's even willing to take the time to talk to him," Rich said. "Remember, he's not exactly a darling in this town."

Cameron called Ralston. The latter was intoxicated, but lucid enough to be relieved that he wouldn't be alone.

Evan turned to McIntyre. "What requires our attention?"

"Too much to explain now. It's late, old boy," Chuck chided. "I'll fill you in when we get back. In the meantime, why don't you guys make Dougie comfortable? I'm sure you've got some catching up to do."

Chuck followed Cameron and McIntyre out the door. They beckoned the elevator.

"You were a bit rough on Doug back there, Cameron," Chuck said.

McIntyre agreed. "I was just going to send him home! You really went after him."

"Who, me?" Cameron smiled. "No way! He needed it, trust me. I know that goofball better than he knows himself. He needs direction, focus, and a goal to keep him out of trouble. What worked as a roadie doesn't fit here. He's got to understand that. It's going to take me a long time to forgive him, but it doesn't mean I can't trust him."

McIntyre shook her head vehemently. "He didn't make himself known to us. He was alive, for Christ's sake. The way you're handling him isn't going to help. He's beyond help."

"No, he's not. I've got him right where I want him. He knows he blew it, so he'll work hard to redeem himself. As far as Doug's concerned, our troubles are over."

"As far as everything else is concerned," McIntyre sighed, "our troubles are just beginning."

CHAPTER THIRTY-NINE

"Open and Shut"

When Chuck, McIntyre, and Cameron arrived at Jack Ralston's hotel, they happened upon a hive of activity. Reporters, police, crime scene technicians and forensic evidence specialists, and personnel from the coroner's office were buzzing about in organized chaos. The reporters instantly recognized Cameron and Chuck. A flurry of flashes from cameras ensued, along with demands for statements.

"We have no comment!" Chuck barked.

He led Cameron through the crowded lobby and followed the hotel manager and McIntyre to a cordoned-off room, where three men in suits were deeply entrenched in conversation. Cursory introductions were performed, which revealed that two of the men were federal agents; the third was a Seattle police detective. The hotel manager, to his great relief, was immediately released and he scurried away. His vexation over the public relations nightmare haunting his establishment was evident on his face, as well as on those of the hotel personnel.

Cameron stood to the side as Chuck and McIntyre explained their presence to the officers and detectives, one of whom looked at them with great scrutiny. Cameron wondered if Chuck and McIntyre would have to present their credentials, then remembered that they were undercover.

Damn…getting used to this more and more everyday…

The two federal agents conferred with the detective, then led Chuck and McIntyre to another room. Cameron followed, but Chuck gestured for him to stay where he was. Cameron did as he was told. Chuck and McIntyre were in the other room for almost fifteen minutes. Chuck returned, but was alone.

He eyed Cameron. "Come on. They'll bring us to see that fellow now. Apparently, he's one heck of a mess."

I can imagine…

They followed a woman from the police department, who led them to Ralston's suite. Cameron knew from his telephone call with Ralston that the man had hit the bottle pretty hard. Cameron couldn't blame him. Ralston's manager's assistant died, followed almost immediately by his manager's death. Those incidents, coupled by the press incessantly vilifying the Boney Jack band rendered the situation, to the public, devoid of sympathy. Despite the fact that Cameron hardly knew Ralston, Cameron felt sorry for the bassist. When they finally reached Ralston's suite, Cameron discovered that calling Jack Ralston a mess was an understatement.

Cameron's previous encounters with Ralston were brief, yet momentous enough for Cameron to discern that Ralston possessed a robust personality. Without having to be loud, Ralston projected a formidable presence. However, when Cameron and Chuck entered his suite, Ralston struggled to focus on them. In his current condition, having faced enormous tragedy, he was literally a shadow of his former self. Barely able to keep his head up, he slumped upon the couch, spoke with slurred speech, and drooped like a marionette.

"Who are you?"

Cameron introduced himself, speaking loudly and slowly to make sure Ralston could process the information. He was having trouble understanding who stood before him, and why they were there in the first place. Ralston continued to slur and babble incoherently. Cameron stooped down to face Ralston in an attempt to gain his attention, but to no avail. Frustrated, he rose to leave.

"The Sons…Roadhouse Sons. Yes! I know you," Ralston blathered, and immediately returned to his former state, his mind wandering and his conversation tangential. In his alcohol-induced fog, Ralston's mental meanderings were perfectly understandable to him. To Cameron, though, the diatribes were the chaotic and random musings of a drunk. Ralston mentioned interviews he'd read about the Roadhouse Sons, then talked about unrelated circumstances, including Boney Jack's shows, then moved onto topics completely unbeknownst to Cameron, such as former bands with whom he'd played, and people from his past. Cameron couldn't keep up with Ralston's chatter and gave up trying. Chuck, too, made valiant attempts, but met the same fate as Cameron.

"We don't have to stay," Cameron told Chuck. "We can go if you want. He doesn't even know we're here, and probably won't even wonder if we showed up."

Cameron made no attempt to conceal his sentiments; it was evident that Ralston was in his own world. Even the police officer who escorted them left the premises. As they were about to leave, though, Ralston experienced another burst of lucidity and became increasingly agitated.

"I called you! I couldn't find any of those fuckers! No one, nowhere!"

"Who? Your band?" Cameron asked, stooping down once more.

"Quinn," Ralston hiccupped. His face turned to an expression of surprise he began to shout. "Donny, Boney Jack—I looked and looked everywhere. I couldn't get a hold of Gibson, either. I found Stanley, though… Blood, bullet holes, and his eyes wide open! I found him."

Ralston raised a bottle to his lips, gripping it tightly. He tilted his head back and gulped the clear brown liquid.

"Man, I think you've had enough of that," Cameron said, reaching for the bottle. Ralston yanked it away from his face and out of Cameron's reach, which caused the drunken bassist to fall back onto the couch cushions. Nevertheless, he maintained his grip on the bottle, and awkwardly propped himself up again.

Ralston leaned in toward Cameron and whispered in a conspiratorial fashion. "Have you ever seen a dead body before?" Ralston's breath reeked of alcohol. Cameron gagged. He nodded in response to Ralston and covered his nose and mouth with the top of his shirt.

"You have?" Ralston gasped in disbelief. "I found one, tonight. Horrible…" Ralston was not only drunk, he was traumatized.

Change the subject…

"Hey, man. Where are some of the places you've played?" Cameron spoke loudly to keep Ralston's attention.

Chuck, also anxious to change the subject, winked at Cameron, who had to repeat and explain each subsequent question before Ralston could answer. He'd stammer the name of a town and Cameron responded with another. Soon, they conversed fairly well about bands whom they both knew, as a result of Cameron asking Ralston if he'd ever played with a band other than Boney Jack. They continued to swap names and divulge details about their respective adventures until the burden of the conversation fell predominantly on Cameron.

Chuck, meanwhile, became restless, muttering and sputtering about Ralston's inability to maintain a coherent path of thought, or that garnering new information from the poor drunkard was akin to pulling teeth. When Ralston's slurs and thought gaps increased, Chuck gestured slashing his throat, and smacked Cameron on the shoulder when, at last, Ralston fell asleep, his eyes half-opened and glassy from booze. Cameron worried that Ralston suffered some medical mishap, but the bassist's steady breathing assured Chuck and him that Ralston was simply passed out. Cameron removed the liquor bottle from Ralston's hand and placed it on the coffee table. He covered Ralston with a blanket. Then he and Chuck stepped silently from the suite, switching the light off as they left.

Ralston remained still, listening for several moments. He heard the noises of people departing, and sounds in the hallway, which soon faded. Ralston was confident that he was alone. To be sure, he carefully stirred from his ersatz sleep and groggily opened one eye. No one else was in the suite. With a satisfied smile, he yawned and stretched, then rose to use the bathroom.

"That was easier than anticipated," he said aloud to himself.

Cameron had been the perfect unwitting musician, more than willing to provide to him a wealth of information. He, on the contrary, having behaved like a traumatized inebriate, had provided nothing to Cameron. Cameron's prattling would assist Ralston in compiling cover stories and establish camaraderie, thereby nudging himself closer into Cameron's confidence.

Ralston stood at the bathroom sink. He studied his face in the mirror. His eyes, nice and bloodshot due to constant rubbing all evening long, had given him the exact appearance he'd desired.

"I look like a bloody derelict!"

He cupped his hand over his mouth and exhaled. "I smell like one, too!"

He smiled, for that was the easy part. He had gripped the bottle by the neck, raised it to his lips and made swallowing motions, convincing Cameron and company that he was drowning his sorrows; in all actuality, he'd really swallowed only once for every four or five tipples. That helped maintain the reek of alcohol on his breath. He had to ensure, though, that nobody examined the bottle too closely; they would have noticed that the level of alcohol didn't diminish much. It had been a risky maneuver, but definitely worth the trouble and, by not offering anyone a drink, as well as the clever technique of constantly swinging the bottle about to keep its contents moving, he'd made it difficult to discern its actual contents.

Ralston desperately wanted to use eye drops and rinse the foul taste of liquor from his mouth, but he knew that he couldn't afford to appear at all fresh the next morning.

"Just a few hours away…"

The iota of sleep available to him would further authenticate his performance. He understood that in order for the plan to be successful, an unkempt, hung-over Jack Ralston had to make an appearance the next morning in front of a sea of press correspondents and respond to inquiries regarding Stanley's death. Overcome by recent circumstances, he would break down and throw himself beseechingly upon the mercy of the public, all while declaring his personal reformation. For emphasis, he'd publicly renounce the previous antisocial attitudes of the Boney Jack band.

"Then…I will quit!" he reveled out loud. No one could hear him.

He worried not about the implications of his actions; he'd been assured that all resultant details were taken care of. The band would no longer be of any consequence, either. He was glad to wash his hands of it. The band's drummer, Caesare Donatello, was a follower, not an innovator, and wouldn't fight the breakup of the band. Neither would Russ Gibson, the rhythm guitar player, who was such a non-entity that Stanley had to remind himself that Gibson was even a member. Gibson never performed any of the vocals; he left that to the others, and he sometimes didn't even warrant enough ink to be captioned in publicity photos. Just before the Boney Jack band became famous, Gibson had joined the ensemble in order to improve his guitar playing. He was no leader then, and he certainly wouldn't become one to try and keep the band together. The truth of the matter was that the band didn't know what to do with him, or how to get rid of him. Since the arrest, Gibson remained incognito and out of the public eye. Per the terms of his bail, he checked in privately with the authorities.

"Ultimately, he'll probably just disappear…"

Jack Quinn was another story. Still, he didn't present too much of a problem. Quinn would likely feel relieved, which he would manifest via some nasty remark to the press, then flip his middle finger at the world as he trekked off, solo. Quinn was talented and ambitious enough to make it on his own; he, along with everyone else, knew it.

Boney Jack remained. Seemingly, he'd be the biggest problem if the group disbanded. In all actuality, though, he'd be the least of any problems. The superiors had decided long ago that while the band's successes had indeed garnered a great deal of revenue for the cited operations, the group quickly became unmanageable. As directed, Boney Jack's excesses and antics were encouraged, in hopes that the singer would either humiliate—or annihilate—himself. Either way, come the following morning, Boney Jack would find himself out of a job.

"So, too, for poor Jack Ralston…"

To make matters worse, while Stanley's estate affairs were processing through probate, there would be no royalty payments. Therefore, poor Jack Ralston would have to depend upon the kindness of strangers.

"Or upon the kindness of the Roadhouse Sons…"

He could learn so much more as a harbored waif than as a casual drinking buddy of Cameron Walsh.

Ralston longed to bathe and wash the filth of the day off, but knew he had to look his absolute worst for the reporters. With a weary sigh, he strolled into the living room and made himself comfortable on the couch before making his last telephone call of the night. He dialed the number, let it ring three times, and hung up. Redialing, he let it ring once. Someone on the other end picked up, but said nothing.

"Tell Jake thanks for dinner," Ralston said. "It was delicious. I tidied up a bit for him." Without waiting for a response, he hung up. With another yawn and stretch, Jack Ralston fell sound asleep.

* * * * * * *

Elsewhere in the hotel, McIntyre awaited Chuck and Cameron in the hotel manager's office. From the look on her face, Cameron knew she wasn't at all happy. He was about to offer an apology for how long they'd been away when McIntyre shook her head, almost imperceptibly.

Not now…

Bidding good night to both the manager and the night clerk, McIntyre followed Chuck and Cameron out to the car. Cameron briefed her on their bizarre interaction with Jack Ralston.

McIntyre waved her hand at him. "It's to be expected, what with everything that's transpired. I'd be on a bender, too."

Cameron laughed. "You! I can't picture that!"

McIntyre shot him a sly look. "I suppose you invented it?" Her reply smacked of sarcasm.

Cameron laughed even louder, his mirth triggering his memories of the early days in Vermont when McIntyre and her former partner, Gordon Dwyer, hung out at the Roadhouse Sons' clubs, just prior to recruiting the band.

Cameron was snapped away from his reminiscing when McIntyre spoke right into his ear. "Hey! I talked to the two agents. We had to wait a millennium until we were all alone, with such high traffic, people going to and from the crime scene. I don't even have to mention how much this complicates our assignment..."

Chuck shook his head, concurring. They climbed into the car.

Cameron voiced his confusion. "I don't get it."

"We're supposed to work with Stanley to find out Simms' connection to Collier, the Soviet agent," Chuck said. "We were also assigned to find Collier's contact in the bases and the refugee camp. Unless you have a Ouija board, that's going to be a little difficult."

Oh, that...

Cameron sank back into the seat.

"But, didn't Stanley check out?" he asked. "I mean, obviously he did...but you guys said you couldn't find anything on him. So, maybe there isn't any connection?"

"If that was the case, then why would he commit suicide?" countered Chuck.

"According to the police, Stanley left a suicide note, saying that he did it because of his guilt over killing Simms," McIntyre explained.

"What was his motive for *that*?" wondered Chuck.

McIntyre furrowed her brow. "According to the note, he killed Simms in a fit of rage. He discovered that Simms had been skimming revenue from the company and confronted him. He stabbed Simms with a pen and left. He realized that Simms had identified him with a clue and that there would be no way out of it. Between that and the drama lately with his band, he decided enough was enough."

"Clue? What clue?" Cameron asked.

"That's what I want to know," McIntyre grumbled. "They weren't certain what Stanley meant by that, so I asked what they found. The forensic technicians' notes indicate that Simms appeared to have been working on some accounting task and was killed while performing it. There were numbers punched into the calculator and on the print roll, but no indication of their significance, if any."

"Do you think that had anything to do with his murder?" Chuck mused.

"At first, I thought it was nothing. On a hunch, though, I asked if they knew what the numbers were. The police detective we met was the investigating officer for Simms' case. He showed me his notes. Simms had entered 52257 on his calculator."

Chuck whistled. "Five hundred twenty-two dollars and fifty-seven cents... fifty-two thousand two hundred fifty-seven dollars. It could be anything. Were there any receipts to account for it? Checkbooks, account books, anything like that?"

"No," McIntyre replied. "Apparently, Simms didn't handle any money except nominal sums sent in by fans requesting pictures and autographs, and those remittances certainly weren't that large. The big money was handled by the corporate accountants."

"They got paid for pictures and autographs?" Cameron blurted. "We've been doing that for free."

Chuck glared at him. Cameron, sheepish, dropped the subject.

"Have they checked any of the bank statements to verify?" Chuck asked McIntyre.

"They've subpoenaed the statements, but haven't had a chance to go through all of them yet. So far, nothing's contradicting Stanley's suicide note."

Cameron cleared his throat. "Do you think...is that number a clue? It could have been Simms just tapping the keys before he died. Like a chicken running around after you cut off its head."

"Like I said, I didn't think so...at first," McIntyre repeated. "Then, I made a phone call. It was crystal clear."

"How the hell...?" asked Cameron. "Did you call someone who had the answer?"

"No!" McIntyre laughed. "I called on *something* that had the answer!"

Chuck slapped his forehead. "Of course," he moaned. "So simple, its stupid!"

"Must not be stupid," grumbled Cameron. "I have no idea what you're talking about."

"One of the easiest codes ever," laughed McIntyre. "My girlfriends and I used it when we were in school. It was a great way to keep secrets from our parents and teachers. Use the letters on the dial of the telephone. The number one represents A, B, or C. Get it? And so on."

Why didn't you say this before?

"Five two two five seven would spell out the first initials of who attacked him," Chuck interjected. "J, A, C, K represent the first four numbers, and the seventh key?"

"The letters P, Q, R, and S," said McIntyre. "He was spelling out Jack S.! Jack Stanley!"

"McIntyre, didn't Stanley have an alibi?" Cameron queried. "He was at the press conference when Simms was killed."

"Initially, that's what authorities surmised, based on the estimated time of death. Now, though, they realize he may have had time to commit the murder. No one else has confirmed his alibi. His driver reported a different pickup time for him than he provided for police."

"There's a Jack Q. and a Jack R., too. Were you able to confirm Quinn's and Ralston's whereabouts?" asked Chuck.

"Yes. Remember, Quinn was at the press conference," McIntyre revealed. "He was purportedly having a nice romantic liaison with that girl from housekeeping. Just as we suspected! As for Ralston, the maid confirmed that she saw him asleep in bed when she cleaned his suite."

"At least that part of the scenario checks out. I'm not in love with the idea of trusting the statements of hotel maids…" Chuck whistled again. "But we're still left with the conundrum of Simms, Collier, and the Russians. What's the connection? And what are they scheming?"

McIntyre pulled over to the side of the road. She turned off the ignition.

"That, my friend, is how our jobs become even more complicated."

"I want to go home!" Cameron bellowed from the back seat. "Come *on!*"

"Not so fast, rock star!" Chuck said. "We've got work to do."

"*Drive!*" screeched Cameron to McIntyre.

She turned the ignition and drove. When at last they reached the Roadhouse Sons' living quarters, Cameron was so exhausted that the very act of holding up his head was too formidable a feat. He bid them adieu and went to bed.

Chuck stopped Cameron dead in his tracks. "I said we've got work to do."

Cameron gaped at him.

"No! No reports tonight! No fucking way! I'll jump into Puget Sound first!"

"Not reports…"

"Then what?" Cameron was fading fast. Chuck smirked.

"Check for bugs."

CHAPTER FORTY

"Nevermore To Go Astray..."

Cameron opened his eyes. He couldn't focus and he was tangled up in his bedclothes. Panic set in.

Where am I?

He wrestled with the sheets and blanket and managed to kick them away. He was sweating profusely. He sat up and eyed his surroundings.

Calm down! You're in your own bed...

He fell back onto his pillow and attempted to will himself to sleep, but to no avail. Cameron stretched and yawned and looked across the room to see if Chuck was there. He wasn't. His bed was unmade.

He must be downstairs.

He glanced at the clock on the nightstand.

Noon. God, I need a cigarette...

Cameron lit a cigarette and sat on the edge of the bed. He watched the waft of smoke as it rose to the ceiling, and pondered the events of the previous evening. A noise from downstairs jarred him from his thoughts. He grabbed a tee shirt and a pair of jeans from the floor and put them on. He stumbled to the top of the stairs. Chuck and the Roadhouse Sons surrounded the television set.

"Man, you gotta come see this!" cried Evan.

Cameron ran down the stairs. The look on Evan's face said it all. Something was awry. Myriad scenarios coursed through his mind.

The war...new attack on the front?

Suddenly, he remembered Jack Ralston.

How could I forget that?

Upon returning to the suite the previous evening after his and Chuck's visit to see Ralston, Chuck was prompted to conduct a detailed search. The results were fruitless and Cameron was exhausted. Chuck had already performed a cursory search before they left. That search turned up nothing. He'd corralled the whole band to help, despite the fact that Evan and Clyde had been carousing on the town all evening. With all of the unexpected activity, Cameron didn't go to bed until five o'clock in the morning. He slept straight through until noon, but his body was still screaming from fatigue.

He sank into the couch and watched the television. The announcer was a young woman who also appeared to have been up all night.

"Turn it up a little," Cameron ordered.

Clyde turned the volume knob. The announcer's voice boomed into the room.

"At this time, there is no word on the cause of death."

The scene shown behind the announcer was the front of the hotel where Jack Stanley and the Boney Jack band were staying. The camera shifted to Jack Ralston standing on the steps, squinting into the harsh sunlight, the wind blowing through his hair. For someone who made his living as an entertainer, Jack Ralston was surprisingly uncomfortable in front of a camera. He was obviously reading a prepared statement, and he interrupted himself by constantly clearing his throat. His delivery was halting, to the point of reminding Cameron of Doug's struggle through the *Sackett* passages the night before. Cameron wondered if Jack Ralston had some sort of learning challenge. He was ripped from his thoughts upon hearing Ralston's next words.

"Boney Jack was a good friend of mine. We've been playing together for a good long time. When you're with someone that long, you become very close."

Boney Jack? What about Jack Stanley? Did I dream last night happened?

"If I believed in curses, I'd have to say that band has a hex upon 'em," Evan said. "First their assistant manager, then their manager, then they find the body of their lead singer, all in less than a week."

"You've got to admit, that is pretty friggin' strange," agreed Rich. "It reminds me of Agatha Christie. *And Then There Were None...* It was about all these people that went to this island and got killed in all kinds of ways. Some freaky shit in that book, a lot like this. A murder, a suicide, and someone choking on their puke. What's next?"

"Shhhh! Be quiet, man," Cameron admonished.

He listened with great interest as Jack Ralston stammered through his statement. Cameron realized that the bassist's difficulty wasn't due to a reading disability; Ralston was at the mercy of his emotions. As Ralston read the statement, he made no effort to hide his tears. He sniffled and wiped at his nose, and his hands trembled. In desperation, he threw the paper to the ground and sputtered an apology, rueful for his behavior and for that of the band, and for their lifestyle and derisive attitude. Ralston apologized for mocking anything and everything that "regular people" held so dear.

"Look where it's got us!" he shouted. "People are dropping like flies all around me! I don't want to end up like that. I'm sorry for what I've done and how I've behaved. I'm starting fresh…I'm starting fresh!"

Ralston wiped his eyes, turned his back to turned the camera, and scurried into the hotel. The camera switched back to the announcer continued who continued with the broadcast.

"Turn it off, Clyde." Cameron stared at the television.

"He's bullshitting," said Doug.

"How do you know?" Cameron was aghast. "You've never even met the guy! You've never talked to him; you've never worked with him. How in hell would you know if he was bullshitting or not?"

Doug stared at Cameron, but said nothing.

"Keep your bullshit opinions to yourself because no one's interested in them. You weren't even here, man. You weren't even here…"

As soon as the words popped out of his mouth, Cameron knew he'd made a mistake. Doug's face flushed. His eyes narrowed and, for a brief moment, Cameron wondered if Doug was about to punch him. Doug, still silent, turned and walked into the kitchen. The other band members were stunned and Cameron felt as though their eyes were boring into him. He hurried into the kitchen. Doug was at the sink, rinsing his coffee cup.

"Look, man, I'm sorry," soothed Cameron. "I don't know what came over me. It must be because I'm so tired. I just wasn't thinking."

"Don't mention it." Doug whirled around, right into Cameron's face. His voice was harsh, tinged with finality. Cameron knew he had to tread lightly.

"Really. I'm sorry."

"I said don't mention it. I mean that. Don't ever mention it again."

Chuck was sitting at the table. He'd witnessed the entire exchange. He was studying Doug's hat, turning it inside out. The *Sackett* book was on the table. Cameron realized that Chuck was monitoring the situation to prevent it from escalating. He winked at Chuck and poured the last of the coffee into his mug.

"Now, tell me again where you got this," Chuck said to Doug. Doug sat across from Chuck, back to normal and conversing as though no argument had transpired.

"I told you, Gus gave it to me. That was the hat he was wearing when our softball team won the championship the summer before he left. He sent it back with the rest of his stuff before he shipped out, along with a note saying the hat and the book were for me. His mom said they weren't allowed any personal effects on the Mustang, so everything had to be inventoried and sent home."

"That was it? Nothing else?"

"Nothing else. Just that the book and the hat were for me and I was to hang onto them until Gus got back."

Doug picked up the book and perused the cover.

"I'm curious about that book," Chuck said. "Did your friend know that you—"

"Did he know what? That I couldn't fucking read or write? Yeah, he knew. But he never threw it in my face."

"I'm not throwing it in your face." Chuck remained calm and reassuring. "But, it would seem to me that if your buddy knew that, he'd've sent a book to someone who would have put it to more use, that's all."

"I don't know," Doug grumbled. "Maybe he wanted me to go back to school or something. He didn't say. His mom just said he wanted me to hang on to these two things until he came back for them. How many friggin' times do I have to say it?"

Chuck ignored Doug's vitriol and pointed to the sweatband in the hat. The front panel of the trucker cap was black, but the rest of the hat was a white mesh, with white fabric forming a portion of the sweatband. On a section closest to the front were numbers, handwritten and barely legible.

"What's this writing in here? There's a three, a five, and a seven. Do they mean anything to you?"

Doug shook his head.

"Didn't you ever wonder about them?"

"Sometimes," Doug admitted. "But I never thought about it too much. I know he had a .357 Magnum. I thought it might be that."

"That makes sense," Chuck concurred. "I'm curious to know why you put up such a fuss at the thought of losing this, but you never once thought about that book."

"I didn't put up a fuss about that hat," Doug insisted.

"I read a report about the night you and D'Lorenzo were drugged. In your delirium, you became hysterical at the thought of losing this hat."

Doug blushed, embarrassed at the memory. "Look. That hat is a souvenir from a close buddy of mine. I didn't want to lose it. That's all. You're making a big deal out of it."

"Then why did you come back for this instead of that book? It must mean something more to you than you're letting on."

Doug was exasperated. "I didn't come back for anything!" he shouted. "I thought I lost it in the fire. When they let me go in Washington, they gave me all of my stuff and that was sitting on top, with an orange under it. I thought it was a joke from one of you guys at first, but when I realized you left me, I figured it was a kiss-off."

Chuck stared at him. "Wait a minute. What do you mean when they gave you back your stuff?"

"When they released me, they gave me back all of my clothes and personal stuff. And my hat, with an orange under it. It felt like, don't let the doorknob hit you…"

"Were you naked or something?" Cameron interjected.

"When the cops arrested me in Burlington, they made me strip. They put me in a jumpsuit and irons. When those agents showed up, they loaded me in a van and took me away. I ended up in Washington and was there for months. I didn't get my stuff back until I got released."

Chuck stared in disbelief. "You were in a jumpsuit and irons?"

"What?" Cameron asked.

"I was under the impression that Doug was taken in just for questioning," Chuck said. "But he was taken into custody. Were you ever advised of your rights, or charged with anything?"

"Nope. Nothing." Doug was angry. "They didn't even let me leave the room, except to answer questions. I never got my one phone call or a lawyer and they never let me go outside for weeks."

"What did they say when they released you?" Chuck queried.

"They just said I was free to go and all my stuff was waiting. My hat was on top of the pile of clothes and there was that fucking orange under it."

"An orange—"

Cameron interrupted. "The morning after the fire! I left Doug's hat on my stereo. The hat was right there when I went to meet with you guys that morning. When I got back, it was gone. There was an orange in its place. I also found an orange on the front seat of my car, right before the shit hit the fan in Burlington, remember?"

Chuck nodded, absentminded. "Yes, I remember that... No time for citrus now. Doug, show Evan where you're staying so we can bring your stuff back here. It'll be a little tight, but we'll manage."

He turned the hat right side out and handed it to Doug.

"Thanks, but no thanks. I've already got a job and a place to stay and you've already got a roadie. He's got everything under control. You don't need me."

He rose from the table, donned his hat, and headed out of the kitchen. Chuck stepped in front of him and waved the battered copy of *Sackett*.

"There's a connection between you and Gus Kalbe's belongings. I don't know what it is, but my gut tells me it's important. Why else would he give you, of all people, a book?"

"Go wipe your ass with a cactus."

Chuck clenched his teeth. "I wasn't the only one to make this connection. Whoever incarcerated you did, too."

Doug's jaw jutted forward. Cameron knew that he was readying to hit, and that with Herculean effort, Doug was quelling his desire to scream at the top of his lungs. Doug smacked the book out of Chuck's hand.

"I don't know anything. I told you, Dwyer and those men in Washington all I know. Here! Keep the damn hat if you think it's so important!"

He threw his hat onto the table. Chuck grabbed it and tossed it back.

"Put your hat on, sit down, and shut up. That is an order."

"I don't take orders. Not from you. Not from anybody."

Cameron was stunned; Chuck reached into his rear waistband and drew his gun.

"You and I are going with Evan, retrieving your belongings, and returning here. If you continue to resist or try anything funny, I'll have no choice but to defend myself and everyone here."

"You can't do this to me!" Doug snarled. "I haven't done anything wrong! I haven't broken any laws and you don't have anything to charge me with."

"Hmmm. What about your rations?"

"What rations?" he spat. "I don't have any, in case you've forgotten! I'm dead, remember? I get paid for honest work. I don't use ration books. I use hard-earned cash."

"Have you declared that income to the Internal Revenue Service? Are you working under your real name, or an alias? Does this alias have a Social Security number?"

Doug's face turned ashen. "You prick."

"I didn't think so," Chuck growled. "Any one of those infractions is actionable. Hell, some are felonies, carrying fifteen to twenty years in federal prison. I'm taking you into custody right now." Chuck nodded toward the living room. "You can have this nice jail, or the one in Washington. You pick."

Doug's shoulders sagged in defeat. He sat at the table, conceding.

"I only have a backpack," he whispered. "What little I've got, I can get on my bike. I don't need help."

"But I need to keep an eye on you," Chuck stated. He was completely devoid of sympathy.

"If we're going, then let's go."

Chuck called for Evan. "Evan! You guys head down to the van. Take Doug here with you. Don't let him out of your sight. I need to talk to Cameron alone. I'll be down in a minute."

Doug seethed at them both. Cameron looked away.

Clyde, Rich, Snapper, and Evan appeared at the kitchen door. Throughout the entire exchange, they remained silent, except when Clyde, in an attempt to bring levity into the situation, whispered that he felt like he did as a child when his parents were fighting. His joke had landed with a thud.

"Come on, Doug," Evan beckoned.

"Good to see you, man." Clyde took Doug's arm. Surprisingly, Doug allowed it. All five of them left the suite.

"Well," Chuck offered. "Looks like your work's cut out for you."

"I can handle Doug," Cameron assured him. "We've had our ups and downs before. It'll smooth over."

"I'm not worried about Doug."

"What—" Cameron stopped himself. He held no quarter for Chuck when he waxed cryptic.

I fucking hate it when he does that!

Chuck continued talking as though he'd merely asked for a glass of milk.

"Why don't you go back to Ralston's hotel and see how he's doing? We have to keep a close eye on him. Give him a call and let him know you saw the news."

"What am I, a babysitter now?"

"He's the only connection we have to the Collier and Simms network. We can't let this opportunity slip away. We still have no idea of their reach or size. Ralston contacted *you*. So, I want you to go to work on him while we're situating Doug."

"Doug said Ralston was bullshitting. I don't believe it. You were there last night. You saw him."

"Welcome to the big league." Chuck sighed. "Like I say, you've got your work cut out for you."

He held Cameron's gaze, to the point of discomfort, then turned on his heels and left.

What the hell?

Cameron mixed a glass of Tang. He longed for real orange juice, even a real orange.

Oranges...

After Dwyer's death and Chuck's subsequent arrival, Cameron had discovered an orange on the seat of his car. After Doug's death, an orange was left in place of his hat. When Doug was released, an orange was hidden in his belongings. Why? Their previous agent superior, Gordon Dwyer, had established the color orange as the Roadhouse Sons' alert that they were officially contacted. All of their initial contacts somehow employed the color or the word orange, or the fruit. Cameron shuddered.

The warning Dwyer received on the day of his death...written on orange paper.

Chuck had denied any knowledge of the oranges left in Cameron's car, or in his room. Subsequently, Cameron's concern with the color orange dissipated once they left Vermont. Once they, of Dwyer's team, were passed to Chuck Lamont, any relevance of the color orange was seemingly moot. Why, though, did the color orange surface at all, including while Doug was incarcerated in Washington?

Is Dwyer...? No! Ridiculous...he's dead. I saw him with my own eyes...his pants were soiled. He's dead...but I thought I saw Doug's dead body, too...

At one point, Cameron was sure that his quandaries were the same as those of McIntyre. Chuck, on the other hand, wasn't sharing all of his information.

Why did Chuck keep saying I had my work cut out for me? If not with Doug...

Cameron felt completely unsettled. Every nerve in his body was screaming in alarm. His gut was going off. Why couldn't he pinpoint the reason? Was it because he'd almost made an enemy of Doug? No. He meant it when he told Chuck that he could smooth everything over. Was it Ralston? Not really. How was a man supposed to behave when three people close to him end up dead within a week? Cameron drained his glass. What was Chuck holding back?

I can't think straight...

He saw the *Sackett* book on the table.

Chuck knows something...